The Cowboy from Tipperary

by

Toni V. Sweeney

The McCoys, Book 3

The Cowboy from Tipperary

Cover Art by *Lisa Dawn MacDonald*

The Wild Rose Press, Inc.
PO Box 708
Adams Basin, NY 14410-0708
Visit us at www.thewildrosepress.com

Publishing History
First Edition, 2024
Trade Paperback ISBN 978-1-5092-5931-1
Digital ISBN 978-1-5092-5932-8

The McCoys, Book 3
Published in the United States of America

Dedication

To the memory of Milburn Stone, for twenty years as
Gunsmoke's "Doctor Galen Adams"
(1955-1975)

Chapter 1

Tipperary, Ireland
1850

The clip of horse's hooves pierced Padraig's lust, jerking him from his desire for the woman he held in his arms.

"What was that?" He glanced to the mullion windows opened to the night air.

"What was what?" she asked, reviving from eye-glazed passion.

In a flash, he was out of her arms as well as her body, and off the bed. Naked flesh gleaming palely in the lamplight, he darted to the open casement.

"I thought you said your husband was gone for a fortnight." Padraig peered through the window.

"He is." She sat up, brushing back tousled hair.

"Does he ride a dapple with black points?"

"Yes."

"Then he lied." He hurried back to the bed, searching. "Where'd I leave me clothes?"

Bending, he scooped up the garments, tossing them onto the bed.

"What are you doing?" she asked.

"Leavin'." He hopped on one foot, then the other, pulling on his stockings.

"But…you can't," she protested.

"'Fraid I can, darlin'." He brushed a quick kiss against her lips, dodging her grasping hands. "It was good, *acushla*…what there was o' it, don't get me wrong…but not enough for me t' risk a bullet."

He wrapped his cravat around his neck.

The clomp of boots on the stairs told him he didn't have time to dress further. Clothing in hand, Padraig dashed to the window, peering out again. He didn't hear the faint metallic tinkle as the threads on a button broke and the little object fell to the floor.

The front wall of the manor was densely covered with generations of ivy. Thinking he'd be exiting the same way he entered, he hadn't bothered to check for an escape route when he came to the manor an hour earlier. Now it was climb out the window and trust the strength of the vines or face Lord Cornwell's pistol.

"Will I see you again?" her ladyship asked.

"Extremely doubtful," he flung over his shoulder.

Wrapping his garments around his neck, he seized a branch and swung up and out the window, silently praying it would support his weight. The ivy vine gave, stretched, and held. Breathing a quick sigh of relief, Padraig went hand-under-hand down it as his lordship burst through the bedroom door.

****

"Clarence, you're back." That inane statement was startled out of his wife.

"Obviously. Where is he?" he demanded, gaze darting around the room.

"Where's who?" His wife clutched sheets to her bosom and attempted nonchalance.

"Your lover." He started to the window, raising his pistol.

"Why, you've just arrived, my darling," she said, holding the sheets tighter.

"Don't try to cozen me," he accused, whirling to look back at her. "I'm no cony and I won't be a cuckold. Where's that McCoy bastard?"

"Mr. McCoy?" She managed not to show how startled she was that he remembered Padraig's name. "The young man who came to dinner with his parents?"

"The young man you flirted with the entire meal," Cornwell corrected.

"Dearest, you're mistaken," she protested. "I didn't…"

"No?" His lordship wasn't to be fooled. "Why then are you lying there in all your naked glory, my lady?" His lip curled in a near-snarl. "It's all *I* can do to get you to raise the hem of your nightshift."

"I…I was…" Her ladyship swallowed and chanced a statement belying her usual attitude toward her husband. "…I confess…I missed you, Clarence…I suddenly realized how alone I was, and…I didn't think I could bear fourteen days without your…attention…so I decided to…"

She shrugged, letting the sheet drop. Clarence's gaze went immediately to full, heaving breasts. Taking a deep breath, she cupped one globe in each hand. They bounced and jiggled, riveting his lordship's gaze, as she'd hoped.

"But you're here now, so I needn't…" She opened her arms. The naked bosom rose and beckoned.

"Lord, I love your teats, Eleanor." His lordship pulled loose his neckpiece.

His subsequent groans masked the sound of Padraig's horse making its getaway.

3

Chapter 2

"Master Padraig. Are you awake, sir?"

Padraig groaned and turned his head, staring through a vision-obscuring mop of hair at the ornate hand-painted china and brass oil lamp on the table by his bed. Raising himself on one elbow, he discovered he was lying crossways of the bed. Naked. No, not quite. One stocking was still on, though slipped halfway to his ankle, the other missing.

Damn, I must've been more coopered than I thought.

He didn't remember falling into the bed, barely recollected arriving home and putting his horse into its stall.

It was a long ride from Cornwell House to his father's home. Both he and the horse were near-exhausted when they arrived. He'd stumbled to the house, using his key to get in through the door to the kitchen, then crept up the backstairs to his room on the third floor—remarkably not meeting any servants still abroad tending to late-night duties—where he apparently collapsed upon the bed without even turning back the covers.

The only memory he had was of the wine he'd consumed—they drank from the same goblet so there would be no second telltale glass for a sharp-eyed servant to see—as well as Lady Cornwell's soft, eager

4

body, and its wet warm interior. Oh, that was good, while it lasted. Too bad their little seduction—and who was to say who was the seducer and who the seducee?—was so rudely interrupted.

Damn it.

Padraig luxuriated briefly in remembered sensation.

"Master Padraig?" Cormac's knock on the door intruded, cutting the short memory even shorter.

"I'm awake, Cormac." His answer was reluctant and difficult.

He had to cough twice to get the words out. *Damn, me throat's dry.* His tongue felt as if the Queen's entire army had tramped across it, after dipping their feet into the mud of a pigsty.

"Why are you awakenin' me…?" He squinted in the direction of the window. *Hm, sun's up, must be morning.* "…so early?"

"'Tis near noon, sir." There was mild reprimand in the butler's voice. "Your father wishes t' see you. Immediately. In his study."

Uh-oh. *In his study.* That didn't bode well. Quinton McCoy never spoke to any of his sons in his study unless it was for a dressing-down.

"Very well." Padraig breathed a deep sigh. "Tell Da I'll be down soon's I'm dressed."

"I'll send Sean t' assist you, sir."

Padraig heaved himself from the bed, staggering to the commode with its ironstone washbasin and pitcher. *Oh damn…*a glance in the mirror told him her ladyship had marked him with her pent-up passion. Halfway up his throat, a large red splotch fairly glowed on his skin.

"Ne'er mind," he called. "Since Da's impatient t' see me, I'll tend meself this mornin'. Tell him I'll be down directly." He dismissed the butler. "Thanks, Cormac, that'll be all."

"Very good, sir."

He pictured the butler turning away, scowling in disapproval. Cormac was an old stick, as rigid as his father in some respects. Adherence to the rule that a gentleman never shaved or dressed himself but allowed his manservant to do that chore for him was one of his basic tenets. Sometimes he was too much like Quinton McCoy, Padraig thought, especially in his attitude toward the master's second son.

Since his father was waiting, probably impatiently, fuming with each passing second, if Padraig knew the old man, his son took his leisure in shaving, selecting his garments and putting them on, delaying the moment as long as possible. Last night's clothing, dropped into a pile at the foot of the bed, was tossed into a chair for Sean to later gather and see to making presentable again.

For now…

After the necessary ablutions and *toilette*, Padraig studied his image in the cheval glass, deciding he not only looked acceptable but would convey to his father the image of the young gentleman his parents so wished him to be. Tall for an Irishman, his height was inherited from mercenary forebears, themselves possessing Viking blood. They'd immigrated from Scotland into northern Ireland and then downward to Tipperary in the south. He was red-haired and green-eyed, and possessed of the temper and passion one might expect from someone so imbued with a Gaillich legacy…to Padraig's delight and his father's chagrin.

He ran fingers through his hair, decided it would pass inspection, and went out the door.

****

At his father's call, Padraig opened the study door and paused on the threshold.

"Padraig, come in."

That was part of the ritual, as was knocking and saying, "You wished t' see me, sir?" before entering. It was very obvious Quinton did want to see him, because he had sent Cormac to fetch his son, but any child summoned to the study had to go through this redundant ceremony.

Padraig came inside.

"Shut th' door."

That was also part of the rite, and it gave Padraig a momentary quiver, for it meant this was something dire and Quinton wanted to keep as much of it from the rest of the household, and especially his wife, as possible. Padraig could only surmise what it was his father wished to suppress, no matter how momentarily, and was certain he knew the answer.

Quinton's next words confirmed his thought.

"What th' hell am I t' do with you?" He didn't go into his usual preamble this time, of how he tried to be a good father, how Padraig was obviously a bit of a bad seed but he felt he could still be salvaged. Today, that was bypassed completely as he got to the crux of the matter.

"What do you mean, sir?" Padraig attempted the ignorance ploy.

It didn't work.

"Nay, don't play that note with me."

Quinton was incensed, and on his way building to more. He was a big burly man, appearing more like a laborer than the upperclass landed gentry he was, generally sounded the same way in his speech, and at the moment was a very incensed one.

"Lord Cornwell was here this mornin'." He paused, drew in a deep breath, and continued, "He wanted t' call you out. I managed t' persuade him away from that idea."

"Why?" Padraig realized that didn't convey what he meant. "I mean, why would he wish t' do such a thin'?"

"Don't play th' innocent, Padraig. You know very well."

"I swear, I…"

"You young idiot!"

Quinton was up from his chair and around the desk, face-to-face and nose-to-nose with Padraig, so close anyone not knowing their relationship to each other could immediately mark their resemblance, though the son was a good two inches shorter than the father.

"Because you were with his wife last night. He missed catchin' you by a hairsbreadth, but he knew you were there. You flirted with her ladyship at dinner, had her hangin' on your e'ery word. Hell, lad, you practically shucked th' lady with your eyes. Don't interrupt," he said when Padraig again started to refute that. "I noticed it, as did your dear maithur, an' I regret that, believe me, her now knowin' her son's such a womanizer, an' everyone else at th' table, too. Can you imagine how embarrassin' that was? When Lord Cornwell mentioned he was leavin' on a trip th' next day, I thought both o' you would stand up an' cheer…so don't deny it."

Padraig didn't. He was too busy thinking, *Damn an' blast. How did Cornwell get here so fast?*

"Aren't you aware Cornwell's His Majesty's representative here? That he says who does an' doesn't run thin's in this part o' our world an' 'tis in his purview t' say I'm no longer steward for Lord Alisdaire in this corner o' Tipperary? What'll happen t' th' villages under me control if they bring in someone else? An Englishman, p'rhaps? Did you ever think o' that while you were tuppin' his wife, you randy young *cü*?"

Padraig visibly quailed under his father's wrath. He'd never seen Quinton so angry. Where before he'd paid off Padraig's debtors, soothed angry fathers, furious sweethearts, and cuckold husbands with double-talk and occasionally mild threats of his own, this time he appeared to be having none of it. His son realized this time, what he'd done was serious, very serious, and no excuse he made would suffice to cool the paternal ire.

He didn't answer, simply stared at his father in mute expectation of what was coming...and realized he had no idea what it might be. Abruptly, his neckpiece felt too tight. He inserted a finger inside, working it loose.

"An' there's th' proof o' it!" Quinton burst out, pointing a finger at Lady Cornwell's little love bite. "A passion mark...as plain as th' nose on your face. Have you no shame?"

Padraig hastily tried to straighten the neckcloth to hide the incriminating mark.

"I could've gotten that anywhere," he protested. "That li'l dolly at th' tavern in th' village, for instance. Besides, if his lordship missed me by a hairsbreadth, how does he know 'twas I? If indeed there was any man there?"

"By this!" Quinton picked up something from the desk and lobbed it at him.

Padraig caught it, looking down at what he held. A button...with the initials PM in an entwined design. Damn, those same buttons were on all his jackets. Lady

Cornwell had remarked on them at the dinner and his lordship heard.

"The Lord knows I've tried to be a good faithur, raisin' me sons t' be God-fearin' men…"

"An' your daughter," Padraig put in, attempting any kind of distraction. Mentioning Quinton's only girl-child always softened him a bit. "Don't forget Brigid."

"Leave your sister out o' this," his father snapped. "Bridey's a good obedient girl an' ne'er given me a moment's worry."

That was true. She'd married a man he'd chosen, another landholder, strengthening Quinton's claim to this part of Ireland.

"I've tried t' teach you right an' wrong," Quinton went on. "The ithurs…they listened. They're good boys, but you…"

It was at this point Padraig could've reminded his father how he'd heard tales of Quinton's own forays into misbehavior as a youth, that he'd been a bit of a rip, and anything in petticoats hadn't been safe from that particular McCoy lad, even in his adolescence. Quinton's losses at the card table and his reputation for how much good Irish whiskey he could hold were near legendary, but it all stopped the moment he married…at the grand old age of twenty.

Though the marriage was an arrangement made by his father and that of the bride's, he and the lass found themselves compatible in a good number of things and settled down to producing three sons and a daughter. He became a good agent to his tenants and one of his aims in life was to stay landholder to protect his people from English maltreatment.

Being a husband and its accompanying fatherhood

tamed Quinton's wild spirit before it got him into real trouble, and now only manifested itself in his temper. He failed to see, *refused* to see that Padraig was indeed his son in all respects, a son following the path his father had blazed before him.

"…you'll have nane o' it. You gamble an' lose more than you win, an' expect me t' settle your markers. You gull Englishmen with wild schemes an' take their money, which *I* have t' pay back when they call in your debts."

Quinton stopped, heaved a sigh seeming to come from the innermost depths of his soul, a sigh speaking volumes…of a father driven to his wit's end, despairing of what to do, and left with only one choice.

"Do you know how many times I've saved you from gaol? Or transportation?"

He didn't wait for an answer, not seeing his son's slight blanch at mention of that.

"You drink an' stumble in at all hours an' don't try t' be quiet about it. More than once you've awakened your maithur an' then I have t' soothe her an' convince her you've come t' no harm. You're a rake with th' females…I thank God I never allowed you t' go t' London as I did your braithur. You'd probably have lasted only long enough t' get yourself done in a duel or had t' cut a scarper an' become a fugitive for bein' th' one survivin'." He shook his head. "P'rhaps that wouldn't have been such a bad idea."

It was a bone of contention between father and son that eldest son Donal was sent across the sea to England. He'd been given an English education, a Grand Tour, then furnished with a townhouse in London. Donal comported himself as a young Englishman, with the following attendance at balls and society's seasons, a bit of gambling at Almack's, the installation of a mistress (though at this particular point, that part wasn't known to Quinton), and the other usual actions. He was also expected to soon get himself betrothed to a well-to-do English lass.

If Donal had been available, Padraig imagined he would've been at his father's elbow, adding his own sanctimonious condemnations to Quinton's.

To Padraig's way of thinking, Donal betrayed them all by becoming more English than a John Bull Englishman.

He didn't say that, however, because it would've only angered Quinton more, while reminding his father he was responsible for attempting to make his sons into Englishmen by sending them away for their educations instead of allowing them to be good sons of Erin…simply so he could keep his position in Ireland.

"You're a menace, Padraig, an' I see no hope o' you changin'. Is there?" Quinton paused, giving his son a gimlet stare out of eyes as green as the serpentine in Connemara marble. "*Is there?*"

Padraig pretended to think, then shook his head. "No, Da, I don't believe there is. I'm enjoyin' it too much."

He could've said what Quinton wanted to hear, but his own actions would've proven him a liar soon enough.

"Ah!" Quinton threw up his hands, then recovered. He stalked back around his desk but didn't sit. "I'm afraid you leave me no choice."

Briefly, his anger fell away. His gaze wavered, then he appeared to force himself to speak.

"Padraig, lad…I'm turnin' you out."

Padraig didn't understand.

Turning me out? Surely he'd misunderstood. *What?* The full import struck.

"Da...no!" He didn't have to inject anguish into his voice. It was there. For real.

"I'm sorry, son. I see no ithur way if you refuse t' control this passion you have for misadventure."

"You...you're disownin' me?" Padraig's voice trembled. To his own ears, it didn't sound like himself but a stranger saying those words.

"Ah, I'd ne'er do that," Quinton said.

"Then, what *are* you sayin'?" Padraig demanded.

"I'm sayin' I want you t' leave this house, indeed this country, an' ne'er come back."

"But if that isn't disownin' me, what is it?"

"You'll always be me son, lad. You just won't be in me sight. I'm makin' you into a remittance man, boy." Quinton sat, opened the middle drawer of his desk, and brought out a thick ledger.

Padraig recognized it, the book containing the bank draft slips his father meticulously completed each month after going over the accounts. He didn't have a clerk do them but always kept the books himself.

Disbelievingly, he watched as Quinton flipped open the cap of the brass inkwell, selected a quill, and dipped it into the ink. He watched the pen as it moved over one of the sheets of perforated paper. Quinton finished writing, returned the quill to the stand, tore out the draft and shook it briefly to dry the ink.

He held it out.

Padraig didn't move.

"What's that?" He wanted it said plain and clear that his father was paying him to leave and stay away.

"Your first month's allowance." Quinton's voice was steady, almost as if he were clenching his teeth. "I've sent one of th' footmen inta th' city t' th' station t' get th' schedule for th' next train t' Dublin, an' also th' next ship leavin' there for England. When he brings back that information, I want you packed an' on your way."

"But, sir…" Padraig was truly at a loss for words. He'd never believed his father would do such a thing. Sending away a child for mere high spirits?

"Whene'er you get t' your destination, let me know, an' a cheque'll arrive at th' nearest bank e'ery month."

Quinton raised the hand holding the draft a little higher and shook it.

If I refuse t' take it, what'll he do? What can I do? Beg, grovel, bawl like a babe…promise t' be a good lad an' do what he wishes…I can't become somethin' I'm not, an' I can ne'er be th' gentleman he wants. I can't be Donal.

"Does Mama know about this?"

"Aye…an' she's resigned."

With a sickening rush through his guts so heavy he was afraid he'd puke, Padraig pulled the cheque from his father's hand. Quinton paled as he did so.

Padraig spun and ran from the room.

****

He was hopin' I'd recant, that I'd beg him t' let me stay. What would've happened if I did? I could play th' game for a while, but soon…

Padraig knew he'd be back to his old tricks quick enough. He couldn't help it. People were so gullible, why shouldn't he teach them a lesson? He'd never fleeced anyone who couldn't afford it. As for the gambling and drinking, that was only good fun. And the women? Hell, if a man didn't give his wife what she needed, someone else had to. It was his humane duty.

He'd never give up all that. *Perhaps 'tis better this way, for all o' us.*

He knew he'd miss his mother, perhaps his brothers, too, especially Colin, who was still young enough to revel in his older brother's escapades and envy them.

Sudden insight dawned. *Da's getting' rid o'me t' protect Colin. He doesn't want me influencin' him as he grows up.*

He consoled himself with the thought he hadn't been forbidden to correspond with his family, though perhaps that ultimatum might yet come. If he could keep abreast of what was happening, perhaps it might not be so bad...wherever he was.

Where will I go? He'd be leaving Dublin and sailing for a port in England...Cardiff? Dover? Liverpool? Briefly, he felt a sense of loss nearly overwhelming in its totality. From there to...where?

Certainly not to Australia. Perhaps the United States, or Canada? There wouldn't be much of a language barrier there, and the Canadians were still under British rule. Perhaps that wouldn't seem so much a foreign country, but...

Thought of the U.S. intruded, with its tales of wild Indians and cowboys, the buffalo hunts he'd heard some of his father's English contemporaries speak of attending, the sheer breadth and beauty of the land...

Aye, that's where I'll go.

Padraig sat on his bed, sudden visions blazing through his mind. He allowed them to overwhelm and obscure the despair he felt, filling him with eagerness and expectation as he prepared to leave the land of his birth forever.

'Tis a young nation, still havin' its fun...like meself. We'll suit each other.

He went to the door, calling for Cormac to have one of the footmen bring his traveling trunk from the attic.

Chapter 3

Nebraska Territory, United States
1852

Climbing out of the stagecoach, Padraig briefly stood looking around.

Two men on horseback galloped past, sending a cloud of dust billowing so thick and dense it reminded him of London's pea-soup fog. That was really an obscuring vision, so thick one literally couldn't see a hand before his face.

He thought back over all that had happened since he'd left his father's home that day seeming so long ago now.

Upon his arrival at Cardiff, he'd traveled to London, staying some time in the city. He found it a place well-suited to the style of living he was accustomed to, as the child of landed gentry, but that fog...

Once venturing from his hotel, he actually blundered head-first against a lamp post. For days afterward, he sported a goose egg on his forehead and spent a good portion of his time denying he was accosted by footpads or been in a fisticuff bout.

Though he visited Colin at school because he felt he owed his younger brother an explanation, he hadn't gotten in touch with Donal, mainly because he knew to expect a lukewarm greeting there. Whenever they were together, his brother reluctantly introduced him because as soon as he opened his mouth, the question usually followed, "I say…are you certain you're ol' Don's brother? I mean…really, old chap, that accent…"

Everyone always looked askance at him because of the disparity between his delivery and the way his older brother spoke.

In order to stay in *ol' Don's* good graces, Padraig always managed to refrain from flattening the speaker then and there. As it was, he merely grimaced and explained, "I'm the second son. I didn't rate a good English education like me braithur had."

That was a lie, of course. Padraig went to Eton as Donal had. He'd then chosen to matriculate at Oxford instead of Cambridge, because he swore that institution had seduced his brother into becoming an Englishman. Before he voluntarily left school short of being expelled, Padraig clung to his accent like a man to a log in a raging river.

That fact, plus London's fog, settled it for him. England wasn't the place to stay. Besides, hadn't Da specified he had to leave the country? Though he might've meant merely Ireland, Padraig had a feeling he was including the entire United Kingdom under that one designation. After enjoying London's entertainments a bit, and carefully avoiding running into Donal during that time, Padraig did as he'd originally planned and booked passage on the *HMS Borealis,* bound for America.

On May 17, 1850, with a second cheque written on his father's bank in London, ne'er-do-well Padraig McCoy was out of his family's hair, and on his way.

He arrived in New York, decided to stay a bit, as

much to sightsee as to get a feel for the city and determine if perhaps it might become his new home.

That was decided rather quickly for him one night as he was returning to his hotel from a nearby theater.

He saw a figure dart out of an alley, pausing beside a gas-lit street lamp where he placed something on the sidewalk. Then, the man ran back into the shelter of the shadows.

In a few moments, an elderly couple walked by. The old man appeared to be in his late sixties, white-haired and rather shabbily dressed, walking with a cane. His wife was a wizened little creature, clinging to his arm. He saw the object lying on the sidewalk.

It was a wallet.

Oh no. Padraig knew what was going to happen next. Sliding into the shadows, he leaned against the building, waiting.

"Look, Martha," the old man said. "Someone's lost his wallet."

Before he could pick it up, the man in the alley darted out, scooping up the wallet. He opened it. "Hey, this is my lucky day."

"Is that yours?" the old man asked.

"Is it yours?" the stranger countered, clutching the wallet as if he thought it was going to be snatched from him.

"No, but we should try to find its owner," he answered.

"Little chance of that," the man said. He pretended to check for some identification. "Nothing here to show who it belongs to. Look, we both found it. Why don't we split whatever's inside?"

"That wouldn't be honest," the old man protested.

"We should turn it in to the police."

The stranger considered. "I suppose you're right. If it isn't reclaimed in two weeks, then we can ask for it back."

"I guess that's fair," the old man agreed. He held out his hand, "I'll take it to…"

"Wait a minute," Again, the stranger pulled away. "How do I know you'll take it to the police? How do I know you won't simply take the money and run?"

"I wouldn't do that," the old man protested. Beside him, the old woman shook her head.

"Right," the stranger sneered. "There's fifty dollars in this wallet. The minute I hand it over, you'll be fifty dollars richer and I'll be out."

"If you don't trust me, what can we do?" The old man appeared both affronted and bewildered.

At that moment, a policeman came walking up the street.

"I've an idea." The stranger looked at the passerby. "You, sir!"

He stopped. "Are you speaking to me?"

"You're an officer of the law?" The stranger motioned him over, looking him up and down.

"Yes, sir," the man answered, indicating his uniform. "I consider myself such."

"We have a problem."

"May I help?"

"Would you take this wallet to the police station for us? I'll give you our names and you can say we found it. Then in a week, if it isn't claimed, we'll go and ask for it back."

"Well, I… We generally turn such monies in to our widows and orphans fund."

"I don't know." The old man was still uncertain.

"I tell you what," the stranger said. "To show you I'm trustworthy, I'll give this gentleman half of what's in that wallet." He nodded at the policeman. "From my own pocket. I'll give it to him to hold for me. You do the same...to make sure we get it back. Then, when we reclaim the money, he gives us back our money plus half of what's in the wallet. Sound fair?"

"That's only if no one claims it," the old man pointed out. "What if someone does?"

"I'm pretty sure no one will," the stranger said. "But if someone does, then this gentleman—what's your name, sir?"

"George," the man supplied. "Officer George Carmichael."

"Officer Carmichael will give us back our original amount." The stranger looked at Carmichael. "In fourteen days, we'll meet outside this hotel and you either give us back our money and the cut or we get our own money back and no hard feelings. Sound good?"

"Very well," the old man said, looking abruptly eager, obviously seeing an easy twenty-five dollars coming his way. Even his little wife had a greedy gleam in her eye.

He reached into his breast pocket, bringing out his own threadbare wallet.

"All right!" Padraig emerged from the shadows. He'd seen all he needed to see. "That's enough o' that!"

The stranger jumped. "Who are you?"

Both he and Carmichael looked apprehensive. The old man and woman merely appeared confused.

"Someone who knows a confidence scam when I see one." Padraig pulled the wallet from Carmichael's hands. He spoke to the old man. "These two are in cahoots, sir. As soon as you hand over your hard-earned money…"

He thought he was right in assuming the old couple couldn't afford to give away twenty-five dollars.

"They were going t' scarper off an' count their ill-gotten gains."

"What?" The old man looked outraged.

"Here now, you've no right to…" the stranger began.

"You want t' turn this over t' th' police?" Padraig glanced up the street. "There's anaithur constable in th' next block. A *real* one. Why don't we call him over? That'll save a trip t' th' precinct station."

He raised a hand.

"Oi! Officer!"

The stranger broke away, making a mad dash up the alley, Carmichael at his heels.

"Didn't think they'd want that," Padraig said, in satisfaction.

"They were going to cheat us?" The old man seemed unable to comprehend that.

"They were going t' rely on your greed t' get somethin' for nothin an' steal from you," Padraig corrected.

"But…how did you know?"

"I've played that game meself on occasion, sir…but not anymore," he added as he saw fear cross the wrinkled face.

"You…you aren't with one of those Irish gangs, are you?" the old woman quavered, recognizing his accent.

"No, ma'am," Padraig answered, truthfully. "I've always been a loner." He held out the wallet to the old man. "Here. This one's in better shape than yours, an' 'tis got fifty dollars in it. I think you can probably use that."

He watched the old man transfer his own money into the new wallet and place it in his pocket.

"Thank you."

"Think naithin' o' it, sir. Just don't talk t' strangers from now on…an' remember, if it seems too good t' be true, it usually is."

Padraig walked on down the street and to his hotel, but that little episode decided for him. The gangs of New York, especially the Irish ones, were giving his people a bad name. He didn't want to stay in a place doing that. The Irish were having a bad enough time of it at home without it spreading to the New World also. He'd go west as he'd planned, and soon.

****

…and he had.

With the passengers disembarked, the stage was gone, driven to the nearby livery stable where a fresh team would be substituted for the one carrying them this far. Then, the driver and his armed companion would be on to their next stop with whatever passengers remained.

Padraig glanced at the portmanteau the shotgun-wielding rider had helped him heave from the top of the coach and set on the ground. It now sat on end, a fairly small box holding all his worldly possessions. He'd made some heartrending choices as to what he would take with him, other than his clothing.

He was tired, in both body and spirit. He'd taken trains as far west as they went, but from there on, it seemed he'd been sitting in various coaches forever…rocking and swaying on wooden seats covered with scantily stuffed cushions almost as hard.

As soon as the driver called down to the passengers that they were entering this town, his body couldn't take any more. He decided to depart the coach, cutting short his proposed trip farther westward. Now, as he took in his surroundings, Padraig wondered if he'd made the right decision.

He was at the edge of town. A small building nearby announced, on a boarded sign nailed to its front, that it was the *U.S. Post Office*. In front of it was a single pole driven into the ground, a metal ring attached.

Pitiful excuse for a mail depository, Padraig thought. *Looks more like a privy.*

A short distance away stood a building three times as big and twice as long. The sign above it announced, *Olsen's Livery*. To one side, a small corral offered a view of several horses dozing in the shade of a long eave projecting from the stable's side.

There was a space of perhaps thirty feet between the livery stable and the next building where the town actually began.

The coach driver said the place was called Four Corners. It didn't appear to consist of much. From where he stood, Padraig could see only four buildings, two on the left and two on the right, facing each other across an expanse of what might be considered the main street. Far in the distance was the steeple of a small white building…a church, if the cross on its apex was any indication.

Oh Lord, an' I'm bettin' it ain't a Catholic church, aithur.

Padraig might not consider himself extremely religious, but he'd been christened, taught his catechism, been dragged to services by his parents, and enjoyed the Sacraments as a child. That in itself had been a tricky business, since the McCoys had long ago converted to Church of England to further their positions, though they privately held to Catholicism for many generations until recently. Either way, Confession hadn't been a very large part of this particular McCoy son's life after he set his feet on the path of scandal and nefarious activities, but deep inside it had been instilled in him that a place without a Catholic church, even one no longer attended, was nowhere for a decent Irishman to be.

He forced himself to ignore that small, still voice telling him to wait for the next coach, to get in it and out of this heathenish town. He was curious as to what those four buildings were…when someone rode up on a compact little sorrel.

The rider stopped the horse at the hitching post, slid from the saddle, and made fast the reins. With one hand on the horse's flank, he went around the animal, untying and pulling a set of bags from behind the saddle. Slinging the bags over his shoulder, he aimed himself for the post office.

Padraig picked up his portmanteau and hurried over, blocking his progress.

"Excuse me, sir…" He tapped the brim of his hat with his free hand.

The man stopped. He was short, stocky, and sandy-haired, about Padraig's age, with eyelashes of such a light color they made his blue eyes look shortsighted. Under his broad-brimmed hat, his hair curled around the cloth circling his neck, an oddity looking more like a large colored handkerchief than a neckpiece. His shirt was of threadbare fabric, faded and soft from many washings, and his trousers were of some material strongly resembling canvas duck, with slightly flaring hems covering slant-heeled boots.

The thing most impressing Padraig, however, was the revolver resting on his hip in a brown leather holster.

"Somethin' I can do for you?" the man asked.

"Aye, I'm wonderin' if you might answer me a couple o' questions?"

"Maybe." The man was cautious. He looked Padraig up and down, noting the very stylish frock coat and the now-dusty pointed toes of his high-button shoes, as well as the portmanteau. "You just leave the stage?"

"That's right." Padraig set down the case and held out a hand. "Padraig McCoy."

The man caught the hand, giving it a hearty shake. "They call me Buck."

"Why?" As the man scowled, Padraig went on, "I mean…a buck's a deer an' they're tall, beautiful craitures. If you'll pardon me sayin' so, you're naithur tall nor in any way what I'd call beautiful…so why do they call you Buck?"

"Because it's short for Buchanan." The man laughed, the scowl disappearing. "Buchanan Wallace, but that's too much of a mouthful when someone's in a hurry, so I'm Buck to one and all." He winked. "A word of advice, if you're planning on staying around here, McCoy…it ain't wise to question a man's chosen handle. You said you had a couple of questions. Was that one of 'em?"

"Not exactly. I'm wonderin' if you can tell me whether anyone in this town is hirin'?" Padraig looked past Buck to the sorrel, switching its tail against a couple of horseflies. "I'm guessin' you're one o' those cowboys

I've heard about. Do you have a ranch around here?"

"That's two questions," Buck acknowledged. He stroked his chin where a bit of blond fuzz had escaped his morning razor. "Which should I answer first? Hmm." He smiled.

"No, I don't own a ranch, but I work at one. Circle J. And, yes…my boss is hiring, matter of fact. We had two hands quit during the last drive…"

"Drive?" Padraig interrupted. "What's that?"

"Cattle drive…where are you from, anyways? You don't know what a drive is?"

"I'm from Eire," Padraig supplied.

"Ire? Where's that? Somewhere Back East?"

"A li'l farther than that," Padraig explained. He would soon learn that when referring to the east coast of the country, either in speech or writing, everyone capitalized both words. "Across th' Atlantic. Ireland."

"Ireland, huh? Well, I'll be." Buck grinned. "Why would an Irishman be 'way out here in Nebraska?"

"Why is *anyone* in Nebraska?" Padraig countered, not wanting to go into detail just then. He was uncertain whether an explanation of how his father was paying him to stay away might make these westerners consider him an outlaw of some kind. He didn't want that.

"Guess you've a point there," Buck conceded. "Won't argue, since it ain't always safe to ask about a man's background. That goes along with questionin' his name."

"Do you think your boss might consider hirin' me?" Padraig asked.

"Depends. Know anything about herdin' cows?"

Padraig shook his head.

"Ropin'?"

27

Again, Padraig gave a negative shake.

"Brandin'? Wranglin'?"

"Sorry. I don't e'en know what those words mean," he admitted.

"What use are you, then?" Buck wanted to know, smiling to show he meant no insult. He glanced at Padraig's waist. "Good thing you're so thick in the middle. With your lack of skills, you might need to live on some of that fat." He thought a moment. "Are you familiar with horses?"

"Horses…those I *do* know," Padraig said. "Me da— me faithur, I mean—has a stable o' thoroughbred hunters an' carriage horses, an' I had a couple o' me own."

They were reluctantly left behind because no passage had been paid for horses to go on the ship with him.

"That's one thing in your favor, anyways," Buck agreed. "Tell you what, you can ride out to the ranch with me and talk to the boss, and if he wants to take a chance on a greenhorn, then you're set."

"Thank you." Padraig didn't ask what a greenhorn was. He decided it must mean someone completely ignorant of the Nebraska vernacular.

"Right now, I've got to pick up the mail, and do a few other in-town chores, so why don't you tag along and I'll introduce you to the postmaster and get you acquainted with the town?"

With that, Buck walked to the post office and went inside.

Picking up his portmanteau, Padraig followed.

"How's your name pronounced again?" Buck asked as he neared.

Padraig told him.

"Paw-drick, huh?" Buck drawled the word. "They call you anything other than that?"

"Me braithurs call me *Paddy* on occasion."

"Patty?" Buck laughed. "Better not let any of the other hands hear that. Out here, Patty's a girl's name, and believe me, you don't look anything like a girl. Unless you're one of those sweet mollies." He took a step back, giving Padraig a squint, eyes narrowing. "You ain't...are you?"

"If I thought you meant that in a derogatory way," Padraig answered, "I think I should be insulted." He shook his head. "Nay. You can relax. I'll settle for being called Patrick, if pronouncin' it th' Irish way's too much o' a bother."

"Right then, Patrick." Buck slapped his shoulder. "Let's get that mail."

Chapter 4

After meeting Elton Trent, the postmaster, and being given an interrogation he thought he deftly answered without giving away much incriminating background, Padraig followed Buck outside.

"Curious ol' geezer, isn't he?"

"That's because he's town folk," Buck answered. "You won't catch a cowhand asking such questions. Like I said, out here, it ain't good policy to delve too closely into a man's background, 'less he volunteers it."

"That's good t' know," Padraig murmured. As Buck gave him a brow-lifting stare, he explained hastily, "I mean, so I won't be committin' a social error."

"Don't know how social it'd be," Buck countered. "Though it could possibly be a downright fatal one."

While Padraig was digesting that fact, Buck started down the main street.

"Next stop, bank," he called over his shoulder. "I'll leave my horse here and come back for him."

Padraig caught up to him about three yards from the post office. "That answers me ithur question—does this town have a bank?"

"Guess I did already answer that, didn't I?" Buck increased his speed.

Padraig did the same, swinging his portmanteau.

****

The bank was as unimpressive as the post office. A

plain clapboard building with a sign over it proclaiming it the *Four Corners Bank & Trust*, it had the distinction of being painted white, though that color was long since tinged gray by dust, wind, and rain.

Inside, there was barely room for four people. The single teller in his little cage took up a third of the space. Another man sat at a desk to one side with a small floor safe beside it, using the second third and allowing precious little space for patrons to line themselves before the teller, if there had been any patrons. At the moment, the bank was empty, except for the two employees.

"Afternoon, Buck," the teller greeted them. "Heard y'all got back from the drive. That the sale price for the cattle?"

He nodded at the saddlebags.

"And right glad to get it outen my hands," Buck confirmed. He swung the bags off his shoulder and dropped them into the window's opening. "Count it and write me out a receipt for the boss. I'll be back to pick it up when I leave."

Nodding, the clerk slid the saddlebags out of the window and opened one flap. He began to take out greenbacks, banded together by paper strips, stacking them on the counter in front of him.

"You were carryin' around that much cash?" Padraig was astonished.

"Couldn't leave it on the horse while I was getting the mail."

"But…why didn't you come here *first*?"

"Because I always get the mail first." That explanation was delivered as if it should've been obvious. Buck faced the door. "Come on."

"Wait."

Buck looked back at him.

"While we're here, I think I'll do a bit o' bankin', meself." Padraig turned to the clerk who had unbanded the money and was sorting it into stacks of various denominations. "I'd like t' open an account, please."

"Certainly." The clerk hid his astonishment very well. He glanced at the man behind the desk. "Mr. Bainbridge can help you with that."

"Mr. Bainbridge?" Padraig took the five steps placing him before the desk while Buck leaned against the wall, watching.

The man had already gotten to his feet. Unlike the clerk, who was in shirtsleeves with sleeve protectors and an eyeshade, he was dressed as nattily as Padraig and looked just as out of place in the little bank.

"Milton Bainbridge." He held out a hand that Padraig grasped. "You say you wish to open an account, Mr...?"

"McCoy...Padraig McCoy."

"Please, sit down." Bainbridge gestured to a chair beside the desk and Padraig dropped into it.

"Hey, Patrick..." Buck spoke up. "Ain't you getting the cart afore the horse? Shouldn't you get a job before you worry about putting the money into a bank?"

Bainbridge stiffened. "You aren't employed, Mr. McCoy?" His tone was icy.

"Nay," Padraig answered. "But don't worry about me money." He patted his waist. "I've a money belt. I want t' use its contents t' open an account."

"Oh, well, then..." Bainbridge warmed considerably. Opening a drawer of the desk, he pulled out papers, opened his inkwell, and grasped a pen, poising it over the top sheet. "How much would you like to deposit?"

Padraig considered. Upon arriving in New York, he'd had his cheque cashed and converted into dollars, carrying it in a money belt wrapped around his waist under his shirt, hoping if anyone noticed, they'd simply think him a bit well-padded in the belly area. Buck's previous comment confirmed that fact.

"About…oh, around two thousand, I guess."

He was completely unprepared for their reactions.

"Two thousand? Jehosephat, Patrick," the cowhand exclaimed. "With that much cash, what do you need a job for?"

"We'll be most happy to open an account, Mr. McCoy," Bainbridge gushed. His hand shook as he wrote in the amount on the paper.

From sheer joy, Padraig didn't doubt. He'd already pegged Mr. Bainbridge as one who judged a man's ability by his financial worth and realized he'd climbed considerably higher in the banker's estimation with those few words.

"Thank you." He gave Bainbridge a slight dip of his head in acknowledgement. To Buck, he said, "Money doesn't last long if there's nane t' replace it."

He had no idea how long it might take for a wire to reach Quinton and for his father to send another draft to the bank…if he hadn't been gulling his own son and no more were forthcoming.

Would Da be that cruel to me? A little tit for tat, perhaps? Letting Padraig see how it felt to be conied? He decided he was going to trust his father to keep his word.

"Good thinking." Buck resumed his stance against the wall.

It didn't take long to get the transaction done.

Bainbridge allowed Padraig to go into what turned out to be a coat closet behind the desk to unbutton his shirt and remove the money belt. Emerging from the closet, he placed the belt on the desk, where the teller, having completed counting the money brought in by Buck, was called over. Apparently, accepting money was part of Bainbridge's job but counting it wasn't.

"Here." The teller thrust the empty saddlebags and a slip of paper at Buck as he walked past. "Here's your receipt. Since you're still here, you may as well have it now. Then you won't have to come back for it."

Buck folded the receipt and stuck it into a hip pocket, then draped the bags over his shoulder.

The teller proceeded to sort and count Padraig's money. "Two thousand five hundred and thirty-two dollars," he announced.

"In that case, I'll deposit twenty-four hundred, an' ask for a hundred an' thirty-two back," Padraig decided.

"You sure you want to carry around that much cash?" Buck asked.

"No one's going to know I have that much," Padraig answered. He looked from him to the teller who still stood by the desk, and then at Bainbridge. "Unless someone blabs."

"Mr. McCoy…" Bainbridge managed an affronted bluster. "Be assured, we don't talk of our patrons' transactions."

"Good." Padraig got to his feet. He picked up the empty money belt, snapped open the portmanteau, and dropped it inside. "If there's nothing else…"

"That should do it," Bainbridge announced. He took a small folder in which he'd written something and presented it to Padraig with a bow. "Your passbook, sir.

Welcome to Four Corners Bank & Trust."

"Thank you." Padraig accepted it, placing it in a breast pocket. "Now, if you'll excuse us? Mr. Wallace has ithur business t' tend." He walked out, Buck following.

Outside, the cowboy hooted with laughter. "*Mr. Wallace?* I don't think anyone's ever referred to me that way. Bainbridge sure looked dumbstruck for a minute. I don't think he knew who you meant."

He struck Padraig on the shoulder.

"Damn, Patrick, you've got a wicked sense of humor!"

Not wanting to tell Buck he hadn't intended speaking of him in such a way as a joke but a courtesy, Padraig merely grinned back. "Where to now?"

"My *other business* is at the general store." Buck led the way down the boardwalk.

That didn't take long. Buck merely left a list. In between introducing Padraig and explaining he was new in town, he told the storekeeper someone would bring the buckboard into town later in the week to pick up everything. Afterward, they were out on the street again.

"What next?" Padraig asked.

He looked up and down the street, finding there was more to Four Corners than he'd thought as he stood before the livery stable. Besides the bank, there was another building with a sign declaring, Eats, Breakfast, Dinner, and Supper. Next to that was a slightly larger building, a sign suspended from a nail over the front porch, Ruff's Boarding House. Across the street was the Four Corners Barber Shop and Bath House, and another building with double swinging doors through which music could be heard. The placard above it read Trails

End Saloon.

Next to the saloon but across the alley was a small building distinguishable from the others by the fact that its one small window had Sheriff's Office written in white paint on a single dusty pane.

"Nothing," Buck answered. "That completes my chores for the boss. I have to start back for the ranch in two hours, but until then, the rest of the time's my own." His blue eyes abruptly took on a gleam. "You got anything you need to do, Patrick?"

"I'm too much o' a stranger t'answer that," Padraig said.

"In that case, let me introduce you to one of Four Corners' most famous landmarks." Taking his arm, Buck led him across the street and onto the opposite boardwalk.

They stopped in front of the swinging doors where Buck released Padraig and spread his arms wide.

"The Trails End Saloon...the place for the weary cowhand to escape the toils of his everyday life and take in some leisure in the form of..."

"Don't tell me, let me guess," Padraig interrupted. "Gambling...women...an' booze?"

"...and not necessarily in that order." Buck finished for him. "You a drinking man, Padraig?"

"I've lifted a few tankards in me time," Padraig admitted. "An' before you ask...aye, I've cut a couple o' decks, too."

More than a couple, truth be told, but he wasn't about to tell this new acquaintance *that.*

"What are we waiting for?" Pushing open the doors, Buck stalked inside.

Currently, the saloon held only six men. In a corner

under the mezzanine, a piano player was plinking away at some tune Padraig didn't recognize but decided was catchy enough. The bartender was behind the bar, polishing glasses. The four customers played cards.

It appeared to be a friendly game because matchsticks littered the center of the table instead of money or chips. Two women, one an improbably pale blonde and the other, an equally impossible redhead whose locks were even more brilliant than Padraig's own hair, stood behind a couple of the men.

Padraig gave the two women an appreciative eye, taking in the frilly wrappers open to reveal tightly-laced black satin corsets, and black stockings peeking from under white pantalettes to disappear into calf-high buttoned shoes.

The blonde poured drinks whenever glasses were emptied, occasionally stroking a flannel-sleeved arm, or kissing a leathery cheek. When one of them raked in the matches, the redhead grabbed his hand, dragging him from his chair and toward stairs leading up the mezzanine, pulling off her wrapper as they went.

"Lord, they're ready for action, ain't they?" he muttered.

The game started over, as three-handed poker this time.

Buck was so well-known the bartender didn't bother asking what he'd have. He simply poured whiskey into two shot glasses.

Raising his, Padraig said, "To your good health, Buck."

He downed it in one gulp.

A second later, he was gasping and demanding, "What th' hell's that supposed t' be? You call that *whiskey*?" he asked the bartender.

"I do," the man answered. He straightened so Padraig could see he was well over the six-foot mark. One hand went under the bar's counter.

Figuring he probably was reaching for a mallet or something as deadly as a shillelagh, Padraig deftly turned his insult into something else.

"I'm thinkin' you've got a better brand o' whiskey under th' bar than this benzene you're foistin' on me," he said. "An'…so…"

He brought out his wallet, managing to get out the smallest bill without letting anyone see how many it held. Laying the greenback on the bar, he said, "I'd like t' buy everyone here a drink…o' th' good stuff…an' leave Buck an' me th' bottle."

"Hey! I like that." The card player had reached the top of the stairs.

Pulling away from the blonde, he galloped back down to the bar. Receiving a glass from the bartender, he nodded to Padraig, "Thanks, gent," tossed it down, and ran back up the stairs again.

Putting his arm around the blonde, he disappeared into the first room with her.

"You're welcome," Padraig called.

A raised hand acknowledged his words before the door shut.

As the others bellied up to the bar, the piano player changed the tune to something more melodious, a ballad of some kind. Buck took the bottle and gestured to a nearby table. While Padraig dropped into a chair, he poured two generous slugs into their glasses.

"Now that's more like it." Padraig declared as he lowered his glass. He picked up the bottle, studying the label. "Don't recognize it, but 'tis much better than that other swill."

"If you do stay around here, you've just won a few friends for life," Buck said, nodding to the three who were now resuming their game. "'Course they'll expect you to stand them to drinks every time you see them from now on."

"An' if I don't get th' job?" Padraig asked, pouring another.

"Then they'll be buying you one to commiserate."

"Do you think I've a chance of bein' hired, Buck?" Padraig became serious. "I've money now, but like I said, I don't know how long 'tis goin' t' last."

"Can't say for sure, Patrick. It all depends on the boss."

"Maybe I should have somethin' waitin' in th' wings."

"Sam Barlow owns Trails End," Buck said. "He can always use someone to sweep the sawdust and sprinkle new, and empty the spittoons."

He glanced at the floor, with a kick disturbing the sawdust piled around the table leg.

"Floor ain't been re-sprinkled in a week," he said disapprovingly. "Not since his last tender up and left for California. Don't pay much, but I understand he allows a sleeping cot in the storeroom."

"Does it come with any benefits?" Padraig glanced up at the mezzanine.

"Don't count on it." Buck laughed. "Those girls are only available if you've got four bits. Glad to see you like the ladies."

"Why?" Padraig sipped his whiskey. He decided two glasses would be his limit. He didn't want to meet his prospective boss two sheets to the wind, a mighty temptation since the liquor was very smooth. Not Bushmills, but good enough.

"Because it eases any doubts I had concerning your earlier answer about being a molly."

"You doubted me word?" Padraig pretended insult.

"Hey…men can get tarred and feathered and run out of town on a rail for admitting to such a thing," Buck said. "Who'd be that stupid? I figured you might be lying. Those fine clothes of yours…"

"…are what any decent gentleman in Ireland wears," Padraig interrupted. "Oh, I love th' ladies, Buck, don't e'er doubt it…sometimes a li'l too much, I'm afraid."

"Better not let any husbands in Four Corners hear that, either." Buck laughed.

"Hey, 'tis beginning t' sound as if I'm damned if I do an' damned if I don't," Padraig complained. "I don't truck with married women, be assured, Buck me lad…ne'er again, anyway," he added, in a slight mutter.

"Let's slow down on the drinking," Buck suggested. "It's getting time for me to start back to the ranch, and I don't want to show up pie-eyed. Boss doesn't allow that except on Saturday nights."

"In that case, by all means…" Padraig downed his drink and got to his feet, picking up his portmanteau. "Let's be on our way."

"There's only one thing left to do," Buck said as they reached the door to a chorus of farewells from the card players.

"An' what's that?" Padraig turned to wave at the three men.

"We've got to get you a horse."

"A horse?"

"How else d'you expect to get to the ranch?" Buck paused as the doors swung shut behind them. "You didn't think you were riding behind me, did you?"

"Been a long time since I rode pillion behind anyone," Padraig said.

"Pillion? What's that?"

"Ne'er mind. I noticed we passed a livery stable on th' way in. Think they might have a horse for sale?"

"We can find out."

They started up the street in the direction of the livery stable and the depot.

Chapter 5

After a brief stop at the general store, where Padraig was quickly and properly outfitted by the proprietor with trail clothes, they were on their way. Though he didn't change garments, tucking everything into his portmanteau with the explanation he'd save them until he learned if he were going to be a cowhand or not, Padraig exchanged his shoes for boots and his top hat for a broad-brimmed one similar to Buck's. The topper wouldn't fit into his portmanteau so he reluctantly left it with the storeowner, who immediately put it on the counter as a sale item.

As he paid, he said, "How about throwin' in anaithur shirt for Buck here? That one he's wearin' looks as 'tis goin' t' be lettin' in th' wind soon."

"That's not neces..." Buck began a protest but Padraig interrupted.

"Nay, now. You've been so helpful, 'tis only right I repay you somehow."

"Well, in that case..." Relenting, Buck accepted the folded shirt, tucking it into his saddlebag. As they left the store, however, he said, "Padraig, I've got to tell you right now. Stop being so generous. It ain't healthy."

"What d'ya mean?" Padraig stopped, wavering back and forth on his new boots, and wondering how he was ever going to learn to walk on heels two and a half inches high and slanted as well. How did any of them manage it?

"I mean, it ain't a good idea to wave your money around like you were doing at the saloon, or in the store." He paused a moment as if trying to decide how to say the next thing on his mind. "And…well, I'm grateful and all, but don't buy me any more gifts."

"I was merely showin' me gratitude…" Padraig protested.

"In that case, a simple *thank you* is enough. Out here men don't buy men presents."

Padraig thought about that a moment. "Are you going to take it back?"

"No." Buck heaved a sigh. "Truth be told. I need a new shirt."

"Consider it a birthday present."

"My birthday ain't 'til next February," Buck said.

"Early Christmas gift, then."

"All right," Buck relented and held up a warning finger. "But nothing else. Understand?"

He swung the saddlebags over his shoulder again and started up the street.

"Got it." Stride heavy and firm to make certain he didn't turn an ankle until he learned to maneuver in boots, Padraig followed.

At the stable, he allowed Buck to dicker with Olsen about the price of the horse he was to buy. Buck picked out one from those in the corral, a bay-and-white animal he called a pinto, that Padraig might have mistaken for one of his own country's Gypsy Vanners, except for its conformation. Buck pointed out its good qualities to Padraig and its bad points to the stable owner.

Studying the sturdy pinto and its muscular shoulders and hindquarters, Padraig commented, "Damn, that animal looks more like a bulldog than a horse."

"Don't turn up your fine Irish nose at him," Buck warned. "That bulldog'll go a quarter of a mile faster than any of those thoroughbreds you say your pa owns."

Impressed with that fact, Padraig shut up and quietly forked over the amount settled upon, which also included the price of a saddle, bridle, and blanket. He saddled the pinto, impressing Buck with how he managed that without asking for assistance, though he was a little dismayed by the configuration of the saddle and the high pommel. Tying the portmanteau to the horn, he swung into the saddle, gathering the reins.

With a tip of his new hat to Olsen, he said to Buck, in a parody of his brother Donal's acquired accent, "Now then, my good fellow, shall we be on our way?"

That was met with a hoot of laughter as Buck touched heels to his own horse's sides and guided it away from the stable.

Chapter 6

"You're looking mighty pleased with yourself," Buck commented.

They'd been riding for some time, but except for Padraig's occasional comments about the landscape and the heat, neither man had spoken since leaving Four Corners.

Padraig looked away from his contemplation of the flat grassland before them. Though he was certain it looked odd combined with his clothing, he was grateful for the wide brim of his hat, shading his eyes and protecting them from the sun glaring off the brown prairie grass.

"I'm thinkin' me da would be whoopin' with laughter if he could see me now...ridin' a horse that looks as if someone poured white paint o'er him, an' sportin' this...what'd you call it? *Sombrero*?"

"After he stopped laughing, your pa'd find out quick enough pintos seem to have better stamina than most horses, and quarter-mile horses even more so," Buck replied. "He'd learn how necessary a *sombrero* is, too."

"I've a feelin' me education's about t' be enlarged considerably." Padraig shook his head, trying to envision Quinton wearing clothing similar to Buck's.

He couldn't.

"Say, Patrick...mind telling me what brings you to Nebraska, anyways?" Intent on breaking the silence by making conversation, Buck asked. "I mean, we don't get many Irishmen around here. Got a few with Irish names, but it was their grandpas or such that came from the Old Country, and them from Back East somewheres."

"Didn't you tell me 'twasn't good form t' enquire after a man's antecedents?" Padraig stopped the pinto and looked over at his friend. "Could be downright dangerous, I think you said."

"You're right." Buck looked chagrinned. "I spoke afore I thought. Ignore my nosiness. Sorry."

"…but seein' as you're a friend, I'll tell you anyway," Padraig continued. "'Twas a steamship as brought me th' first leg o' me journey. After that, 'twas train, then stagecoach th' rest o' th' way." He paused as Buck laughed. "An' I think that answers your question while not really tellin' you anythin' at all."

Kicking the pinto into a gallop, he rode away, smiling as he heard the sorrel's hooves behind him.

Presently, he slowed the horse to a walk. No sense wearing out the animal by running him when he wasn't certain how long they'd have to ride.

Ahead, something bright made him again halt the pinto, putting up a hand to shield his eyes.

"What is it?" Buck asked, pulling his own horse to a stop.

"Up ahead." Lowering his hand slightly, Padraig peered around it at the white expanse before them, reflecting back the sun so brightly it made his eyes water. "Is that snow?"

His tone indicated he couldn't believe it at this time of year, but had no idea what else it could be.

"That's a salt flat," Buck explained. "Little Salt Creek's near here. It's a run-off of Salt Creek, which I've heard is somehow connected to that big salt lake they've got over in Utah, but I've never understood how that can be."

"Salt flat, huh?" Padraig stared, attempting not to blink.

The sand-like deposit was fascinating, so white and shining, covering the prairie. It reminded him of some of the beaches he'd seen in Eire, where the high sheer cliffs dropped down to little inlets giving way to miles of sandy seacoast. Ships would anchor off shore and send in longboats, taking passengers and crew to land.

Here and there, cattails protruded from the white soil, as well as little green patches growing through the salt. The wind wafted toward them, bringing with it a remarkably ocean-like scent.

He thought of the fishing boats and the smell of salt-soaked timbers on those times his father had taken him to Dublin. Closing his eyes, he inhaled deeply, momentarily transported back to that scene at the mouth of the River Liffey where it opened into Dublin Bay.

"Over at Lancaster, they've got bigger salt flats," Buck continued. "That's why people started settling there. There's salt mines there now, but I hear most people are getting their salt from the mines down in Kansas. Some of the sodbusters around here still harvest the salt and use it."

"You mean, you can cook with th' stuff?" Padraig was astounded.

"Them what can't afford boughten salt do," Buck replied. "The boss gets ourn from the general store."

Padraig decided he was thankful for that.

"See those little green spots?" Buck pointed.

Padraig nodded.

"Plants. Most of them are some kind of cactus, I reckon. Only things can survive a salt flat." He waved a hand at the other grasses rippling in the breeze, the salty ocean smell getting stronger.

Fighting the near-overwhelming wave of homesickness flooding over him, Padraig gathered his reins. "We've spent enough time talkin' about salt flats an' such. Let's get goin' before it gets any later. How many miles farther do we have t' go, anyway?"

In four more hours, they arrived at the Circle-J. By that time, Padraig was mentally debating asking Buck to stop and let him dismount to walk around a bit, before his backside was fooled into thinking it had become part of his saddle. Certain as he was that he'd be ridiculed for doing such a thing, he was saved from the embarrassing admission by the road to the ranch coming into sight.

"We're here." Buck looked up at the sky where the sun was slowly sliding behind some far-off foothills. "Looks like we're in time for supper. Good thing, too. I'm getting hungry, how about you?"

"I am feelin' a li'l belly-empty," Padraig admitted.

The ranch house came into view, a small unimpressive single story, its only outstanding feature a porch running the length of the front. On the porch, a man leaned against one of the supports of the porch overhang. He was holding a tin cup, sipping from it.

"There's the boss." Buck trotted the sorrel to a hitching post in front of the house with Padraig following.

When the cowhand dismounted and tied his reins to the post, Padraig copied his action, hoping that wouldn't be breaking some unspoken Nebraska rule since he was with someone living at the ranch.

"Well, Buck. See you got back all right." The man acknowledged their arrival. "In time for supper, too. Cookie tells me he'll be ready to ring the bell in a bit. Got my bank receipt?"

The rancher was another short, stocky man, making Padraig wonder if all Nebraskans were so much smaller than he. He'd never considered himself tall. In fact, both Quinton and Donal towered over him, but since his arrival in Four Corners, he hadn't met a man whom he could look straight in the eye, and none taller, other than the bartender at Trails End. Those treacherous heels to his boots now made him feel as if he were a giant.

"Yes, sir, Mr. Jessup." Buck dug into his hip pocket and produced the receipt the teller had given him, going up the steps and handing it to his boss.

Jessup took it, tucking it into his own shirt pocket without glancing at it. He raised the cup, taking a long swallow, then lowered it to gesture at Padraig.

"Who's this?"

"This is…"

"Padraig McCoy." Padraig stopped on the second step so he was lower than Jessup and looking up at him. He'd decided it might not be a good idea to point out how much taller he was than his prospective employer.

He held out a hand. With a quick glance at his clothing causing raised brows, Jessup shook it.

"Samuel Jessup."

As he released it, Padraig continued, "I'm looking for employment an' Buck said you're hirin'."

"Oh?" Jessup's brows went even higher…and the interrogation began, the same questions Buck had asked, to which Padraig gave the same answers.

As he thought he saw rejection in Jessup's

expression, he said quickly, "I admit I know naithin' about cattle in particular or ranchin' in general, but I do know horses, an' anyway, how difficult could it be t' learn t' tend a bunch o' cows?"

That made Jessup stare at him as if he'd said either the smartest thing or the dumbest he'd ever heard. When he laughed, that encouraged Padraig, who smiled tentatively.

"You know…I like you, young feller, though you're about as ignorant as a newborn babe about certain things." Jessup took another swig of coffee. "It's true I need another ranch hand, two if I could find them. Tell you what. We won't be having another drive until the current crop of calves grow up, so Buck here'll have plenty of time to show you the ropes."

"You mean, I'm hired?" Padraig looked at Buck, who appeared disbelieving Jessup was actually going to take on the greenhorn.

"Tell me one thing, and I want the truth." Jessup lowered his cup to give him a stern stare.

"Yes, sir," Padraig nodded. "What is it?"

"Are you wanted by the law? In any way, shape, or form?"

"Nay, sir." Padraig felt compelled to raise one hand as if taking an oath. "I'm not. I swear."

"Then you're hired." Jessup shook a finger, reminiscent of Buck's action in town. "But if I find out you've lied…you'll be out on your ear and cooling your heels in Four Corners' jail so fast it'll make your head spin."

He looked at Buck.

"Get him settled into the bunkhouse and introduced around. By then it should be time to eat."

"Right, Boss." Buck untied his horse and led it away, motioning for Padraig to follow.

"Thank you, sir…uh…Boss," Padraig called as he pulled the pinto's reins from the post.

Jessup raised a hand and went back to his coffee.

"I didn't think he'd do it," Buck muttered as Padraig caught up to him. "I figured he'd turn you down flat, let you bunk here overnight, and send you on your way in the morning."

"Shows you what a good judge o' character th' boss is," Padraig murmured.

Chapter 7

The bunkhouse was a small clapboard building looking more like one of the out sheds on his father's property than living quarters. It was a fifteen-by-twenty-foot rectangle with a barely slanted tin roof, one window next to the door, and no porch. Beside the door was the expected hitching rail.

"How many employees does Mr. Jessup have?" Padraig asked, tying his horse next to Buck's.

The pinto raised its head, looking around as if assessing its new home and finding it acceptable. It switched its tail and snorted, stamping a hoof.

"Counting me and the cook…nine," Buck answered. He pulled the bags from behind the saddle. "Or, I should say…ten now, since he just hired a certain Irish dude…and we call them *hands.*"

He gestured to the horses.

"We'll bed down our mounts after supper. For now, let's get inside and acquaint you with your fella cowpokes."

He pushed open the door and went inside. Pulling the portmanteau from the saddle horn, Padraig followed.

The first thing he saw were six two-decker bunks ranged around the walls, three head-to-foot on a side wall, the other three at the back.

Tucked into a corner on the opposite wall next to a potbellied iron stove, four men were playing a game of cards. Another sat in a lower bunk, laboriously writing a letter, a short length of board doubling as a lap desk balanced precariously across his knees. At his feet was an open bottle of ink. He leaned forward, dipping his pen into it, then straightened and began to write again.

In the bunk above him, the flannelled back of another man was visible, blanket pulled to his waist, his head burrowed into a pillow. Someone was also asleep in the lower part of the next bunk.

The next sets of bunks were empty, the bottom of the last one filled with a big man propped on a pillow set against the bunk's head. He was fully dressed except for his boots, bare feet crossed at the ankles. His nose was buried in what Padraig at first thought was an almanac such as he'd seen in New York, until he turned a page and the book shifted so he could see it was actually a magazine. *Naughty Ladies* was the title emblazoned across the front cover with a detailed sketch of a woman carrying a parasol and not wearing as much as the shakes at Trails End, little more than a camisole and stockings, in fact.

Damn, Padraig thought. *This place has more o' th' amenities o' civilization than I expected.*

He'd seen such a magazine while browsing through a bookshop in New York and had been astonished that the city had such items since he'd only thought places like London and Dublin bookstores carried literature "for discerning gentlemen" in their back rooms. His surprise increased when the proprietor told him he had some other rarities in his stockroom…"if the gentleman would care to peruse them?"

The gentleman did.

Padraig followed him and was astounded to discover

a veritable treasure trove of pornographic literature, at some fairly exorbitant prices. He purchased the least expensive pamphlet and hurried back to his hotel to savor his find. It now rested in the bottom of his portmanteau.

"Boys," Buck called out. "Want you to meet our new hand." He tossed his saddlebags onto one of the empty bunks and gestured to Padraig. "Padraig McCoy."

Padraig took a step and stopped beside him.

"That's Sam…Will…" Buck waved to the men at the table.

Each nodded or raised a hand in acknowledgement as he introduced around the room. Padraig did the same.

"…and that's Big Jack." Buck indicated the man reading the magazine.

Big Jack looked up but didn't speak. He eyed the newcomer quietly and speculatively, with a slightly malicious stare that gave Padraig an odd quiver.

"Pleased t' meet you all," he said, trying to stifle his accent as much as possible and failing.

His words were met with a couple of raised brows but no one commented. Adhering to that *No questions asked* code, he decided. All except Jack, who swung his sockless feet over the side of the bunk and stood up, dropping the magazine to the bed where it fell, pages bent, revealing an actual lithograph of a woman in an odalisque pose, her bare shoulders and full-figured backside presented to the viewer while she peered coyly over her shoulder. Remembering the price of his little pamphlet, Padraig surmised the cowboy must've handed over a good bit of his wages to obtain the magazine. He wondered who in Four Corners was the seller. That also reminded him he hadn't asked how much his own salary would be.

"Well, now…" Big Jack took a step away from the bunk. His bare feet made a soft slap on the rough boards. "Who have we here?"

Other than the bartender, he was the first man Padraig had met who came anywhere near his own height. His pose, feet slightly apart as if bracing his body, fists against his hips, seemed intended to point this out as well as to intimidate slightly.

Thinking he hadn't heard Padraig's name because he'd been so immersed in the titillation of the magazine's illustrations, as the slight peak in the front of his denims bore witness, Padraig again said, "I'm Padraig McCoy, an' I'm th' new hand."

"I know *who* you are, pretty boy." Jack sneered his answer. There was no other way to describe his expression. "What I'm asking is…*what* are you…molly?"

"What did you say?" Padraig stiffened, not only at the insult but in wonder that the man was verbally attacking him for no reason.

"Ignore him." Buck's caution came in a fierce whisper as he put a hand on his arm. He dropped his voice even lower so only Padraig heard. "Jack's a bully and a troublemaker, but he's the trail auger and a good one, so the boss tolerates his meanness."

"Don't bother saying anything, belvedere boy." Jack raised his voice slightly. "That fancy vest and that swingy-tail coat answers my question for me."

Across the room, the card players fell silent, looking from Padraig to Buck in something pretty close to dread. It certainly wasn't anticipation, so whatever was about to happen, they were obviously not going to be part of it. In his bunk, the letter writer stopped scribbling. Carefully, he picked up the ink bottle and capped it. Everyone waited for Padraig's reaction.

"Can you tell me where I can put me portmanteau?" Padraig made his question as mild as possible. He raised the case in case Jack wasn't aware of the meaning of the word.

"Portmanteau, is it?" There was another sneer, even more hateful than the first. Jack seemed to think Padraig's calm answer even more condemning. "You too good to carry a warbag like the rest of us? But a la-de-dah portmanteau? Well." He gestured to the last bunk near the door. "That one's empty."

"Thanks." Relieved that he'd diverted trouble, Padraig turned to regard the two bunks. He heard a step behind him. Out of the corner of his eye, he saw Buck step forward.

"Trying to decide whether you want to be on top or on the bottom, molly?" Jack grated out the insult.

What ails him? Padraig couldn't understand why the cowhand seemed determined to start a fight. *I'm a total stranger. Is it me accent or what?*

He wondered if this was some form of hazing a newcomer. Once, while home on holiday, Donal had told him they did such at school. Some of his older brother's tales of public school life had been hair-raising, making Padraig in no hurry to follow him to Eton. Obviously institutions of higher learning were not merely halls of academe but were also fairly dangerous.

From the others' behavior, he had a feeling Big Jack did this often, and the outcome would determine how he fared as one of them. He also was certain they wouldn't interfere unless he was definitely endangered.

He set the bag on the bottom bunk and flipped open the leather strap securing the lock.

"Whatcha got in there, dearie?" Jack asked. "Something to go with that pretty vest? Some more city slicker duds, maybe?"

Padraig didn't move, continuing to bend over the bag, hands on its handle. There was another step behind him, a third.

Jack moved closer.

"What ails you, man?" Padraig asked, looking over his shoulder. "An' why have you taken such a dislikin' t'me? We're ne'er met afore."

"Maybe I just don't like the way you talk," Big Jack snarled. "Or those fancy duds of yourn."

"Can't much be done about me accent," Padraig replied. "As for me clothes, I'll be changin' them soon enough..."

"You're such a sweet little daisy-belle I'll bet your drawers are silk with lace on them."

A hand on his shoulder spun Padraig around so swiftly he was nearly knocked off his feet. He struggled to regain his balance.

Buck drew in a sharp breath. It was echoed by someone at the card table.

"Think I'll just take a peek and find out for myself." Jack hooked three fingers into Padraig's belt, dragging him forward. "Are they pink or..."

Padraig hit him in the belly with his fist.

With a loud whoosh of breath, Jack doubled over, gasping for air. Padraig's knee came up, catching him under the chin.

There was a loud *click* as the cowboy's head was knocked backward, his lower jaw colliding with his upper, teeth snapping together, a move Donal had condescended to teach him in case the older boys at whichever university Padraig went to got serious about their hazing.

Big Jack's body followed, and he flew into the air. He landed flat on his back on the floor, sprawling.

"Oh, me goodness." Padraig spoke in mock dismay. "You seem t' have slipped. Here, let me help you up."

While the others watched in shocked consternation, Padraig seized Big Jack by his shirt front, hauled him upright, and slung him into his bunk. Other than to curl into a ball, hands clutching his belly, the cowboy didn't move. The only sound in the room was the harsh sucking-in of air as he tried to breathe without pain.

"Now then." Padraig turned back to the others. "Anyone else got any aspersions t' cast?"

Whether they knew what he meant or not, no one spoke. Even Buck seemed transfixed. Jack still gasped in his bunk. Padraig decided he'd hit him harder than he intended.

"I'm takin' th' lower bunk. Whoe'er comes after me can have th' upper." He reached for the portmanteau, then stopped, looking back. "By the way, I sleep bare, so when I get ready for bed tonight, then you'll see me drawers are o' the same fabric as everyone else's…an' what's inside them is, too."

With that, he flipped open the lock on the portmanteau and began to take out the clothing he'd bought at the general store. At that moment, a loud clanging came from outside. Padraig looked up.

"Is that th' supper bell?" He slapped his stomach. "I hope so. I'm famished. Buck?" He looked at the foreman. "You want t' show me th' way?"

Silently, Buck nodded and gestured to the door. Padraig started toward him, then paused, looking back at Jack.

"Hang on."

Going over to the bunk, he eluded grasping hands as Buck tried to stop him. "Padraig, don't…"

"Hey there, you look a li'l peakish." He seized Jack by the arm. "Need some help?"

Jack gave him a dazed stare.

"Hope that li'l tap I gave you didn't spoil your appetite."

With that, he threw an arm across the cowboy's shoulders and dragged him out the door. Halfway there, Jack got control of his feet and pushed away, walking the rest of the way by himself, though he continued to rub his belly. Buck and the others stared at the door. Then Buck came to life.

"Well? Are you gonna sit there? Supper's getting cold. Come on!"

Later that night, the bunkhouse was quiet. Everyone was asleep except Big Jack. Padraig, in the bunk across the way, was also awake. Too much excitement, he guessed, as well as too much food, perhaps. He was still curious as to why Jack had treated him so. Perhaps it had been an initiation after all, and Padraig had passed with flying colors.

He certainly hoped that was all it was.

Jack was still reading his magazine, hunkered down in his bunk, a kerosene lantern on the floor providing light but not enough to keep anyone else awake. He was also doing other things, if the moving hand under his blanket was any indication.

As Padraig had said, when he got into his bunk, he

shed all his clothes, not being blatant about it, but giving everyone a view of his drawers as he removed them, then of his privates and backside as he tossed his clothing to the foot of the bed. Lying there, he kept thinking of something to do to ensure Jack didn't keep this feud, if such it was, going.

Granted the cowhand had seemed a little friendlier while eating and hadn't started anything when they returned to the bunkhouse, but he had no idea what kind of temperament any of these men had.

At last, he thought he had the answer. Throwing back his blankets and sitting up, he reached for his denims, pulling them on. Approaching Big Jack in the altogether wouldn't be a good idea, Padraig figured. Once his trousers were buttoned, he rolled over, easing the portmanteau from where he'd stashed it under the bunk. Thrusting his hand inside, he rummaged through it, found his own magazine, and pulled it out. Then, he stood and walked on bare feet across the slight expanse to where Jack lay.

At first, the cowhand didn't realize he was there, his gaze fixed on the bare-breasted sketch of a female on the page before him. His face was slightly strained, breath labored, the hand beneath the blankets moving vigorously.

Padraig could see the buttons of his flannel underwear were open from just above his waist, disappearing under the blankets. He shifted his weight slightly, making a board creak.

Jack's hand stopped. He looked up, taking a deep breath, anger flaring. "What the hell you want?" It was a near gasp.

"Thought you might like t' look at somethin' new."

Padraig held out the magazine. "Care t' swap for a while?"

Jack stared at what he held. Without answering, he held out his magazine. Padraig took it. Jack pulled the other from his hand. He tilted it toward the lantern, scanning the cover.

"Where's you get this?" His question was suspicious.

"Bought it when I was in New York." Padraig studied the magazine he'd just swapped his for. It was wrinkled, the edges of the pages torn. It had been read quite a bit. He imagined Jack knew the contents by heart.

"You mean, this came all the way from New York City?"

There was obvious awe in Big Jack's voice. He opened the magazine, turning a page. There was an audible intake of breath at the illustration. This magazine was certainly of much finer quality and definitely more prurient than his own.

Without looking up, he said, "I'll take good care of it."

Nodding, Padraig returned to his bunk. It was dark on his side of the room so he couldn't look at the magazine. He tucked it under his pillow.

"Hey, Patrick." From across the room came a soft call.

"Yeah?"

"Thanks."

"Think naithin' o' it."

Enthralled, Big Jack peered at the lithographs, holding the magazine in both hands. Padraig fell asleep to the sound of pages being turned.

****

17 July, 1853
Quinton Aloysius Francis Xavier McCoy, Esquire
McCoy Hall
Tipperary, Ireland
The United Kingdom of Great Britain

Beloved and Esteemed Father,
I am in hopes this letter finds you in good health and faring well.

I write this to inform you of my arrival at my destination. I am in the United States of America, specifically the Nebraska Territory, which is a vast plain west of the Mississippi River. My place of residence is some miles east of the town of Lancaster and south of Omaha City. I thought of settling in Lancaster but that had too much of an English ring to it, so I settled for the village of Four Corners.

You will be gratified to know I am also gainfully employed as a cowhand at the Circle-J, the ranch of Mr. Samuel Jessup. I am now officially a cowboy, not to be confused with a cowherd, though I do indeed herd Mr. Jessep's cattle. I also assist in tending and branding them, and doing various other chores involved with preparing the beasts for driving to market in Sedalia, Missouri, several hundred miles south.

I have placed the remainder of the money you so generously gave me in that second draft into the Four Corners Bank & Trust. I further intend to live off my wages from Mr. Jessup and let the balance remain untouched except for emergencies. If you send further cheques to me, they should be addressed directly to the bank for deposit into my account.

I hope you will permit me the opportunity to

occasionally write you and advise you of my well-being.
Please kiss my mother for me and offer Donal and Colin
my well wishes.

    Your son, always loving, if perhaps a bit errant,
    Padraig Aloysius Francis McCoy
    Circle-J Ranch
    Four Corners, Nebraska Territory
    United States of America

Chapter 9

The lariat loop encircled Big Jack's head, falling around his shoulders. A jerk tightened the rope and a second tug pulled him off his feet and into the dirt. Before he could move, his hands were twisted behind his back, a second length of rope knotted around them. His feet were caught, another quick loop securing them to his hands.

"Done!" Padraig straightened, raising his own hands. He looked at Buck. "How long did that take?"

The foreman consulted the pocket watch in his hand. "Ten seconds."

"Not bad," Padraig decided.

"Not bad?" Jack looked up from his vantage point in the dirt. "I'd say that's damned good for a greenhorn."

He looked around at the other hands perched on the corral fence.

"An' I'd say you can't call me a greenhorn, now," Padraig retorted.

"Agreed. So how about cutting me loose?"

"Nay, I think I'll let you stay there a while longer," Padraig replied. "It'll keep you out o' trouble."

"You know, I'm beginning to regret teaching you how to swing a lariat," Jack groused. He twisted in the dirt, raising little puffs of dust. "Dang it, Patrick. Cut me loose!"

"Calm down, ol' son." Padraig sauntered over, no hurry in his step. "No need t' get yourself inta a lather."

He fell to one knee, pulling on the slip-knot that fell open at his touch. "'Tain't good for your blood pressure."

"You let me worry about my blood pressure," Jack rolled over and sat up, then accepted Padraig's hand, allowing himself to be pulled to his feet. "You just think about never letting one of those loops fall over my head again."

He wiped the dust off his chest and the knees of his denims, then gave Padraig a sideways stare.

"All right, I admit it. You're getting good with a rope."

"That's because I had a good teacher." Padraig slapped Jack on the back. Picking up the rope from where it lay in the dirt, he began to recoil it.

"In that case…pupil…it's time for us to get our horses and ride fence," Jack reminded him. "East acreage's waiting."

Climbing over the corral fence, he started to the hitching post where his horse and Padraig's pinto were tied.

"Rattle your hocks and let's get going."

Lariat in one hand, Padraig followed.

Padraig had now been with the Circle-J nearly a year. He was under Buck's tutelage and, surprisingly, that of Big Jack's, for the same length of time, becoming a fair-to-middling ranch hand. Though Buck informed him he'd probably never become a ranny, a skilled cowhand, he was now knowledgeable enough to do whatever job he was assigned without getting himself maimed by an irate cow.

After having his gut massaged with Padraig's fist, Big Jack turned out to become fairly sociable and a good friend, especially after the magazine swap. Apparently, the fact that Padraig didn't let himself be intimidated and afterwards maintained a semblance of friendship by half-carrying him to the mess hall, struck the proper chord with the ranch hand. Discovering they had the same tastes in pornographic literature, if Padraig's was a bit more refined, didn't hurt.

From then on, Jack became determined to transform the dude into an acceptable cowpoke. While his first offers to help were met with suspicion, Padraig soon realized the trail boss was sincere in his overtures and not planning some retaliation for his comeuppance in the bunkhouse.

He listened intently to whatever Jack had to say and soon surprised both him, Buck, and the rest of the hands by remembering what he'd been told and developing a bit of skill at throwing a lasso, as well as riding western-style.

They had ridden some fifteen of the east acreage when they came upon a fence post leaning dangerously, the wire strung across it slack, though not yet low enough for a steer to walk over. Hair adhering to the wire suggested one of the cattle had used it as a scratching post, pushing it half out of the dirt in the process.

Padraig slid out of the saddle, grabbing the post and straightening it so the wire was pulled taut again. While he held it in place, Jack took a shovel from the pack tied to the back of his saddle and began digging.

"You going into town tomorrow night, Patrick?" he asked as he shook the dirt from the shovel, depositing it around the post's base.

"Nah, guess not." Using the heel of his boot, Padraig tamped the dirt into the hole.

"Why not?" Jack wanted to know. "It's Saturday,

and payday."

"I'm aware o' that," Padraig replied. "'Tis always Saturday this time o' week, I've come t' understand, an' once a month, 'tis generally payday, too."

"You've been working at the Circle-J for nigh on a year now…"

"'Tis hard to believe, I know," Padraig cut in. "Toss a li'l more dirt on this side."

"…and I can't remember you going into town with the boys once during all this time," Jack ignored his interruption. "Either on a Saturday *or* a payday."

He emptied the shovel, then drove the blade into the dirt and leaned on the handle, watching Padraig stamp the dirt hard so the post wouldn't fall over again.

"The rest of us let off some steam and get a little happy hoorah, but you? You stay holed up in the bunkhouse with one of those books you borrowed from the schoolmarm."

Having discovered Four Corners had a school, Padraig quickly made the acquaintance of the schoolmistress, a Miss Abercrombie. That lady, a fiftyish spinster, was delighted to meet someone who could half-intelligently discuss literature. When he asked if he might borrow one of the books in her meager library, she gladly agreed. The times Padraig rode into the little town, mainly to relieve Buck of the chores of collecting the mail or bringing in the buckboard for carrying supplies back to the ranch, he also returned a book he'd borrowed, then asked for another. Pretty soon, however, he realized he'd have read all those Miss Abercrombie owned.

"That's got me to wondering…" Jack stopped as Padraig straightened, head coming up.

"Wonderin' what?" he prompted, eyes narrowing slightly.

"I'm wondering…now don't get me wrong," Jack went on, holding up a hand as if to fend Padraig away. "I got no doubt about your leanings but…to tell the truth, Patrick, the way you seem to shun having any fun in town makes me wonder if you're…afraid of women?"

That last was definitely a question, though Jack looked as if he were preparing to duck if Padraig's answer was delivered with a fist. That was odd in itself, considering the things he had said on their initial meeting.

"Afraid?" Padraig stared at Jack, then burst into laughter.

After a moment, certain now he wasn't about to get a fist to the side of his head, Jack laughed also.

"Oh no…" Padraig brought his laughter under control. "'Tisn't fear keepin' me away from th' females, Jack, but because I like them *too* much."

"That don't make a lick of sense," Jack protested. Satisfied Padraig wasn't angry, he began shoveling dirt into the hole again.

"If you knew more o' me background," Padraig answered, "you'd understand."

"In that case, since I ain't about to question that statement, or pry," Jack retorted—he gave the dirt around the post a couple of extra stamps—"I guess I never will."

"Let's just say, women trouble was one o' th' reasons I left Ireland." Padraig released the post, studied it, then nodded. "I think that's steady enough. So I decided givin' th' ladies a wide berth would keep me out o' trouble in Nebraska."

"But...a whole year?" That, to Jack, seemed the most amazing point. "As far as I can tell, you ain't asked for your magazine back, or...done anything else to...uh...relieve the tension..." He paused, then dared ask, "Have you?" Without waiting for an answer, he went on, "I mean, God knows I'm certainly not one to look down on you for it, but it just ain't natural for a man not to..."

"Jack, I think you an' I can speak plainly with each ithur after all this time." Padraig ran his hand along the wire, then plucked at it as he would a guitar string.

It vibrated slightly, giving off a high-pitched metallic whine. He nodded as if that confirmed something.

"In spite o' th' way we started off, I consider you a good friend, so I'll tell you why I stay away from town."

He gathered the reins and swung into the saddle. Jack didn't move, looking up at him.

"I'm listening."

"There's quite a few pretty ladies there." Padraig stopped, nodding to Jack's horse.

The trail boss tied the shovel to the back of his saddle and mounted, following as Padraig turned the pinto down the track, continuing to check the rest of the fence.

"And?" he prompted.

"An' if I got involved with any o' th' nice ones, I'd probably find meself soon on th' way down th' aisle in that li'l church just outside town."

"Would that be so bad?"

"You can ask that?" Padraig pretended astonishment. "I don't see you sittin' in anyone's parlor sippin' tea."

"That's different," Jack protested. "No one would want an ugly, hulking galoot like myself, but you…now you're fairly good-looking, for a foreigner, and…"

"Thanks for that, but no thanks." Padraig shook his head vehemently. "Th' last thin' I want at this stage o' th' game is a wife. Therefore, th' only one o' two ithur outlets for me…tension…as you put it…is me own fist…" Here he waggled his gloved fingers. "…or th' girls at Trails End, an' I've no wish t' catch th' clap an' end me amorous adventures then an' there."

"Tanner's girls are pretty safe," Jack protested. "Otherwise, *I* wouldn't risk them."

"*Pretty safe* don't sound safe enough t' these ears," Padraig answered. "*You* might want t' take th' chance, but I don't want me dingus fallin' off because it got stuck in a clap-filled snatch."

He'd picked up quite a bit of cowpoke slang over the past year, and, except for his accent, sounded like the rest of Jessup's wranglers now. Padraig was fitting in better than expected.

"Well, hell, Patrick!" Jack laughed, a short bark of a sound. "If that's all that's stopping you… Ain't you never heard of fishskins?"

"You mean, they have those 'way out here?" The surprise in Padraig's expression wasn't pretended. "Why didn't someone tell me?"

"Maybe because we didn't think we needed to explain the nature of things to a man who can handle his fists like you do," Jack answered.

"Ordinarily, no one would." Padraig gave him a grin. "I've been laid more times than I care t' admit, but…I thought they stopped sellin' those thin's when we reached th' Mississippi…or usin' them, for that matter."

"Sorry no one gave a thought to cluing you in to that fact," Jack answered. "Fishskins may lessen the pirooting a bit, but what's that to keeping your privates attached as long as possible?"

"So? You gonna tell me where I can get some?"

"I'll do better'n that," Jack promised. "Come into town with us tomorrow, and I'll show you myself."

****

"There it is." Jack gestured to the sign above the little building across the street from Trails End and two doors down from Ruff's Boarding House.

"Crossroads Barber Shop & Bath House..." Padraig read aloud. "I guess I know now why Will and Pete are always in such a hurry t' get here an' have a bath."

"Right," Jack agreed. "We'd have to go there anyway, what with it being Saturday night and bath time, so..."

"...make one trip count," Padraig finished. "Get bathed, shaved, an' outfitted with protection in one stop. An' t' think I passed it e'ery time I came t' town." He slapped Jack on the shoulder. "What are we waitin' for?"

"Do I ask now?" he wanted to know as soon as they were inside.

"Got to do things in the right order," Jack explained. "A bath, a shave, then say, casual-like, 'Oh by the way, Mr. Billings, there's something else I need...' and he'll take it from there."

There was a moment's confusion as they decided who was going to bathe first. Though Buck stayed behind with Samuel to go over the month's accounts, there were still nine of them crowding into the little barber shop that was the entrance to both establishments.

Finally, coins were flipped. The winners got the tubs

first, while the losers stayed behind for shaves. Then, they exchanged places.

In the bath house, Padraig dropped his five quarters into a glass jar sitting on the counter where flour sack washcloths and towels were stacked next to a bowl of square knife-cut soaps. Baths were fifty cents, hot water, four bits more, and soap twenty-five cents extra.

"Hey, I'm puttin' in a dollar and a quarter," he called to the teenage boy standing by the door. "I want hot water, and soap, too."

The boy, Billings' son, who swept up hair clippings and mopped up the wet bath house floor when customers dripped water from the tubs as they redressed, nodded.

Padraig took one of the bars from the bowl, started to unbutton his shirt, then stopped. Raising the bar, he sniffed at it.

"Damn, this smells like…roses?" He picked up another bar. It smelled the same. "Aren't there any plain ones?"

"Sorry." Jack shook his head. He'd already shucked his shirt and started on the buttons to his dungarees. "It's roses or nothing."

"So…we'll all smell th' same." Padraig appeared to be working out some puzzle in his head. "I guess that's all right, then. As long as no one makes any wiseacre comment."

"Can't," Will answered. He was sitting on a nearby stool, pulling off his boots. "Not without including himself in the insult."

"Dibs on the first tub," Jack called out.

He'd skinnied out of his jeans and flannels, dropping both them and his shirt atop his boots. Clutching a washcloth and a towel plus his own bar of soap, he ran to the tin tub, stepped in, and lowered himself into the water, leaning back with a sigh.

"Ahhh…that feels good…hot, but good."

The next instant, he was dodging a splash as Padraig practically jumped into the second tub.

"Hey!"

Will and Pete were already in the water. There were moments of slight roughhousing as they tossed water at each other like children, splashing themselves, the floor, and the boy also. He didn't look too happy, carefully removing their clothing to keep it dry. All settled down to the business of bathing away a couple of weeks' worth of dirt and sweat.

"Kind o' hate t' put back on those same old denims an' shirt," Padraig complained, industriously scrubbing the back of his neck.

"Unless you've got another set somewheres, guess you'll have to," Will answered, rubbing the soap between his hands and lathering an armpit. "We all will. You know, this soap ain't half bad. Leastways, it's better'n that yellow stuff Cookie makes us use when we wash in the crick."

"Why do we have t' wear th' same clothes?" Padraig asked. He raised a leg, bristling with copper hair, dripping water back into the tub as he rubbed the bar against his calf.

"Hey, you gone deaf?" Jack questioned. "Will just said…"

"I mean, like you reminded me yesterday," Padraig interrupted. "I haven't spent much o' me wages in a whole year." He wasn't going to mention he'd received twelve cheques from Quinton during that year, also. "What say I buy us all new outfits…shirts, dungarees, an' socks?"

"Why would you want to do that?" Will asked.

"Because you're me friends?"

"If you've got to ask if we are, maybe we ain't," Pete spoke up. He splashed his face, washing away suds.

"You needn't get carried away because this is your first trip into town," Jack cautioned. "Besides, buying us clothes don't seem right, somehow."

"Forget that...Buck already warned me men don't buy men gifts," Padraig answered. He got very busy rubbing the sole of one foot with the washcloth. "However, since this is a momentous occasion...namely being me first trip into town t' hoorah it up with you boys...an' I know you won't turn down a stand o' drinks at th' Trails End...why don't we call this a prelude t' goin' t' th' saloon?"

He stood up in the tub, looking around.

Everyone stared at him, not looking away, deliberately ignoring his nakedness.

"Hell...we go into Trails End wearin' clean clothes an' smellin' like roses, an' those shakes'll be fighting t' get t' us."

"When you put it like that..." Jack looked thoughtful.

"Just did," Padraig replied. He settled back into the water again, rubbing the soap through his now shoulder-length hair, then ducked his head, coming up with bubbles and water streaming down his face.

Jack looked past him to Will and Pete. "What say?"

"Hell, I'm for it!" Will agreed.

"Does this go for the others, too?" Pete wanted to know.

"For e'erybody," Padraig affirmed. He looked at the

boy now holding a mop. "Hey, kid!"

"Yes, sir." The boy jumped as if he'd been prodded.

"Get me denims."

The boy hurried over to the piles of clothing he'd placed on a wooden bench, hand hovering over them.

"That one, with th' blue shirt."

Picking up the dungarees, the boy brought them to him. Padraig dug into a pocket, producing his wallet. After all this time, he still carried it. He pulled a greenback, returned the wallet to his hip pocket, then handed both money and denims to the boy.

"Put me pants back, then take this an' go t' Delsey's general store an' pick up nine shirts, nine denims, an' nine pairs of socks an' bring 'em back here."

"That's damned decent of you, Patrick," Will said.

"Think naithin' o' it."

"Don't worry, he won't," Pete laughed and ducked as Will threw his washcloth at him.

****

The stack of clothing lying on the table was pointed out to the other four as they came through the door, clean-shaven and taking their places in the tubs.

"Early Christmas," Padraig explained with a straight face. "Since you've all been such good li'l boys this year."

"Is he talking about us?" someone asked.

There was only one chair in the barbershop, so they had to wait their turns. Padraig was last. Where the others asked for both shaves and haircuts, he ordered the barber to merely rid him of the growth of copper bristles and leave his hair be for the time being.

As the barber patted some bay rum onto his face, then whisked the protective cloth from around his neck,

Padraig glanced at Jack, who nodded.

"Say, Billings, looks like Padraig here needs a little something from your back room. Hope you've got plenty of supplies."

"Certainly do." Billings didn't bat an eye. "Got in a new shipment last week. All in brown-paper wrappers." He folded the cloth and dropped it into the chair Padraig vacated, indicating a curtained doorway behind him. "Step this way, please."

Padraig followed him, Jack bringing up the rear. "Be right back, boys," he told Will and Pete.

"Think I need someone t' hold me hand?" Padraig asked.

"Maybe, for moral support." Jack snorted.

"I'm thinkin' you just want t' see what I'll do," Padraig retorted. He walked over to the cupboard Billings had opened, and peered inside. "I'll take that one."

As Billing handed him the object, he studied it, a smoothly sanded and varnished wooden dowel with a rubber sheath stretched over it.

"*Dr. Boudreau's Préventif Français*," he read the label aloud. "Good enough. What's th' price?"

"Three dollars," Billings answered.

"A bit steep, but a bargain at twice th' price…but don't get any ideas about raisin' it." Padraig handed over the three bills, and pocketed the condom.

"Hey, Patrick!" Pete chortled as he came through the door. "Looks like you're already eager to see the ladies." He pointed to the bulge the dowel made in Padraig's pocket.

"That ought t' get me a trip upstairs fast." Padraig didn't slow his course to the barbershop door.

Being a Saturday night and payday besides, Trails End was filled, as many cowhands from the neighboring ranches and several unattached young men, as well as a few married ones, made the saloon their meeting place. The piano player was kept busy with requests, someone or other supplying drinks as bribes to play the songs they wanted. Most of them had scurrilous lyrics, making Padraig laugh as they sang along.

"Damn, I haven't heard that one since I left Tipperary!" he exclaimed, slapping his knee.

By this time, the girls had discovered the newcomers, especially the red-haired cowboy whom none remembered from that first day over a year before. The saloon owner had four girls and they were kept busy that night. Somehow, two of them managed to elude grasping hands and make their way to the table where Padraig, Jack, Will, and Pete were settled with a bottle, their second.

"Don't look now." Jack nudged Padraig. "The she-wolves have got your scent."

"You mean, me sweet-as-a-rose smell?" Padraig, well into his fifth shot of whiskey, smirked.

Unlike the girls, the bartender remembered him and asked if he wanted another bottle of the "good stuff." Assured they did, it was given to them with the label carefully covered so the other patrons wouldn't know how they were being cheated.

"The blonde's Sadie, the redhead Mary," Jack whispered. "She's got green eyes, too."

"Hello, ladies!" Padraig was on his feet before they got to the table.

Both stopped, looking at each other as if they didn't know what to do with a man who stood and performed a slightly drunken bow in their direction.

"Come on," he beckoned. "Don't be shy. We've been waitin' for you."

"You have?" Mary sidled closer, immediately caught by an arm around her waist, and pulled onto Padraig's lap.

"You wouldn't be Irish, would you?" he asked. "With that beautiful hair like a Connemara sunset?"

"More likely that hair came outten a bottle." Will laughed.

"Give me a chance to find out for certain?" Padraig nuzzled against her neck, whispering the question into her ear. "Let me inspect your collar an' cuffs, an' I'll let you see if I'm a real redhead, too." He raised his head, giving her a direct stare with eyes as green as her own. "I'd like to go upstairs with you, lass."

"Why…uh…sure," Mary answered, shivering slightly as he blew into her ear. Her expression reaffirmed that she wasn't accustomed to someone asking for her services in such a polite way, nor being so sensually restrained.

"Good, then." Standing, Padraig gently pushed Mary off his lap, then seized her hand. "Lead on, me dear."

"Hey!" Sadie came to life, placing a hand on Mary's arm and pulling her away from Padraig's side. "No fair. I didn't even get a chance to talk to him."

"Why, no problem, darlin', though talkin's not what I had in mind." Padraig looked back, placing an arm around Sadie's waist and drawing her close while the other hand reached for Mary. "I imagine there's enough o' me for both o' you."

He kissed Sadie's neck, ignoring the hum of

conversation circling the tablet as the other men reacted.

"Do I get a discount for two?"

"Sorry." Sadie pulled away to stare into his eyes. Briefly, she appeared as lost as Mary. "Fifty cents, for each of us."

"Ah, well…" Padraig released them and returned to his chair, though he didn't sit.

Amid the noise and music, the silence at the table was ignored. The men's expressions were curious, waiting to see what he was going to do next.

Both women looked disappointed, as if for once they'd been looking forward to getting this particular customer upstairs. Now that he seemed to be turning them down, they were dismayed.

"You drive a hard bargain." Padraig turned back, hugging both against his chest. "Done! One dollar t' split 'twixt th' two o' you."

With that, he strode toward the stairs, dragging the two women with him, making them run to keep up with his long strides. He went up the stairs two at a time.

"Ain't eager, is he?" Jack muttered.

"Lord," Pete broke the silence. "He's taking on both of 'em? Can't believe it."

"Believe it," Jack affirmed. "Fella's been without a woman for a year. He's probably got so much joy juice stored up, it'll take two to handle it all."

****

It was two hours before Padraig reappeared. The others studied him silently as he made his way back to the table, the two whores trailing behind him like followers of a prince. The men gave him the eagle eye as if trying to find signs of fatigue or downright exhaustion. Nothing in his demeanor or actions revealed either.

"Damnation, Patrick," Jack said. "If those gals were tossing flower petals at you, I wouldn't be surprised. What the hell did you do for two hours?" He shook his head as Sadie reached the table and started to answer. "No, I don't think I want to know."

Padraig dropped into his chair, picked up the bottle, and poured himself a healthy swig of whiskey.

"T' you, Mary…" He raised the shot glass. "An' you, Sadie… Thanks for a very pleasant evenin'." He put the glass to his mouth and slugged down the whiskey, then reached for the bottle again. "Damn, but such action makes a man thirsty."

"Patrick, did you use…" Jack didn't go any further, stopping in mid-sentence. "Nah, none of my business."

"See any bulge in me pocket?" Padraig got to his feet. "I feel like a different kind o' action now. Anyone playin' cards?"

He looked around as if searching for a table with cards and chips on display. At the moment, none were in sight.

"No? Then guess I'm for th' boarding house an' some sleep before we ride back in th' mornin'."

"You'll be coming back next week, though." Mary spoke up, catching at his sleeve as he turned away. "Won't you?"

"O' course, darlin'." He looked back, catching her hand and pressing a kiss on her fingers. "Now that I've discovered th' delights Trails End holds, wild horses couldn't keep me away."

Releasing her hand, he walked through the crowd to the door, leaving Jack and the others, even the two women, staring after him. Sadie put her hand on Mary's shoulder. The blonde cupped the one Padraig had kissed with her other, as if hiding it from anyone's sight.

"Oh, I hope so," she murmured.

Thus, Padraig McCoy made his first conquest in the town of Four Corners, the women of the Trails End saloon.

Chapter 10

Anything involving ranch work was grueling, some of it downright rough, and even more so for a young man who'd been raised in relative gentility as had Padraig McCoy. He'd already shown he wasn't afraid of hard work, however, and attempted to meet each challenge working at the Circle-J with what he was privately coming to call *the McCoy stubbornness*, a trait he thought Quinton would've been proud to see his second son display.

It was that stubbornness bringing him out of his bunk on winter mornings when a fresh snowfall covered the ground two feet deep during the night. First one up had to make sure the fire, banked in the cast-iron stove the night before, hadn't gone out, and then feed it more logs to warm up the bunkhouse.

Huddling around the little stove with the others, attempting to get warm before dressing, all clad in flannel long johns and woolen socks, some even sleeping in mittens with their heads wrapped, then running to the outhouse and hearing Jack's complaint, "Damn, it's cold enough to freeze my water!" engendered a camaraderie and feeling of family Padraig hadn't experienced even when at home.

That shook him a little, to think he felt more of a kinship with this group of strangers than with his own relations.

Nevertheless, when he joined the shovel brigade to clear a path from bunkhouse to ranch kitchen through snow piled six feet high and drifted so tight against the bunkhouse door it took three of them to push it open... When he rode out on those frigid mornings, braving below zero temperatures, wrapped in a sheepskin trail coat with the wool on the inside and goat hide chaps covering his legs, hands encased in fur-lined leather gloves, with a muffler wrapped across the lower part of his face, while a second encircled his head and ears under his hat, and his horse's shoes capped with pointed calks to prevents his slipping on ice under the snow... When he had to dismount and slog through knee-deep drifts to a trapped steer, then take a hammer to break off frozen breath blocking its nostrils so the creature could breathe...or drag bales of hay into a cleared area to make certain the cattle had plenty to eat during the winter...

Padraig did it, not merely because he had to, but also because he enjoyed it. He was startled to realize that fact.

He enjoyed every cold, hot, freezing, baking, dangerous, wonderful moment of his life in the Nebraska Territory, working in a country alternately hostile and welcoming. He liked the land and he liked the people and he had absolutely no desire to go back to being the elegantly clad, gently mannered young ne'er-do-well causing his father to despair and send him away.

Quinton McCoy had done his son a favor, though neither realized it at the time.

Anyway, he'd take a Nebraska blizzard any day over having to escape a pistol-wielding husband by climbing bare-assed down an ivy vine with his clothing slung around his neck.

Of all his chores on the ranch, however, branding

time was the one thing he disliked most. In fact, Padraig would be the first to admit he hated that act.

He'd been a thorn in his father's side, he'd confess, if asked. He'd gambled, bilked men out of money, though he always clarified that statement with the further explanation they were all English and could afford to lose whatever cash he pocketed, and anyway, 'twas merely for the fun of it, never with any malice. He'd cuckolded many a complacent and unappreciative husband and seduced several lasses away from their doltish sweethearts, but the women involved were spoiling for a little romantic excitement and no force was involved in any of his trysts.

In spite of all that, Padraig had never been in a duel, thanks to Quinton's paternal intervention, and aside from an occasional fisticuff scrap, never physically harmed anyone, Big Jack excepted. He was a fairly peaceful soul in an adventuresome body, would never deliberately hurt another person, and most especially never maim or kill an animal merely for the fun of it.

That's why he didn't like branding. Having to be one of those cutting a calf away from its mother and dragging its fighting body to the branding fire, hearing the calf's pain-filled wails as the hot iron was shoved against its flank, and the cow's panicky moos as well as inhaling the smell of burnt flesh and hair…

The first two days, it was all he could do to keep his gorge from rising and spilling his breakfast into the grass. Somehow, he managed, however, swallowing continuously and keeping his head turned while studiously coiling or uncoiling his rope. If the others guessed, no one said anything. Perhaps they were thinking of their own initial reactions, perhaps cutting him a little slack because he was a foreigner. Whatever the reason, Padraig hid his revulsion well, while telling himself it had to be done.

The cattle were Jessup's bread-and-butter, the way he made his living, and they had to be protected and kept from harm, and that meant marking them so if they were stolen, they could be identified and gotten back.

There were plenty of men not wanting to go to the trouble of getting money the honest way. They preferred to let someone else do the work, then rob them of their hard-earned gains. Rustlers were plentiful, and branding was the easiest way to prove who owned what stock.

Almost any brand could be changed, however. All it took was a running iron, but if the criminals were caught fast enough before they could convert a brand, most of the animals could be recovered.

Of course, there was always the starving farmer, shooting a stray cow to feed his family after a crop failure. Jessup didn't count those, and even went so far as to instruct his men if they found someone in that dire need, to ignore the crime and suggest to the man he take up a new occupation...like becoming a ranch hand for a certain Circle-J ranch.

Jessup had acquired several new workers that way.

This time, it was Padraig's ill luck to be one of the cutters, the men singling out the calves unfortunate to be chosen for branding. There were a lot of them, over three hundred head in this particular pasture alone. It was going to take weeks to get them all branded, and he was already wishing it was over when it had only begun.

While he was being taught by Buck and Jack how to be a cowhand, the pinto was being trained as a cutting horse and learned his job faster than did his rider. The two of them were now a team working together to herd a calf away from its mother, keep it from running back, and then get it roped and tied.

That part was up to Padraig. It was the pinto's job to stop once the rope landed around the calf's neck, then back away, keeping the tension on the lariat taut so the animal couldn't slip the noose and escape. Once it was roped and tied, another cowhand would drag it to the fire and afterward, pull loose the ropes and send it, bawling, back to its ma.

Today, Padraig and the pinto, with Will on his big-chested buckskin, were given that assignment. Padraig was cutter and Will brought the calves to the fire. Padraig nearly laughed when he heard Buck's choice because Will was the shortest of the lot, barely five-six with his boots on, thin and wiry. Nevertheless, after the first calf was roped, he discovered the cowhand was a lot stronger than he looked, and an expert at hauling the calves quickly as well as letting them go.

Sometimes speed was a necessity where a wounded calf and an infuriated cow were concerned, as Padraig learned the hard way.

He had just roped a spindly acorn calf, half the size of the others. The pinto stopped so quickly he was thrown against the pommel, grunting as it jabbed into his groin through the leather of his chaps. He ignored the sudden pain to his side, though the thought came, unbidden, *Damn, bet that sent a bruise t' me ghoolies!*

As the calf was jerked off its feet and thrown sprawling into the grass, a second thought followed. *A wonder some of these li'l fellas don't get their necks broke.*

So far, none had. They were tougher than they

looked, apparently.

As soon as the calf was down, before it could recover and scramble to its feet again, Padraig was off the pinto. By the time he got to it, the calf was sitting up. Thrusting the twist of rope into his mouth, he seized a foreleg, jerking it out from under the creature and sending it tumbling to the ground again with a tremulous bleat. He pulled the length of rope from between his teeth, wrapped it around both fetlocks, then hauled up a hind leg and tied that also. Then he stepped back as he heard Will approaching.

Unlooping the rope from around the calf's neck, Padraig stepped out of the way as Will scooped up the calf and hauled it to the fire. Padraig recoiled his rope and headed back to his horse.

That was when it happened.

Neither was watching the cow. The calf had run a good distance before Padraig's lasso brought it down, and they thought the cow was too far away. She'd followed the pinto, watching silently.

As Will half-lifted the bawling calf, she gave a tremendous moo, frightening in its volume and suddenness, put her head down, and charged.

Weighed down by the calf, Will reacted by dropping the little animal and spinning to run to his own horse a few yards away, placidly cropping grass, its reins loose. A couple of the others, seeing what was happening, began to yell and wave their arms, trying to distract the cow from her target. She didn't give them a glance, simply kept thundering in Will's direction.

By this time, Padraig had reached the pinto, getting into the saddle faster than ever before. The cow's head was down, her horns thrust before her, two thick, deadly points aiming for Will's body. If she struck him…

Once, Padraig had seen a tenant on one of his lordship's farms gored by a bull. The man survived but he had a great, ugly scar marring half his belly and wasn't able to do much farm work from then on.

Kicking the pinto into a gallop, he aimed the horse at the cow. As if anticipating its rider's intent, the pinto caught up with the animal, galloping alongside. Raising the coiled rope, Padraig brought it down against the animal's shoulder with as much strength as he could muster.

The creature galloped on, the horse keeping pace.

Glancing over his shoulder, Will abruptly stopped in consternation. In the next instant, he looked around wildly as if uncertain which way to go as he realized he was now in danger of being run down not only by a stampeding cow but also by Padraig and his horse.

"Move, Will!" Twisting the reins, Padraig sent the pinto careening against the cow, ramming her in the shoulder. He kicked the horse, preventing it from slowing its pace.

Thrown off balance, the cow turned slightly, forelegs crossing. It tripped over its own feet and, as the pinto continued to push, went down with a crash, hooves waving in the air as it rolled over and got to its feet with a startling nimbleness.

Its momentum and intent now broken, the cow shook her head. The calf chose that moment to rush to it. Nuzzling her baby, she nosed it back to the herd.

Padraig pulled the pinto to a halt and sat with head down, breathing heavily. Back at the fire, he heard the others cheering. As Will came running up to him, he twisted in the saddle.

"Let that one go for now. Let's get anaithur an' come back for th' li'l troublemaker later."

Will nodded. Padraig turned the pinto's head.

"Patrick?"

He looked back.

"Thanks. You saved my bacon."

"Think naithin' o' it." Padraig raised a hand as if swatting away a fly. "You're too good a cowpoke t' waste on the horns o' an angry mama cow."

Will's laugh carried all the way to the branding fire.

Later in the day, Padraig again roped and tied that calf, and this time, he kept an eye on Mama, while Will took care of Baby.

Chapter 11

It was getting close to time for Jessup and his men to drive the herd to Sedalia. The current calves had grown up, the last crop now ready for market. As usual, Jessup added a couple of extras to help out, a pair of waddies, itinerant cowhands who always appeared whenever more help was needed, or farmers who were cow-savvy and currently in need of cash because the latest drought had killed off most of their gardens and crops.

The Great Plains seemed to be getting drier and drier.

Pretty soon, Padraig thought, if something didn't happen, if there wasn't a big, gulley-washing rain, everything was going to dry up and blow away, and men like Jessup who were apparently too soft-hearted for their own good were going to have a bunch of sodbusters working for them and all the farmsteads would be empty.

That morning at breakfast, Jessup told Padraig he would be going on this drive. He'd missed the last one by arriving in Four Corners shortly after the riders returned.

Immediately, Buck spoke up. "Are you sure you want to do that, Boss?"

Buck doesn't want me along? Padraig started to protest, then remained silent as the foreman continued, "I mean, Patrick's learned a lot in a short time, but he's never been on a drive before, and I don't know if it's a good idea to take a newcomer on a long one like that."

"You don't think I'm up t' it?" Padraig demanded. He felt betrayed by the man who'd brought him to the ranch and been his best teacher.

Is Buck sayin' he isn't a good teacher, if he's doubtin' me skills after he taught 'em t' me?

"Sorry, Patrick." Buck gave Padraig an apologetic glance. "But it has to be said. I don't think you're ready for a trail drive." . He looked back at Jessup, who hadn't spoken. "We've got enough extra this year, what with the waddies and farmers hiring on. We don't need Padraig…"

"I think we do," Jessup interrupted. He looked at Padraig. "You'll come, Patrick. He's got to start some time, Buck. Now's as good a time as any."

Buck didn't argue, though his expression said otherwise. Padraig nodded and tapped the brim of his hat.

"Thanks, Boss." In the next instant, Padraig asked himself, *Why am I bein' so grateful? 'Tis two hundred an' thirty-five miles from Four Corners t' Sedalia. Me arse'll be pounded t' jelly by th' time we get there, an' I'm lookin' forward t' it? I must be crazy!*

And yet…he *was* looking forward to it, eagerly.

Chapter 12

14 June, 1854
Quinton Aloysius Francis Xavier McCoy, Esquire
McCoy Hall
Tipperary, Ireland
The United Kingdom of Great Britain

Beloved and Esteemed Father,
This letter will serve to inform you I am going on my first cattle drive. I must also let you know I received your letter of two years ago, in which you informed me Donal has made the fateful decision to take a wife and also that you are chagrinned at the thought of a McCoy being nothing more than a glorified cowherd. I find myself wishing you could be here to witness an actual drive. I believe this would change your opinion considerably about both that event and my involvement in it.

Please realize, sir, we aren't speaking of a mere group of five or six cows being driven down a country lane to the barn or to a pasture. A herd in this part of the world may contain as many as five hundred to three thousand of the creatures. They are not placid and easy handled as dairy cows but flighty, excitable, and quite prepared to gore and trample someone as to look at him.

They have to be watched at night, in case a coyote, which is a wolf-like though more cowardly animal, should try to attack one straying, or a sudden snap of a twig or the hoot of an owl send them into a panic and a stampede that may possibly kill the riders and scatter the cattle over the plain. Because of that, we look over the herd in shifts. I've been chosen as bobtail guard, one of those taking the first shift of duty. We ride around the cows, seeking to soothe them by speaking to them softly and sometimes even singing as a mother would to a fussy babe. Be amused, sir. They seem to appreciate my voice, though I know Donal once compared it to the sound of a hog call.

At night when not riding herd, we sleep on the ground near the campfire and the chuck wagon, which is where the camp cook keeps our supplies and water. Cookie is also our doctor while we're on a drive. There are no trees on the Great Plains, so we burn what the natives call Round Browns, that is cow dung, instead. It makes a warm fire but fragrant blaze.

We have stopped in Dodge City, Kansas, for the night and a little relaxation before continuing our journey on the morrow, so I am mailing this letter from there. Please give my love to my mother and Colin, as well as my regards to Donal.

Your son, whom I believe you might now not recognize,

Padraig Aloysius Francis McCoy
Circle-J Ranch
Four Corners, Nebraska Territory
United States of America

****

They were only a few miles outside a little town called Rosewater, last stop before reaching Sedalia.

They'd been traveling steadily but slowly, the cattle going fifteen miles a day. That was to keep them from losing any more weight than necessary, Mr. Jessup explained, as well as to keep any of the weaker cattle from sickening and dying.

"Every head is that much more money in each of our pockets," he said.

He'd also declared a ten-dollar bonus for everyone at the end of the drive. Since they were receiving forty dollars a month already, each man, Padraig included, considered that a windfall.

The drive had been without incident, except for a brief encounter with a group of farmers the other side of Dodge. Fearing the herd would trample their crops, as well as perhaps bring in an epidemic of tick fever, a dozen belligerent sodbusters met the drovers. They were armed to prevent them from going any further.

"You don't have to worry about tick fever," Jessup told them. "That only comes from those Texas longhorns. These are Herefords."

"Don't make no never mind," one grizzled farmer spoke up. "Ain't you heard the territorial legislature passed a law? Diseased cattle can't be brought into Kansas."

"My cattle are healthy." Insulted, Jessup drew himself up in the saddle. He waved a hand at the herd as well as his men, who were sitting their horses placidly enough, if impatiently. "Go ahead. Check them if you don't believe me."

The farmer did exactly that. Motioning to a couple of the others, he pushed his way among the cows, stopping to study this one, run a hand over that one's back. When he returned to where Jessup waited, he acknowledged, "They look good enough, but I don't want them running over my crops. It's been a hard year, what with the drought and all."

"The trail to Sedalia's pretty clear," Jessup said. "I intend to keep my cattle on it. None of them'll be straying if I can help it." He looked thoughtful. "I imagine the drought's made farming tough this year."

"That's why we've got to protect our crops," one of the other men answered. "This year's provisions are getting low, and if anything happens, we won't have enough to sell or put up for winter."

"Would a couple of steers help out?" Jessup appeared to be mentally counting how many men were in the little group.

"Hell, if we had a few of these cows of yours, we could smoke the meat and have enough to last all of us through next spring," the man laughed, then sobered. "But we don't."

"Jack." Jessup didn't look around. "Have the boys pull four steers from the herd."

"Boss?" Jack looked as if he didn't understand.

"You heard me." Jessup continued, looking at the farmer who seemed to be the leader of the little group. "Cut out four steers...and herd 'em over here."

"But that'll cut down on how many you have to sell," Jack protested.

"We won't miss four out of two thousand," Jessup answered. "Get to it."

Nodding to Padraig, Sam, and Will, Jack obeyed. When the four steers were standing outside the herd, surrounded by their horses, Jessup said, "There they are. Take 'em."

"You're selling us four cows?" The farmer was disbelieving. "Sorry to tell you this, but we ain't got the money..."

"Nope," Jessup interrupted. "Givin' 'em. Free of charge."

The others looked at each other and muttered to themselves.

"I'm doing this to show my good intentions and because I don't want to cause anyone harm by my actions. Don't expect every man who drives a trail through here to act this way, though," Jessup warned as he thought he saw a crafty expression cross the farmer's face. "The next one might decide a bullet would be quicker than debating the subject."

He turned his horse's head, riding back to the herd.

"Come on, boys. We've got lost time to catch up."

"Hey!" came from behind him.

Jessup looked back.

"Thanks." The farmer raised a hand.

Jessup returned the gesture.

They left the farmers chasing the cows in the opposite direction.

****

A slight breeze sprang up, wafting the prairie grasses in long, undulating waves, making it seem they were wading through a sea of yellow water rather than stalks of thick vegetation.

To one side of the trail, a clump of brown-eyed sunflowers waved their many-petaled heads in the breeze. As the cattle moved along, for once in a slow, docile herd, their hooves kicked up clouds of dust.

That night was clear with few clouds obscuring the stars. When they stopped to make camp, the cattle continued grazing while the men not on duty slept around the campfire and the night guard kept watch.

The next day was as as steady and monotonous as

those before.

The cattle ate as they walked, biting off mouthfuls of grass.

At present, Padraig was riding the pinto. Each cowboy was given five horses in his string so he could switch from time to time during the drive. That way no one horse was ridden continuously...*into the ground,* as Big Jack put it.

During the day, a wrangler tended the horses, driving them behind the chuck wagon so they'd be far enough from the herd not to excite or send them into a panic. At night, they were kept in a rope pen with the chuck wagon acting as a barrier between them and the cattle.

Padraig's string consisted of two sorrels, a buckskin, a skewbald chestnut, and the pinto, his favorite. He and the horse worked together well, while the others were occasionally difficult to manage. He often found himself wishing the pinto had enough stamina to be ridden the entire day instead of merely eight hours. After that long, he sometimes wished he, or rather, his arse, had a replacement, too, so he could ride in the wagon with the cook and rest his weary hindquarters.

At present, the sun beat down, making everything warm and sleepy. If not for the wind blowing around them and stirring soil into miniature dust devils, Padraig was certain he might've actually nodded off and tumbled from his saddle, awakening to find himself rooting in the dirt.

Shaking himself from his doze, he raised his head, glancing around to make certain no one had noticed. When he saw Pete doing the same, then giving him a sheepish grin as he caught Padraig's eye, he realized the others were as lulled by the monotony and warmth as he.

"Guess we'd better watch it," he said, loud enough for Pete to hear. "Don't think it'd do t' fall asleep."

"Right," Pete agreed. "I've a feeling that's all these four-footed critters are waiting for...to catch us unawares. No telling what they might do..."

He didn't finish.

There was a loud snap, as if someone had broken a very dry twig in half. From a mat of trampled brush and sunflower stalks emerged a small gray form, a jackrabbit, running for its life. Behind it, from a hiding place in the shrubs where it had been waiting for the rabbit to make its dart for freedom, loped a coyote.

"Looks like someone's going to have rabbit stew for supper tonight," Pete commented, nodding toward the two speeding figures.

The jack darted across the prairie, hopping in long, distance-eating leaps, erratically, this way and that, while the coyote attempted to follow, keeping a straighter course.

The rabbit abruptly swerved. As if it didn't see the oncoming line of cattle, it circled, running directly toward them.

What happened next was so sudden and unexpected, everyone was briefly stunned into immobility.

At the last moment, the rabbit seemed to realize the long wide obstacle before it was made of living bodies. It skidded to a halt, flipped in midair trying to stop its forward progress. Its effort to retreat sent it colliding with the lead cow. With a frightened squeak, it kicked out with those strong, overdeveloped hind legs, pushing off against the cow's chest and falling to the ground as the coyote, rapidly gaining, leaped.

Finding itself attacked by something on the ground and out of its sight, and seeing the doglike creature running toward it, the cow actually leaped into the air. Rearing unbelievably on its hind legs, it careened sideways into the one next to it, which in turn, was thrown off balance, staggering and going to its knees.

Clambering to its feet, it was stepped on by the one following. The cow spun, remarkably nimble for something of such size, lashing out with a hind hoof, then ducking its head and butting the offending cow, who fell again as it attempted to straighten and back away.

Abruptly, there was a loud bellow and the first cow began to run, escaping its angry fellow. The one behind stumbled against another, and that one leaped forward. Before any of the hands could react, they were running in all directions, mooing and bellowing while the jackrabbit struggled in the coyote's jaws and that animal bounded back the way he'd come, out of harm's way.

"Stampede!" Big Jack shouted, pulling his rope from where it was tied to his saddle. "We've got to head them off." He spurred his horse forward, attempting to reach the head of the line.

By now, it was chaos within the herd, cattle bellowing and fighting against each other, pushing and shoving with shoulders and horns, knocking each other aside. Kicked up dust and clods of dirt obscured the cowhands' sight as they attempted to keep pace with the herd.

Behind them, Cookie stopped the chuck wagon, knowing its unwieldy bulk would only get in the way. If overturned, both he and the supplies would be trampled. He sat on the wagon seat, watching the herd scatter and the riders race after them.

Pete and Padraig were on one side, attempting to herd back into line the cows breaking off in that direction. The pinto showed how well it had learned its lessons, darting in and out, leaning against a cow so roughly sometimes their bodies actually collided. Padraig was holding the reins but not bothering to guide the animal. He gave it its head, turning his attention to the cows as he realized he was now surrounded by frenzied, galloping bodies all rushing forward blindly. He swung his rope, swatting one cow on the nose, sending it swerving to the left. The pinto followed, pushing both it and the one beside it into the line again.

Across from them, Jessup waved his coil of rope, shouting, "Slow the leaders. Padraig…Big Jack, get to the front!"

The pinto found an opening and burst through, galloping to the head of the herd. From the other side, Big Jack on his sorrel, did the same. He swung his lariat in a wide loop over his head. Dropping his reins over the saddle horn, Padraig used both hands to form a coil. Out of the corner of his eye, he saw Pete copying his action.

Raising the rope above his head and swinging it, he seized the reins in his left, giving Pete plenty of room as he aimed his rope at one of the cows running madly in front of him.

A strip of brush and prairie flowers loomed ahead. The herd didn't hesitate. They thundered over the obstacle, trampling the stalks of the flowers into shattered reeds, grinding petals and brush into the soil.

Behind them, a horse screamed. Padraig glanced back. The animal disappeared into the heaving bodies, his rider thrown from the saddle. The cows rushed over it, heavy, meaty thuds echoing as they trampled the animal. Its body was flung from the herd, rolling over, kicking once, then lying still.

The rider was nowhere in sight.

"There's supposed to be a river up ahead. If they hit that, most of them'll probably drown," Big Jack shouted. He slung his rope. It sailed through the air, catching on a set of horns. "Damn it."

Wrenching his horse's head around, he guided it away from the front of the line as quickly as possible, dragging the cow by its horns.

Padraig realized he was gripping his horse with his knees, fearful he might lose his balance and fall, or be knocked from the saddle by the rushing cows. He and his horse were body-to-body with the fright-blinded cattle, the pinto galloping as fast as it could, unable to slow or stop because of the animals rushing behind it.

If he stumbles…if he goes down…or one o' th' cows decides t' swerve…

Both Padraig and the pinto would be crushed, like the unfortunate horse and rider behind them.

What'll they tell Da? His thoughts were frantic, colliding like the cattle, as he struggled to keep himself and the horse upright. *Dear Mr. McCoy, Sorry to tell you your son's dead… Will anyone even know where t' write him? Will Da care?* Another thought intruded. That fallen rider. *Oh God, who was it?*

He made his choice and threw his own rope. Behind him, he heard the whistle of another lariat and knew Pete had roped a cow also. Padraig saw his loop go past the steer's horns, over its neck. He tried to guide the pinto in the same direction Jack had gone, kicking out at the cattle surrounding him. Miraculously, they moved, in spite of their supposed terror, fanning out and giving him room to maneuver. He dragged the cow toward Jack's horse, hearing Pete follow, the cow he'd roped giving an abruptly breathy bellow.

The banks of the river came into sight. Wind blew the coolness of water across them. The murmur of rushing current sounded above the cattle's cries.

The herd veered, following the three roped cows. Jack kept his horse turning, riding in a circle. Padraig followed, keeping as close as possible, Pete behind. They continued to circle, seemingly in the same spot around and around, until the horses slowed to a trot and the cows followed, milling together, and the roped ones quit fighting...

...and it was over.

The herd calmed, becoming docile again, looking around as if wondering what the fuss had been about, and why some of them had been roped. They began grazing.

"Thank God we stopped them before they got to the river," Big Jack said. He glanced at Padraig. "You did good, Patrick."

Padraig nodded his thanks. "How far did they run?"

He looked back. He could still see the chuck wagon sitting in the settling dust.

"Damn. You mean, we didn't e'en go a quarter o' a mile?" He couldn't believe it. It seemed he'd ridden leagues.

His gaze traveled from the wagon to a large dark shape lying to one side, and a few yards away, a smaller one. He saw Cookie climb down from the wagon, running toward it.

"Who got hurt?" He kicked his horse toward that figure lying in the dirt. "Who is it?"

"Will...Sam! You and the others watch the herd."

Big Jack spurred his own horse after Padraig.

By the time they got there, Cookie had the body off the ground, cradled in his arms.

"Cookie, who is it?" Padraig fell from the saddle, jumping from the stirrups before his horse had time to stop.

The cook looked up. The hands clutching the broken body were bloody. Padraig was startled to see tears in the man's eyes. He shook his head. "Nothing to be done." He spoke through a throat filled with tears. "He's dead."

"Boss?" Padraig fell to his knees beside Jessup's body as Jack arrived.

Though it was obvious Samuel Jessup was dead, Jack insisted on sending a rider into Rosewater to fetch a doctor.

The doc, arriving with Will hours later, found a group of men hovering around a body covered by a couple of saddle blankets. He dismounted, lifted the blanket, and blanched. Looking as shaken as the men, he confirmed Jessup was dead.

"No way he could've survived these injuries," he said, justifying his announcement. "Both arms broke, as well as his legs, crushed ribs, skull fracture…"

"We don't need t' hear that," Padraig grated.

The doc shut up quick enough. He looked as shaken as the men, but whether it was at Padraig's outburst or Jessup's injuries, no one was certain. He attempted to offer sympathy, then merely fell silent.

Big Jack got to his feet. He didn't look ashamed as he wiped his eyes, glancing around at the others, daring them to comment. They were too busy wiping away their own tears to notice.

"Will, you and Sam help Cookie put the boss in the

back of the chuck wagon," he ordered. He turned to the doctor. "You got a graveyard in town where we can give Mr. Jessup a final resting place?"

"Of course," the doc answered. "Rosewater's got an undertaker, a church, and a cemetery."

"Then I'd be obliged if you'd ride back with us and help us make arrangements." He looked at the men gathered around, as well as the ones still keeping watch on the cows. "You got a place we can bed down the cattle?"

"Got stockyards," the doc said. "Now that the train comes through, lot of cattlemen are making Rosewater a stopping-off point and shipping their cows from there instead of going on to Sedalia. Couple of meatpacking companies got representatives in town offering top prices."

"I'd be obliged if, when we get to town, you'd advise me on who I need to speak to in order to keep our herd safe until after we get the boss taken care of."

"Be glad to." The doc looked around for his own horse.

Catching the reins, Will walked it over.

"About payment...?" Jack continued.

"Don't need any." The doctor brushed away that thought. "All I did was pronounce that poor man dead. Wasn't any doctoring involved."

Jack nodded, then looked around, raising his voice. "All right, let's get going. We got to give the boss our last respects, then decide what we're going to do."

He swung into the saddle. Without speaking, the others followed.

Chapter 14

The ceremony around the graveside was short. Too short, to Padraig's way of thinking.

Mr. Jessup should've had a grand funeral, with everyone in Four Corners there. He shouldn't have died out here on th' prairie, far from home, with no one but a handful o' cowpokes t' mourn him.

Luckily, Silas Wilson, the undertaker had a spare coffin handy.

"Made it for a really sick gent who decided not to die," he explained. Because of that, he sold it to Big Jack cheap. "Three dollars...to pay for the nails."

Jack handed over the money out of his own pocket without arguing.

The doc had gone to the church while they were at the funeral parlor, coming back a short time later with a man dressed in as much black as the undertaker but without the sorrowful look. He was introduced as Pastor Hutchens.

"I understand there's been a death," he said, looking them over as if trying to decide which to talk to.

"That's right," Jack spoke up. "Our boss...herd stampeded."

"You'd like me to speak a few words at the grave?"

"The boss wasn't part of your congregation, being a stranger and all," Jack replied. "Don't even know if he was much of a religious man, though he did attend church at home on occasion."

"That doesn't matter," Hutchens replied. "I'll give him as good a send-off as I would one of my own people."

A short time later, the undertaker ushered them into the front room of the funeral parlor where a plain wooden coffin, nailed shut and set on two sawhorses, was on display.

"Went ahead and closed it," he explained. "Didn't figure you wanted to have your last glimpse of your boss to be the way he looked." He nodded at the coffin.

"We've already seen him anyway." Padraig spoke up. "Goin' t' take a long time t' get that out o' our heads. Don't need t' see it twice."

The undertaker nodded. "Shall I help you carry it? I need to go along anyway. I'm also the cemetery caretaker."

"We'll handle it," Jack answered. He looked around at the others, "Will…Pete, Padraig…help me."

Together, they hoisted the coffin onto their shoulders. It was remarkably light to be made of wood and holding a body.

Maybe that's because his soul's no longer weighin' it down. Padraig was shocked by that thought. He'd never considered death, until now, but in that moment it came at him, full gallop, that his parents, his brothers—hell, even *he*—could die at any moment. He forced himself to listen to what Jack was saying.

"Lead the way, Preacher."

Nodding, Hutchens opened the door and stepped onto the boardwalk, starting down the street. The four men followed, with Wilson bringing up the rear, stopping long enough to grab his shovel from where it stood propped against the wall by the door.

There were a few people on the streets. They all stopped as the miserable little procession passed. The men took off their hats and the ladies looked down. A couple muttered to themselves. Padraig hoped they were saying prayers for Jessup's journey.

The cemetery was a small plot of land behind the church, which was a remarkably tiny building compared to the one in Four Corners. They slid the coffin from their shoulders and set it on the ground. The pastor opened his Bible. They took off their hats and stood with heads bowed.

He began to intone Psalm 13. *"Out of the depths I have cried to thee, O Lord, Lord, hear my voice…"*

When he finished and closed his Bible, no one spoke for a very long moment. Abruptly, Padraig took a step forward.

"I can't let Mr. Jessup go without sayin' somethin'. He was a good man…t' all o' us, but t' me especially. He took a chance on a greenhorn, an' made him inta if not a ranny, at least a passable cowboy, an' I'll always be grateful t' him for that." He looked around at the red-eyed, sad faces, and sniffled slightly. "We all will. He was a fair man, too. Th' way he helped out others—like those farmers—showed that."

Stooping, he scrabbled a handful of dirt from the ground and held out his hand over the coffin, letting the soil sift through his fingers.

"Goodbye, Mr. Jessup, have a safer trip than you did in this life."

"Amen, Patrick." Big Jack scooped up another handful of dirt, copying Padraig's action. "Goodbye, Boss."

One by one, the others did the same. Then they all put on their hats and walked through the little picket gate, not looking back. The pastor followed. Willis stayed behind. They heard the sound of the shovel digging into the dirt.

"How much do we owe you, Preacher?" Big Jack asked.

"Nothing, son," Hutchens answered. "It was my duty to help out. I was glad to do it."

"Then I thank you, sir."

"Jack," Will asked plaintively. "What do we do now?"

Padraig likened his tone to that of a calf finding itself without its ma. *God, we're supposed t' be men, trail-toughened an' hard.* At least, the others were. He wasn't certain he should count himself in that lot. Not yet. *How did we so suddenly turn inta children again?*

Jack looked around at the others. "We go to the saloon and get drunk," he said decisively and glanced back at Hutchens a little guiltily. "Sorry, Preacher…"

"No apology necessary." Hutchens shook his head. "Everyone mourns in his own way. If that's yours…"

"It is, this time," Jack said with determination. Without another word, he started at a run toward town.

Once in the Prairie Star saloon, however, each man took one drink, then simply sat, staring at the table.

"What do we do now?" Will repeated. "I mean, the boss is dead and we've got two thousand head of cattle in the stockyard pens. What do we do with them?"

"We see about sellin' 'em," Padraig answered, unconsciously sounding more like a trail boss than a mere hand. "Tomorrow, after we recover from this binge o' drinkin', which we ain't started on yet…"

He glanced at the empty glasses and the full bottle.

"I hear there's a slaughterhouse set up in Abilene where they ship dressed carcasses instead o' th' whole cow. They're even trying t' figure a way t' keep the boxcars cold with ice so th' meat's in better shape when it gets t' Chicago."

"Who cares about that?" Pete put in. "Once they're sold and out of our hands, keeping the meat from spoiling's not our problem."

"My thoughts exactly," Padraig agreed. "Frankly, I wish the boss had given all o' them t' those farmers."

"That would've left us in a spot...no cows...no money...and two hundred miles from home," Will argued.

"But th' boss would still be alive," Padraig shot back. He was startled by the anger surging through his body, as if Will's remark insulted Jessup somehow. His hands clenched into fists.

So did Will's.

"Hey, calm down." Jack put a hand on each shoulder. "I know how you both feel, but taking a swing at each other ain't going to bring back the boss. We need to make a plan and stick to it. Abilene's over a hundred miles from here. We'd probably lose half the herd if we push them that far. We're lucky they've all survived up to now."

"I say, we'll get inta our saddles an' ride on t' Sedalia," Padraig said decisively. "Drivin' them murderous beasts before us. We owe that much t' th' boss anyway."

"Excuse me." Someone spoke behind them.

They looked around to see a well-dressed gentleman standing behind Jack.

"This is a private party." Jack swiveled to look at the man. "No offense, but we're all mourning a friend and don't want to talk right now."

"I understand." The man looked apologetic. "Trenton spoke to me, and…"

"Who?" Padraig interrupted.

"The doctor, Edward Trenton," the man explained, patiently. "He said you lost your employer while driving a herd of cows…"

"That's right." Jack looked belligerent, but whether it was at the man's interruption or the fact none had asked the doctor's name, no one was certain. "So?"

"Ordinarily, I wouldn't bother you, but I heard what your young friend there said, and…"

"Just get t' th' point," Padraig snapped, touching his glass and twirling it in his fingers.

"Right." Looking nervously as if expecting someone to draw a gun if he dallied longer in his explanation, the man hurried on.

That made Padraig wonder if he'd ever been west of the Mississippi before. Judging by his clothes, he probably hadn't.

"I represent the Harrington Packing Plant from Chicago."

"Hey, that's right." Padraig snapped his fingers. "The doc did say some o' th' plants were sendin' people ahead t' catch herds before they got t' Sedalia." He looked hopeful. "Are you saying you want t' buy Mr. Jessup's herd?"

"I'm saying I'd like to look at it," the man answered. "Which of you gentlemen do I talk to?"

All looked at Big Jack.

"And you're…?" the man said.

"The trail boss. Come on." Jack got to his feet. "Doubt we're going to do any drinking tonight anyway. I'll take you there. Now."

He pushed back his chair and turned to the door. The man and the others followed.

****

"They seem like pretty good stock," the man said, looking out over the various corrals where the cattle were penned. On the way, he'd introduced himself as William Walters. "Plenty hefty, too."

Rosewater's stockyards were bigger than the town itself, acres and acres of pens a few yards from the depot where the trains ran through. It was muddy and smelly, but no one complained when the wind blew from the other direction, and neither when it wafted the scent of cows, mud, and dung into the town. A few of the townsfolk merely called it *the scent of money* and turned their heads and breathed the other way.

"Should be," Jack said. "We drove them slow, so they wouldn't walk off their fat." He paused, waiting for Walters to comment, then asked, "So? Do we have a deal? What're you offering?"

"My company's authorized me to pay two dollars a head…"

"Two dollars?" Jack cut him short. "These are prime Herefords, not Texas longhorns. We can get three dollars in Sedalia." He looked around. "Guess we'll drive them there. Thanks anyway…but no thanks."

"Wait," Walters thought about it. "This is the best herd I've seen yet. Two fifty."

Jack shook his head. "Two seventy-five."

There was a momentary silence, then Walters nodded. "Agreed. In the morning, meet me at the bank at nine o'clock and I'll give you the money."

"Would you mind writing out a draft?" Jack asked. "When the boss came with us, he always asked for a bank draft so he wouldn't have to be carting a wad of cash back home."

"I can do that," Walters said. He held out his hand. Jack shook it.

"See you at the bank."

Chapter 16

The bank meeting was short but complicated. Without Jessup to handle things, it seemed fate was throwing as many obstacles as possible into their paths. While the others returned to the Prairie Star where food was served in the mornings, Jack met Walters at the Rosewater Bank.

He asked Padraig to come along. "Since you're from Europe and probably more up on these legal things than I am."

Padraig didn't tell him the only "legal things" he'd ever been faced with was determining how far he could go in bending laws before actually breaking them. Nodding, silently, he followed the two men into the bank, standing to one side and deciding to remain silent unless directly spoken to.

"I'm sorry,'" the bank president said. He'd been called in specifically to facilitate the transaction Walters had assured them shouldn't take over twenty minutes. "If you're not the owners of those cows, I can't allow a draft to be written on this bank for them."

"Jehosephat!" Jack could barely contain his annoyance. "We've driven those cows this far and lost our boss. Now you're telling me we can't collect the money he died for?"

"I'm certain there's something that can be done," Walters said, raising a pacifying hand. "Harrington

Company has an account here, and I'm legally authorized to write checks, or I could simply draw out the cash."

"Don't want that." Jack shook his head stubbornly. "If I go back with cash, there's probably going to be some busybody who'll say I helped myself to more than my share and call in the sheriff and make a big stink. I'm honest, but a lot of people look down on us drovers." He glared at the banker. "As I imagine a certain someone in this bank is doing right now."

The banker remained silent.

Walters thought about that. "Surely it would be legal for me to write out a check to the estate of Mr. Jessup?"

"Well…" The banker considered, giving Big Jack a cautious glance, then looking away. "If the money were deposited instead of being cashed. We could honor a check written on our bank that way. It would go into his estate and you men could be paid from that."

"Do it, then," Jack exclaimed. "So we can get out of here and start home. Lord, I just want to be done with this."

Once on their way, however, Jack turned to Padraig. "Say, Patrick, you still carrying around that leather wallet?"

"Sure." Padraig slapped one of his breast pockets. He'd started carrying the wallet there because he was afraid it might fall out while he was riding, and the button on his pocket kept it secured.

"Would you keep this check in it until we get home?" Jack held up the paper. "In case we run into a rain, it might get wet, or I might lose it somewheres."

Padraig carefully folded it smaller and slid it into the bill section of the wallet. He returned it to his pocket and fastened the flap.

"Now then." Jack looked around at the others. "Let's round up the boys and see how fast we can get outen here and home without killing our horses."

****

Once back in Four Corners, Jack found himself saddled with the chore of notifying people of Jessup's death.

"Who all do I have to tell?" he wondered aloud. "The bank, I reckon, when I deposit the money. Maybe the general store? 'Cause he's got an account there."

"Does he have a solicitor?" Padraig asked, thinking back to all the people Quinton did business with.

"What's that?"

"A...what are they called here...a lawyer?"

"Lawyer. Yeah...Josiah Blackstone." Jack looked relieved. "See? I knew I was right about you knowing legal things, Patrick."

While the others rode on to the ranch, he stayed in town with Padraig, going to the lawyer's first.

"I'm shocked," Blackstone said. "Samuel...gone? It doesn't seem possible."

"It's possible," Jack confirmed. "We buried him three weeks ago, and a sad time it was, too. What we want to know now is what we need to do about the money we got for the cattle, and about the ranch."

"Did Mr. Jessup have any relatives who might inherit?" Padraig asked. "Did he have a will?"

He decided perhaps he did know a bit about legal things, as he remembered how Quinton had made a big to-do about drawing up his will. He wondered if it had been changed after he paid off his second son and sent him on his way. *Did Da disinherit me, after saying he wouldn't?*

Blackstone appeared hesitant. "Generally, I'd say that's none of his employees' business," he answered. "Neither is the contents of any will I might've drawn up, but in this case…"

Getting up from his desk, he went to a picture hanging on the wall above a cabinet. Pushing it out of the way, he revealed a small safe built into the wall. Blackstone twirled the dial and swung the door open, taking out a document tucked into a green baize folder and tied with a black ribbon.

He returned to the desk, untying the ribbon and opening the document.

"This is Samuel Jessup's last will and testament," he announced, tapping the sheets of foolscap. "Samuel was one of my first clients. I'd just hung out my shingle," he reminisced. "I don't remember all that's in his will, but I do know he had no close kin and he wanted his ranch to be sold and the proceeds going to the betterment of Four Corners…building a bigger schoolhouse, a library or some such."

"That means we're all out of a job," Jack interpreted. He looked as if Blackstone had just hit him in the belly.

"Not necessarily," the lawyer answered. "If someone buys the ranch, he'll no doubt need hands to help run it, and if there are already men on the job…" He didn't finish.

"How do we go about this?" Padraig asked. "Puttin' th' ranch up for sale, I mean? Do we handle it, or do you?"

"As Samuel's attorney, I will," Blackstone answered. He studied the will as if reading the section before him. "That'll make it legal and aboveboard. I suggest you go over to the bank and get that draft deposited. Tomorrow, I'll have flyers printed up and posted around town stating the ranch is for sale, as well as notifying Samuel's friends of his demise. I'll put a notice in the paper, too. I imagine they'll want to have some kind of memorial for him. If no one in Four Corners is interested in buying, then I'll advertise in the Omaha paper."

"Thank you, Mr. Blackstone." Jack got to his feet.

Padraig followed him out the door.

"Guess you better give me that check back," Jack said.

Silently, Padraig dug out his wallet and produced the folded bank draft. Jack took it.

"Let's get this over with. Then we can go home and see how much longer we can call it that."

At the bank, there were more exclamations of surprise and condolences, then an unexpected announcement from Banker Bainbridge.

"I don't know if I can accept this draft for deposit, Jack."

"What do you mean?" Jack didn't look in the mood to be told such a thing. "The banker in Rosewater told us it was acceptable for the check to be made out to Jessup's estate."

"Then he slipped up, because this check's made out to Samuel himself," the banker explained. "We need it endorsed and Samuel's not here to do that."

"What kind of fool talk is that?" Jack wanted to know. "Of course he ain't here. We left his mortal remains in Rosewater, Kansas."

Padraig put a hand on Jack's shoulder. The big cowhand was trembling, in suppressed fury and frustration, he was certain. He wondered why things had to go so wrong when they'd been so right up until the moment those cows stampeded.

Jack looked up, glaring at him so furiously he jerked his hand away.

"Jeff," Bainbridge looked at the teller. "Run down to Blackstone's and ask him for advice in a case like this. How do we accept a check when the owner of the account is deceased?"

The teller nodded, left his cage, and dashed for the door, slamming it behind him.

"You're a banker." Padraig made it an accusation. "You should know these things. Haven't you e'er had a case like this before?"

"Can't say that I have," the man admitted. "I'm certain they do it all the time in big cities like Chicago and New York, but out here...I've never had someone die who didn't have another relative or an executor handy to take over the account."

"Oh, damn." Padraig swung around, hitting the desk with his fist.

"Hey, now, young fellow, don't take your frustration out on the furniture."

"Better than takin' it out on you," he retorted.

Bainbridge looked startled. "This isn't my fault. I merely want to make certain everything's legal so there's no accusation of mishandling on my part. I also need to know what's to happen to the money of a deceased patron."

"Will you quit that 'deceased' business?" Jack exclaimed. "I'm getting damned tired of hearing it."

Both he and Padraig were close to letting escape the grief they'd kept bottled inside, and it threatened to be an ugly sight when it happened. Jack bit his lip and clenched his fists, trying to regain control. Beside him, Padraig did the same.

"I admit I'm not as up on all the banking regulations as far as something like this is concerned." The banker made that statement in apology. "After we've spoken to Josiah Blackstone, I intend to get out the federal rules and regulations and give them a thorough going-over so this won't happen again."

"Don't help us in the meantime," Jack muttered. "How could Mr. Jessup entrust his money to someone so stupid?"

Fortunately, the banker didn't hear that.

"What's takin' him so long?" Padraig demanded. "How long does it take to ask a question an' get an answer?"

The door opened. The teller stood there with Blackstone behind him.

"I should've come with you," Blackstone said, looking at Jack and Padraig. "After you left, I read through the will to refresh my memory. Samuel named me executor of his estate because he had no relatives or anyone he considered worthy. I'd forgotten that. I was on my way here when I met Jeff. Sorry about this, boys."

He looked at Jack.

"You're Samuel's trail boss, aren't you?"

Jack nodded. "So?"

"If Samuel hadn't been along, you'd have been authorized to accept the money in his name and pay off the hands, wouldn't you?

Again, Jack nodded. "I did that on the last drive, then brought back the rest of the money for him to deposit, but we were paid in cash that time. The boss always preferred bank drafts." He glared at the banker. "Said it was easier that way." He snorted.

"It'll work similar now." Blackstone turned to the banker. "Milton…here's the way it goes. Jack gives me the draft. As executor of Samuel's estate, I'll endorse it to be put into his account. Actually, Jack could do the same as his representative, as long as the check is deposited in its entirety and he doesn't attempt to cash it."

"In that case, why all this happy hoorah?" Jack burst out.

"Jack…" Padraig spoke up.

"I mean it, Patrick. If I could deposit the check, why are we going through all this?" Jack stopped, shaking his head.

"After that, I'll withdraw enough from the account so Jack can pay the drovers their wages and give them their cut of the sale. If you go through your records, you'll find my signature on file on Samuel's account." As the banker started to interrupt, he added, "You know, Milton, it might be a good idea for you to make certain this is kept quiet."

He gave Jack and Padraig a knowing look.

"The people around here might not like it if they thought their banker was so ignorant of laws concerning the money they've left in your safekeeping. They might want to take it out and put it somewhere safer."

That brought a startled splutter from Bainbridge, who turned red-faced.

"The rest will stay in the account until the ranch is sold," Blackstone continued. "Then it'll go to the town of Four Corners as per Samuel's will." He shook his head. "This may be going against the usual forms of legality as far as telling all of you these things before the will's probated and become public knowledge, but I don't know what else to do. These are unusual circumstances." He looked at Jack. "Give me the check."

It was handed over. Blackwood took a pen from the banker's desk, wrote something on the back, and handed it to the teller.

Bainbridge counted out the money due the men and Jack pocketed it, handing Padraig his share.

"Guess we'll be on our way."

Now that everything appeared settled, Jack was a little calmer, though still anxious to get back to the Circle-J and tell the others what he'd learned.

"So we sit and wait? Until we hear from you about the sale, or not?" he asked Blackstone.

"That's right. I doubt it'll take long," he assured him. "Getting probate done will be the lengthiest part."

"I don't know what that is," Jack admitted.

"Don't worry about it," Blackstone answered. "It's one of those things that has to be done. The Circle-J's a good spread. As soon as people hear it's for sale, it'll probably go fast."

"I hope whoever gets it wants us to stay," Jack muttered. "Come on, Patrick."

He started to the door. Padraig didn't move.

"Uh...Jack...I need t' deposit this cash you just gave me." He'd been thinking hard and fast since they left Blackstone's office, coming to the conclusion there was only one way to keep the ranch safe and the men he called friends from the possibility of losing their jobs when the new owner took possession.

Padraig had heard Quinton rant enough about property being bought and then let fall into waste because the buyers had no knowledge of how to handle it. He'd seen his father struggle to help out tenants who'd been turned out when that happened, also.

Jack stopped. "I'll wait, then."

"No use you waitin'. You go on an' get started t' th' ranch. I'll catch up with you when I'm finished."

"I can wait." Jack persisted but Padraig shook his head. "All right, see you in a bit, then. I'm looking forward to gettin' into my bunk. This has been the worst time of my life and I just want some sleep."

He went out.

"Just step over here and I'll fill out a deposit slip," Jeff said, walking back to his cage.

"I'm not makin' a deposit," Padraig denied. He looked at Bainbridge and then at Blackstone who had also turned to leave. "I'm makin' a withdrawal. Don't go, Mr. Blackstone. As Mr. Jessup's executor, this is definitely going' t' concern you, too."

Chapter 18

When Jack and Padraig tied up their horses outside the bunkhouse, they were greeted at the door by twelve anxious faces.

"What took you so long?" Will demanded. "We were beginning to think someone had ambushed you and stolen the boss's money."

"Nothing like that," Jack denied, pushing his way into the room. "It just got a little complicated. Seems that fool banker didn't know as much about what to do as Patrick here did." He nodded at Padraig.

"Oh, I didn't..." Padraig began a denial.

"The bank has these rules about taking money from a dead man." Jack snorted his derision.

"Did you go to the lawyer's?" Pete asked.

"Yep. Got more rules there, too, but I did find out this...the boss left all his money to the town. He wanted the ranch sold, so now all we have to do is wait for Mr. Blackstone to advertise it and then hope the new owner keeps us on."

"Blackstone isn't goin' t' be advertisin' th' ranch for sale," Padraig said.

"What do you mean?" Jack whirled to stare at him. "Of course he is. He said..."

"He isn't goin' t' advertise because th' ranch has already been sold."

"How? Who bought it?"

"I did."

That brought a silence as everyone stared at him.

"That ain't nothing to joke about, Patrick." Jack's growl questioned his sense of humor.

"No joke, Jack. I've been savin' me money…"

"Ain't no way you could buy this ranch on a cowpoke's salary," Jack argued. He looked startled. "Did you rob the bank after I left? Sure hope not, because then the sale wouldn't be legal."

That made Padraig laugh and everyone else relaxed…a bit.

"There's a few thins about me you don't know, an' I guess 'tis time t' 'fess up." Padraig managed to look slightly ashamed. "Back in Ireland I was a bit o' a mischief maker…naithin' t' get me arrested for, but enough t' make me da throw me out o' th' house," he explained as Jack scowled.

"The devil, you say!" Pete exclaimed.

"I think me da said that a lot, too," Padraig admitted.

"Hell, Patrick," Will said. "I find that hard to believe. You always been such a quiet type."

"He's been payin' me t' stay away an' never set foot in his doorway again…an' I haven't," Padraig admitted. "I've been livin' on th' wages Mr. Jessup paid me an' lettin' me da's money sort o' lie fallow. Now that money's enabled me t' buy th' Circle-J. I'm your new boss, fellas, an' I want you t' know everyone o' you has a job here as long as he wants. Me first act as new owner is t' say…pay everyone, Jack, so th' farmers can get back t' their families."

Nodding, Jack slid his saddle bag off his shoulder and opened it, bringing out the money the banker had given.

Shouldering his own saddlebags and blanket roll, Padraig walked to the door, opening it.

"Where are you going?" Will asked.

"T' th' ranch house." Padraig turned back to look at him, eyes abruptly lighting with mischief. "Since I'm now boss, I can't sleep in th' bunkhouse with th' hired hands. Got t' leave room for th' waddies." He glanced at the two men hired just before the drive started. "You *do* plan t' stay, don't you?"

Both nodded.

"In that case, one o' you can have me bunk an' th' other can take th' upper. Get some sleep. We'll start work in th' mornin' as usual."

Padraig went out, closing the door behind him.

"Tarnation!" Jack's exclamation came to him through the door. "I don't know which is going to be worse, having that tenderfoot as a cowhand or as our boss!"

At the ranch house, Padraig pushed open the kitchen door and went inside. Jessup never kept the place locked. *Nothing to steal,* he'd said. His money was all in the Four Corners Bank & Trust. He followed the little hallway from the kitchen past the tiny parlor, to the one bedroom at the end of the hall.

The house was quiet, eerily so, as if it knew of Jessup's death and felt abandoned.

"Nay," Padraig said aloud, trying to quell the shiver his own voice gave him as it echoed down the hallway. "You're not abandoned. I'm here now."

He pushed open the door to the bedroom. Inside, everything was neat and tidy, no clothes lay about, the bed surprisingly well made. Padraig didn't know if he could've tolerated it if some of Jessup's clothing had been tossed onto a chair or such, or if the bed still showed the imprint of his body.

Dropping his saddlebags on a nearby chair, he sat gingerly on the edge of the bed. He felt as if he were an intruder, someone not belonging who had barged in and taken over. *Surely Jessup'll come barrelin' in an' demand to know what I think I'm doin'...*

Taking a deep breath, Padraig pulled off one boot and dropped it to the floor. It made a hollow sound as it struck the bare planking.

Rug, he thought. *First thin' I'm doin' is buyin' a rug.*

It'd be good to have something warm under his feet on winter mornings instead of that cold bunkhouse floor. He wished he were anywhere but here, maybe back in town, snuggled down in a bed with Sadie or Mary. In that moment, he wanted a warm body beside him. He didn't want to be alone in that bed.

Nevertheless, he was, and it was going to stay that way…for a long while, at least.

He dropped the other boot.

"I'll do the best I can t' keep th' Circle-J goin', Mr. Jessup. I swear."

He thought he heard a soft sigh, or maybe it was the wind whispering through a crack in the window sash.

Padraig got out of the rest of his clothes and pulled back the sheets.

He slept better than he expected.

Chapter 19

Milton Bainbridge, mayor of Four Corners and president of the Four Corners Bank & Trust, rapped his gavel upon the desk. "The meeting will now come to order."

It was the weekly gathering of the Four Corners town council, taking place in the little building they called the city hall. That self-effacing edifice, consisting of two rooms connected by a minute foyer, shared a single fireplace which, if one looked across the logs from the mayor's office, gave a clear view of the city clerk's room on the other side. There was also a cellar, in which files were archived, but Four Corners had very few of those, as yet, since the town had only been in existence for thirty years.

Samuel Jessup's will had now been filed with the clerk, who, currently ousted from his desk by Bainbridge, sat to one side with a lap desk on his knees, diligently preparing to take minutes of the meeting, if he could prevent the ink bottle from sliding off and spilling its contents onto the floor.

The bequest to Four Corners was to be the main topic of the meeting.

Bainbridge got directly to the point, looking around at his fellow council members. There were six of them: himself, Arthur Delsey, owner of the general store, Elton Trent, Senior, the postmaster/stationmaster, Josiah

Blackstone, and Rance Terry and Steven August, owners of two of the larger ranches outside Four Corners. Terry owned the T-Bar north of town, August the Box-S, generally called "the Rattler" by the townsfolk because someone once said the S inside that little square looked like a snake trying to escape a trap.

The clerk supplied coffee, the pot still heating on the stones of the hearth in the shared fireplace. The members took their first swallow of Arbuckle's and Bainbridge spoke the opening words.

"We're here to discuss the disposition of the money left to Four Corners by our late friend Samuel Jessup." He looked at Blackstone. "Josiah, care to elaborate the contents of the will?"

"As you know…" Blackstone got to his feet. "Samuel Jessup wished to have something built that would enrich the town. He suggested a library…"

"Does it have to be a library?" Elton interrupted.

"Well, no." Blackstone considered. He placed a hand on the will, which he'd brought along to refer to, as if trying to assimilate some of its information through touch. "It doesn't have to be, but that was the deceased's specific wish."

"Because I'm thinking Trails End could use a new roof. It was leaking during the last rain about three months ago."

"How do you know that?" Delsey asked.

"I was…inspecting the building," Elton answered. "I'm building inspector, you know."

"I'm certain you were." Delsey snorted. "Did you give the girl in the bed as close inspection as you did the roof?"

"Hope you didn't get the back of your head too wet."

August snorted.

"That's none of your business." Elton's answer was an embarrassed near-snarl.

"None of your wife's, either, I guess," Terry muttered.

"Gentlemen." Bainbridge picked up the gavel, giving the desk a sharp rap. "We're not here to bicker over who does or doesn't visit Trails End on unofficial business…" He gave both Terry and Elton a sharp glare. "…but of where Samuel Jessup's money might be needed."

"All right, then." Elton huffed a bit and settled his ruffled feathers. "As official building inspector, I vote we use the money to refurbish Trails End…new roof, fresh coat of paint, maybe even paint the inside and carpet it."

"Carpet?" Blackstone looked shocked. "Won't the sawdust ruin it?"

"I hear some of the saloons in Omaha are doing that," Elton defended his suggestion. "They're leaving off the sawdust…and making 'no spitting on the floor' a house rule."

Blackstone shook his head.

"Shall we vote on it?" Bainbridge asked. He glanced at each of the men, thinking he was certain, as frequent patrons of Trails End, all would vote to spruce up the saloon, except possibly Blackstone, who was a teetotaler and rarely went there except for an occasional card game.

"I think we should have a bit more discussion," Blackstone intervened.

"I don't think we need any," Elton challenged.

"Don't see that we do," Delsey agreed.

Blackstone didn't answer, considering himself

already outvoted.

The door opened. Everyone glanced toward it. Padraig McCoy came in.

"Mornin', Mayor. Gents. Sorry I'm late." He swept off his hat, nodding to each man as he placed the hat on one of the pegs affixed to the wall. "Didn't know where the meetin' was held. I tried the bank, Mr. Mayor, an' 'twas closed, so I came here."

"Is there something you need, Patrick?" Blackstone got to his feet, assuming he was on some legal business concerning the ranch. "Shall we go to my office?"

"Don't need a thin', sir," Padraig said amiably. "I merely wanted t' sit in on th' meetin' t' make sure Mr. Jessup's last wishes get carried out proper, an' from what I heard as I was comin' in, 'tis a good thing I'm here."

"What does that mean?" Elton looked guilty.

"I think you might have an idea, sir." Padraig's respect struck the proper ironic note.

"Why…I…" Elton got no further.

"I'm afraid this is a private meeting, Mr. McCoy," Bainbridge quirked an eyebrow as he said that, hinting he didn't consider Padraig worthy of that polite title. "Not open to the public. For council members only."

"Now, Milton…" Blackstone began a protest.

"Since when?" Padraig interrupted. He looked exaggeratedly surprised. "When were Four Corners' city bylaws changed?"

"What would you know about our bylaws?" Elton asked.

"Quite a bit, since I got a copy from your clerk th' ithur day," Padraig replied, glancing at the clerk, who looked apologetic and avoided Bainbridge's gaze. "I'm thinkin' you gentlemen need t' become better acquainted with them. It states…" He pulled a thick pamphlet from his jacket pocket, thumbing through it. "…here it is…" He looked down. "…*all meetin's held by th' city council shall be open t' any an' all inhabitants an' citizens o' Four Corners, t' attend an' put forth their opinions on all matters brought before th' council.*"

He closed the pamphlet and returned it to his pocket.

"An' that reminds me, Mr. Bainbridge, sir, have you had a chance t' refresh your acquaintance on those bankin' rules an' regulations yet?"

"Uh…not yet…" Bainbridge stuttered. "But that's neither here nor there…"

"I think it might be quite a bit *here*. A man who neglects one area might also neglect anaithur, so that's why I'm here," Padraig continued. "As a citizen o' Four Corners, if not a direct inhabitant, an' also owner o' ten thousand acres, making th' Circle-J th' largest ranch in these parts, which I think might just give me a wee bit o' influence in some areas, I've come t' make certain Mr. Jessup's bequest t' Four Corners is used wisely an' not frittered away on somethin' with only prurient interest t' a select few."

All the men stared at him, both for the audacity of his delivery as well as the fact that one they considered a mere cowhand could use words of more than two syllables. With the exception of Bainbridge and Blackstone, none knew of the money received each month from an Irish bank sent by way of New York. At the moment, only Blackstone allowed himself a slight smile, an admiring one.

"See here, you can't…" Elton began.

"'Fraid I can, Mr. Elton," Padraig interrupted. "Bein' a citizen an' all. As such, I propose you

131

gentlemen vote t' build Four Corners a library as Mr. Jessup wanted."

"Why a library?" Elton asked, if a trifle timidly in the face of Padraig's confrontational manner.

"Why not a library?" Padraig countered. "Because libraries hold books an' books is knowledge. Not just for us, but for our children, too."

He looked slightly startled as he said that. Padraig had never thought of children in his life, except how to prevent them. Now, realizing what he'd said, he decided perhaps someday he might consider them, and if he did, he wanted them to have a library.

"All o' you men have li'l ones, don't you?"

There was a group nod.

"Don't you want your sons, an' daughters, too, t' grow up smart an' as educated as their das, if not more so? They'll be that. By readin'." He glanced at Bainbridge.

"That may work in big cities," Terry protested. "Four Corners is a rural area. Most of the men around here are farmers and cowhands. They don't need to be able to read and write to herd a cow or push a plow."

"P'rhaps not," Padraig surprised them by agreeing. "But what if a man needs t' read th' instructions on a bag o' corn before he plants it? What if knowin' his ciphers could help a cowpoke become a foreman, especially if his boss knows he can do accounts?"

He thought how Buck had taken over the business records for Jessup, who had been as poor at math as he himself was. The boss had gone weak with relief every time he'd remembered he was absolved of that chore.

Padraig glanced at Bainbridge. "Wasn't that why you sent your son Back East t' school? What's he studyin'? It ain't calf ropin', is it?"

Bainbridge didn't answer.

"I'm guessin' you did it t' give him an education so he wouldn't become anaithur cowpoke but could maybe follow in your footsteps in the bankin' business. Though I hope he's more knowledgeable o' rules an' regulations than his pa. Bein' able t' read'll help him be, you know."

Bainbridge started to speak, then settled for a glare.

"Anyways," Padraig continued, "I've a feelin' Four Corners isn't always goin' t' be a li'l prairie town. Omaha's getting' t' be a big city, an' I've heard rumors they're thinkin' o' makin' Lancaster th' state capitol. Here we'll be...smack betwixt two cities forgin' ahead with progress. Industries are goin' t' come here, an' Four Corners will get some o' th' run-off an' profit from it. We're goin' t' need civilized amenities t' attract people an' make them want t' stay here. Therefore..."

He gave each man a defiant stare before continuing.

"I strongly suggest you six start by considering th' construction of th' Samuel Jessup Memorial Library as your first step toward that progress. Who knows? If you get someone who'll design an' build it cheap enough, you might even have some left o'er t' make a bigger schoolhouse an' hire a second teacher, too."

Padraig settled back in his chair.

"Now then, don't mind me. Go about your council business. I'm just goin' t' sit here an' watch our local government in action...as is me right, as a citizen o' Four Corners."

His eyes met Blackstone's and the lawyer smiled as Bainbridge reluctantly said, "Shall we vote on hiring an architect to design our new library?"

The next day, the town clerk sent a telegram to the

Toni V. Sweeney

Omaha *Clarion,* advertising for *an architect to design and supervise the building of a public library in Four Corners, Nebraska.*

****

12 August, 1854
Quinton Aloysius Francis Xavier McCoy, Esquire
McCoy Hall
Tipperary, Ireland
The United Kingdom of Great Britain

Honoured and Esteemed Parent,

I am certain you will be astonied to receive this missive from me so soon following my last a few months previous. Several events have occurred in the meantime of which I feel you should be advised.

Firstly, there is the death of my employer, Mr. Samuel Jessup.

I recollect writing to you of the extremely excitable temperament of the cattle we were driving to Sedalia. This point was driven home most dramatically when the animals stampeded outside a town called Rosewater in Kansas. Mr. Jessup was killed and we, his men, found ourselves both bereft and bereaved. I can only compare our sentiments as well as our actions thereafter to those of vassals whose liege lord has been killed. We carried Mr. Jessup's body into Rosewater where we saw to a proper burial with graveside services. Then, we proceeded to continue with our quest, namely the sale of his cattle. That done, we returned to Four Corners to bring the money to his bank and speak to his solicitor, where we learned his will ordered the selling of his ranch.

I'm certain you will applaud our actions up to this

point, sir, but now comes the part I believe you will find most difficult to accept. There was a good chance the new owner might not want to keep the men hired by the previous one. There was also a chance a buyer might not be knowledgeable of cattle ranching, or for some other nefarious reason might let the ranch fall into disrepair. Therefore, I did the only thing I deemed possible in those circumstances... Father, I purchased the Circle-J, whose name I have changed to The Shamrock.

Let me say I didn't do it because I want a cattle ranch. I did it merely to make certain my fellow cowhands have gainful employment, and also because they are my friends.

Father, I am now a cattle baron, as a man who owns much acreage and cattle and the power to go with it, is termed in these parts. Be assured I will not use any power I have gained in any negative way but will follow the examples you set for me during the years I grew up observing you with his lordship's tenants. Even if I am no longer part of your family, I am certain the things I learned from you will keep me in good stead now.

I hope I may be as good a 'boss' to these men as you are to the people on the properties you hold.

Also, though buying the ranch depleted a good portion of the monies you have been sending me, I feel I now no longer require those remittances from you. Their original intent is long past. Upon taking possession of the Shamrock, I have settled myself in this country and made it my home. You have my permission, indeed my request, that the cheques from you should now be discontinued.

Please give my regards to my brothers and my love to our mother.

Toni V. Sweeney

Your wayward son, now perhaps not so contrary but settling into being a responsible land owner,
Padraig Aloysius Francis McCoy
Owner, The Shamrock Ranch
Four Corners, Nebraska Territory
United States of America

Chapter 21

After three weeks, the town council, again with Padraig present, voted on hiring an architect out of the remarkable total of six who answered the ad in the *Clarion*. The site for the building was scouted out and decided on, next to the schoolhouse at the end of town, where it would be convenient for the students. Since fall was now on its way and winter would inevitably follow, the contracts were signed with the expectation work would start in the spring, giving the architect two seasons to draw up his blueprints and determine how much material he would need.

"Winter's a long time off," Padraig complained, exhibiting what the others would patronizingly term "youthful impatience" when not in his presence. "Why can't he start in September?"

"Winter's going to come early this year," Delsey spoke up.

"How do you reckon that?" Padraig demanded.

"Found some woolly worms in the storeroom last night. They only come inside when cold weather's on its way," the storeowner explained. "Crickets been crawling under the floorboards, too."

"Been a couple of flocks of starlings flying over the last few days," Elton put in. "Haven't you seen them? And the geese starting to settle on the Platte?"

"The horses have started putting out winter coats,

too," Terry added. "You haven't noticed how shaggy that pinto of yours is getting?"

Padraig had seen the birds with their speckled brown feathers, the geese flying overhead, too, but hadn't really given them much mind. He supposed he should've, since the birds from summer had disappeared on their way south for the winter. Now he was surprised he hadn't wondered why these particular birds were sticking around. As for the pinto...come to think of it, he was looking a bit furry.

"Don't mean anythin'." He dismissed the worms and crickets' movements as old wives' tales and took the easy way out. "But, since the contract is signed, I don't guess there's any rush. Suppose we'll look forward t' havin' a new buildin' in th' spring, then."

Three weeks later, Padraig found himself wishing he'd paid a little more attention to the signs when he woke to a definite chill in the air.

Throwing back the covers and climbing from the bed, he immediately wanted to crawl back into it as the air in the room surrounded him like an icy embrace.

At least, I'm not standin' on a cold floor. He was momentarily thankful he'd bought a rag rug from the wife of one of the farmers who'd gone on the drive with them...bought one and asked her to make two more, actually. One for the bedroom, another to put by the stove in the kitchen, and a third at the front door so if he ever had visitors, they could wipe the mud off their feet before coming in, though as yet no one had come a-calling.

Reluctantly leaving the rug's warmth, he stepped onto the bare planks and hurried across to the chair where his clothes lay, snatching them up and clutching them against his chest as he ran down the hall to the kitchen. He could've started a blaze in the bedroom fireplace, but the kitchen stove needed to be lit anyway, so he always went there to get dressed.

Since it had been relatively warm the night before, Padraig hadn't banked the stove before he went to bed, thinking to stoke it in the morning before Cookie came to start breakfast. He'd told the cook to wait until he saw smoke coming from the kitchen chimney before he started to the ranch house, giving his boss enough time to warm and pull on his clothes before he arrived. Padraig made that a rule after the cook came into the kitchen one morning, catching him huddled bare-assed before the fire, shirt held to the open stove door before he pulled it on.

While Cookie looked away, stifling his laughter, Padraig hastily dressed and told him thereafter to wait twenty minutes after he saw smoke before leaving the bunkhouse. The cook was scrupulous in obeying that order from then on.

Hastily shoving kindling into the stove and striking a lucifer, he got the fire going and pulled on his denims and shirt, wondering if he was going to regret not hunting for his longies or should go back to the bedroom for them. He thought he'd better see how outside looked and perhaps that might decide for him.

Pulling open the kitchen door, he shivered in a frigid blast of air he'd swear held particles of ice as he stared at a changed world.

Everything was white.

"Snow?" He spoke in disbelief. "How can it snow? 'Tis only th' first o' October."

Outside was an expanse of white, unbroken by

139

footprints of any kind, human, animal, or bird. The roofs of the barn, the bunkhouse, the outbuildings, even the blades of the windmill near the stables were covered with several inches of the stuff. As Padraig stood in the doorway, the wind shifted position, sending a sprinkling of icy white onto his shoulders and down the back of his neck. He shivered and stepped back inside.

Across the way, he saw the door of the bunkhouse open and a head poke out.

"You all right over there, Boss?" Buck called. He was fully dressed, including hat and trail coat, and held a shovel in one hand.

Two snow scoops were kept in the bunkhouse for quick access, in case a snowfall was so heavy the hands had to dig their way out and then clear a path from bunkhouse to the ranch house and also to the stable. That had happened once last winter. Winds drifted snow against the door, sealing it shut. Will and Sam had opened the single window, scooped a tunnel through it and emerged a few feet away, wading around to push snow aside so the door could be opened.

Jessup had also kept a scoop near the kitchen door in the ranch house.

"I will be once I get over th' shock o' overnight winter," Padraig answered, raising his voice so the foreman could hear. "Looks like I should've heeded what Delsey an' Elton were sayin' at that meetin'."

"Those old-timers do know what they're talking about on occasion," Buck agreed. He went back inside a moment, then returned without the shovel. "Don't think this stuff's deep enough to scoop."

Cookie appeared behind him. "Need some hot coffee, Boss?" He grinned.

"Come ahead." Padraig waved him over.

As they dug into hot cornmeal mush and biscuits, Padraig said, "Guess I'd better start thinkin' about layin' in more supplies, in case we get another snowfall a bit heavier. How many bales o' hay we got, Buck?"

"Should have enough for at least three months," the foreman replied. "Especially since the Boss...I mean, Mr. Jessup..."

He looked apologetic at that slip. Padraig nodded.

"...had a barn built so we'd have a place for more hay than is kept in the stable loft."

"I think it might be judicious if I bring in some more," Padraig said. "I'm getting' th' feeling this li'l two inches we got last night's just th' prelude to a much bigger somethin' comin' soon."

"Might be a good idea," Buck agreed, washing down his biscuit with a swallow of Arbuckle's.

"Probably should check on the staples," Padraig went on. "Flour, corn meal, coffee, and such." He savored his own coffee and decided, "I'll ride into Four Corners today, take th' buckboard, an' get what we might need. Cookie, make me up a list?"

The cook nodded. "Not a bad idea, going this early. Everyone else'll probably have the same idea. If you get there first, everything won't be picked over."

Early winter meant things usually done in November and December now had to be done then and there. The cattle had to be brought closer to the ranch so when the time came to drag out the hay bales they wouldn't have to be taken so far. There was always the chance a few cows would decide to have winter calves. Any looking pregnant had to be watched so when the time got close, a couple of hands could be near in case

141

the cow had difficulties and had to be brought to the ranch so she and the calf wouldn't freeze.

Cords of firewood had to be chopped and stored next to the bunkhouse and kitchen door where it would be needed. The wood boxes inside had to be kept filled at all times. Everyone got out their trail coats, gloves, and long johns, checking for any tears or spots needing mending. Padraig had already let it be known if one of the hands needed underwear, socks, flannel shirts, or any other clothing and couldn't buy it himself, he was to be notified immediately.

"I don't want anyone runnin' th' risk o freezin' just because he's too proud t' admit he can't afford winter wear," he said. He'd already checked his own gear, hanging in Jessup's bedroom closet, and was wearing his short trail jacket, thinking soon he might trade it for the longer one.

He'd boxed the former boss's clothing, placing it in the back of the closet. Now, he brought it out.

"This may seem a bit ghoulish," he commented as he set the box on the bunkhouse floor. "But I'm certain Mr. Jessup wouldn't complain, knowin' his clothes are still doin' some good. Check what's in here an' if any o' it fits, take it with his blessin'."

Buck and the boys put every piece to good use.

Three days later, a second snowfall hit, this one heavier than the first, depositing eight inches on the ground as the temperature dropped to a frosty eighteen degrees. Winter had arrived, full force, bringing with it something as equally deadly as freezing weather…

Influenza.

Chapter 22

It might be cold weather, but life and the everyday routines of ranchers and townsfolk had to go on. Once a week, Padraig rode into town to get the mail. When either he or Buck drove the buckboard into Four Corners to get supplies, a little more was added to certain staples so there was no chance they would run out if the weather kept them from getting into town on time. There was now plenty of sugar and flour, cornmeal and coffee, plus an extra barrel of beans in the kitchen pantry, and they slaughtered and dressed a side of beef, smoking and hanging it next to a couple of hams Padraig had bartered from a farmer south of town for a slab of beef ribs.

The first indication anyone had that there was a danger other than exposure to below-zero temperatures came as Padraig was getting the mail one day.

It was cold but sunny, the sunlight reflecting off the snow making it glitter. Elton had shoveled around the post office entrance and riders going to and from the building had churned the snow into slush, so it was easy maneuvering.

"What's the hell've you got over your eyes?" the postmaster demanded as Padraig came through the door, stamping snow off his boots and rubbing together his hands, still encased in gloves.

"You mean these?" He pulled down the brown-lensed spectacles and peered over them at the stationmaster.

"You got anything else on your face you don't usually have?"

"Well, there's me beard…" Padraig ran a hand across his jaw, listening to the rough rasp of bristles against the leather of his glove.

"Huh, wouldn't call that much of a beard." Elton snorted. "Though guess it's good enough for a youngster like you."

Padraig didn't answer, except to laugh. Being a redhead, he was well aware the hair on his face wasn't as noticeable as it would be if it were dark. That didn't bother him. His beard was now thick enough to serve the purpose of keeping the lower half of his face warm, so he didn't mind a bit of guying by one of the old-timers. Elton, he noticed, was still clean-shaven in spite of the weather, but then, being a public servant as he was, Padraig supposed that might have something to do with it…keeping up a respectable appearance and all. Good thing cattle barons didn't have to be so well-kempt.

"You didn't answer me." Elton got back on track. "What are those things? Brown spectacles? Only person I ever saw wear any of those was a man blind from the French sickness."

Elton's expression changed to sympathy mixed with horror. He took a step backward, though the postmaster's cage was between them.

"Oh, Patrick, you ain't got that, have you?"

"Relax." Patrick's laughter was genuine. He seized the glasses by one earpiece and pulled them off. "These are eye protectors. I bought them when I was in New York. Th' sun there's not as fierce as here, e'en when 'tis reflectin' off snow, but it can get pretty bright, an' the

144

rich people find them fashionable. They come in handy when I'm checkin' th' cattle." He studied the smoky-quartz lenses. "I'm thinkin' of writin' th' optician I bought them from an' orderin a pair for each o' me' hands."

"Guess that might be a good idea," Elton agreed. "I've seen a couple of cowpokes get snow blindness. One never did get his vision back completely." He laughed, then the sound changed to a soft cough. "Hell, there might be a good many people around here wanting them. Anyway, I'm glad it's not…the other thing."

"Not as glad as I am," Padraig answered. Silently he thanked Big Jack for telling him about the barber shop and the fishskins in the backroom, though he didn't do as much visiting at Trails End in winter. He replaced the spectacles, and got down to business. "Got any mail for me today?"

"Nothing but a couple of advertising handbills," Elton said. "You expecting a letter from your pa?" He paused, face crumpling into a grimace, nose crinkling before blasting out a tremendous sneeze. "Sorry." Pulling out his handkerchief, he wiped his nose, snorted slightly, and shoved the square of cloth back into his pocket. "Got a dab of a stuffy nose." He coughed again. "Bit of a scratchy throat, too."

"You sure you should be workin'?" Padraig asked. "If you're ill…"

"Not ill, just doing some sneezing and having a little tightness in my chest." He gave Padraig a slightly impatient look. "Comes on every year when the weather changes. I sneeze and snort a bit, then take a couple of swigs of honey and lemon juice to soothe my throat, and it goes away. Now if you want to see someone sick, you should've been here a few days ago."

"Why? Who was sick then?"

"Fella who came in on the stage. He was so bad off I had to help the driver get him out of the coach…coughing, upchucking…felt hot too, like he had a fever." Elton shook his head. "Nose was running, so I offered my handkerchief to mop up the snot. He was coming from his aunt's funeral in Omaha, said the old lady took sick with pneumonia or something and passed away. He was heading home to North Platte."

"Why'd he stop here, then?" Padraig asked.

"He took sick on the road and the driver got him off so he could see the doctor. Neither looked too happy when I told them Four Corners didn't have a doctor."

"There's no doctor here?" Padraig looked up from the flyers.

"Didn't I just say so?" Elton looked a little irritated. "Didn't you know?"

"Why should I? I haven't been sick since I got here. What do people around here do?"

"They mostly take a hot toddy and go to bed for a couple of days, or if it's really serious, like a broke leg or something, they get stuffed into the back of a buckboard and taken over to Lancaster and see the doc there."

"Lancaster? That's near forty miles from here. Hell, someone could die on th' way."

"A couple have, but that's the closest doc. Four Corners can't afford one of its own."

"That's not good, Elton. Not good at all."

"Maybe not." Elton paused to press a hand to his nose and sneeze again. "But that's the way it is, unless we start seeing some of that progress you were spouting off about at that council meeting. Until then, it's Lancaster's doc or nothing."

"Doesn't seem right, somehow." Padraig raised the flyers in a parting gesture. "Guess I'd better get goin'. If that cough keeps up, maybe you'd better take that advice, too."

"What do you mean?" Elton asked.

"Take a hot toddy, heavy on th' lemon juice an' honey, an' go t' bed. You really don't look well."

"I'll consider it, Dr. McCoy."

"See that you do." Padraig opened the door and went out into the snow-filled sunlight.

It was late evening when he arrived back at the ranch. From the smoke billowing out of the kitchen chimney, he surmised supper was in progress.

A knock at the kitchen door confirmed this.

"Boss!" Buck shoved the door open. "Didn't know what time you'd get back, so we started without you."

"I'll get another plate," Cookie pushed back his chair and started to the cupboard where the spatterware tin dishes were stored.

"Need a couple o' you t' help me unload," Padraig answered. He coughed to clear his throat. "Then I'll eat."

With Buck and Will helping, they got the buckboard emptied and the goods stored in the pantry off the kitchen. Afterward, Padraig settled himself in the chair at the head of the long table while Buck and Will resumed their seats.

"What are..." Padraig coughed and swallowed. "Sorry," he croaked, shaking his head. "Seem t' have a frog in me throat." He coughed again. "What are we havin' t'night?"

"Green beans and bacon with biscuits and fried

ham," Cookie supplied, looking around at the others shoveling in the food. "Don't think th' hands like it much, though."

"Aye," Padraig agreed. "I see they're practically spittin' it out. Someone pass me that ham platter."

As he accepted it from Will, however, he sneezed, turning his head.

"Sorry. Must've picked up some dust somewhere." He stabbed a slice of ham and set down the platter. "You want to hand me that bowl of beans and maybe a biscuit or two, Buck?"

"Dust? With all this snow on the ground?" Buck held the bowl in one hand and the biscuit plate in the other.

"I know…seems odd." Padraig spooned beans, then selected two biscuits that he set on his plate. He seized his knife and sliced off a piece of ham. "Elton was sneezin' an' snortin'. Maybe me own nose is bein' sympathetic."

He thought about that a moment.

"He said a sick passenger came in on th' stage from Omaha. He was lookin' for a doctor."

"He was out of luck then, wasn't he?" Buck asked.

"That worries me," Padraig answered. "Do all th' folks around here really go t' Lancaster when they're sick?"

"Most of them head to the ranches," Cookie answered. "To the chuck wagon cooks. We do most of the doctoring in these parts, but so far, there's been nothing really bad any of us have had to take care of." He smiled, though it was ruefully. "I've set many a broken arm or leg in my time."

"Let's hope you never have anythin' worse."

Padraig rapped his knuckles against the tabletop. "Knock on wood."

"Why'd you do that, Boss?" Buck asked.

"'Tis a way o' wakin' up th' li'l people an' askin' them t' grant a wish," Padraig explained. "In this case, that we don't have a terrible sickness come t' Four Corners."

He settled in to eating with gusto. It was only as he was reaching for his second slice of ham that he noticed Will was barely eating. "What's th' matter, Will? You didn't take what Cookie said t' heart, did you? I swear he was joshin'."

"Nah, Boss," Will denied. He balanced a couple of beans on his fork, stuck them into his mouth and chewed, then grimaced as he swallowed. "Truth is, I got a bit of a sore throat. Things go down kind of scratchy."

"Hope you didn't catch whatever Elton's got when you were in town the other day," Padraig muttered.

"When we get through eating, I'll get you some slippery elm lozenges," Cookie said. "That'll take care of a sore throat fast."

"Thanks, Cookie." Will made a pretense of eating, but it was obvious his throat hurt more than he'd said.

"If anyone else starts eating like that," Cookie commented as he cleared away the plates, stacking them near the wet sink, "we'd better ask the Boss to invest in a couple of hogs, because we're definitely going to have garbage to get rid of, and since we don't have a dog..."

"I'm thinkin' a dog'd be more useful," Padraig spoke through his biscuit. "He could help out on th' drives."

"But we can't get ham and pork chops from a dog," Sam pointed out.

"Maybe we should get both," Pete suggested.

"What say we table this conversation for anaithur time?" Padraig suggested. "For some reason, that trip t' town has got th' best o' me. I think I'm callin' it a day. Right now."

Pushing back his chair, he got to his feet and started down the hall at a stagger.

"G'night, Boss," Cookie called. "I'll try to be quiet while I'm finishing up."

Padraig waved a hand to acknowledge his statement and went into the bedroom.

He banked the fire, then shut the door to keep in the heat. Undressing except for his long johns, he fell into bed. Cookie's movements in the kitchen hadn't bothered him at all.

It seemed he'd only been asleep a few minutes when he was jerked awake by someone pounding on the bedroom door.

Raising himself on one elbow, being careful not to let the quilts fall away, he called, "What is it?"

"Boss?"

He thought he recognized Buck's voice through the paneling.

"Come on in, Buck." Padraig sat up and pushed his hair out of his face. *Damn, need a haircut.* Pretty soon he'd be able to braid it if he didn't watch it.

As the door came open, revealing a harried Buck completely dressed including trail coat and holding a lantern, he asked, "What's happened?"

"Will's sick, Boss. Real bad."

"From a sore throat?"

"It's more than a sore throat. He woke up around midnight, rushed to the door and outside in time to throw up. Finished that, turned around to come back in and did it again. He must've spent near twenty minutes outside wearing only his longies."

"Hell, that's enough t' make a man sick right there, considerin' how cold it is."

"I think he's got a fever. Cookie's trying to tend him, but he keeps upchucking. He says if it doesn't stop soon, he's going to be doing something called dehydrating. What's that?"

"It means he's dryin' up." Padraig threw back the covers. "Give me a minute t' get some clothes on an' I'll be right there."

Will was definitely a sick man. He was huddled on the edge of the bottom bunk, wrapped in several blankets. While Padraig and Buck watched, he threw the quilts aside, declaring, "Damn, why's it so hot in here?" A few moments later, he began trembling, snatching them back and wrapping them around his shoulders. "It's so blasted cold."

The others were awake, a couple sitting near the stove, feeding wood into it, while the rest sat in their bunks looking worried and sympathetic, those in the uppers perched on the frames, feet hanging over the edges.

"Boss, can I talk to you a minute?" Cookie put a hand on Padraig's arm and guided him to the closed door.

"Sure, Cookie, what is it?" Unconsciously Padraig lowered his voice to a whisper.

"I don't know what Will's got," Cookie began, "but I think it's more than I can handle. I made a pot of coffee so I can get some liquid in him."

He gestured to the spatterware coffeepot sitting on

the top of the stove.

"He's losing it so fast, his body's liable to dry out. I don't see how any more can come out. He's got chills and fever, and he's been coughing…"

"Cookie, you're all we've got since there's no doctor in Four Corners," Padraig said. "You'll have t' do what you can."

"What if that ain't enough?" Cookie asked.

"We'll have to hope it is," Padraig answered. "Is there anythin' I can do?"

The cook shook his head. "Will's pretty quiet right now, but if he gets worse…"

He didn't get to finish. Will raised his head, throwing back the blankets and reaching for a small washbowl at his feet.

"Cookie…" He vomited into the bowl.

The cook hurried over, reaching for a towel lying on the foot of the bunk.

"Wet this." He held it out to Sam, who had gotten to his feet, hovering anxiously.

The cowhand took the towel to the washstand next to the wall. He poured water from the pitcher there into a small basin. Dipping the towel in it, he wrung it and brought it back to Cookie, who pressed it to Will's forehead.

Once the heaves stopped, he began washing the cowboy's face.

"Thanks, Cookie, but I can do that myself," Will muttered, gasping for breath as he pulled the cloth from the cook's hand and swiped it across his mouth. "Can I have some water to drink?"

Someone produced a bucket of water and a dipper.

Padraig motioned to Buck. "Naithin' I can do here.

I'm going back t' th' house. Come for me if Will gets worse." He raised his voice to call to the others. "We'll work around Will tomorrow an' let him recover. The rest o' you try t' get some sleep. Mornin's goin' t' come early enough."

With that he turned and slogged back through the snow, noting idly that fresh flakes had begun to fall.

Chapter 24

In the morning it was Cookie and not Buck who met Padraig at the kitchen door. Padraig didn't get a chance to ask him how Will was faring because the cook greeted him with, "Will ain't much better, Boss. In fact, I think he's worse. Put my ear against his chest and he sounds real phlegmy. I ain't never seen nothing come on this fast. It sure ain't just that winter cough most of us get at one time or another." He paused, then said, "Couple of the other boys are starting to cough, too."

Padraig thought again of that sick passenger. "Do you think he could've brought somethin'?"

"Don't see how," Cookie answered. "Only one who's been to town lately is you and Will and neither of you met that gent, did you?"

Padraig shook his head. "Nay, but I did talk t' Elton an' he was sneezin' an'… Oh, damn, Cookie, you don't think one of us brought whatever it is t' th' ranch, do you?"

"Cookie!" Buck burst through the door. Behind him, trampled snow showed he'd come across the yard at a run. "We need you. Three of the hands are starting to throw up."

He gestured over his shoulder. They could see three figures standing outside the bunkhouse door, all in their underwear, each bent over, shoulders heaving into discolored spots in the snow.

They spent the next hour getting everyone sorted out. Padraig and Buck helped as much as they could, while Cookie gave orders and told everyone what to do.

"Whatever this is, it's catching," he guessed. "Must've gotten into the air somehow. Maybe that sick passenger breathed out something and the wind blew it this way. Boss, Buck...all you who ain't showing signs of being sick..." He raised his voice. "While you're in the bunkhouse, put your bandannas over your faces. *Now*." He proceeded to pull his own from around his neck and tied it like a mask over his nose and mouth. "Don't breathe in any more of this air directly."

"Right now, anyone who's on his feet get outside an' get t' work," Padraig added. "Ride out an' check th' cows. Make sure they can forage. Otherwise, drag out some hay bales so if we're all sick, they'll at least be fed." He looked back at the cook. "What else do you need us t' do, Cookie?"

"Got to ask you to ride back into town," Cookie replied. "My supply of medicinals is going to go fast, so I need it replenished if I'm going to halfway fight this. Most of what I need can be got at the general store."

"Give me a list then," Padraig said.

"Got it ready." Cookie thrust a crumpled sheet of paper at him.

Padraig glanced at it, not recognizing any of the words on the list.

"I'll saddle me horse an' get goin'," he promised.

****

In town, he was startled to find a small woman behind the counter at the general store.

"Pardon, ma'am, but where's Mr. Delsey?"

"I'm afraid my husband's ill," she answered,

tightening the shawl she was wearing around her shoulders. "I'm Mrs. Delsey, and I'm taking over until he's on his feet again."

"Is he coughing an' feverish?" Padraig felt a sinking in the pit of his stomach.

"Why, yes, how'd you guess?" She looked surprised.

"No guess, Mrs. Delsey. I've got four o' me hands down with th' same thing, an' Elton at th' station was coughin' an' sneezin' yesterday when I was there. He said there was a sick man on the stage passin' through in the mornin'."

"Oh, dear..." Mrs. Delsey looked worried.

"Yes, ma'am," Padraig agreed. "I think we might be gettin' an epidemic." He pulled Cookie's list from his pocket. "I need t' get these things if you've got them."

She took the list, reading it. "We've everything except the licorice and mullein. I've got anise and stinging nettle. Will those do?"

"I suppose." Padraig had no idea whether those two could be substituted or not. "I'll take them, anyway."

Quicker than he expected, she had several glass pint jars lined up on the counter. They were filled with what looked like dried leaves, bits of root or tree bark, and pepper of various colors.

Padraig thought of what Elton had said about lemon and honey, and Cookie's remark about slippery elm lozenges. "You got any lemon, honey, or slippery elm?"

"The slippery elm's right here." She touched the top of a jar. "And there's the honey. She nodded to another. Padraig realized he should've recognized that. It still had the comb in it. "Don't have any lemons, not even any lemon flavoring. Wrong time of year."

She began placing the jars into a small burlap sack.

"Then I guess that's it." Padraig dug out his wallet. "How much?"

"Five dollars."

He paid the amount, carefully hefted the bag so the jars wouldn't strike against each other and break, and returned to the pinto waiting at the hitching rail. He tied the bag to the saddle horn, resting it against his thigh to cushion it. As he rode out of town, it again began to snow.

Once back at the ranch, he handed Cookie the bag, then tended the pinto. In spite of the cold weather, it was lathered and wet. Leading the horse into the stable, he unsaddled it and carefully curried and brushed down the animal. Afterward, Padraig hurried to the house, ignoring Cookie to rush into the bedroom and take one of Jessup's quilts from the closet.

Running through the snow back to the barn, he pulled some hay out of the pinto's feed trough and placed it on the animal's back. Throwing the quilt over the horse, he then took a piece of rope and wrapped it around the animal's girth, securing the blanket into place.

The hay would hold the blanket off the pinto's body, letting it dry without dampening the cloth. As it fell away when the horse moved, the blanket would settle, keeping cold air out and heat in.

After that, he led the pinto into its stall.

"That should keep *you* from gettin' sick," he told the horse, who snorted and turned its attention to the oats mixed in with the remaining hay in the trough.

Padraig went out, securing the stable door behind him.

This time, Cookie met him at the ranch house door.

"Come in and get something warm inside you, Boss."

"I ain't very hungry," Padraig protested, coughing. "Damned cold air." It was a moment before he could catch his breath. "You cookin'? Is it time for supper already?"

"It's past suppertime, Boss. You've been gone a good part of the day." Cookie reached for the coffeepot. "Here, have some coffee. It's good and hot."

Padraig accepted the cup but didn't drink. At the moment, his throat felt so full he was certain he'd choke if he tried to push any liquid down it.

"What's that?" He nodded at a pot of something boiling on the stove.

"Potatoes," Cookie explained. "That bunch in the bunkhouse can't keep anything solid down, so I'm making potato soup. Got to get something nutritious in 'em and I thought potatoes would be easy on their bellies. I peeled 'em while the boys were napping." He didn't seem to realize he was speaking of the cowhands as if they were infants in his care. "Drink your coffee."

Obediently, Padraig raised the cup and took a sip. "Is this Arbuckle's?"

"What else?" The cook replaced the coffeepot on the stove and reached for a spoon to stir the potatoes.

"Just wondered."

It was tasteless. Padraig realized his nose was stuffed and he was having trouble breathing—every breath burned as it entered his lungs. "Anyone else sick so far?"

He stumbled to a chair at the table, pulled it out, and dropped into it, setting down the cup.

"Buck's a little hoarse, but so far he ain't showing no signs of fever."

"I think we should get e'eryone still on his feet out o' th' bunkhouse," Padraig decided. He took a deep breath. A line of fire ran up his chest. "I'll go tell them."

Getting to his feet, he staggered out, leaving Cookie tending the soup. His feet felt as if someone had pounded lead soles onto his boots. He could barely lift his legs.

Damn, I'm so tired. Padraig brushed a hand across his forehead, pushing back his hat. *When did it get so hot? It should be freezin' out here.*

He reached the bunkhouse and went in. The sick men didn't acknowledge his presence. The others, bandannas firmly in place, welcomed him back.

"Did you get what Cookie needed?" Buck asked. He was standing so close to the fire it was a wonder his denims weren't scorching.

Padraig nodded and got to the point. "You men still well, grab your bedrolls an' get t' th' house. You can sleep on th' kitchen floor. I've got plenty o' quilts." He slapped his hands together. "Let's go!"

Chapter 25

"Goodness, Mr. McCoy," Mrs. Delsey looked surprised. "You back again?"

"Yes, ma'am. Need a few more things. Oil o' wintergreen, spearmint oil, an' some mustard seed." He held out the list. "How's Mr. Delsey doin'?"

"Some better," Mrs. Delsey answered as she stood on tiptoe to get one of the items. "I can't reach that." She looked back at Padraig. "Would you mind, Mr. McCoy?"

"No, ma'am, not at all." Coming around the counter, Padraig looked up at the row of bottles. "Which one?"

"The one with the green label."

Padraig got it down, setting it on the counter. He returned to his place on the other side as Mrs. Delsey got the other two items.

"Miss Abercrombie was in today. She says she closed the school because most of the children are out sick. The ranchers have been in getting medicinals their cooks are asking for. I guess it's a good thing you came in so early. I don't have much left until the next shipment comes from Omaha." She indicated the near-empty shelves.

"So th' whole town's infected," Padraig murmured. "We need a doctor."

"I couldn't agree more," Mrs. Delsey said. "But we don't have one, and what could he do? Really? Except prescribe exactly what we're already doing?"

"I guess you're right, but a medical man always knows a bit more than th' ordinary citizen," Padraig answered. "That's why they read those medical journals."

Mrs. Delsey didn't answer. She handed him the three bottles. "One dollar, Mr. McCoy."

Padraig paid and placed the bottles in his trail coat pocket. "Hope next time I come in, things are a li'l better."

"Amen to that, Mr. McCoy."

****

"Boss, there's a rider coming." Holding two cups of soup as he prepared to walk across to the bunkhouse, Buck looked out the kitchen window.

Padraig followed him to the door as the rider pulled his horse to a halt. The animal dropped its head so quickly he thought for a moment it was going to collapse. As its rider slid from its back, it tottered, then regained its balance.

"Hey." Padraig came onto the porch stoop. "Aren't you one o' th' farmers Mr. Jessup hired?" He shook a finger. "Yeah…Jacob Stieglitz."

"That's right," the man agreed, unwinding his muffler so his speech was intelligible. He was a short man, a German, bearded and wrapped under layers of knitted scarf, flannel shirts, and a coat looking as if created from scraps of old quilts. "I haff come to ask for your help, Herr McCoy."

"Patrick," Padraig corrected, automatically. "What can I do for you?"

"Patrick," Jacob amended. "It's…One of *mein kinder* iss *krank*—sick—*und*…"

"Coughin', fever, throwin' up?" Padraig

161

interrupted.

"What are you doing for it?" By now, Cookie joined them at the door.

"Come inside. No sense lettin' th' cold air in." Padraig pulled Jacob into the kitchen.

Buck went on out, trudging across the yard to the bunkhouse as Jacob made a beeline for the stove and its warmth.

"*Frau* Stieglitz has been giffing her tea *und* licorice root *und* keeping her varm."

"That's what I'd say t' do," Cookie said.

"But she iss not getting any better," Jacob protested. "She…she iss haffing trouble breathing." He caught Cookie's arm. "She iss turning blue, *und*…"

"Jesus, Jake. I don't…" Cookie turned a distressed face toward the man. "Damn it, I've never felt so helpless!"

He set down his cup so violently coffee splashed onto the tabletop.

"There's too many people sick and none of us really know what to do. Your daughter needs a doctor, not a chuckwagon cook."

He turned away.

"That does it!" Padraig stamped to where his coat hung from a peg.

"Boss, what are you going to do?"

"I'm goin' t' get a doctor."

"But the only doctor is in…"

"Exactly, an' that's where I'm goin'." Padraig pulled on his coat, wrapping his muffler around his neck and stuffing it into his collar. He strapped on his gun belt, settling it against his hip. "I'm gettin' that doctor an' bringin' him back with me if I have t' carry him!"

With that, he flung open the door and stamped down the steps, then paused and looked back. "Jacob, bring your daughter here. That way, p'rhaps th' rest o' your children won't become infected. Cookie, you can bed her down in th' parlor."

He turned and ran in the direction of the stable.

****

The pinto wasn't happy about leaving its stall. It started off at a plodding walk, stepping high through the drifts, but as soon as they were out of sight of the ranch house, it balked, pawing the snow and sending great swathes of white flying. Nothing Padraig did, whether slapping its flanks with his hat, flailing its shoulders with the ends of his reins, or kicking it in the ribs, seemed to make a bit of difference.

"Come on, you blasted animal!"

Though he struggled to keep the despair out of his voice, it was there, and he was certain the horse would sense his feeling of hopelessness and act upon it.

Da always said animals are smarter than people think. They can tell when we're desperate. That's why they can be as stubborn as humans sometimes.

He was startled to feel tears start in his eyes, knowing they weren't from the cold or the wind. For the moment, there wasn't even a breeze blowing, and the cold had been steady since the second snow.

"Damn it..." Padraig's voice trailed into a mutter. He heaved a sigh so deep it sent a rivulet of fire up his throat and made him cough for several minutes, during which the pinto rumbled a sound within its own chest as if in sympathy. "All right..."

Padraig pulled his hat from his head. Pressing it against his heart, he looked up at the sun. It was still early morning, but the snow was bright and near-blinding. He should be wearing his eye protectors, but he'd forgotten them and definitely wasn't going back after them.

Taking a deep breath, he said quietly, "Lord...I know me da thinks I'm a bad one, but I swear I'm tryin' t' be good. Maybe th' people in Four Corners, an' me own men, an' Jacob's li'l girl...maybe they'll get well without me help, but then again, maybe they won't. I've got t' try...I've got t' get t' Lancaster an' convince that doctor t' come back with me. Even if he says Cookie's doin' exactly what he'd do, I've got t' get his expert opinion. Will you please make this damned animal cooperate? I don't think I can walk that distance...not in this snow..." Putting his hat back on, he wiped his eyes and said, "Amen," waited a moment, then kicked the pinto in the ribs.

To his surprise, the horse started up, picking its way at a smart trot through the snow.

Padraig laughed, looked up again and said, "Much obliged," and turned the animal's head in the direction of Lancaster.

God might've gotten the pinto on its way, but other forces were working contrariwise to His plan. A mile outside of the ranch, the wind started to blow. Padraig, who'd been feeling warm, had unbuttoned the top three tabs of his trail coat and pushed back his muffler. As soon as the icy air hit his chest, he began to cough. Hastily, he rebuttoned the coat and wrapped his muffler tighter.

The pinto plodded on, resolutely continuing through the white until it came to the stagecoach track still visible in the snow. Padraig turned it onto the narrow road, urging it forward.

It began snowing, the wind blowing the flakes into a swirl around him and the horse, an icy maelstrom of air and ice. He shivered and was certain he felt the pinto copy the action. Turning up his collar, Padraig huddled inside his trail coat, settling his hat lower on his brow and pulling up his muffler, protecting his face and ears as much as possible from the icy blast.

The wind blew stronger, pushing the snow and frigid air against them. Flakes formed in little drifts around the pinto's fetlocks. It raised its hooves higher, stepping out of its tracks and making deeper, newer ones, walking carefully. Once or twice, it stopped, shook its head, and gave a loud, wuffling rumble as if in protest before it began walking again.

By now, Padraig was merely a bundle on its back, a heavy weight wrapped in layers of cloth. Occasionally, he moved, trying to restore circulation to his feet or hands. He'd wrapped the reins around the saddle horn, drawing his hands and arms back inside the coat as much as possible, hugging them against his body but keeping his sleeves open so he could reach out and grab the reins if necessary, if the pinto stumbled or decided to become stubborn again. He wished he could pull his legs up inside the coat also, thankful it at least covered down to his boot tops, though his legs felt so benumbed he couldn't feel the coat after a while.

He closed his eyes. It would be so good to go to sleep and simply let the pinto travel where it would. Surely sooner or later it would reach Lancaster where there would be houses and warmth. Then he could wake up and get off its back and make his blood start moving again.

Padraig's eyes flickered and shut. He stayed that

way for several seconds, then lurched forward, forcing his eyes open with a jerk.

"Mustn't do that. Go t' sleep an' I might ne'er wake...don't sleep." He shook his head, sending the ends of the muffler flapping about his face, frozen fringe slapping his cheeks and making them sting.

He looked up at the sky, gray now and leaden with still-swirling snow.

Are we goin' in th' right direction? What if we're lost... What if we hit a drift an' get buried in snow an' no one finds us until next spring? Leaning forward, he stared at the ground. They were still on the track. It was barely visible through the snow but still there.

Padraig relaxed slightly. For some reason, that brought on a spate of coughing. He put a gloved hand over his mouth, the other rubbing his chest through his coat, trying to ease the burn.

How long have we been travelin'? Without the sun, he couldn't tell. It could've been an hour. It might've been five. *I'm so damned tired...so sleepy...me horse is, too...we both ought t' stop an' rest...*

Ahead, through the white whirl, he saw a flicker of light and a gray hulk. As they neared, it became a building. Nearby was another, and a third. A sign... *Adam Galen, MD...*

Padraig slid from the pinto's back, clinging to the saddle horn. Briefly, he couldn't stand, numb feet wouldn't hold his weight. He swung one hand outward. It struck something solid, a hitching bar. He wrapped the pinto's reins around it, then stumbled forward, willing his feet to move. They felt as if they were wrapped in bales of cotton, thick and sensation-stealing. He stumbled across the boardwalk and tripped, coming up against a door, raised a fist and brought it down with so feeble a movement, the sound it made was barely audible to his own ears.

He tried again. This time the blow was louder.

There were footsteps inside. The door was pulled open and Padraig fell into the arms of the man standing there. He fumbled under his coat, pulling out his revolver.

"You're comin' with me," he muttered. "If I have t' kidnap you."

That was the last thing he said for quite some time.

Chapter 26

Someone was sticking needles into his feet and trying to drown him with coffee.

Padraig opened his eyes, staring at the man kneeling beside him.

"You had me scared for a minute there, youngster. Didn't know whether you were going to shoot me or fall flat on your face. Luckily, you didn't do either one."

"Damnation, me feet hurt," was Padraig's answer, delivered in a croak. "What did you do t' them?"

"Nothing. That's just the blood starting to run through your veins again. Be glad it's doing that."

Padraig looked down. He was sitting in a rocking chair and his boots were gone, his feet, bright red and burning, were extended before him in the direction of a blazing fire. His boots rested to one side at the hearth.

"Thought to get them dried out a bit," the man said. "You're lucky you didn't get frostbite." He extended a hand. "I'm Adam Galen."

"Padraig McCoy." Padraig gave the hand a feeble shake.

"What the blazes you doing out in weather like this, anyway?"

He released the coffee cup into Padraig's hand. Padraig gulped it down, feeling it wash away some of the phlegm clogging his throat. He swallowed, coughed slightly and said, "I'm from Four Corners. We've got a batch o' people sick there, an' they need doctorin'."

"And you were the unlucky one chosen to come fetch me?" The doctor shook his head. "Brave...but damned dangerous. How many sick do you reckon?"

"I don't know for sure." Padraig tried to think. His brain must be frozen, too. He forced it to work. "Four o' me men, maybe one or two more by now...me foreman was complainin' o' a sore throat. A li'l girl from a German farm...th' general store owner, th' postmaster... most o' th' children...dunno 'ow many...most of the school, I guess..."

"Symptoms?" The doctor was being very professional and Padraig liked that.

"Sore throat...coughs...vomitin'...fever..."

"Sounds like influenza." He said that definitely enough and stood with a sigh. "How do your feet feel?"

Padraig wiggled his toes. That hurt but not too bad. At least he could feel it. "I'm all right."

The doctor disappeared into another room and returned with something in his hand. He tossed it onto Padraig's lap. It was a pair of socks. "Put those on, get your boots and your coat, and let's get going. I drive a buckboard. You can ride with me and tie your horse to the back."

It had stopped snowing, and the sun was shining again. Whether that was the reason or not, the trip back seemed shorter than the trip there.

They went to the ranch first.

Buck met them, running into the yard without a coat, shouting, "The boss is back. Hallelujah!" then breaking into a fit of coughing.

Throwing back the buffalo hide rug the doc had spread across their knees, Padraig jumped from the wagon. "Buck, you fool. Get back inta th' house."

He caught the foreman by the arm and spun him around as Dr. Galen followed him into the kitchen.

The cowhands were sitting around, looking ill at ease in their inactivity. Two were playing checkers, the others involved in a game of cards. They all looked up, getting to their feet as they saw Padraig and the doctor.

"All right…first off, who's Cookie?" Galen asked.

Padraig had explained to him how the cook was attempting to medicate everyone and felt he was overwhelmed.

"I am." Cookie stepped forward, coffeepot in hand.

"What've you been doing?"

"I've been boiling stinging nettle leaves on the bunkhouse stove and having them sniff the steam," Cookie answered. "I made anise tea and infusion of speedwell, then wrapped everyone in quilts to try to get them sweating, rubbed spearmint oil on nostrils and on the bridges of noses."

"Exactly what I'd do," Galen said, confirming what Mrs. Delsey had said to Padraig two days before…or was it a week ago?

Padraig's head whirled. He pulled out a chair and sat into it. Heavily.

"There are some other things you can do, too. Does anyone still have a fever?"

Cookie shook his head. "Fevers broke after I used speedwell. Mostly, they're congested and all stuffed up."

"Got any garlic?"

Cookie shook his head.

"Sweet basil?"

Again, a negative headshake.

"Hell, doc," Padraig spoke up in a croak. "This is a

ranch, not a restaurant."

"Too bad. Those two are good expectorants." Galen ignored him. "How about horehound?"

"Got that," Cookie affirmed.

"Good, take some, melt it down with sugar and water into a syrup, add a little pounded licorice root if you have it. Use that four times a day. Should break the phlegm loose." Galen thought a moment. "How about echinacea?"

"Don't know what that is," Cookie admitted.

"Purple coneflower. Grows wild hereabouts."

"Don't have it."

"Never mind, then." He glanced around. "Anyone here been coughing or have a sore throat?"

All shook their heads. Padraig looked up, jerking as if suddenly brought out of a deep sleep. "Buck? You..."

"Been sucking on those slippery elm tablets of Cookie's and my throat's all right now," Buck said. "That coughing I was doing in the yard was from sucking in that cold air."

"In that case, show me my patients," Galen said.

Pulling on his coat, Cookie opened the door. Galen and Padraig followed him across the yard to the bunkhouse.

After examining each man, Galen pronounced two of them on the way to recovery. "Going to have to take it easy, though. Give them chamomile tea to make them sleep. At this point, plenty of rest and liquids...coffee, tea, water..."

"How about beer?" Will croaked.

"No alcohol," Galen said, and smiled at the cowhand's sickly, sullen look. He told Cookie, "No heavy foods yet. Broths, soups."

"Been giving 'em beef broth and potato soup with butter," Cookie said.

"That sounds good, though you might go easy on the butter until their bellies heal a bit. Keep using the spearmint. Inhaling some warm salt water will also open those nasal passages. Ordinarily I'd order some tincture of wintergreen, but these men are so dehydrated, they don't need any alcohol in their systems." He thought a moment. "Mustard plasters, for everyone, along with the horehound syrup. That'll break up that congestion quick. Now, let me get a look at these two…" He turned to the other bunks and the men lying there.

"They should be all right," Galen told Padraig. "Your cook seems to be a veteran at this, which is a good thing. He's got it under control, even if he didn't think so."

Padraig breathed a sigh of relief. "Thanks, Doc."

"Now, then, you said there were people in town who were ill?"

"…an' th' li'l Steiglitz girl," Padraig added. "I told her da t' bring her here. She should be in th' parlor on me sofa." He opened the bunkhouse door. "I'll show you th' way…"

"Let one of your men do that. Your foreman can guide me to town, too." Galen's hand on his arm stopped him. "You've done enough. I think you need to get yourself to bed and rest some."

"Rest." Padraig nodded. For some reason, that made a buzzing in his ears. "Very well."

He stepped out into the ranch yard. The snow was very bright, almost blinding. He blinked. The buzzing got louder.

Padraig took a step. His knees buckled and he went

down as the noise drowned out Buck's shout and the doctor's voice.

Chapter 27

Padraig opened his eyes. Once again, Galen was bending over him, holding a cup. He sat up so quickly, the doctor had to jump back to keep from spilling the coffee.

"Doc? Where am I?" He looked around, trying to find something familiar. "I thought…didn't we get t' th' ranch? Are we still in Lancaster?"

"You've been out of it a while," Galen explained. "You collapsed in the yard. You were so busy looking out for everyone else, you forgot yourself."

"I was sick?"

"As a dog, Boss," Buck supplied, helpfully.

"How…how long?" Padraig didn't allow himself time to be embarrassed by the thought he'd probably upchucked as badly as his men, in full view of everyone.

He glanced at the window. It was daylight. *Surely I was only out for a few hours.*

"Four days," Galen supplied.

"Four…"

"We were worried, Boss." Buck stepped up to the bed.

Behind him, Padraig saw Cookie hovering in the doorway, his empty hands looking odd because he was holding neither coffeepot nor cook spoon.

"When you started raving with fever…"

"I had to take drastic measures," Galen said.

"What kind of..." Padraig felt overwhelmed. He wanted to snuggle under the quilts and go back to sleep.

"Your fever got up to one hundred and three," Galen explained. "I tried cold compresses, sponged your body with the alcohol I had in my bag, but nothing seemed to help."

"So we stripped you, took you outside, and laid you on the ground and covered you with snow," Buck said.

"You...what?" That shook Padraig out of his lethargy. "You put ice on me naked body? God!"

His hands moved under the blanket. For the first time he realized he wasn't wearing his long johns.

"Did you freeze anythin'?"

"Don't worry." Galen was laughing. "Nothing got frostbite and I imagine everything is in as good working order as it was before you got sick."

"Thank God for that anyway," Padraig breathed. He relaxed against the pillow. "An' e'eryone else? Th' people in Four Corners? Jake's li'l girl?"

"The little girl's all right. Her father took her home yesterday," Galen said and his expression changed. "I'm afraid I couldn't save everyone. That Mr. Elton? He was too far gone...pneumonia had set in. There were a couple of children...one of the mayor's sons, and a Mr. Terry. I understand he was a fellow rancher."

"Oh, I'm so sorry," Padraig muttered.

"We couldn't save them all, Mr. McCoy." Galen's hand on his arm gave a consoling pat. "But you did save most of the town of Four Corners. Be proud of that."

"I didn't do it for pride, Doc," Padraig muttered. "I did it because this is me town an' I've got t' take care o' them. Like me da does back in Ireland..."

With a shock he realized it was true. He might not

have been given Four Corners as Lord Alisdaire had, nor appointed estate steward as his father was, but he felt as responsible for it and its inhabitants as Quinton did the tenants on the properties in his care.

"These are me people an' I've got t' keep them safe."

E'en I can't keep e'eryone safe, Padraig. He was certain he heard Quinton's voice. *E'en your da fails on occasion. Like I did with you.*

"You didn't fail, Da. You just had t' get me t' th' proper place for me t' succeed..." Padraig's voice trailed away as he drifted back into sleep.

"Is he all right?" Buck asked.

Galen nodded. "He'll sleep for a while, then next time he wakes, he'll be a bit more alert." He looked at Cookie. "Keep pouring the chamomile and horehound into him. Use another mustard poultice for a couple of days, then ease him back into his regular activities." He moved toward the door. "I estimate in four more days he'll be bossing you men around again, good as new, with no residuals. Now, I've got to get back to Lancaster and my own patients and be prepared to meet the infleunza head-on if it hits there."

Chapter 28

"…so it's settled then." Mayor Bainbridge rapped the gavel against the desk.

It was a faint, half-hearted gesture. The mayor felt as if he'd been merely walking through his days since the loss of his second son in the influenza epidemic. "We'll inform Padraig of our decision on both subjects as soon as he…"

The door opened.

"Speak of the devil." Bainbridge forced a smile to his lips. "Here he is now."

"Mornin', Mr. Mayor…gentlemen." Padraig nodded to each man as he shed his coat and hung it and his hat on the peg now automatically reserved for him by the others. He looked at Bainbridge. "Sorry I'm late. Had a couple o' things t' tend t'. Before we go any further, let me offer me condolences t' you an' th' missus on losin' your boy, Mr. Mayor."

Bainbridge nodded, his hand going to the mourning band on his left arm as it did whenever anyone spoke of young Steven.

"An' me sympathy on th' death o' two o' th' council members." Padraig glanced at the empty chairs where Elton and Terry usually sat. "I'm goin' t' miss both o' them."

He took a deep breath, thinking how good it felt not to have his lungs burn as he inhaled, as well as not breaking into a coughing spasm.

"I see you've already started th' meetin'…"

"We weren't certain if you'd be here or not," Blackstone explained.

"Since I'm not a council member but merely an interested citizen," Padraig continued, "'tis been downright polite o' you t' delay your meetin's until I could get here."

"We had a good reason for not waiting this time," Blackstone said.

"I suppose you're goin' t' tell me," Padraig said, frowning slightly.

"That we are," Delsey answered.

He cleared his throat, scowling as the others glanced at him hurriedly. After all the coughing and sneezing, that was everyone's initial reaction if anyone so much as sniffed, and probably would be for some time.

"We had some items on our agenda we had to vote on. Since they concerned you, we wanted to get them out of the way before you got here."

"They concerned me?" Padraig looked startled, and a little worried. "In what way? I thought we'd got it settled that I, or any person livin' in Four Corners, had a right t' attend meetin's."

"It's not that," Blackstone assured him. "We…well, you've been at every meeting we've had for months now and you've always brought up good points and concerns, and…"

"Since we now have two vacancies, we've voted to ask you if you'd fill one," Bainbridge finished.

"You're wantin' me t' be a city council member?" Padraig looked disbelieving.

The four men nodded.

"You lost *two* members," he reminded them.

"We'll think about the other one," Bainbridge said. "We know for certain we want you."

"I...thank you." Padraig blinked.

He was startled to realize he was affected more than he felt he should be. He'd originally come to the meetings merely to make certain Mr. Jessup got his library. He'd continued as a distraction from ranch work and because it was actually interesting. He'd never expected to be asked to become one of the men making decisions concerning the town.

"Thank you, gentlemen." He stood, sweeping them a grand bow. "I'll be greatly honored t' accept th' appointment t' be a council member for th' town o' Four Corners."

"About that..." August spoke up.

"We also voted to change the name of the town," Bainbridge explained.

"Oh?" Padraig thought about that. "I hope 'tis somethin' a li'l grander, in that case."

"We think so." Blackstone smiled. "We want to call it McCoy's Crossing."

Padraig didn't speak. He simply stared at them.

"It's our way of thanking you for what you did during the influenza epidemic, Patrick," Blackstone said.

"Sirs, I..." Padraig sat down, rather quickly. He brushed a hand across his forehead, blinking away tears before anyone could see them. "Excuse me. I guess I'm not as recovered as I thought. Legs don't want t' hold me up."

He saw the men exchange glances and knew he hadn't fooled them for a minute, but also that none would comment on it.

"Well, then…" Padraig got to his feet. "Since I'm now a council member, I've a bit o' business I'd like t' bring up, Mr. Mayor." He cleared his throat, harrumphing a bit as he'd heard the others do, both to remove the lump lodged there and to sound businesslike.

"The floor recognizes newly appointed member Mr. Patrick McCoy." Bainbridge pointed the gavel at Padraig. "Take your seat at the table and speak, Mr. McCoy."

Picking up the chair he'd been sitting in, Patrick pulled it up to the table and sat down.

"After our recent siege o' influenza, an' me own ride t' Lancaster an' subsequent struggle with th' disease, I've come t' a decision." Padraig looked around the table, seeing the curiosity on their faces, knowing they were wondering what he was about to say. "I've taken th' liberty o' askin' Dr. Galen from Lancaster t' refer me t' several o' his colleagues who might have an interest in becomin' doctor t' a small town on its way up. This morning, I posted five letters t' be taken by th' Pony Express an' eventually delivered t' physicians in Omaha, Chicago, Boston, an' New York, invitin' them t' apply for th' vacant position o' resident doctor o' Four Cor…I mean McCoy's Crossin'. That's why I was late."

Padraig smiled and settled himself into the chair, hitching it up to the table.

"Members of th' McCoy's Crossin' town council, we are goin' t' get outselves a doctor."

Thus Padraig McCoy made his second conquest in the town he now called *home*—this time of the people themselves.

****

2 March, 1860

Quinton Aloysius Francis Xavier McCoy, Esquire
McCoy Hall
Tipperary, Ireland
The United Kingdom of Great Britain

Esteemed and Honourable Father,

Please do not think I am trying to establish a correspondence because I am sending you another missive so soon. I do remember you expressed the opinion in a previous communication that one letter a year, to confirm I still lived, would be enough. However, several events have occurred of which I feel you should be apprised.

Several winters ago, Four Corners was visited by an influenza which was particularly devastating because we have no doctor. Some of my hired men were stricken as well as many townsfolk, causing me to undertake the ride to the town of Lancaster forty miles away and fetch their doctor. Because it was snowing at the time and the temperatures were fiercely cold, I was also taken ill though I have now recovered.

I lost several friends to this influenza, two of which were members of the town council. Father, in gratitude for my efforts during this time, the council have asked me to replace one of their lost members. This is a great honour, comparable to being elected to Parliament, though on a much lesser scale. I hasten to add I in no way coerced or used my status to obtain this position. In truth, I was completely flabbergasted when I was informed.

The most unbelievable part, sir, was that they also advised me they were changing the name of the town to McCoy's Crossing, in my honour. Again, I swear I was unaware of their intent.

Now I must ask you a question. I was ill in probably mid-October. Father, did you think of me during that time? I ask because, in my delirium, I could swear I heard you speaking, lamenting your failure where I was concerned. Whether you did think of me or if this was simply the ravings of a feverish mind, I wish you to know you did not fail, sir. You were merely the instrument delivering me from the ill influence of my surroundings into the place where I might become the man I should be. Be assured I am no longer the scoundrel who called himself your son but have taken on the mantle of respectability.

I hope, should anyone now ask after me, you will inform them with some pride that I am a prosperous businessman, well liked by the community in which he lives. I owe my present condition to you, Father, and, where I once lamented your ultimatum, now I am grateful for it.

Please convey my good wishes to Donal and Colin, and my love to my mother.

Your appreciative son,
Padraig Aloysius Francis McCoy
Owner, The Shamrock Ranch
McCoy's Crossing, Nebraska Territory
United States of America

****

McCoy's Crossing
Summer 1860

The world began to change and McCoy's Crossing changed with it. More stores opened, more businesses came to town. As yet, there was no doctor in residence, however.

In spite of Padraig's letters and the recommendations Dr. Galen also wrote, no one had yet agreed to take up residence. Most sent polite but adamant declines. Undaunted, Padraig asked Galen for more names, which were dutifully supplied. Those men also rejected the honor, just as politely. When Padraig came back with a third request, the doctor laughed, stating soon he'd have supplied him with the entire roster of his graduating class.

Padraig was determined, however, and at last, Fortune shone upon his endeavors. Six years after his initial attempt, with luckily no epidemics in the meantime, the recipient of one of his original letters wrote to him, stating his son, a recent medical college graduate, wished to be independent and not go into practice with his father. Would McCoy's Crossing take a chance on a newly graduated physician?

McCoy's Crossing most definitely would.

On a late summer day in 1860, Padraig McCoy and other members of the town council, dressed in their Sunday best, made their way to the stage station to welcome Dr. Elias Sheppard to McCoy's Crossing.

There was also someone else arriving that day, who would change Padraig's life in another way.

Chapter 29

Padraig got to the station first. He'd risen early, dressing in one of the suits purchased from the tailor's shop after he decided the clothing he brought with him and rarely wore was now out of style. A cattle baron and town council member, as well as the man for whom the town was named, had to look up-to-date in his dress as well as his ideas.

Leaving the pinto at the livery stable, he shucked the duster worn over his suit to protect it from pollen and other prairie dust and debris, dropped it over the horn of the saddle set atop a stall enclosure, and walked to the station.

He thought it a fine day. The sun was shining but not too hot since it was still early morning. A breeze was blowing, just enough to lift his freshly cut hair off his neck.

To celebrate Dr. Sheppard's arrival, Padraig had splurged for a haircut and a shave, cautioning the barber to be careful of the handlebar moustache he was cultivating. As he moved in confident strides to the station, he felt revitalized, definitely stylish, and very much the powerful council member and cattle rancher that he was.

He could see a cloud of dust in the distance, the stagecoach approaching. So far, that specific coach had never been late. People in town could set their watches by the 8:10 from Omaha. Out of habit, Padraig pulled his own watch from its little pocket in his vest and checked the time.

Prompt again.

He closed the watch, returning it to his pocket, while making certain the chain and fob were stretched across the vest from one pocket to the other and stylishly looped around the center button of his vest.

The stage came to a halt, dust rising, blending with that blown up by a sudden wind into a grayish haze.

Like London's fog, he thought, startled to think of something he hadn't seen in a decade, the same thought when he himself arrived in Four Corners.

The postmaster's son, Elton, Junior, who'd inherited the position upon his father's death during the epidemic, came out of the building, wearing his "official" uniform of black billed cap, black vest, and white shirt over his denims. He trotted toward Padraig.

"Morning, Patrick. Coach's right on time, as usual." He watched the driver climb down from his perch and hand the reins over to the man from the livery stable, who began unhitching the horses.

"Did you doubt it wo…"

Padraig never finished that sentence as the guard opened the coach door and offered his hand to a passenger. She placed her own in it, allowing him to assist her in leaving the stage.

My God, she's beautiful.

He stopped stock-still, feeling such a sensation of breathlessness in his gut it was almost pain, as if someone had driven a fist into his belly. It came so swiftly he couldn't speak. Padraig inhaled, a sucking-in of air like a gasp.

"Patrick?" Elton looked at him in concern. "You all right?"

Padraig didn't answer. He went toward the stage, walking as swiftly as possible without actually breaking into a run, passing others gathered to welcome loved ones, including Blackstone and Bainbridge, who appeared from somewhere and made their way to him. He left them behind, ignoring their greetings. He had to get to that woman, that angel, before anyone else did.

She stood in the midst of disembarking passengers, looking around.

Please, God, not for her husband.

The other passengers were welcomed with hugs and kisses and walked away with wives, brothers, or sweethearts. She stood alone, abandoned amid the dust rapidly wafting into the air.

Relief washing over him, Padraig approached, holding out his hand.

She looked around, past him, everywhere except at him. As he stopped directly in front of her, she bestowed a dark-eyed gaze upon him.

He was lost.

OkíŋyAŋ Zitkála was a Lakota Sioux, torn from her family by white men's cruel but basically good intentions.

She was so young when it happened that she barely remembered the day the blue-coated horsemen arrived, forcibly taking her and her brother and placing them in a government school, where they were given an education while any vestige of their native culture was erased.

Along with a good many other youngsters, OkíŋyAŋ Zitkála was sent east, where, after her initial schooling, she was placed with a white family and raised to be white. Every iota of her people's culture was prohibited while the adoption of her new family's customs, language, and clothing was forced upon her.

Unlike many of the children who fought this change and suffered for it, being beaten until they gave in or later became outcasts from both cultures because they fit into neither, OkíŋyAŋ Zitkála saw the profit in accepting what she was taught, even at the expense of being considered a traitor to her own people.

At that point, she didn't care. All she was interested in was her own survival.

At the age of eighteen, she was ostensibly returning to her home state after thirteen years of indoctrination. Now she saw her people through white eyes, as ignorant savages needing a superior guiding hand. OkíŋyAŋ Zitkála had no desire to reconnect with her people and definitely didn't want to again settle into their way of life. What she wished was to find a white husband and continue living as a white woman.

With that in mind, she bade her adoptive family goodbye, albeit with some reluctance since she did have affection for them. They'd been good people and sympathetic to a small child being forcibly taken from her home and given into the care of strangers. Truly, they hadn't wanted her to leave, and there were a couple of young men who were disappointed that she refused their proposals of marriage to board a train taking her back to a life of what they assumed would be savagery.

That was the way everyone thought, but Maria, as she was now called, had a plan. She had to get away from anyone who knew of her background, which meant abandoning the family and people she could truly call friends. The ticket she purchased was for a ride the length of the stagecoach system, and when it was used up, she was determined she'd find another way taking her to Sacramento.

Alta California was now out of Spanish hands. While the Gold Rush was officially over, there were many who'd struck it rich and now were living grandly because of that. In spite of the fact that Alta California was now an American state, there were still a few Spanish grandees living in *haciendas* around San Juan Capistrano, Cuidad de las Nuestra de los Angeles, and other cities.

Maria's plan was to go to a place where her dark looks wouldn't garner so much attention, pass herself off as Spanish, and entice one of the now well-heeled miners, or perhaps a *Californio*, marry him, and escape her heritage forever. To that end, she'd saved every bit of the meager monthly stipend allotted to her. She hadn't foreseen how she was going to live in the meantime or how everyone would regard an unmarried, unescorted young woman in a state considered even more wild and lawless than the West. All she saw was the goal she'd set.

To that end, she endured the uncomfortable ride west, braved advances by men seeking to take advantage of a female traveling alone, and was tired, wishing her journey were over and also that she'd never allowed herself to undertake such an insane endeavor. At that exact moment, she wished she'd accepted one of those young men's proposals, even if he was aware she was Lakota.

Then the stage pulled into McCoy's Crossing and she spoke to the driver about leaving it briefly, to move about on a surface not rocking beneath her feet, to breathe some air not filled with dust and sweat and cigar smoke and let her cramped legs and back muscles relax a bit. He told her they would be there long enough to switch teams and allow passengers continuing on to avail themselves of the outhouse behind the livery stable, and to pick up any new passengers.

With a thought to the irony that she was momentarily entering the town so close to where she'd been taken from her family, Maria stepped from the stage, looking up to see a well-dressed young man coming toward her at a near run. She stiffened, got a better look at him, and forgot the stage, Sacramento, and anything else.

He stopped before her, panting slightly as he swept off his broad-brimmed hat with a flourish. Maria was dazzled by red hair, copper-bright in the sunlight. She blinked, actually taking a step backward.

"Welcome t' McCoy's Crossin'." He bowed, then replaced the hat, shading eyes of the brightest green she'd ever seen. "May I say our town's bedazzled t' have someone with your beauty grace it? Are you stayin' long?"

To Maria's way of thinking, both questions were impolite bordering on brazen, especially coming from a stranger. Nevertheless, there was something attractive and impudent in his smile, as well as the twinkle in those eyes….and his accent intrigued her.

Irish? Here? She decided to answer him, but not let him know she was the least bit attracted.

"You're rather impertinent, sir, to comment on my appearance, and also rude to ask me such a question." Briefly, she wished she had a fan to shake at him, then to hide behind, but since she didn't, she looked away, turning her back slightly.

She was aware of a man in shirtsleeves and black vest standing a few feet away—the stationmaster, no doubt. He was watching them and scowling. Two other men, also well-dressed though much older than the man before her, were also looking on with curiosity, though not at *her*.

The man was their subject of scrutiny.

"In that case, I beg your pardon," he answered. "For 'twasn't me intent t' be ithur impertinent or impolite." He walked around her so they faced each other again. "Shall we start over?"

Before she could answer, he again doffed his hat.

"Good mornin', miss. Welcome t' McCoy's Crossin'." He replaced the hat. "Would you permit me t' introduce meself?"

She studied him a moment, then made her decision. She nodded.

"Padraig McCoy, at your service. I'm a wealthy cattle ranch owner hereabouts, an' th' town's named after me, so you can see I'm a trustworthy type. May I have th' honor o' knowin' your name?"

He smiled again.

"Maria. Maria Citcála." She'd kept part of her Lakota name, transforming it into a Spanish-sounding one. Since she couldn't resist his smile, she gave him one in return.

"Are you a new resident t' our fair city?" He made it sound as if it would be the city's loss if she wasn't.

She found herself answering reluctantly. "I'm afraid I'm continuing on to California."

"California?" he exclaimed in a tragic tone, as if his heart were breaking. "Ah, nay, 'tis such a long way t' travel when me town's got more t' offer."

"Such as what, Mr. McCoy?" She looked directly into his eyes as she spoke.

"Such as meself, for one thing," he replied, so promptly she felt as if he'd been waiting for her to ask. "Have you had breakfast?"

"Well, no, but I'm…"

"Will you let me treat you t' a meal at th' Sylvestre House, our finest restaurant?" He leaned a little closer, confiding, "Our only restaurant at th' moment, though we do have a diner, but I've been told several ithur eateries have inquired about openin' establishments here."

"Well, I…" She had to refuse. If she were foolish enough to go into town, she'd miss the stage. Already, people were climbing onboard. Still…he was so handsome, and his smile so beguiling. She decided it was true, what she'd heard about Irishmen.

"Padraig?" One of the men she'd noticed spoke.

McCoy looked over his shoulder. "What is it, Mr. Blackstone?" His question was a trifle short.

"I believe that's Dr. Sheppard." Blackstone nodded to someone standing a few feet away, another young man, nattily dressed, and carrying a portmanteau in one hand and a heavier suitcase in the other.

McCoy gave him a blank look.

"The man we came to meet?" Blackstone supplied. "Our new doctor?"

"Oh." McCoy glanced at the young man and dismissed him with a shrug. "You an' Bainbridge can be th' welcomin' committee, Josiah. I've somethin' more important t' do." Turning back, he ignored anything else Blackstone said. "Now, then…Miss Citcála, may I…"

"Padraig." Blackstone spoke a little more forcefully. "I really think you should meet him, since you were the one to…"

"I can meet him later, Josiah." McCoy's voice became sharper. "After breakfast. I'd forgotten Miss Citcála here was comin' in on th' stage also. Bein' th' gentleman I am, I can't abandon her, can I?"

"Well, no, I don't suppose…" Blackstone shrugged and smiled. It was the slightly indulgent expression of an uncle for a favored but unruly child. He glanced at his companion. "Come, Milton, let's greet Dr. Sheppard. He's standing there looking lost."

"Give him me regards an' tell him I'll see him later," Padraig called as they walked past. He looked back at Maria, offering his arm. "Shall we?"

"The coach…" She made a halfhearted final protest.

"You can exchange your ticket for anaithur," he answered, adding, "or not."

"Yes," she agreed, then realized that was an ambiguous answer. She was being foolish, letting her plans be sidetracked, but there was something about him… "I can."

She slipped her arm through his.

****

As soon as they were seated, Maria decided to tell her fabricated story, beginning with the explanation, "I suppose I should thank you for rescuing me from boredom. That's why I asked the driver for permission to leave the stage. It was so hot, and tiring."

"You've traveled far, then?"

"A bit." Her answer was rueful. "I'm returning home to California."

"Ah." McCoy looked intrigued.

"I'm an orphan. My guardian sent me Back East to be educated." That wasn't so much of a stretch of the truth. Didn't the president consider himself custodian of all native peoples, and hadn't that *guardian* caused her to be taken east to be schooled, even if she hadn't wanted to go? "Now I've finished and I'm returning home, though…"

Here she heaved a distressed sigh and looked away.

"I truly don't want to go."

"Why not?"

"My guardian and I have never seen eye to eye. I fear he's planning a marriage for me."

"An' you're not wantin' th' man he's chosen," he guessed.

Maria was certain she could see his mind busily considering this, and also his interest growing.

"I'm certain he's chosen himself," she answered. "He has control of my parents' money, and I believe he wants to continue spending it." She began wringing her hands slightly as if unaware of the gesture. "I might not complain, if he weren't so old."

"Ah, that's bad news," McCoy sympathized. "What I don't understand is how he could let you travel alone."

"I don't think he cares how I get back," Maria answered, realizing she was painting her imaginary guardian a very wicked shade of black. "As long as I come home." She gave a theatrical shiver. "I admit I was afraid, because of this talk of war I've heard. I feared we might be fired upon by some of those rebellious Southerners."

"Ah, now, if there is a war, I doubt they'd be comin' this far west," Padraig soothed. "They'll have enough t' handle in their own part o' th' country."

They fell silent. Maria gave her attention to their surroundings.

The Sylvestre House advertised it had a "genuine French cook," giving it definite competition to the diner. There were eight tables in the room, all covered with white cloths looking, if not genuine linen, at least a very high-grade and thick weave of cotton. All were occupied by diners obviously enjoying their meals.

The walls were papered instead of painted, and there were several paintings—still lifes strategically placed— with tables holding large double-globed lamps giving considerable illumination.

Someone had put a great deal of work into the Sylvestre House, making it into a very nice restaurant. Perhaps it wasn't as fancy as some she'd seen in New York, but it was good enough to look out of place in a little Nebraska town.

"Aye, but McCoy's Crossin's not always going to be a small Nebraska town," McCoy said, as if he'd read her thoughts.

"How did you…"

"'Tis what visitors always say, first off," he explained. "They believe we're at a standstill when actually we're as progressive as Lincoln or Omaha…maybe even more so because McCoy's Crossin's got meself behind it."

"You certainly think a great deal of yourself, don't you, Mr. McCoy?"

"That's because I'm full o' ideas an' burstin' t' put them into action," he replied. He studied the menu, giving her time to look at hers also. "I recommend th' eggs and braised beef tips with julienne potatoes."

That startled her. She'd expected he'd ask for baked

beans, salt pork, and a mug of beer. She studied him as the waiter took their orders, accepted back their menus, and walked away.

Tall, red-haired, and Irish…definitely handsome, and a stylish dresser…a little older than she, perhaps by ten years, but what did that matter? Maria had been prepared to set her cap for someone she considered actually elderly, a man in his fifties or more, if necessary, and endure his attentions in exchange for status, but…

This Mr. McCoy was definitely well-off, if he had a town named after him. That was better than she expected, to find a man good-looking, fairly young, as well as rich, and not have to travel across the entire country to do so.

She tried to be cold in her appraisal, ignoring the little tingles of delight she felt every time he glanced at her. *Why am I trying to fool myself? I like him. Possibly I could love him.*

Unaware of her scrutiny, Padraig raised his cup, sipped the coffee it contained, and set down the cup. "Now then, what would you like t' know?"

"About what?" She looked puzzled.

"About me, o' course. It appears t' me you're not th' type o' lass t' go off with a stranger, so I'm for makin' certain I'm no longer that, an' th' way t' do it is for me t' tell you about meself."

"I already know about you," she said.

"Oh? An' exactly what do you know?"

They were flirting, Padraig realized with a shock. Something he hadn't done in a decade. Saloon girls didn't require flirtation, so he was surprised he hadn't forgotten how. This time, however, it wasn't a mere dalliance he had in mind but something much more serious…and permanent. That shook him even more.

"You're Padraig McCoy," she answered, looking down at her hands as if stricken shy. "You're obviously an Irishman, so I might wonder how you got *here*. You're also a gentleman and, by your own admission, well-liked by this town."

"Well then, t' answer that question you didn't ask, I came here almost a decade ago, tryin' t' find me way out o' being a scamp an' a scoundrel…"

"Did you succeed?"

"I believe I have." He sounded surprised to discover the fact. "I started out as a cowhand for th' Circle-J, th' largest ranch in these parts…still is for that matter. Then me boss was killed on a cattle drive." Here Padraig paused and took a deep breath. "An' I bought th' ranch. 'Tis now th' Shamrock. I suppose I'm well-liked by most o' th' people around here. I've certainly tried t' ingratiate meself, an' I truly love this town."

He paused, thinking a moment.

"Let's see…what else should I say? I'm thirty-one years old, still got all me hair an' me teeth, an' haven't been sick since th' influenza epidemic of '54."

"An' you're a terrible flirt," Maria added.

"Oh, nay," he disagreed. He realized he was rapidly recovering all the qualities he'd once used on women and thought he'd forgotten. Gaillich words spoken in amorous conversation came back to him, lurking and preparing to be launched into this one. His speech patterns were also becoming more like the licentious lad he'd been. "I'm a *great* flirt."

"What does your wife think of that, Mr. McCoy?" Maria decided she'd better find out his marital status before she went any further. No need to waste attention on him if he was already taken. She had no desire to become a mistress, no matter how tempting the man. "Does she approve of your whisking young women off stagecoaches and taking them to breakfast?"

"I've no idea." Padraig met her eyes in a direct stare shaking her in its intensity. "You haven't married me yet."

"Wh-what did you say?" Surely she hadn't heard correctly.

"I said, will you marry me, Miss Citcála?" He placed his hand over the one lying on the table. "I ne'er thought o' takin' a wife until th' moment I saw you. Now, it seems th' natural way o' things, but th' woman I marry has t' be *you*, an' no one else."

"You can't be serious."

"I assure you I am, me dear."

He certainly looked that way, Maria thought.

"I want you, Maria Citcála, an' bein' th' honorable man I now am, that means lawfully wedded."

"But...why me?" She hadn't meant to say that, simply blurted out her first thought. "I mean, I'm a stranger."

"What better way than marriage t' not be a stranger for long?" Those eyes were twinkling at her obvious confusion, perhaps enjoying her distress a bit. "I'm captured, *muirnín*. You're a siren, woman, a Circe...you've bound me heart with gossamer, an' I can ne'er break those silken strands."

"That's very poetic, Mr. McCoy." Luckily, Maria had adored reading myths and fairy tales and was very familiar with everything he'd mentioned. "I suppose I should be flattered, but I do believe you've mixed your characters a bit. Circe didn't bind men with gossamer, she turned them into swine."

"In that case, I'll gladly root in the mud an' accept swill if poured by your dear li'l hands," he replied grandly. Again, that sincere green stare bored into hers. "I mean it, lass."

"I...but..." She was stammering like a fool. For once in her life, Maria didn't know what to say. She told him exactly that.

"Say, *yes*," Padraig urged. "Become Mrs. Padraig Aloysius Francis McCoy an' put me out o' me misery, for I swear I haven't been able t' breathe properly an' me heart's been a-poundin' since you stepped out of the stage. Truly, I may expire soon if it keeps up this way." His eyes crinkled at the corners as they lit with mischief. "I promise I'll ne'er beat you an' I'll make love t' you e'ery night."

"Oh." Maria put her free hand against her heart, taking a deep breath. "With a promise like that, how can I refuse?"

"I daresay you could," Padraig replied calmly. "But it definitely would be both our losses." He winked. "I'm a very accomplished lover."

"Can you provide letters of authenticity attesting to that fact?" Maria dared laugh aloud, startled by her own audacity.

"I wouldn't dare." He looked earnest. "Once I'm married t' you, I'll forget e'ery woman I've e'en glanced at. I swear."

"There's something I must know, Mr. McCoy," Maria drew in a deep breath.

"Ask." He looked at her the way a child might who was being given a quiz by a stern teacher. "Whate'er 'tis, I'll tell th' truth."

"I understand there are Indians in these parts." She paused, trying to form her question in a way that wouldn't betray her.

"Aye," he agreed. "Lakota, mostly, though I've ne'er seen one in all the time I've been here."

"They're not…dangerous?" What she wanted to ask was, *What do you think of them? Do you believe the only good Indian is a dead one, as some white men do? Would you shoot me if you married me and then learned I was Lakota?*

"Ah, now." He considered that before speaking and when he did, his words came carefully. "I suppose anyone can be dangerous if pushed far enough. I know me own people back in Ireland…they've been down-trod enough some Englishmen don't dare turn their backs on them, but Lakota? Unless one was comin' at me full-tilt with one o' those tomahawks, I'd leave him be. I've naithin' against them. Fact is, I'd like t' meet some, t' show them all white men aren't bad."

He thrust out a forearm, pulling back his suit cuff and revealing a brawny tanned wrist whose copper hairs were almost the same color as his skin.

"Matter o' fac' I'm probably near th' same color as a Sioux by now, me self."

Maria felt herself relax. She didn't speak.

"So…how about it?" His question held a tinge of anxiety. "Will you stay here, let that guardian keep your money, an' stay with me? I've enough for both o' us."

"Yes, Mr. McCoy. I will." Maria felt as if she'd thrown herself from a high cliff into a raging ocean. Her stomach clutched from the swiftness of the fall.

Briefly, everything went black, and when she surfaced through the darkness, McCoy was staring at her as if she'd handed him not only a basket of golden eggs but also the flock of geese laying them.

"Thank God." He breathed a sigh. "I was afraid you'd come t' your senses an' turn me down an' me life would be o'er."

At that moment, the waiter returned with their breakfasts. McCoy waited until he'd placed the plates on the table and left before he spoke again.

"Come, Miss Citcála, eat up." He picked up his fork, and stabbed it into one of two fried eggs. "We'll have breakfast, then make our way t' th' preacher's."

"Now?" She nearly dropped her fork.

"No time like th' present," he replied, eating with relish. "You may think me eager. Well, I am…t' put you in me bed an' prove th' truth o' what I've been sayin'."

"Mr. McCoy…"

"Nay, 'tis Padraig now, an' Maria, *leannán*. After we're husband an' wife, there'll be no need for such formality, except in front o' visitors."

"In that case, Padraig…" Maria raised her coffee cup, holding it out. *I pray I'm doing the right thing.* "…here's to us."

"Couldn't have said it better." He tapped his cup against hers and drank. "*Sláinte,* me darlin'."

And so, for the first time in his life, Padraig McCoy became the one who was conquered…and conied.

Chapter 30

If Pastor Willis was surprised to discover Padraig on the other side of his door, he gave no sign.

"Well, Mr. McCoy, to what do I owe the honor of this visit? And bringing a young lady with you." He stepped back. "Please, come in."

"Thank you, Preacher," Padraig removed his hat and stood twirling it between his hands. "I've come on a kind o' business."

"Business?" Willis frowned.

Like everyone else, he knew of Padraig's history in McCoy's Crossing, and was well aware he was one of the council members.

"It must be town business," he guessed, trying not to sound accusing. "Because I've not seen you at church since you settled here."

"In a way, it is," Padraig answered, managing to look like a youngster being chastised by an elder.

He hoped the preacher wasn't going to give him a sermon for his laxity. He'd had enough of those by the Tipperary minister, as well as the vicar teaching him his catechism, when he was growing up.

He caught Maria's hand. "This is me affianced an' we'd like you t' marry us."

"Well, now." To say the pastor was surprised was an understatement. He hadn't been aware of a betrothal announcement, but rationalized that since Padraig wasn't much of a churchgoer, perhaps he might be excused his ignorance about that little formality. "When would you like the happy event to take place?"

"Now." Padraig glanced at Maria, who hadn't spoken.

She blushed.

"So quickly?" Willis decided to risk a question. "May I be so bold as to ask if there's a rush?" That was the most delicate way he could put it.

To his surprise, Padraig laughed. "Ah nay…not like you might be thinkin', Preacher. 'Tis just that I love th' lass so, I'm tryin' t' prevent us from committin' that sin you're thinkin' of. Will you marry us? Now?"

"I'll be glad to perform the ceremony," Willis answered.

"Then, let's get to it," Padraig exclaimed.

"Let's go into the church." Willis gestured to a door leading down a small hallway to the church itself. "Mattie!" he called over his shoulder. "Take breakfast off the stove, get Walt, and you two come be witnesses."

Once in the church proper, with an aproned Mrs. Willis smelling redolently of fried bacon and baked bread while eighteen-year-old son Walter looked dazzled and important to be a witness, the pastor glanced at Maria.

"You haven't spoken a word, my dear. You *do* wish to marry Mr. McCoy? He isn't forcing you into this marriage in any way?"

"Goodness, no." She appeared surprised he might think that.

"I had to ask. Generally, young women prefer a wedding with friends and relatives sharing the joyous day."

"I'm an orphan, sir," Maria answered. "As for friends, any I might call that are back in New York."

"Surely, you wish to participate in the parties and celebrations given a bride before her wedding, as well as the wearing of a wedding gown?" Mrs. Willis spoke up, eying the young woman's travelling suit.

"Those things don't really matter, ma'am." Maria caught Padraig's hand. "All I wish is to become Padraig's wife."

It shook her as she realized that was the truth. She did want to become his wife, for more than the mere opportunities that status offered her. Foolish as it sounded and startling in view of the shortness of their acquaintance, she meant it.

"In that case..." Willis sighed. "...may I have the ring to bless it?"

"Ring?" Padraig yelped.

Walt suppressed a snicker.

"You don't have a ring." Willis made it a statement.

"It seems I didn't have this very well thought out, Preacher."

"Undoubtedly." Willis' answer was dry.

"Can we be married without a ring?" Something akin to panic touched Padraig's expression. "Will it still be legal?"

"My dear boy, of course it will." Willis allowed himself a gentle laugh at Padraig's distress. "It'll be lawful the moment I pronounce you husband and wife, but a young woman does need to have a ring on her finger, especially if you intend to celebrate your wedding night here in town and not at your ranch."

Padraig's change in expression told him he hadn't thought of that, either. Willis found the young man's concern slightly endearing, especially since he was aware of Padraig's feats of bravery as well as being adept in doing things for the town…and he'd also heard rumors of his activities at Trails End, though he tolerantly considered those mere gossip.

"The clerk at the hotel may not allow you to have a room if you take your wife there without the proper credentials," he added gently.

"Credentials? Lord, what else have I overlooked?"

"Shall I take that to mean you don't have a license, either?"

At his blank look, the pastor explained.

"A certificate of marriage…of which I have several," Willis added as Padraig started to speak. "I'll prepare one for you as soon as the ceremony's over, but I advise you to get that ring as soon as you can."

"Don't worry," Padraig assured him. "I plan ta."

"In that case, if you'll join hands…"

Gently, Padraig took Maria's hand in his. She gave him a tremulous smile and both turned their attention to the pastor.

"Dearly beloved…"

****

"How much do I owe you, preacher?" Assured they were truly married and lawfully bound, with the signed certificate in hand and a promise from Willis that he'd register it at city hall, Padraig became very businesslike, reaching into an inside breast pocket for his wallet.

"Just put a couple of dollars in the collection box," Willis told him.

He wanted to smile, struggling to keep a serious demeanor. He was certain the moment his lips curved upwards he'd break into outright laughter at the near-comical relief on the young rancher's face that the ceremony was now completed.

Padraig pulled out the wallet, carefully extracted a five-dollar greenback, and leaned past Willis, dropping the bill into a small wooden box on the altar table behind them. The pastor's gratitude for such a large donation was evident, since most offered only a dollar, while a few brought eggs or live chickens to pay for their ceremony.

As Padraig replaced the wallet, he laughed and took something else from the pocket. "I'd forgotten...I had a ring all the time."

"What do you mean?" Maria spoke her first words since her *I do*.

He held up a narrow black-enameled case, flipping it open. Inside lay three cigars, dark oblongs about six inches long, all decorated with gilded paper bands.

"I ordered these for one o' me ranch hands who's got a birthday soon. He's always goin' on about ceegars an' envying th' men rich enough t' smoke them. I decided t' get him a few so he could have that pleasure, too. Here, me darlin' wife..."

Taking out one of the cigars, he slid the band from around it, then returned the tobacco to the case and the case to his pocket.

"You're going to use a cigar band for a wedding ring?" Pastor Willis was aghast.

"Only until I can get a real one," Padraig answered. Taking Maria's hand, he said, "What's the words I should've said, Preacher?"

"Uh..." Willis thought of the sentence he'd omitted from the ceremony because of Padraig's oversight. "With this ring I thee wed, and all my worldly goods I do endow."

"Right." Taking Maria's hand, Padraig looked into her eyes and repeated Willis' words. He slipped the band onto her finger, then raised her hand and kissed the piece of paper. "'Twill do for now, don't you think?"

The lantern light reflected off the metallic ink on the band, making it gleam as if made of genuine gold.

"It's beautiful." Maria held up her hand, studying her finger.

"Then, I guess we should be goin' so Mrs. Willis can get back t' cookin' your breakfast." Putting his arm around Maria's waist, Padraig drew her to the church's front door. "Thank you, again, Preacher."

"Hope to see you in church some time, now that you've a wife, Mr. McCoy," Willis replied.

"Guess we'll have to see," came Padraig's noncommittal answer. He turned toward the church's entrance. "Come, *achusla*."

Mrs. Willis moved to the pastor's side, watching Padraig push open the church door and step aside for Maria to walk through. Behind them, Walt wandered back into the house and the breakfast the couple's arrival had interrupted.

As the door swung shut, the pastor's wife sighed. "I think that paper ring was a very romantic gesture. Mr. McCoy is a resourceful young man."

"We already know that, don't we?" Willis was moved to seize his wife's hand and give it a squeeze. "If their entire married life is anything like the start to it, those two are in for some very exciting times."

Chapter 31

The walk back into town was a remarkably short one, too short as far as Maria was concerned. She wasn't frightened by the way this man she now found herself married to was dragging her by the hand. Rather, she was startled to realize she was excited by the zeal he was displaying in taking her to the Crossroads Hotel, as well as anticipating their arrival.

"Mr. McCoy…" Halfway there, she pulled her hand from his. "Wait a moment. Please."

"Nay, didn't I say 'tis Padraig now?" As her hand left his, he whirled. "What is it?"

"You're taking me to the hotel?" she queried. "Now? In the middle of the day?"

The sun hovering brightly overhead told her it was nearing noon.

"Of course." He appeared surprised she'd ask. "Lovemakin' has no timetable, *a chroi*. It can be done in th' blaze o' noon as well as at midnight."

He reached for her hand.

She moved away.

"But…I've no real wedding ring." As he started to protest, she pointed to her finger, shaking her head. Now that the marriage was a fact, Maria wanted to make certain there was nothing to prove it unlawful. "Do you think any desk clerk is going to believe this is a true wedding band? The first time I wash my hands, it'll dissolve."

"In that case, I'll make certain you do naithin' requirin' hand washin'," he retorted.

Again he tried to take hand. Again, she dodged.

"It's simply that…I don't want there to be a doubt in anyone's mind what I am to you, and a cigar band for a ring isn't going to do that."

"No one had better dare…"

"I'm sure they won't. Not within earshot, anyway," Maria went on. She saw she'd struck a nerve. Padraig's pride.

"So 'tis a ring now or naithin' later, eh?"

She didn't get a chance to answer. Seizing her hand, he spun and went in the opposite direction, not at a run but fast enough on those long Irish legs to cause Maria to nearly trip several times as she attempted to follow. He stopped in front of a little shop whose large square front window announced, in gold script, Koenig's Jewelers.

Padraig pushed open the door and stalked in. The shop wasn't large, but since it had only two display cases, perhaps it was large enough.

Bracelets, necklaces, brooches, and earrings lined the shelves, not as many as she might've seen in a jewelry store in New York, but nevertheless quite a large inventory for a small Midwestern town. There weren't many jewels in sight, either, but those that were glittered in the sunlight streaming through the display window.

Padraig released her hand as the man behind the center display case looked up.

"Mr. McCoy. You're in town early today."

"Had things t' do, Mr. Koenig," Padraig greeted him. "Meetin' th' new doctor, attendin' weddin's an' such."

"A wedding?" Koenig looked interested. "Who got married?"

"I did, an' I forgot t' get me bride a ring." He whirled, looking at Maria, who'd stopped a few feet inside the door. "Well? Go ahead, darlin', pick out whate'er you want."

She didn't move, glancing around, searching for a display of rings among the bracelets, necklaces, and earrings.

"What's your best ring, sir?" Padraig was looking around, also. He gestured at a lone ring, displayed by itself in a small glass case on a counter. "That one. How much is that?"

"That's definitely my most expensive ring, Mr. McCoy."

Koenig hurried to open the case and bring out the ring resting in its little black velvet box. It had a wide gold band with a single emerald-cut diamond in the center, four smaller ones in a row on either side.

"It's too costly for anyone around here. I ordered it merely for display. Don't ever expect to sell it."

"But it *is* for sale?" Padraig asked. When Koenig nodded, he said, "How much?"

"Five hundred dollars."

"Sold." Padraig didn't hesitate but drew out his wallet, counting out the bills and tossing them onto the counter.

A goggling Koenig scooped them up. With a trembling hand, he rang up the sale and placed the money in the cash register. Neither saw how wide Maria's eyes became.

"Now, then." Taking the ring out of the box, Padraig

took Maria's hand. He glanced back at the jeweler. "You can be a witness, Mr. Koenig. I'm placin' this ring on me beloved's finger, as I should've at our weddin'."

Sliding off the cigar band, he dropped it onto the glass countertop.

"How did it go? *With this ring I thee wed, an'...*" He scowled. "Somethin' else... I forget." The scowl deepened. "Seems I forgot a good many thin's today. No matter."

He replaced the paper band with the ring, nodding in satisfaction as he released Maria's hand. "Well, lass. 'Tis better now?"

"You really didn't have to." She studied the ring. "I rather liked the other one."

"Now she tells me!" He began to laugh. "Lord!"

Maria took a step toward him, hand going to his cheek. Padraig put his hand over it, pressing her palm against his face and savoring its warmth. She put her arms around his neck. He swung her off the floor, hugging her tightly. Koenig looked away, slightly embarrassed by the love he saw in Padraig's expression.

"Got t' be goin' now, Mr. Koenig." Padraig set Maria on her feet. "Thank you, sir."

"Mr. McCoy?"

Padraig paused at the door.

"May I tell anyone of your nuptials?"

"Mr. Koenig, you can send a telegraph t' th' capitol in Washington, if you wish!"

With that, he dragged Maria through the door, slamming it behind him.

Once outside, however, Maria again wrested her hand from his. "Padraig. Wait."

"What is it now?" he asked, scowling. "I'm getting'

th' feelin' you're havin' second thoughts, lass, an' if that's so, I'd best remind you it might be a struggle t' get out o' this marriage." Briefly, he appeared insulted. "Could you really prefer some dried-up ol' Spanish *don* instead o' *me*?"

"No, of course not," she denied, "but…my luggage…all my clothing. They're still on the stage, on their way to who-knows-where. I've nothing to wear."

"Is that all's botherin' you?" Visibly, he relaxed. "You won't need anythin' t'night," he told her. "Tomorrow, I'll buy you an entire new wardrobe, from silk stockings an' all those pretty li'l under-fripperies t' th' most beautiful gowns. Let th' Spaniard have your clothin'. That's *all* he's goin' t' get."

"There's a dress shop there." She nodded across the street.

"Why, so there is." Padraig looked at the sign over the little shop's door, then back at Maria. "It'll still be there tomorrow, too. No delayin', *acushla*. 'Tis t' th' hotel we're goin', with no more stops."

With that, he swung her into his arms and carried her at a brisk walk toward the Crossroads Hotel.

Chapter 32

Padraig was beginning to wonder if every man he met was going to look astonished at seeing him with a woman. A good many of the men in McCoy's Crossing were usually present at Trails End when he and his men rode in on Saturday nights. They'd seen him swiggin' beer and whiskey, with a bar girl perched on his knee. They'd also watched him going, sometimes a bit unsteadily, up the stairs with one, also, on several occasions, so why were they all in some form of shock to see him in broad daylight with a pretty girl on his arm?

Or, in this case, *in* his arms?

The Crossroads Hotel wasn't much to look at, being a very plain whitewashed building of three stories, but it was already displaying pretensions of grandeur.

Its guests were separated financially by whichever floor they could pay for. The first-story rooms were the cheapest with only a bed with a chamber pot beneath. Second-floor bedrooms had the same amenities as the first but also a dresser and closet for clothing. The third floor held the luxury suites…bed, dresser, free-standing wardrobe, and a dressing room for bathing and other sanitaries.

The Crossroads employed two maids and a handyman to keep the hotel clean. It advertised that its bedding was changed once a week whether the rooms had been used or not. Each bed was guaranteed free of bedbugs, fleas, and lice.

"Good morning, Mr. McCoy."

The day clerk was very formal, as stiff and starched as his high-buttoned collar. It was the night clerk who called Padraig by his first name, treating him more like his old schoolmates had…winking in conspiracy when he came in late, assisting him in climbing the stairs if his vision suddenly played tricks and made him see more than one set of steps.

"Mornin'," Padraig replied, and got to the point. "Is me room ready?"

"Yes, sir," came the prompt response. The clerk reached behind him and pulled the key to the room Padraig had begun reserving on a monthly basis as soon as he became owner of the Shamrock. "I thought you might be staying in town tonight since the new doctor was arriving."

He set the key on the counter.

Padraig reached for it, only to have the clerk pick it up and move it out of reach.

"I'm sorry, sir, but you aren't thinking of taking that young woman upstairs, are you?"

"What young woman would that be?" Padraig asked.

"Why…the one in your arms, sir." The clerk gave him a stare as if he'd started raving.

"Oh. This one?" Padraig set Maria on her feet.

She bestowed a glare on him much more stringent than the clerk's look.

"Aye, as a matter o' fact, I was. So?"

"I'm afraid the management doesn't allow a woman in a man's room, sir." That was delivered so stiffly it sounded as if it hurt the young man to speak the words.

"Not even if th' woman's me wife?" Padraig pretended outrage. "In that case, I may have t' make arrangements t' find anaithur place t' stay."

"Your wife? Oh, no." The clerk was prepared to argue. "I'm sorry, sir. You may be quite the power in McCoy's Crossing, but I can't allow you to go against the rules. The whole town knows you're a bachelor."

"Th' town doesn't know e'erythin'," Padraig replied. *Where is this lad from?* "You...what's your name?"

"Charles, sir." The young man nodded slightly. "Charles Brighton."

"Well, Charles Brighton, let me introduce you t' Maria Citcála McCoy, me wife." He glanced at Maria, who was alternating glances between him and the clerk. "Maria, lass, meet Mr. Brighton, who appears t' be a stickler for th' rules, generally a commendable trait, except in these circumstances."

Maria didn't answer.

"Wife? Since when?" Charles did everything but sneer.

"What time is it?"

The clerk glanced at the clock on the wall behind him. Before he could answer, Padraig pulled out his pocket watch, consulting it.

"Ten o'clock. T' answer that very rude question, since an hour ago." He returned the watch to his vest, and brought something out of his coat, waving it under the clerk's nose. "Here's me certificate o' marriage, if I have t' prove anythin' t' you, an' here..." Seizing Maria's left hand, he held it up. "...is her weddin' ring."

He released her hand and carefully and ostentatiously folded the paper and returned it to his pocket.

"If you've any more objections, send up the manager. Tomorrow. Because I'll be celebrating me weddin' all day today an' t'night an' I don't want t' be bothered by trivialities."

With that, he plucked the key from the young man's abruptly nerveless fingers, again swept Maria into his arms, and started up the stairs.

"Y-yes, sir…" came weakly behind him.

On the first landing, Padraig paused.

"You'd better lighten up a bit, son, an' relax. Right now, you're as stiff as if someone's shoved a very thick stick up your arse, an' that ain't goin' t' work around me."

Maria's forehead rested against Padraig's cheek, her arms around his neck. Her shoulders were shaking. As soon as they were out of sight of the clerk, he stopped.

"Here now, lass. Don't cry. I'm sorry that happened, but as soon as e'eryone's aware…"

"Oh, Padraig." The face she raised to his wasn't tearful, however.

"You're laughin'?"

"That poor young man. You have such a sharp tongue. You whittled him away to nothing."

"Ah, well, me tongue's not always sharp," he answered. "You'd be surprised what else it can do."

"Do you always throw your weight around like that?" She ignored his innuendo.

"Afraid so. Best get used t' it," he warned. "I'm not a bully. I simply set people straight when they're wrong."

He started up the stairs again.

Chapter 33

Though Maria protested she was able to walk, Padraig carried her up the three flights.

The hallways were dim, lighted only by fuel lanterns inserted into wall sconces, the Crossroads not yet fitted with gaslight. As they traversed the stairs, flickers made their shadows dance grotesquely upon the walls. There was a strong smoky smell of burning kerosene floating in the air.

"Here we are."

Padraig stopped before a door, inserting the key, then pushed it open. He stalked inside, tossed the key onto the dresser top, and kicked the door shut.

"Welcome to me permanent residence when I'm in town." He set Maria on her feet.

She looked around. This was definitely one of the best suites. The quality and quantity of their surroundings attested to it. The room held not only the expected bed, dresser, and wardrobe but also a closet plus two chairs. The bed was a cast-iron four-poster painted dark green. It was covered by a beautifully sewn quilt in a wedding ring pattern.

Very appropriate, Maria decided. She was abruptly aware of the ring on her finger, its weight growing heavier.

"Now then…" Padraig caught her by the shoulders, pulling her toward him. "I've been waitin' t' kiss th' bride."

"Why didn't you kiss me before?" she asked, remembering how he'd surprised her by shying away when Pastor Willis told him he was now allowed to kiss her.

"I didn't want an audience," he replied. "Besides, it might've embarrassed th' preacher, an' his wife, too, for me t' demonstrate in public how I feel about you."

With that, he pulled her toward him, pressing his mouth to hers. His moustache tickled her upper lip. She managed to suppress a giggle.

When he released her, Maria didn't move, except to glance at the bed, then back at the stranger who was now her husband.

He moved away, taking off his frockcoat, and placing it and his gun belt onto one of the chairs.

Until that moment, she hadn't realized he was wearing a gun. That shook her slightly.

Padraig dropped his hat atop his coat and turned back to her.

"Well now, shall we get down t' th' business o' makin' ourselves husband an' wife in fact?"

Maria didn't answer. Taking a deep breath, she very carefully and slowly unbuttoned the jacket of her traveling suit. She moved to the chair where Padraig's coat lay and placed her own beside it. Underneath she was wearing a batiste blouse with a high, lacy collar and the same pattern of lace on the cuffs and sleeves.

"That's a lovely waist, darlin'," Padraig remarked. "But I don't think you need it now."

Maria swallowed, very loudly.

"I-I think I may need help..." She turned her back so Padraig could see the row of tiny mother-of-pearl buttons running the length of the blouse. "C-could you…"

"Me pleasure."

She shivered as his fingers touched her back. Briefly, they rested against her shoulder blades. She could feel their warmth through the light fabric. Padraig pulled the first button from its little embroidered hole, then the second…and the third…

She started with a little squeak of surprised as his lips brushed against the nape of her neck.

"Oh!" Her hand went to the spot. "I-I'm sorry. You startled me."

"Didn't mean t'." His voice went quiet. "Best get used t' that, however. I intend t' kiss you often."

He worked on the other buttons. They seemed to take longer than had the first three. Maria glanced over her shoulder. He was frowning in concentration, lower lip caught between his teeth as he fumbled with the fourth button, got it free, then went on to the next.

"Sorry." His apology was soft, a near whisper. "Been a while since I got a woman out of her clothes."

Bar girls didn't usually undress.

"I'd forgotten how many buttons you ladies have."

"You said you wouldn't remember your other women," she reminded him. "Once we were wed."

"I meant it." He continued speaking in that same whisper as if his voice had gone weak. "Once we're in that bed, there'll ne'er be anaithur woman in me heart or me mind."

The bed…

Maria glanced toward it as Padraig got the last button opened. He worked the fabric out of her skirt's waistband. The skirt slid to the floor and the blouse fell from her arms, joining it. Maria stood before him in nothing but her chemise, corset, and petticoats.

"Maria…" He touched her shoulder, fingers trailing up her back to the corset top.

She turned to look at him, whispered, "Padraig…" gave a soft little gasp, and burst into tears.

"Maria, love, what is it?" He touched her cheek, wondering if she were about to faint.

She didn't answer, simply backed away from his grasp, covered her face with her hands, and continued to sob.

"Here now." He caught her hands.

Maria pressed her face against his shoulder. "Oh, Padraig, I'm so afraid," came muffled against his chest.

"Afraid?" He sounded as if he'd never thought of that. "Not o' me?"

She shook her head, lifted it and looked at the bed again. "Of that."

"Th' bed?" He considered that, then said quietly, "…or o' what's t' happen in it?"

She nodded, the movement burrowing her forehead into his chest.

"Oh, lass, you've naithin' t' fear from me. I'll ne'er hurt you." He pushed her away, putting a finger under her chin and forcing her to raise her head. "Didn't I promise that?"

"You said you'd never *beat* me," she corrected. She nodded at the bed. "This is different."

"I agree but it can't be helped, I suppose." He hugged her tightly, rocking back and forth. "Can't make a cake without breakin' eggs, y'know."

"You're not very encouraging," she replied, in a tearful protest. Her shoulders began shaking again.

"Shhh, now." Padraig swung her into his arms and sat in the second chair, cuddling her in his lap.

Pressing her head against his shoulder, he crooned to her as if she were a fractious baby. Maria huddled against him, curled in his arms. They stayed that way until she quieted and the last sob gave way to a watery sigh.

"There's no law says we have t' hurry this." He kept his voice quiet, trying to sound reasonable. "We can take it slow, darlin'."

"Promise?" She looked up at him.

He nodded and stood, hefting her weight easily. "Come now, let's get you out o' these things." Setting her on her feet, he pulled at the corset's lacings, getting rid of them remarkably fast, as well as her chemise and slip.

As the last garment fell away, he pulled the pins from her hair. It fell, straight, dark, and thick, past her shoulders. Padraig gathered her hair in his hands, pressing it to his lips. He turned her to face him.

"Lord, you're so beautiful, Maria. I'm thankin' God I was th' one comin' t' th' depot this mornin' an' not some other man who might've ignored you an' let you get back on that stage."

He put his arms around her, hugging her naked body against his. His hands slid down her back, resting on the roundness of her buttocks, savoring briefly her warmth and the softness of her skin beneath his fingers.

When her flesh quivered under his touch, he released her and stepped back, saying quietly, "Get int' bed. We'll take it slow. We'll just lie there an' let our bodies become accustomed t' each ithur."

Hurrying to the bed, Maria pulled back the quilt and

sat on its edge, holding the covers against her breast. Padraig walked around to the other side. His hands went to his vest-front.

"Best turn your head, love, for I'm about t' take off me clothes. I'm such a fine figger o' a man, I don't want you overwhelmed."

Obediently, she looked away, sliding her legs under the covers, listening to the sound of buttons being opened, the whisper of fabric brushing over skin, the crackle of the starch in his shirt as the garment fell into the chair. The other edge of the quilt was lifted. Her body tilted as a heavier weight pressed down the bed.

She looked around. "Stop."

Padraig froze, quilt held up, one knee on the mattress.

"Let me look at you."

He didn't move, waiting patiently while she stared. As if his body could sense her eyes on him, a slight flush tinted those parts not tanned by the sun.

When her gaze rested on his again, dark eyes holding his green ones, he asked, something in his tone hinting the question was more important than he made it sound, "Well? Do I pass inspection?"

"You're a beautiful man, Padraig McCoy," She gave him her first smile since entering the room. He relaxed slightly and raised the quilt higher as she continued, nodding in the general direction of his groin, "Except for that."

That stopped him. Cold. He truly had no idea what to say, except to stutter, "Wh-why…"

"It's so…silly-looking. I can't believe *that*…" Again a nod. "…is the thing my foster mother in New York warned me against. She told me it was so fearsome." She actually gave a short little laugh, then shook her head, ignoring the twinge at even mentioning the woman who'd been her government-appointed guardian—and taken her real mother's place—gave her. "What was she thinking?"

"Darlin'…" Remarkably, Padraig managed to ignore the anger he should've been feeling at this insult. "Don't slight me John Thomas. Aside from me brain, 'tis me most prized possession." He took a deep breath. "Doubtless your maithur was thinking ahead. It may be a bit of a disappointment now, but hold your judgment until you've seen th' lad in action."

"May I touch it?" She raised a hand.

Padraig leaned across the bed, careful to keep one foot still on the floor in case he had to move back quickly. He truly had no idea what his bride was about to do.

Gently, she slid her hand under his member, fingers closing around it. Now, it was he who shivered, encased in that warm grip. She stroked against the foreskin with her other hand. Helpfully, he slid the enclosing folds back so she could see the crown, fighting back the first tinglings of desire at her touch. She released him.

"Hold me. Please?"

He did that gladly. Pushing back the quilts, he took Maria in his arms, snuggling her against his chest, briefly wishing it were winter so they could wrap themselves in the quilts and be bundled all bare and warm inside layers of goose down.

They lay that way for several minutes before he felt a very light kiss pressed against his chest. She snuggled closer against him. Unconsciously, he began to stroke her back, fingers straying to her waist, then down across her flanks.

"We'll take it slow," he whispered. "We've got fore'er t' be husband an' wife…"

Padraig wondered if all wedding nights were like his. If they were, he reasoned, surely there would be more happy men and women in the world. It couldn't be called a true wedding *night*, of course. After all, their joining actually happened at noon with the sun high overhead, but since the night was rapidly approaching, he decided to include the act in the general vicinity of the term.

He spent a great deal of time caressing and kissing, delving into that forgotten inventory of lovemaking he'd employed in the seduction of other men's wives and sweethearts, a performance he'd not required in quite some time since he mistakenly didn't believe saloon girls would appreciate his techniques because they were being paid for the privilege, and didn't demand as much gentleness and delicacy as he now employed.

Now, he remembered and joyfully did all the deeds he'd once delighted in. Hearing a woman all his own moan and sigh and knowing he was the cause gave him more than one tremor of gratification as well as pride.

When they finally came together, it was Maria who made the overture. She'd been lying passive under his touch, except for those near-panting sighs and heaving breasts telling him she was no longer afraid and not merely tolerating his touch, as he thought she'd done at first, but was now eagerly awaiting the next. He had her body warm, wet, and trembling. She sat up, threw both arms around his neck, and pulled his body against hers.

"Do it, Padraig. Now!" It wasn't so much a command as an entreaty.

It happened so quickly they were both shocked. With a single thrust and an equally sharp cry from Maria, he was inside her.

Her damp-dark eyes looked into his. "Love me, Padraig. Love your wife."

When he leaned across her body instead, pulling open the drawer of the bedside table, her question was a whisper, but a harsh one. "What are you doing?"

He didn't answer, simply slid from her body to take the dowel from the drawer, remove the fishskin from it, and pull it over his now upright and glistening tool.

Maria sat up, staying at the sheath. "What is that?"

"'Tis t' prevent th' babes," he explained

"You don't want babies?"

Was that relief or surprise in her expression? He hoped it was the latter, expecting her, in her maidenly ignorance, to be shocked by this admission.

"Oh, aye," he assured her. "Just not yet. I'm thinkin' we should get t' know each ithur better afore we go creating a li'l one."

She caught his hand, pulling him back to her, then brushed her fingers across the shiny rubbery casing fitted around him like a gray second skin. She giggled. Padraig scowled. A giggle wasn't the expected response, but considering how she'd reacted to seeing his naked member, perhaps it was.

How was he to know? Admittedly, they were still strangers to each other. He waited for an explanation.

It came quick enough. "It looks as if it's wearing a stocking."

That made him smile, also. "Well, then…John Thomas is very fashionable, isn't he?"

After that, there was no conversation for quite some

time.

Much, much later, when it was truly night, and he had officially made Maria his wife three times over, they cuddled together under the quilts, body-to-body, flesh warming each other.

"I was right," he whispered.

"About what?" She was drowsy now, resting her cheek against his shoulder.

He could feel the soft brush of her lips against his skin as she spoke. That made a momentary tremor of desire course through him, a sensation he was too contented to pursue at the moment.

"About you havin' captured me heart."

He kissed the top of her head, nuzzling the dark hair. She smelled of lavender, sweet and a bit heady.

"You've bound me in gossamer, all wrapped an' tied in a neat little bow-knot. So tight I'll ne'er be able t' unravel it." He pulled her up to face him, kissing her on the mouth. "Not that I'll e'er want ta."

She rolled away, pulling him with her, so they lay face-to-face. "Tell me about your ranch."

"What do you want to know?"

"All about it…the cows, the men…anything you want to tell me."

"I hadn't expected t' talk about me ranch just now," he protested.

"Please," she said. "Tell me about the Shamrock, and then…" She hesitated. *I'll tell you the lies I've manufactured about myself.* "You can ask me questions."

"Sounds fair enough." Padraig settled himself upon the pillow, beginning a recitation about the Shamrock. He was going pretty well until he got to the description of the ranch house.

As he finished, Maria said, injecting just the right amount of disappointment into her voice, "It sounds like a lovely *little* place, so *small*, and cozy." She paused, then added a final unspoken criticism, "…and we'll have so much privacy."

There was a slight silence as Padraig thought about that. He remembered the time Cookie walked in on him while he was warming his bare backside by the stove…of Buck pounding on his door during the influenza epidemic…the many times he'd been sprawled in the parlor, boots off, feet resting on the andirons and one of the hired hands barged in wanting to know something.

Then, he thought of how he'd feel if someone came in while he was in the parlor with Maria on his lap, or in bed with her and a battering of fists sounded on the door.

No, oh nay…

"The house is too small." It came out like an accusation. "Oh, lass, 'twill ne'er do for you t' live in that place."

"Of course, it will," she protested, thinking that, for such an intelligent man, Padraig was already very easily led where she was concerned. Briefly, she felt pity for him as she thought of the plans she had…for *him*, for herself. "It's my home now."

"Nay. You need a better place than that. 'Twas all right for me, when I was an unmarried man, but now…it has t' be enlarged. We'll need an upstairs with more bedrooms for when the li'l ones come…an' th' kitchen. You need a better stove. That one I have now, 'tis all right for Cookie, but me wife…she needs a newer one, an'…" He stopped. "That settles it. I'm havin' th' house torn down an' rebuilt."

"But Padraig…"

"Nay, Maria. We've an architect here in town." The man the council commissioned to build the library had finished that project, then decided to stay. "I'll hire him t' draw up plans for a fine house. Th' best for me wife. An' when 'tis done, I'll take you…"

"Where am I to be staying while it's being built?" she interrupted.

"Here, o' course." He looked as if the answer should've been obvious.

"No." she said firmly. "In the morning, when you leave here and go home, I'm going with you." If he was hiring an architect, she was going to be there to tell the man exactly *how* to plan the house she wanted. "While the house is being built…"

"Where will you sleep when the bedroom's in splinters an' th' new one's not yet ready?"

"Wherever you do."

"That might be on th' floor o' th' bunkhouse." Under his moustache, his mouth quirked. "Think you'd like t' sleep in a room with thirteen men?"

"If they'll let me."

Maria didn't tell him she could still remember sleeping in a tipi with her mother, her brother, and ten other family members. Besides, if she had to endure a little hardship to reach her goals, she would.

"I'll help, too, and when it's finished, we'll have a grand housewarming, and invite all your friends, to see your new house and meet your new wife. No arguments," she said as he began a protest. "That's the way it's going to be. I'm your wife and I won't sit around in town while you're having a house built for me."

"Aye, love. 'Tis the way 'twill be, then," Padraig agreed, softly, adding, "Don't think this is givin' you th' right t' boss me around, though. I'm me own man an' no female's e'er done that."

"I wouldn't think of it." Maria kissed him, then tightened her arms around his neck. "Why don't you make love to me again and then let's get some sleep? I imagine tomorrow is going to be a rather hectic day, what with all the explanations you're going to be giving everyone we meet."

It was remarkable how her fear of the marriage bed had so quickly disappeared.

Chapter 34

Padraig came awake with a great many questions in his mind.

The first one was: *Where am I?*

A bleary look around established he was in his room at the Crossroads Hotel.

The second question followed: *What did I do last night?* He struggled through blurred memories...

Did I go t' Trails End? Perhaps take th' new doctor there? Nay, not on a weekday, certainly not during th' daytime.

Getting drunk before noon definitely wasn't the way to impress a new citizen of McCoy's Crossing, nor was taking him to the local brothel.

Movement against his back and a soft murmur made him roll over quickly.

Lord God, I brought one o' th' girls here?

As he saw the glorious thickness of black hair tumbled about her shoulders, memory flooded in, with relief.

Maria, me wife...

He reached for her, then forced his hands to stop. They hovered over her shoulders. He wouldn't awaken her, let her sleep a bit longer. He'd get up, make himself presentable, and come back and relish the sight of her lying there so beautiful in sleep. Afterward, he'd wake her and they'd be on their way.

The days ahead were going to hold a great adventure for both of them.

Cautiously, Padraig eased himself out of the bed. Feeling clumsy and awkward, he tried to be quiet as he tiptoed to the sanitary room.

The sanitary room held a washstand with ironstone basin and pitcher, as well as a quincy—a commode chair with metal slop jar beneath—and a wall rack with towels. Behind the door in its own little nook was a corrugated tin bath tub. Only the rooms on the upper floor had tubs. Other residents wishing full baths had to go to the Crossroads Barber Shop and Bath House.

In his hotel room, Padraig kept duplicates of any item he might need while in town...two changes of clothing, one for work, another for business, and toiletries, such as a razor and shaving soap and a small vial of oil of sandalwood.

He availed himself of the commode, wondering what his bride would've made of the early-morning hard-on he sported, then washed his face in the ironstone basin. Briefly, he thought of calling down for some hot water to take a bath, for he had a feeling his days of Saturday night bathing were at an end. No doubt Maria was going to be just like his mother in insisting he bathe frequently. Rationalizing they didn't have time for that frivolity just then, he took his razor and shaving mug and brush from the little cabinet behind the wall mirror, glancing at the sandalwood bottle as he did so.

He'd purchased the latter while in New York, from a very upper-class tailor's shop, being assured by the clerk the oil was to be used as an aftershave refresher. He was cautioned to apply it sparingly because it was "a most potent aphrodisiac."

Padraig had bought the item mostly out of curiosity, since he truly didn't want women to be more attracted to him than they might normally be. There had been enough of that in Ireland, without the assistance of the oil extracted from an Indian tree's wood.

Nevertheless, he was intrigued, specifically since it had the same scent he'd often noticed about his father in the mornings when he appeared after his own *toilette*. He had the money, so he gave in to a whim. The little glass vial traveled with him to Nebraska, stayed in his portmanteau when he lodged in the bunkhouse, was transferred to the ranch house when he took possession, and eventually found its way to his hotel room.

It had never been opened in all those years.

Now, however, he took the little bottle out of the chest, studying it.

What would Maria have done if I'd been wearin' e'en a drop o' this stuff? He had a feeling her reaction might've been more than either of their bodies could've survived. *Put it back, lad. You don't need it.*

Carefully he replaced the bottle in the cabinet.

He was busily applying lather to his face, being careful not to cover his moustache, when he heard a soft pattering behind him.

In the mirror, he saw the reflection of a pair of hands and slender arms appear under his own. They hugged him tightly, then the hands stroked his belly gently, wandering around and down his thighs.

"If that's th' lass who's been in me bed all night," he said to the mirror, "best get yourself dressed an' out o' here before me wife shows up. She might not want t' see a naked woman rubbing against her husband's bare backside."

"Too late. She's already here," Maria answered. "And she doesn't mind."

"No?" He picked up the razor, wondering if he dared try to shave while that delicious caress continued near his groin.

"As a matter of fact, she's enjoying it." There was a laugh trailing away into a delighted giggle. "Very much."

"Oh, Maria…" Dropping the razor, Padraig whirled, capturing her in his arms. "What happened to that li'l woman who was so afraid of th' things we'd do in that bed?"

"You taught me how good it was, Padraig." She pressed her cheek against his chest, giving him a startlingly strong hug. "That what I felt when I saw you at the depot wasn't wrong, to desire you wasn't wicked." Her eyes met his. "I *do* desire you…and love you."

"And I you, *acushla*." He swung her around and onto the dresser top. Unmindful of soap lathering his cheeks, he kissed her, lifting her thighs and guiding them around his waist.

Afterward, when they were composed again, and Maria was calmly using his bath towel to wipe soap lather from her face, breast, and thighs, Padraig finished his shave and got dressed.

"I didn't use *that*, you mind," he pointed out, nodding to the fishskin abandoned on the bedside table. He made a mental note to take it with him and make certain it was cleaned.

"It doesn't matter." She reached for her stockings and proceeded to put them on.

Padraig paused in his own dressing to enjoy the sight of the finely-knit cotton tubes being drawn over those slender legs.

"I've decided I don't want anything inside me but you, my husband. I want to feel you and not some piece of whatever that thing's made of."

"Your wish is me command, dear lady." He swept her a bow. "I'd much prefer it that way, too, though 'tis been a long time since I went bare int' anyone, but…we won't speak o' that," he continued hastily as she frowned. "If you want t' risk a babe so soon…"

"I will." She stood, putting her arms around him, raising her lips to be kissed, which he did eagerly before pulling away.

"Don't start that, or I'll be draggin' you back to that bed."

"You won't have to drag me."

"…an' we've too much t' do today for that kind o' nonsense."

"Oh? It's nonsense now?"

He grinned at her. "Not in th' least."

"What are we going to do today?"

"I believe I said something about seein' an architect…an' we need some breakfast. I don't know about you, but I have t' replenish me strength after yesterday, an' there was also talk of visitin' a dressmaker? Or can that wait?"

"No. Definitely not." She tied her stockings with narrow silk ribbons, walked over and picked up the chemise and corset, stepping into them. "I don't like to wear the same clothing more than once before it's laundered. Except for stockings. I will wear them two days."

"Why don't you simply go out in your stockin's, then?" he asked. "You'd look most fetchin'."

"Oh, you'd like that, would you?"

"Definitely. Though I'd probably have t' shoot every man we met, for I'll have no one oglin' me wife th' way I know they would."

"You'd better start with that starch-stiff desk clerk. Goodness, what a rigid young man he is." She settled the garments and turned her back.

"I may have t' do something about th' lad." Padraig looked thoughtful. Without prompting, he tightened the laces on the corset. "Take him t' Trails End an' get him drunk an' let th' ladies have their wicked way with him. That ought t' loosen him up a bit."

"You wouldn't?" She pretended shock.

"Aye, I would." He gave her a smile with a glint in it. "I'm a terrible person, aren't I?"

"Time will tell on that. In the meantime, we were discussing my clothing?"

"Aye. Why do you wear this corset thing anyway?" He pulled the last string tight, watched her take a short breath as he tied the laces in a large bow at the small of her back. "You're slim enough without it."

"When I'm old and fat you'll be glad I wear a corset."

"Ne'er," Padraig swore. "When you're fat, there'll merely be more for me t' love." He pressed a kiss against her shoulder, urging in a whisper, "Go without it now, me dear."

"A lady never goes without her underpinnings." An impish smile touched her lips as she stroked her fingers against his cheek. "Except when she's with her lover...or her husband."

She slid on the waist. Padraig buttoned it, also.

"I'm damned lucky your husband an' your lover are

th' same man."

"I wouldn't have it any other way." She spun, pulling the blouse and its buttons from his fingers. "Thank you, Padraig."

"You're entirely welcome, me dear. For what, exactly?" He put his arms around her.

"For wanting me…for marrying me…and teaching me how good love can be." There was a brief niggle of guilt as she said that. She quelled it, telling herself it would be worth it to lie, to get the things she wanted from him, but he was so good-natured and so easy to love, it wasn't really a lie…was it?

"Darlin', 'twas me pleasure." He kissed her.

Chapter 35

They went first to the dress shop where Padraig informed the owner, a Miss Sammons, "Let me introduced me bride, Maria. Her luggage was lost from the stage an' she needs a new wardrobe. E'erthin'. Do you have somethin' she might wear today while you sew th' other dresses an' things she needs?

Alice Sammons had several display dresses Maria declared marvelous. One soon found its way onto her slender body. Out of the other items in the shop, she also selected a second chemise and another pair of stockings, these the most expensive, bought only for display, just as Koenig had purchased the diamond ring now gracing Maria's finger.

Padraig waved aside Miss Sammons' protests and pronounced them *sold.* Maria also asked for a parasol. Padraig studied, then agreed with his wife's assessment it was "the most enchanting thing I've ever seen." He stifled his laughter at the flimsy creation, thinking the first stiff breeze would whip it to shreds, then choked back an exclamation at the price, telling himself the look on Maria's face as she held the item was well worth the two dollars and fifty cents.

After that, Padraig sat and had the educational and completely enjoyable experience of watching the seamstress take his wife's measurements and browse through the latest magazine of women's fashions with his wife to select the style of the other dresses to be made.

With her old clothing carefully boxed, they left the shop with Miss Sammons' promise to have everything completed within the week. Carrying Maria's purchases, Padraig told her he'd return at that time to get them.

"No one better guy me for bein' a porter." He pretended to grouse as he tucked the box containing her traveling suit under one arm. He offered her the other, and she grasped it tightly. "But if they do, I'll tell them 'tis what a gentleman does for his lady an' they'd better sit up an' take notice."

****

The architect was summarily hired.

"You want the entire house torn down and rebuilt? From the ground up?" The man was incredulous.

"Isn't that th' usual way a house is built?" Padraig queried.

"Well, surely, Mr. McCoy." There was a flick of irritation at that facetious question. "However, one generally renovates and adds on to an already standing structure."

"Th' house has a kitchen, which is th' largest room, a hallway, a parlor, an' a bedroom," Padraig answered. "Come out, view th' place, then draw up some prints incorporatin' that, an' take it from there."

With the architect's promise to ride out the next day, they proceeded to the Sylvestre House for breakfast.

****

At Olsen's livery stable, Padraig retrieved the pinto, then decided, "There's no way I'm takin' you t' the ranch ridin' pillion. Nay, Maria," he continued as she began a protest. "I'll not have that pretty frock for which I just paid th' grand sum o' eight dollars ruined by horse sweat

237

an' prairie dust…an' I don't want me men's first glimpse o' me wife t' be o' a lass ridin' astride a horse with her stockin's showin'.'" He paused to take a breath, adding, "Besides, how are you goin' t' handle that parasol thingie if you're usin' both your hands t' hang on t' *me*?"

"Oh, Padraig."

Her laugh reminded him slightly of the way his mother always reacted to things he'd said as a child. Padraig scowled slightly. He didn't want anything about his wife to make him think of his mother. That sounded too odd.

"You're such a dear." Her hand went to his cheek in what would come to be an automatic gesture whenever he said something Maria found touching or loving. "How else am I to get there, if I don't ride? Though I would prefer to ride sidesaddle."

"Sidesaddle! Now there's a thought. Olsen…" He spun around, facing the stable owner, who waited patiently to be paid for keeping the pinto overnight. "Would you by chance have a sidesaddle amongst your tack?"

He fully expected a negative answer.

"As a matter of fact…" To his surprise, Olsen nodded. "I do. My wife had a bee in her bonnet that she was going to ride that way, so I had Johannsen make it for her."

Einar Johannsen, the local cobbler, was also the saddler. Though most ranchers had one cowhand who could take over the chore of patching leatherwork, the cobbler manufactured new harness or did repairs requiring an expert. When he wasn't building or mending saddles, he tended to the footwear of McCoy's Crossing's citizens.

"Bring it out an' let me see it," Padraig ordered.

The saddle was duly hauled from Olsen's tack shed and set on the top plank of a nearby stall.

"Well?" Padraig glanced at Maria. "Will it do?"

She touched the saddle. "This has two pomels. The saddle I used in New York had only one."

"That's right," Olsen agreed. "Johannsen told me he'd heard of them and suggested it as being safer for my Sofia, so I told him to go ahead and build it that way. Apparently, this is the latest thing in ladies' riding equipment."

"Latest thin', huh?" Padraig studied the contraption, thinking it looked more like the saddle had slipped sideways and someone had sewn a second horn into place directly below the first.

He was familiar with sidesaddles. Back in Ireland, his own mother had ridden with one, but he'd never seen one like this. He'd always been uneasy when Quinton and his mother rode to hounds because he feared the horse might overbalance during a jump and fall on his mother.

"Maria, I'll bow t' your opinion. Is this what you want, lass?"

She ran her fingers back and forth over the saddle skirt, fingers caressing the tooled leather in a way reminding him of how she's touched his cheek that morning. Briefly, a twinge of resentment flared. *Damn it, I'm better than some bit o' saddle leather.*

She nodded, looked at him, and smiled. Padraig's resentment faded.

"Sold! Now then, let's find you a horse t' put this contraption on. I was thinkin' that bay mare e'eryone's been turnin' down because she's so small."

The little bay was brought out, pronounced acceptable by Maria, and saddled.

Before they set out, Olsen pulled Padraig aside. "Somethin else I need t' tell you." He spoke in a whisper, glancing back at Maria, who was busy stroking the mare's neck and speaking to her. "Johannsen recommended I have a second saddle made, too…a right-sided one."

"What the hell for?" Unconsciously Padraig also lowered his voice to a whisper. "'Tis bad enough she's going t' be ridin' on one side o' th' horse but t' have a saddle where she has to mount Indian-style?"

"Johansson claims a doctor once told him sidesaddles are bad on the thigh muscles, and they…"

Here the stable owner lowered his voice even more so Padraig had to lean forward to hear.

"…they can sometimes damage a…" Olsen hesitated, then plunged on, "…a female's privates and cause complications when she's birthing. Excuse me for mentioning such a delicate subject, Padraig, but…" He glanced back at Maria again. "I thought I should tell you, since you're new-married and all."

"An' a right-sided saddle counteracts that?"

Olsen nodded.

"I appreciate th' warnin'," Padraig replied. He handed Olsen the money for the pinto's stay, the saddle, and the mare. "If I have much t' say about it, me wife will be usin' th' same saddle as th' rest o' us soon, or find hersel' ridin' in a buckboard."

He winked, a conspiratorial gesture, and swung around, walking back to where Maria stood.

"Well, darlin', goin' t' have t' stuff your clothin' inta me saddle bags, an' then we'll be on our way."

Chapter 36

The ranch hands' reception of Maria wasn't as bad as Padraig expected. He'd believed there would be plenty of sly glances, elbow nudges, and suggestive statements. Instead, he got goggling stares at the fashionably dressed—if slightly dusty—young woman sitting on the bay mare, that ridiculous parasol held high and tilted to protect her from the sun.

As he helped her dismount, there were shy smiles, hats hastily jerked from heads and clutched in hands, and a surprising show of manners.

Walking past each, he introduced Maria, giving a summary of the cowboy's work on the ranch. He could hardly believe these were the same men with whom he'd heehawed and hoorahed at Trails End on any Saturday night and rode with aching head and bleary eyes back to the Shamrock the next day.

"This is Big Jack." He indicated the tall cowboy, after introducing Buck who appeared bedazzled if not downright dumbstruck, muttering a "How do, ma'am" so faint it was barely audible. "Jack's me trail boss."

"Jack." Maria nodded, offering her hand as she had to Buck.

"John, Miz McCoy," Jack corrected, seizing her hand and giving it a vigorous movement as if priming a pump. "John Durwood Gregory."

"Durwood?" Padraig spoke before he realized it.

241

"John Durwood?"

Behind Big Jack, a couple of the others began to hoot.

"Oh, shut up!" Jack growled. He appeared to be rapidly regretting revealing his real name to the boss's wife.

"May I call you Big Jack, as the others do?" Maria asked.

Immediately everyone quieted, seeming to cling to each word she spoke.

"Yes, ma'am." Jack actually blushed. There was nothing else that bright red flooding his face could be. "I'd be honored."

"Thank you." Maria bestowed a smile upon him and looked at Will, hovering beside Jack.

When she got to Cookie, the chuck wagon driver immediately spoke up. "You getting rid of me as cook now, Boss? I hope Miz McCoy here ain't planning on going on trail drives with us. Don't think she'd fit in."

He didn't smile as he said it.

"Goodness, no." Maria spoke before Padraig could make a sound, even before he could take a deep breath to lambaste the cook for his rudeness. Catching Cookie's hand, she squeezed it, making him glance anxiously at his boss. "I sincerely hope you're going to continue cooking for my husband and the others, Cookie…may I call you that?" At his slight nod, she said, "Both on the…uh…trail and here at the ranch, for I don't know how to cook. At all." Maria spoke the lie without a blink. "I'm afraid my dear Padraig will starve if it's left up to me."

With that, she placed a hand on Padraig's shoulder so gently he felt his own face grow warm. Aware of the others crowding around, enjoying his brief moment of discomfort as well as the look of love he gave her, Padraig remained silent.

"Well…when you put it like that, ma'am…" Cookie saved him from further embarrassment. "I'll be glad to keep doing that chore here at the ranch. I imagine you're going to have your hands full taking care of the boss." He glanced at Padraig and smiled, a glint of mischief in his eyes. "As well as decorating the ranch house when that architect fella finishes with it."

Padraig had announced to the hands the architect's coming arrival so they wouldn't mistake him for a trespasser.

"You're right," Maria agreed. "And when he's done, we'll have a grand party…for everyone." She looked around, including all the hands, then back at Cookie again. "In the meantime, do you have anything prepared now? I'm afraid my breakfast has disappeared, and the ride out here has left me famished."

"As a matter of fact…" Cookie gestured toward the kitchen door. "I've beans and beefsteak on the stove, and I was getting ready to ring the dinner bell."

"Then, please…" Marie waved her hand at the large metal triangle hanging from a bracket by the back door. "Go ahead."

With surprising nimbleness, Cookie ran up the steps, seized the straight piece of metal attached to the triangle by a string, and struck the triangle several times, producing a surprisingly musical clanging. The cowboys trooped into the house, but as Maria and Padraig entered, Buck held up a hand.

"Hold it, Boss. Did you forget? You got to carry your bride over the threshold. Otherwise, it's bad luck."

"Frankly," Padraig retorted, "I ne'er knew. You think I get married e'ery day?"

"I certainly hope not," Maria murmured so softly none heard but he.

"Let's do it right, then. I don't want any bad luck t' follow you here." He swung her off the floor and into his arms, stalked into the kitchen, and set her down. "Welcome t' th' Shamrock, Mrs. McCoy."

Maria turned and caught his face in her hands and kissed him.

Everyone applauded.

It was then Padraig remembered. "Hey, I carried you inta our room at the hotel, so this one shouldn't count!"

Cookie brought the platter of steak to the table, preventing Maria from answering. "Set down, everyone, and let's eat!"

****

Much, much later, alone in their bedroom, Padraig asked, "Well, what do you think?"

"About what?"

"About e'erythin'…th' ranch, me men…me, as a boss."

"You know what I think of you, Padraig. Are you simply wanting to hear it again?" Her eyes gleamed, mischievously. "As for the men… They all appear capable of doing the jobs you've hired them for. I suppose I shouldn't pass judgment until I've seen them at work, but from the little I saw of them at table, I imagine people in New York would consider them crude and ill-mannered…" She paused and when Padraig started to defend his men, hurried on, "Myself, I found all congenial, good-hearted, and with a surprising show of gentility in spite of their rough appearances."

Maria made certain almost everything she said, while it appeased her husband, also had a modicum of truth in it. She liked the men, though they were definitely rough-cut compared to the well-bred youngsters she'd known in New York. Nevertheless, she saw they were all loyal to her husband and ready to extend that loyalty to her. She also realized they were equally glad of Padraig's happiness.

"I like them, Padraig. All of them, especially that darling Big Jack."

"Better not let anyone else ithur than meself hear you call Big Jack *darlin'*," he warned. "Else he might get laughed off th' ranch."

"I stand corrected," She swept him a curtsey. "As for the ranch itself, you must take me on a tour tomorrow, but I'll tell you now that I do agree the ranch house must be changed. A man with your influence in McCoy's Crossing definitely should have a statelier abode."

As should his wife, she added silently. Already she was planning the features she was going to tell the architect the house had to have. Padraig was completely unaware of the steps his new wife was going to take to make certain he would retain his status in McCoy's Crossing and acquire an even more important one.

"Glad we see eye to eye on that, anyway."

"My darling husband." Maria put her arms around his neck. "We see eye to eye on a great many things, and one of them is currently waiting for us." She nodded at the bed. "I wish you to show me how you make love in your own bed in your own home."

Padraig did that gladly.

****

245

Quinton Aloysius Francis Xavier McCoy, Esquire
McCoy Hall
Tipperary, Ireland
The United Kingdom of Great Britain

Honourable Father,
Please forgive this influx of letters I've sent you recently, but many things have occurred of which I wished you to be abreast. Now, another occurrence has happened, and while I'm certain this will shock you, be assured I am even more shaken by it.

Father, I have taken a wife.

I must make that a single and solitary statement on this page, for it deserves to stand alone in its uniqueness. Surely you see the irony here…after all my womanizing and playing fast and loose with many females' hearts, my own has been captured and is now held prisoner.

Her name is Maria and she's from Alta California, a territory in the far western part of the country originally settled by the Spanish. She's gently bred, a lady, and… I fear you will laugh at me, Father, for I find there is not enough foolscap in the world to hold all the words I would need to extol her virtues or describe how I feel about her. Yes sir, I have fallen, very violently and permanently.

Please be happy for me, sir, and give me your blessings in this foray I am about to make into totally uncharted waters, that of being a husband.

Convey this news to my mother and my siblings, and also give them my affection. Speaking of marriage, sir, did my older brother ever get himself to the altar? It's been some ten years now since his betrothal to that lass from London was announced.

Your son,
Padraig Aloysius Francis McCoy
Owner, The Shamrock Ranch
McCoy's Crossing, Nebraska Territory
United States of America

Chapter 37

Bellows, the architect, came and went.

Padraig listened to his suggestions, adding his own, which were reluctantly accepted. Maria had the final say on the house's design and it wasn't surprising that whatever she wished, or didn't wish, the architect was only too happy to change.

Padraig didn't mind if other men catered to his wife's wishes. That was all right. The house was being built for her, so it was only proper she keep the features she liked and do away with those she didn't.

When Bellows said he would begin building in the spring, Padraig was adamant.

"Nay, I want it started *now*." He wanted his new home ready for his bride as soon as possible.

As when the library was built, Bellows reminded him winter would be coming soon. Already in summer, there was a coolness in the morning air, especially when the wind blew.

"If you and your men apply themselves, the house could be ready before the first snowfall," Padraig protested.

"Perhaps," Bellows replied. "However, you won't be too happy if there's an early blizzard and your roof and wall are gone and the bedroom fills with snow."

He added that the starlings were already making their appearances. Prairie grasses were turning brown.

He'd heard there was a chance of frost soon, had found ants marching a trail up the wall in his own pantry, and caught a couple of crickets trying to crawl under the front doorsill.

By now, Padraig had learned not to ignore those signs he'd once laughed at. He conceded winter was on its way...early. It was agreed that after the spring thaws were over, Bellows and his construction crew would begin their work.

"Sorry, lass," he told Maria after the architect was gone. "Once they start, we'll be sleeping in the kitchen, as it is, but it'll be better to do it when the weather's good."

****

That winter was a mild one, as Nebraska winters went, several snows falling quick and melting quicker. Surprisngly soon, it was spring again.

Grass began turning green under the white covering, prairie flowers popping into bloom. For a change, there was no danger to the cattle and the crop of new calves was healthy with not a one being lost.

Bellows returned and his men got to work. Padraig ordered the parlor and bedroom furniture stored, Buck and a couple of the hands lugging all to one of the outbuildings. New furniture would be ordered from Chicago to go with the new house and the old furnishings could be donated to someone who needed it.

Padraig personally carried the feather mattress into the kitchen, storing it in the pantry during the day, then dragging it out at night. Settling it on the floor near the stove, he and Maria slept there while the work was being done.

He warned Cookie to always knock and make a lot

of noise before entering the kitchen in the mornings. *In case the missus an' I are discussin' domestic matters.*

Cookie assured him if he didn't get a *Come in* after his third knock, he'd go back to the bunkhouse and try again later.

Padraig marveled how Maria never complained during any of it. He couldn't know she grumbled mentally quite a bit, consoling herself with the image of how the house would look when finished, while forcing herself to become lost in his enthusiasm, which she soon actually shared.

The house was finished in a remarkably short time, the workers no doubt spurred on by Bellows' encouragement to get the house done "so Mrs. McCoy can move into her bedroom."

The new house was everything Padraig wanted, and everything Maria could've wished for. It was a grand building with beautifully routed balusters and railings, and a wide front veranda on which Padraig set two white-painted Boston rockers, one stenciled with roses and vines along its high back.

"Where we can sit after supper an' watch th' sunset," he told Maria.

The original kitchen was kept much as it was, though the pantry had been enlarged. The new stove Padraig mentioned was now in place and being used, much to Cookie's delight. Though there was a table in the kitchen, there was a separate dining room seating thirty, with a matching china cabinet and hutch in which delicate china, crystal, and silver cutlery was housed.

The parlor was a masterpiece, with an entryway and a coat closet as well as a settee and matching chairs, plus a liquor cabinet now holding an assortment of wines and brandies. The bedroom Padraig and Maria had shared was made into an office, with the fireplace rebuilt to reach to the second floor and warm the master bedroom above it as well as the room next door. At the other end of the hallway, a second chimney rose from the parlor to another bedroom. Only the middle ones on either side of the hallway had no heat.

Once the new furniture arrived and was unloaded, they went upstairs for the first time.

Maria was delighted with everything. As she glanced into the second bedroom, the one sharing a hearth with the master one, Padraig startled her by saying, "This is your room, darlin'."

"*My* room?"

She whirled from touching the quilt covering the bed—a wooden bed, she noted—giving him such a shocked stare, he thought she was about to burst into tears.

"Aye," he nodded across the hall. "An' that one…'tis mine."

"Why would you say such a thing?" she demanded. "Are…are you tiring of me, Padraig?"

Fear shot through her at that.

He can't. Not yet.

She was realistic enough to admit he might one day, as she got older, if she allowed herself to get fat or become too demanding. She was prepared to accept that he'd look for younger, more attractive game, but not this soon.

No, please.

"Nay…nay, *a chroi*," he hurried to assure her. "But…well, 'tis the custom where I come from, for husbands and wives t' have separate sleepin'

251

arrangements…only comin' together when they want t'…" Mentally, he sidled away from that, wondering why he was being so delicate about it when he was always so outspoken about loving her…until that moment. "…you know. Me maithur an' da have separate bedchambers," he finished, as if that settled the matter.

"We're not your mother and father," Maria answered, fear vanishing as she realized Padraig was merely suggesting they continue a custom his old way of life had followed. "Is that what *you* wish?"

"Oh nay, lass, but I had t' ask."

"It might be nice to have my own room," she looked thoughtful. "Where I could sit and read, and sew…and daydream." Abruptly, she looked eager. "Could I use it for that?"

"You can use it for whate'er you wish," Padraig replied, thankful the storm he thought he'd seen approaching had disappeared. "As long as you're in me bed e'ery night."

With the house finished, Padraig was ready for its housewarming, giving Maria the opening she needed to put into action the one idea she'd had the moment she realized he wanted to marry her. During this time both homesickness and curiosity had seized her. Because of their proximity, where she'd before been prepared to go to California and abandon any attempt to get in touch with her Lakota family, now she saw a way to do that without revealing she was one of them. His renovation of the ranch house had been the first step in her plan. It was time to take the final one.

It wouldn't be difficult, she reasoned. He'd already made several remarks, more hints actually, about housecleaning, which she parried with the reply that such hadn't been on the curriculum at finishing school. Remembering the many times while living in a dormitory with the other girls when she'd scrubbed floors, and done laundry and other chores, before being sent to the foster home where she was actually loved and treated kindly, Maria swore she was now going to do as little menial labor as possible.

Cookie still took care of the meals, taking that chore out of her hands. When it came to doing laundry or tending the garden behind the kitchen, she played the weak and helpless female in such a way the men remaining behind at the ranch to work the horses and do equipment repairs practically fell over themselves offering to help.

They carried the laundry basket outside for her, built the fire under the wash pot, stirred and rinsed the garments, then hung them on the line strung next to the garden. Maria looked on, lamenting loudly how worthless she felt asking for help, then begging them not to tell Padraig what a weakling she was. All assured her she wasn't weak, merely unaccustomed to western life, and all gladly lent their hands to doing her work for her.

Now, however, Padraig wanted a party to show off his new house and his new wife…and, since she'd been the one originally suggesting a housewarming, Maria couldn't very well back out. Besides, planning parties and menus was something she knew how to do. She simply didn't intend to do anything except *plan*, however.

As Padraig rambled on about who he wanted to invite, with Maria making certain every influential man in McCoy's Crossing and outside it was on his list, she waited for him to pause for breath. Then she sighed and said, very quietly, "I do so want this to be a grand affair, my dear, but…"

She shook her head, and forced herself to look sad when inside she was trembling with anticipation at thought of the party.

"What is it, love?" He broke off, looking concerned at her change in expression.

She was silent a moment, as if trying to decide whether to speak or not, then, "Oh, Padraig, I don't think I can do this alone."

"You won't be alone, *acushla*," he protested. "You'll have Cookie t' help with th' meal, an' Buck an' th' ithurs…"

"That's not what I mean." She paused, and continued with obvious reluctance, "I hadn't wanted to say this. I truly thought I could do it by myself…"

"What do you mean?" Her tone gave him a bit of a quiver in his belly. He tensed, realizing he was bracing himself as if he thought she intended to strike him.

"We need a housekeeper."

That wasn't what he expected at all. He didn't know what he thought she was going to say, but it certainly hadn't been *that*.

"Housekeeper?" he repeated. "T' do what?"

Maria pretended reluctance, then burst forth in a torrent of complaints and explanations as vehement as Padraig hadn't heard since the last time he witnessed a clash between his mother and father.

Hadn't he noticed the hands were doing the laundry and tending the garden because she was too delicate and fragile to handle those chores? Yes, Cookie did the cooking. Before, he'd handled what little housekeeping was done, but now that the house was bigger and of a much better quality, there was more work. Did Padraig truly expect his wife to get down on her hands and knees and scrub floors like a charwoman, or suffer raw chapped hands from plunging them into boiling soapy water?

Servants did that.

Maria turned Padraig's past life against him. He was raised in gentility, he should be aware of this...why wasn't he?

Padraig had definitely grown up with servants. Being a rich man's son was part of his problem. He'd watched his mother do nothing more strenuous than go over household routines, plan menus, and a thousand other domestic activities with the butler and their housekeeper, though there was much more she did for their tenants than he ever realized, since learning about it would've interfered with his own misadventures. Their home in Tipperary had upstairs and downstairs maids, 'tweenies, grooms, and footmen, but he'd never transferred that idea to his current home.

Now that it was brought to his attention, he was apologetic and eager to make amends. He had the money to pay servants. He had a house demanding them. His men were good cowhands but neither they nor Cookie were trained for such work, and by damn, his wife certainly wasn't going to do it. She was going to be waited on as his mother had been...and still was.

That brought up a problem.

"I don't know as there's many women in these parts who'd want t' do such work," he told Maria. "Th' farmers' wives as well as th' ranchers' are doin' it for their own families. Most of the wives o' th' townsfolk are sendin' their daughters away t' those eastern finishin' schools so they can become ladies themselves, an'...

Well, really, darlin', th' only ithur available women in town are th' saloon girls, an' I don't know as I'd want you associatin' with them."

There was also a chance one of those might say the wrong thing about when he'd availed himself of their services. He caught her hands, kissing them gently.

"I could advertise in some o' th' eastern papers, but that'll take a while, an'…"

"I know of someone," she interrupted. *My dear Padraig. I do love you but, truly, dearest, you are so easily led on occasion.*

Where she should've been clapping her hands in triumph by how quickly he'd fallen in with her plans, she was momentarily ashamed by the ease of it all. Maria told herself she mustn't take advantage of his love for her too much, mainly because every time he did as she wanted, she found herself falling more in love with him.

"Who?" He looked confused.

"At the Lakota encampment." As he frowned, she explained, "When I was in school, there were several Lakota girls enrolled also."

"Really?" He frowned at that, letting her know he was unfamiliar with what her people had gone through.

Maria forgave him his ignorance. He was a foreigner. He couldn't be expected to be aware of all the injustices that she had experienced. She imagined that if he'd been present at the time, Padraig would've protested loudly the removal of children from their homes in such a brutal way.

"It was part of some program set up by the government." She brushed it aside in the way she'd seen her foster mother and other women Back East do. It was government, therefore too complicated for female minds to follow. "I didn't really understand it…but I became friends with one girl. She told me she came from a settlement near a place called Four Corners. Wasn't that the name of McCoy's Crossing before it was changed?"

"Aye, but…" Padraig paused, remembering. "There's some Lakota near th' Platte, but I've ne'er seen any o' th' tribe. Maybe they're her people."

"Her name was *OkíŋyAŋ Zitkála*…Flying Bird."

She hoped he didn't comment on how well she pronounced the foreign-sounding words, prayed he wouldn't notice the similarity between the last name she'd fashioned for herself and the fictional friend's.

"When I graduated and prepared to return home, she begged me to promise her…" Maria paused, taking a deep breath. "…to promise if I got a chance as I traveled through Nebraska, I'd try to get a message to her mother that she was all right. That she was married now."

"Well, now, darlin', that's a commendable thing t' do." Padraig plainly didn't see where any of this was leading. It never crossed his mind that his beloved wife might be lying.

"I didn't think I'd be stopping in McCoy's Crossing," Maria hurried on. "I had no idea I was going to be swept off my feet by a handsome Irishman."

May as well flatter him a bit because it was the truth, after all.

"Can you imagine how I felt when I realized this was where Flying Bird came from?" Maria caught his hands, appealing to his pride. Again. "You said you'd like to show the Sioux all white men aren't bad, didn't you?"

"Well…aye." He made a mental note to be careful what he said in future.

"This is your chance. Ride out there, ask for Flying Bird's mother. Her name's *Čik'ayela Wanáhča*. Say her daughter is all right, and...say you want to hire her to take care of your home and be a companion for your wife."

She bit her lip and allowed it to quiver slightly as the abrupt thought that she might soon see her mother again almost overwhelmed her.

"I do get lonely. I need another woman to talk to, of..." She looked away, "...womanly things...things I can't speak about even to my husband." She gave him a limpid look. "Please, Padraig. It's the least I can do for my friend. Won't you do that...for *me*?"

That settled it.

Padraig had encountered those womanly things already, endured the monthly mood swings, the days when Maria stayed in bed with a hot rice pillow on her belly, then huddled away from him at night. If it would ease those awkward moments to have another female in the house...he knew how it felt to be estranged from family...if it gave that Lakota woman some peace of mind about her child...*if it would make Maria happy...*

"I'll do it," he decided.

When he rode away, Maria stood on the front porch, watching.

Chapter 38

Padraig wasn't alone as he rode toward the encampment. He had a second saddle horse and two others, part of his new remuda, with him, all on leads. The saddle horse followed patiently, the two-year-olds were anxious and a little rambunctious, being green-broke and still not accustomed to being led.

Maria had suggested he take the horses.

"Why?" he asked.

"It's something Flying Bird told me," she explained. "When Čik'ayela Wanáhča comes back with you…" She didn't dare allow herself to think her mother might refuse. "…you must offer the chief something in return, to give to her family to fill the space her absence will make."

"I see." He nodded to show he understood. "Kind of a dowry."

"In a way." She obviously hadn't thought of that. She placed a hand on his shoulder. "Be polite when you speak to the chief."

"Do you know his name?" he asked. "Did the girl tell you?"

"She did," Maria replied, "but I don't remember it." She wasn't going to tell Padraig too much, fearing she'd somehow reveal *she* was the girl. "Anyway, it was so long ago when Flying Bird left, there may be a new chief now. Whoever it is, show him respect," she returned to her admonitions. "Let him know you're an important man in McCoy's Crossing, but don't brag…"

She paused, hand tightening on his shoulder as if realizing she was sending her husband into a potentially dangerous situation and also that he was willingly going.

"…and be careful."

"Don't worry, lass," he laughed, patting her hand. "I'll go out there, deliver me message, an' this Čik'ayela Wanáhča an' I will be back before you know it."

With that, he kissed her, mounted the pinto, gathered the leads of the other horses, and rode away.

Now, however, Padraig wasn't so certain of his confident words. *What th' hell am I doin'? Ridin' inta an Indian encampment by meself? Takin' a message from a woman I ne'er knew t' a woman I've ne'er met? An' expectin' t' hire her as me housekeeper as well?*

Though Indian attacks had sent the First Nebraska Calvary and the Seventh Iowa Calvary to Ft. Kearny to escort wagon trains, currently any conflict between Indians and white settlers seemed to have shifted farther west as settlements grew more plentiful. The first fort had been built near Nebraska City, fairly close to Four Corners, but as more and more settlers came along the Oregon Trail, the barracks was moved to a more southerly and central location.

Padraig had heard rumors that orders came from Washington to abandon the fort. It was to be torn down and any remaining structures removed to North Platte and Sidney in the far western part of the state. The soldiers themselves were reassigned to Omaha.

Some people protested this, thinking the Lakota and others were merely waiting for the area to be left unprotected and then they would attack again. Others argued the government wouldn't leave everyone in jeopardy if it was thought such a thing would happen.

Padraig had never thought much about it. Just as he'd never seen an Indian, he'd also never considered the Shamrock or his men being attacked.

Now he did, but memory of how Maria looked as she spoke kept him from turning back.

She's keepin' a promise, an' that's a good thin'. If he'd known someone from McCoy's Crossing was going to Tipperary, he'd have asked him to deliver a personal message to *his* mother, so…

She's a good friend, me Maria. How can I not do this for her?

The camp came into view, and Padraig experienced his first twinge of disappointment. It was extremely small, surely not more than a dozen conical tents arranged in a circle thirty or forty feet from the banks of the Platte, just far enough to keep from being washed away if a sudden rain or a flush of rapidly melting snow sent the river flooding.

Even as far away as he was, Padraig could hear voices, people speaking, the shouts of children. He saw a small group of youngsters running in what appeared to be a game of tag, women moving about. It was startlingly like a scene from market day in Tipperary, only instead of being dressed in gowns and wearing flower-decorated bonnets, the women wore buckskin dresses with antelope-skin leggings, with their hair in braids. The children might've been himself and Colin with some of their cousins, running and shouting in play, except these children were barefoot and near-naked with narrow apron-like clouts covering their privates.

It looked very peaceful…and very harmless.

261

He touched heels to the pinto's sides, urging it to move faster.

No sooner had he reached the edge of the village, where the nearest tent stood, when a sharp whistle sounded, so shrill it made his ears tingle.

The effect was startling.

The children stopped their play, the women broke off their chatter. Within moments, they all disappeared, leaving only tent flaps waving in the breeze to show where they'd gone.

Almost immediately, a group of men appeared in the center of the little avenue between the tents. They were armed. At least, Padraig thought the long poles some of them held might be weapons...lances, perhaps, or spears. He slowed the pinto, thinking he shouldn't go any farther, and tightened his grip on the reins, preparing to turn the horse's head.

Out of the corner of his eye, he saw a figure dart from behind a tent and knew it had stopped behind him. The brush of moccasins on prairie grass told him a second man joined the first.

Padraig took a deep breath and rode his horse toward the little group before him. When he was about ten feet away, he stopped the animal.

The pinto snorted. The three horses on their leads also snuffled loudly. One pawed the dirt.

"Good mornin'." Padraig aimed his greeting at a man standing at the front of the little group, deciding he was the leader.

He wasn't certain why he thought this, for there was nothing to distinguish him from the others. He might be a bit older, perhaps, in his mid-fifties, the two long braids resting against his shoulders streaked with gray. His face was lined and leathery from exposure to the harsh Nebraska sun, but so were most of the others. He wasn't dressed a bit differently, wearing a buckskin shirt, moccasins, and a breech clout but no leggings.

"I'm…"

"What do you want here?" the man interrupted in fairly understandable English.

The others drew a little closer together.

Tightening their ranks, Padraig thought. *Why? Do they think I'm a threat? A solitary white man? Facing at least a dozen Indians?*

"I was gettin' t' that," Padraig continued amiably, trying not to show how the man's abruptness sent a warning chill through him. "Are you th' leader, the chief here?"

Cautiously, the man nodded. He touched his chest. "Eagle-of-Iron."

"Good, then, Mr…uh…Eagle." Padraig gave him the smile that usually melted any hostility. Apparently it didn't work on Indians. He pressed on. "I'm Patrick McCoy and you're th' man I wish t'see."

There was no answer. The man merely nodded, not very encouragingly.

"Me name's Padraig McCoy, an' I'm lookin' for a woman…"

"Leave here now," the chief said. He sounded as if he were speaking through gritted teeth. "We don't give our women to be white men's whores."

"What?" Padraig was shocked. He recovered, hastily explaining, "Nay, you misunderstand. I'm lookin'…"

"Go, white man." A hand went to a knife in a beaded scabbard at the man's belt.

The young man standing next to him copied the action. Behind him, others tightened their holds on their spears.

"Go, before I kill you."

"You wouldn't dare do that." Padraig was shaken out of his explanation. "Not with th' soldiers here."

"If we kill you, you'll never be found." The chief didn't look particularly worried. Abruptly, he smiled, though it wasn't friendly.. "Besides, the soldiers will be leaving soon."

That shook him. More than ever, Padraig wanted to run. Even if it made him seem a coward, he wanted to drop the other horses' leads, wheel the pinto, and kick it into a gallop and get away as fast as he could.

Asking himself why he was being a fool in the face of such a blatant death-threat, he forced himself to say, mildly, "You misunderstand. Will you let me explain?"

The chief hesitated, thought it over, then reluctantly nodded. The others looked impatient.

"May I dismount?" Padraig asked, thinking perhaps if he were on foot, he might not appear such a threat. He imagined someone behind one of the tents aiming an arrow at his back.

The chief gestured. The young man next to him looked as if he thought the white man was crazy, getting off the animal giving him his best means of escape.

Looping the reins over the pinto's neck, Padraig tied the leads to the saddle horn and slid out of the saddle. He took two steps away from the horse and toward the chief.

Be polite, Maria had said. *Show respect.* He removed his hat.

Sight of that flaming hair made several of them blink. He wondered if they were envisioning it hanging from a scalp pole, then forced that thought out of his mind and got to the point.

"As I said, me name's Padraig McCoy. I'm from McCoy's Crossin'." He thought he saw a twitch of recognition. "Do you know o' it?"

The chief nodded, a bare inclination of his head.

"'Tis named for me, but that's no matter…just mentionin' it in passin'," Padraig hurried on. "I've a message for a woman named Čik'ayela Wanáhča."

That brought an unexpected reaction. "You know Čik'ayela Wanáhča?"

"Not meself I don't," Padraig denied. "Me wife…she went t' school with her daughter…Flying Bird."

"Your wife…she's Lakota?"

Padraig thought he saw a slight melting of the stern features.

"Nay, she's from California. Spanish. She said she was in school with Flying Bird. Somethin' about a government program?" He didn't have to sound vague. He had no idea about that.

"Government program." The young man spoke, his tone bitter. "Government brutality, you mean."

"They took our children," the man said. "Flying Bird was among them. So was my son." He nodded at the young man standing next to him.

"I survived their torture," the young man said. "I came home. Flying Bird did not." He looked anxious. "She's alive? Well?"

"I don't know about that," Padraig answered. "Apparently, she *was* nine months ago when me wife last saw her. She asked Maria—that's me wife—if she came through McCoy's Crossin' t' try t' get word t' her maithur. I've come t' do that."

For several minutes, the chief stared at him. Then he gestured. Another young man spun and ran down the row of tents, stopping before one on the far right. He called out.

The tent flap was thrown open and a small woman peeped out. The young man said something else, and briefly, they appeared to argue.

To have something to say, Padraig spoke to the young man. "You speak English very well."

"I should. I have a degree from Harvard School of Law." There was a cynical laugh.

Beside him, his father muttered, "For all the good it does."

"Why do you live here, then?" Padraig was astonished. A Harvard lawyer? Wearing buckskins and living in a tipi?

"Where else would a Lakota live?"

"You should..." Padraig took a deep breath. "You should go into McCoy's Crossin', see Josiah Blackwood. He's a lawyer an' a friend o' mine. Tell him who you are an' that I ask him t' take you on as an associate."

He knew he was sounding grandiose, but he was plainly shocked at the waste of education he saw standing before him.

"You could...represent your people in law disputes...an' ithur thin's."

His voice trailed away as he realized that last sounded incredibly lame, even naïve.

"You truly believe that?" It seemed the young man thought so, too. "You're really a stupid white man."

"It wouldn't hurt to try," Padraig told him.

By now, the woman had emerged from the tent and

followed the other young man back to where Padraig stood.

"This is Čik'ayela Wanáhča." He again took his place behind the chief.

The rest of the men relaxed a bit, though none turned their spears aside or pointed the tips at the ground. They all looked very interested in what was going to happen next.

The woman looked up at Padraig. She was very small, reminding him of Maria in her slenderness and the long, slight curve of her nose.

"You have word of my daughter?" Her voice was very soft and stilted, as if she didn't speak English very often. Certainly the chief's son was much more fluent. "My Flying Bird?"

Padraig nodded. "Me wife was a friend o' hers at th' school they went t'." He hurried on as he saw the shadow crossing all faces at mention of that, as he repeated the lies Maria had told him. "She asked Maria t' tell you she's doin' well, an' happy, an..."

"Will she be coming home?" There was such hope in that small copper face, it put the lie to that stern, stoic redskin image Padraig always had in his mind.

"I...don't think so." He said it as gently as possible, repeating the story his wife had told him. "Maria said she was married now."

"To a white man?" That was a whisper.

"I suppose." He shrugged slightly. "She didn't say about that."

She sighed. He couldn't tell if it was in despair of learning of the marriage, joy over knowing her daughter was still alive, or disappointment that she wasn't coming back.

"Thank you for telling me." She turned to go.

"Wait." Unthinking, Padraig put out a hand to stop her.

Someone raised a spear. The young man touched his knife. Padraig dropped his own hand. Čik'ayela Wanáhča looked back at him.

"Maria wants me t' ask you...will you come t' me ranch, an' work for us...be a companion t' her? She's the only woman there an' she gets lonely. She wants anaithur woman around."

She didn't answer. Instead, she turned and spoke to Eagle-of-Iron in their own language. He answered and, for several moments, words flew fast and sharp. The young man continued glaring at Padraig while they talked.

At last, the chief shrugged and Čik'ayela Wanáhča looked back at Padraig.

"Your wife is young? Like my Flying Bird?"

"I...well, I suppose they might be th' same age." Padraig looked a little sheepish. "Truth t' tell, me Maria's probably too young for me, bein' about eighteen an' all, but I love th' lass, an'..." He stopped as he felt his face getting warm.

He looked down, slapping his hat against his thigh, a little angry he was blushing in front of these savages. To have something to do, he put on the hat. When he looked up, they were smiling, all of them...and that made the flush even brighter.

"I will go with you." She made it a flat statement. "I will take care of the friend of my Flying Bird."

"Thank you." Padraig became aware of the horses. "I brought a gift for your family."

What was it Maria had said? To fill the space her

absence would make?

"I know a family member can't be replaced, but p'rhaps these horses will help ease th' pain o' your leavin'."

He gestured at the two unsaddled horses.

"They're new stock," he explained, directing his words at the chief this time. "Two-year-olds, green-broke."

The chief said something and his son untied the leads from the saddle horn. He gestured and another man took the ropes from him.

"My husband's brother," Čik'ayela Wanáhča explained.

"Your husband…" Padraig told himself he shouldn't be surprised. If she had a daughter, surely she'd had a husband. He looked at the brother-in-law, then back at her. "You can keep th' horses, sure…but I don't want t' take you away from your husband."

"You won't." Her voice was flat. "He's dead. Long time ago. I want no other man." She dismissed his offer of sympathy. "I go with you."

"You can come back t' visit whenever you wish," he said. He looked at the chief again. "I won't stop her from comin' back if she decides not t' stay."

The chief nodded. He spoke again to Čik'ayela Wanáhča, then turned, said something to the other men, and they all walked a few paces away. Abruptly, Padraig and Čik'ayela Wanáhča were alone.

"I'll also pay you for your work," Padraig added. "That way you'll have money if you wish t' buy yourself anythin'."

"What would I buy?" Čik'ayela Wanáhča looked surprised.

"Well…" Padraig had no idea. "You can save it, or give it t' your family. It'll be yours t' do with as you please."

She glanced at the chief. He shrugged. Apparently, the idea of a Lakota having money was unheard of.

"Do you have anythin' you wish t' take with you?" Padraig wasn't certain what personal belongings a Lakota would have, if any.

She spoke to her brother-in-law. He ran to the tent and went inside. In a moment, he returned, handing her a small and very bedraggled cloth doll. She took it, then turned back to Padraig.

He caught her about the waist. She stiffened.

"Relax. Just goin' t' help you get ont' th' horse," he explained. "You're a li'l short t' be climbin' inta that saddle."

To his surprise, she smiled. "That is my name. Čik'ayela Wanáhča. Little One."

"Please t' meet you, Little One." Padraig set her down and held out his hand. "Padraig McCoy."

She grasped his hand, nodding. He swung her into the saddle and untied the lead from the horse's bridle. Then he mounted the pinto and rolled the rope into a coil, tucking it into his saddle bag.

"Think about what I said," he told the young man. "I…I don't know your name, I'm sorry."

"Once I was called *Iníla Uŋ*, the quiet one," the young man said. "While Back East, I was called Benjamin. When I came home again, I took the name *WákhiyA Wówičakhe*, He Who Speaks Truth." He laughed again. "That was the closest equivalent to lawyer I could find. It didn't help."

Padraig didn't push the matter, deciding to leave it

up to him. Gathering the reins, he turned the pinto's head and guided it out of the camp.

Behind him, the other horse followed.

Once they were out of sight of the camp, Padraig felt it his duty to tell Čik'ayela Wanáhča about his ranch.

She didn't speak during his entire explanation, except once, when he was in the middle of describing a trail drive and paused to take a breath.

"You are like a bird with many songs. Do you never stop talking?"

That made him stop, stutter, and then say, "Me apologies. I was simply tryin' t' put you at ease."

"If you wish to do that, tell me about your wife, the friend of my Flying Bird."

"Very well…" Padraig inhaled, thought a moment, then said, "I was in town on business, an' th' stage had stopped, an' there she was…"

By the time they arrived at the ranch, he'd fully convinced Čik'ayela Wanáhča that no matter what else he might be, he was truly in love with his wife.

Chapter 39

As they rode into the ranch yard, he saw Maria standing on the porch. She was in the same place she'd been when he left and briefly he had the odd idea she hadn't moved from that spot the entire day, that she'd stood right there, waiting for him to return.

Seeing him, and that there was someone with him, Maria felt her heart begin to pound so fast in her chest it hurt.

Mother? She's still alive and Padraig has brought her to me! She'd been certain he would return with an empty saddle and the news Čik'ayela Wanáhča had died, either of grief at losing her two children or from one of those frigid Nebraska winters.

Maria refused to believe what her eyes were telling her. They were still too far away for her to see the woman's features clearly. *I won't believe it until I hear it from her own lips.*

He slowed the pinto, then pulled it to a stop and dismounted.

"Hello, *a chroí*. I'm back," he said the obvious.

She ran down the steps to him and was caught in a tight hug. He got a brief welcoming kiss, Maria forcing herself not to act too eager to see his companion. As he released her, she turned to the woman seated on the second horse. Padraig helped Čik'ayela Wanáhča from the horse's back.

As he turned back to her, Maria felt a wave of dizziness sweep over her.

"Sweetheart, are you all right?" His hand on her arm brought her back.

"I'm fine." She smiled at him, then looked past him to the woman standing there in her pale buckskins.

She was smaller than Maria remembered. *But I always had to look up at her.* Now they were almost of a height. *Her features…* For a moment, she wasn't certain. *Is this my mother? I can't remember…*

Maria felt shame wash over her. Thirteen years had destroyed her memories of her mother's face.

"Maria, this is Čik'ayela Wanáhča."

She pushed past him, taking in the black hair, as yet untouched by gray, staring into eyes as dark as her own.

"*Taŋyáŋ yahí.*" She wanted to add "*iná*," *mother*, but knew she didn't dare. Instead, she forced herself to smile when what she wanted to do was cry. "Flying Bird taught me that," she lied.

"You will tell me of my Flying Bird." Čik'ayela Wanáhča said.

"I will. I promise." Maria took a deep breath, inhaling unshed tears of joy.

Padraig took her arm and the look she gave him held so much gratitude she thought he looked shocked.

If I didn't love you before, Padraig McCoy, I do now.

"Thank you," she said aloud and placed her hand over the one on her arm.

****

Inside, she showed Čik'ayela Wanáhča through the house, explaining what her duties would be. The little woman didn't say much, taking in her surroundings in

273

that expressionless way Padraig would've said was more in keeping with his idea of how an Indian should look.

Once upstairs in the room at the end of the hall, Maria said, "This will be your room. Did you bring anything with you?"

Čik'ayela Wanáhča shook her head. "I had nothing I wished to bring except this." She held up the doll. "It was my Flying Bird's."

"You'll need some clothes, then." Maria looked away so her expression wouldn't show.

She remembered how she had cried because the soldier who took her from her father's tent wouldn't let her go back for her doll. Later, she rationalized she probably wouldn't have been allowed to keep it anyway. In that moment, she wanted to take it from Čik'ayela Wanáhča and hug it to her heart. *Now I have you back, too.*

"Will you mind wearing some of my old dresses? I think we're almost the same size."

"I will wear whatever you wish." Čik'ayela Wanáhča studied the face of the young woman looking anxiously at her. "You are so like my people, but your husband says you are Spanish."

"That's right." Once again, Maria repeated the lie she would forever tell. "I'm from California. That's many miles away from here."

"They are white?" Čik'ayela Wanáhča seemed to find this difficult to believe, that someone so dark was not Lakota.

Maria nodded.

Impulsively, Čik'ayela Wanáhča seized Maria's hand. "No matter. Miz Maria, you will be my Flying Bird."

Later, alone in their bedroom, Maria turned to Padraig. "How can I ever thank you?"

"Darlin'," he seemed surprised she was so grateful. "I love you. You know I'm going' t' do anythin' in me power t' make you happy. All you have t' do is ask."

That was the moment Maria decided she would never again take advantage of Padraig's love. From that day on, she was going to do her best to make *him* happy.

Chapter 40

Čik'ayela Wanáhča fit remarkably well into Padraig's household. Once Cookie was assured she wasn't supplanting him in the kitchen, he and the little Lakota shared the stove and pantry. Other than the fact that now someone other than the ranch hands did the laundry and gardening, and had taken over care of the ranch house, the only thing really changing was that Padraig no longer ate with his men.

"We have a dining room now." Maria met his arguments calmly, because she'd expected them and had her reasons well rehearsed. "You see your men all day, Padraig. You work with them from sun up to sun down. I like them, too," she continued as he began a spluttered protest. "However, I want you with *me* at mealtimes. I want our meals to be intimate…"

Here she touched his hand and smiled up at him with the barest twist to her mouth as if suggesting the meals would be something more than merely consuming food.

"…not shared with a dozen or so ranch hands."

"When you put it like that…" Padraig immediately capitulated.

He was like melted wax in Maria's lovely little hands. As they sat in the dining room, with the area lit by an overhead chandelier in which fifty candles were fitted, their flames reflecting in the crystal drops and beads adorning it, he had to admit being alone with his wife was much more enjoyable than eating with Buck and Big Jack and the others, even if he did miss the men's joshing and carryings-on.

Maria never made any other request of him as far as his association with his men. She was smart enough to know she'd very quickly alienate all of them if she kept Padraig from his duties at the ranch. She had a beautiful home, a husband who adored her, and now her mother, even if she couldn't tell Čik'ayela Wanáhča who she really was. As far as she was concerned, she had everything she wanted.

****

The housewarming party was a rousing success.

With Maria reading recipes from the cookbook Padraig bought at Delsey's General Store, Čik'ayela Wanáhča prepared the menu she had chosen. Cookie was called in to assist, the chuck wagon cook gladly helping out. He and the little Lakota were in a friendly rivalry to see who could prepare the tastiest dishes, and they both considered the party a chance to do exactly that.

Maria insisted Padraig not only invite the other ranchers and their wives, but also their foremen and trail bosses. A couple of the more important farmers in the area were added onto her guest list, as well as the mayor and members of the town council. No one was being slighted on this very important night for the owner of the Shamrock ranch.

His wife made certain of that.

The men and their wives arrived bedecked in their very best, though Padraig in evening wear he'd brought with him and never worn until now, and Maria, in one of the gowns Miss Sammons made for her, outshone them all.

The guests were shown into the ballroom where the strains of Johann Strauss II's "Wine, Women, and Song" filled the air. The orchestra consisted of several musically inclined townsfolk Padraig had hired for the evening, and they were doing a very competent rendering of the waltzes and other music.

When the house was being built, Padraig had wondered aloud why Maria insisted on having a ballroom.

"Why the hell do we need such a thing? Excuse me, sweet," he immediately apologized. "But why…"

"You'll see," she told him. "We aren't always going to have barn dances, my darling. An important man such as you has to be elegant on occasion."

Before he could reply to that with the protest that he didn't consider himself so blasted important, she turned away, speaking to the architect again.

Now, as he swept her around the floor, sending her skirts swirling, they were like two sparkling jewels in the midst of a sea of pearls. All were stunning but they the most striking of all.

"I agree about th' ballroom," he said. "It does pay to be elegant, but frankly, I feel like a peasant allowed t' dance with th' princess. You're beautiful, *a chroí*…"

"Is my gossamer still holding?" she whispered into his ear, breath warm against his skin.

"'Tis wrapped so tight I can barely breathe." His own whisper was as soft.

Maria laughed and he spun her about.

In the kitchen, the hired hands were laughing and eating Cookie's baked beans and ham, with gravy and biscuits, and swigging down beer. Padraig had bought a keg from the Trails End inventory and had it carted to the kitchen from town. His own guests drank one of the Portuguese Madeiras he'd had Delsey special order, a *bual* with a raisin flavor. He'd decided that would go best with the roast and the potatoes, onions, and carrots and other dishes Čik'ayela Wanáhča prepared.

The table had been set beforehand, all place settings upon it before the guests took their seats. Maria felt it would be easier for Čik'ayela Wanáhča that way and, to that end, asked Cookie to assist the little woman in bringing the serving dishes to the table. Each offering was met with exclamations of praise as they were passed around.

"Damn, Padraig, this is the best beef I've ever tasted." August looked up from cutting into the slab of roast on his plate. "Did your chuck wagon cook do this, or did you have the Sylvestre House ship out the food? Tell the truth, now."

"Actually…" Padraig's revelation that he had a Lakota housekeeper surprised everyone.

"There you go, being an innovator again," Blackstone declared, taking a sip of his Madeira. "You know what this means, don't you?"

"That you're going t' be invitin' yourself back for more o' me wine?"

"That, too," the lawyer admitted. "But it also means every wife at this table is going to want a Lakota housekeeper if she can find one who cooks this good, and we poor husbands are going to be run ragged trying to find her."

That was met with laughs and agreements up and down the table.

A little later, Blackstone collared Padraig near the punchbowl. "Got a bone to pick with you, my young friend."

"I deny th' entire episode." Padraig's reply matched the lawyer's playful scowl.

"Maybe you should." Blackstone took a deep breath. "I'm taking a chance, Padraig. I hired him."

"Hired who?

"Benjamin Speaks Truth," came the surprising answer. "Though we're going to shorten that to *True*."

"You mean, he actually came to see you?" Padraig couldn't believe it.

"Rode into McCoy's Crossing about two weeks ago. Told me he wanted to represent Indians in court. Brought his diploma with him to prove he had a degree. Been busy on a case a former Lakota scout's bringing against a Lincoln realty company for reneging on a deal to sell him a parcel of land."

"I'm surprised I hadn't heard o' that. It should be fairly newsworthy." Truthfully, Padraig was more than surprised. "I've been t' town twice since I went t' th' Lakota camp an' no one's said a thin'."

"Guess it isn't as newsworthy as you'd think," Blackstone answered. "Ben's a good lawyer, graduated high up in his class. I hope his credentials overcome the fact of his being Lakota and this venture will turn out well."

The party lasted until past midnight, the last stragglers leaving around two o'clock. As the final carriage disappeared into the moonlit shadows, Padraig came back into the house, shutting the front door.

"Mercy, Maria!" He caught his wife around the waist, swinging her off the floor, and kissing her. "You are a wonder."

"Thank you," Maria said. "Are you just discovering

that?"

"An' modest, too." He laughed as he set her on her feet. "You handled this whole thing with such finesse. Me dear maithur couldn't have done better, an' I've attended many a dinner party she supervised. In its own way, this was as good as any *fête,* promenade, ball, or house party we e'er had back in Tipperary."

"Do you really mean that?" She swung around, eyes meeting his as if trying to determine if he spoke truthfully.

"Aye, sweet."

When she threw herself into his arms and hugged him, he laughed.

"Here now. What's this? Not that I'm complainin', but…"

"I'm just so happy," she said. "Because you said my efforts were a success."

"In that case, we'll have t' have more o' these get-togethers, because I want you t' stay happy, love."

Maria started up the stairs, but Padraig made a detour to the kitchen, where he found Čik'ayela Wanáhča up to her elbows in dishwater while Cookie stood to one side, drying each plate and delicate piece of crystal with a flour sack towel as she handed it to him.

"I figured it'd take her all night to finish this by herself, Boss," he explained. "So I thought I'd help out."

Nodding, Padraig spoke to Čik'ayela Wanáhča. "Everyone sends their compliments to the cook." As she frowned, he added, "That's praise. They liked your cooking. So much, in fact, I'm giving you a raise."

"What is this raise?" Her frown changed to a scowl. She paused, plate in her hands.

"It means the three dollars a month I'm givin' you

is bein' changed t' five."

"What will I do with so much money?" she asked. "I don't want anything, Mr. Padraig."

Padraig would always wonder why, of all the people he knew, his wife and his housekeeper were the only ones pronouncing his name correctly. That made him smile as he answered, "I *have* t' pay you. Otherwise, someone might think I'm indulgin' in slavery. If you don't know what t' do with the money," he hurried on as he saw her about to comment on that. "I'll take you inta town an' you can open an account at th' bank."

"What will that do?" Čik'ayela Wanáhča gave the plate she held to Cookie and returned to the dishpan.

"The bank will keep th' money for you until you want it."

"Very well." She handed Cookie another plate. "This is the last one."

As the cook took it, Padraig stifled a yawn.

"You go to bed, Mr. Padraig," Čik'ayela Wanáhča ordered. "Miss Maria is waiting."

He thought she sounded exactly like his mother. With a nod, Padraig obeyed.

He found Maria sound asleep, or at least he thought so. Somehow she'd managed to wriggle out of her stays by herself, leaving petticoats, stockings, and gown in a beautiful billow of ruffles and crimson satin flowing over a chair. Undressing as quietly as possible, he added his own garments to the pile, then slid into the walnut sleigh bed he'd purchased as part of their new furnishings.

She came awake immediately.

"I was tryin' t' be quiet."

"Don't you know I'll always awaken when I sense you near me?" She opened her arms.

"You want me t' make love t' you now?" He pretended dismay. "As tired as I am from all that dancin' an' eatin' an' drinkin'?"

"I'm tightening my gossamer some more," she whispered. "I most certainly do, my love."

Padraig heaved a sigh of mock resignation. "In that case, guess I can't do anythin' except obey, because you definitely have me enthralled, *acushla*."

Chapter 41

Summer, 1862

The rest of the country might now be in turmoil, North fighting South, brother turning against brother with rebel guerillas waylaying Union troops and blockade runners being chased by warships, but as far as Padraig was concerned, he had entered the happiest and most contented phase of his life.

The ranch was doing well. He and Maria were idyllically happy. They rarely argued, and if they did, it lasted only long enough for them to reconcile quite joyously and physically.

Čik'ayela Wanáhča settled into life at the ranch with surprising ease, idolizing Maria, occasionally sounding like a critical maiden aunt when she spoke to his wife. In contrast, she appeared to completely worship Padraig and attempted to meet his every wish when it came to preparing meals. She became so adept at cooking anything he might mention he had a taste for, if Maria was there to read the recipe, that he joked he soon would become too fat to ride his horse.

Little by little, the Lakota edged Cookie out of the kitchen and out of the ranch house altogether. Although he was always around to help unload the buckboard or do any heavy lifting, Čik'ayela Wanáhča was now the one running the McCoy household, a housekeeper in both name and fact.

It happened so subtly the chuck wagon cook didn't even know he'd been supplanted. When he realized it, he saved himself a joshing from the other hired hands by saying to Padraig, while several of the other men were near, "Boss, it looks to me like that little Lakota has everything under control, so why don't I just do the cooking when we're on a drive and let her handle the meals while we're home? After all, too many cooks can spoil the broth...and she does make a good bowl of soup."

Čik'ayela Wanáhča returned to the encampment occasionally to visit, though she never spoke of what was said or done while she was there.

During that time, Padraig and the men drove another herd of cattle to Sedalia. Though there was a high demand for beef to feed the newly recruited army, he'd been reluctant to leave Maria, the first time they'd be separated since their marriage. She assured him she'd be safe, with Čik'ayela Wanáhča to keep her company and some of the hired hands left behind to protect them and see to the ranch.

Padraig left with a high heart and an eagerness to get the drive done and return to his wife.

There was only one blot of discontent in his life—as yet, he and Maria had no children.

That realization came to Padraig after they'd celebrated their second wedding anniversary with another of the many parties they'd had in the past two years. As Mayor Bainbridge toasted the couple, "To Padraig and Maria...and to many little McCoys to grace their household," Padraig abruptly realized he and his wife were childless.

He was well aware Donal had been born barely a year after his mother and father were married, and Bridget soon after that, with him following a year later, and Colin nearly three years after. Yet here he was, two years into his marriage and not a hint of a child on the way.

That thought jolted him so, he flinched right there in front of everyone, though the movement was so slight no one noticed. No one except Maria, that is. She glanced up at him, frowning and tensing slightly.

He raised his glass, sipped his wine, then gave her an innocent look and smiled. As he slipped an arm around her waist and kissed her cheek, while everyone applauded and raised their own glasses in answer to Bainbridge's toast, she relaxed.

The thought persisted, however. Though he might hide it from the others, the lack of a child in their home stayed with him for the rest of the evening.

That night, after everyone had left and they were alone in their room, Maria confronted him.

"What happened?"

"What do you mean? When?" He kept his back turned, carefully unfolding his cravat.

"Don't do that, Padraig."

She saw right through him. Padraig cursed silently. *Why do I have t' have such a perceptive wife?*

"When Milton gave his toast, your expression...what happened?"

He turned to look at her. As usual, he'd helped her undress, "playing the lady's maid," so he always joked, unbuttoning her gown, unlacing the corset, pulling the ruffles and flounces over her head and draping them over a chair. She stood before him beautiful and bare, and truly he didn't want to talk about it, so…

When he would've taken her in his arms, she pushed him away.

"Here now. Are you rejectin' me, woman?"

"Of course not," she denied. "Perhaps, yes…for a moment or two…until you tell me what was wrong tonight."

"If that's the way you want it." He turned back to unbuttoning his shirt and shedding it while she settled herself in the bed.

After placing his boots next to the wardrobe and sliding out of his trousers, he came to his side of the bed. She didn't speak, simply sat there, looking so delicious and enticing, and…

"That toast… It came to me we're two years wed and we've no babe." He got it out in one sentence. Then he blew out the lamp, climbed into bed, pulled the quilt up to his chin, and rolled away from her.

There was silence for several seconds before he felt a small hand touch his shoulder.

"Does it bother you so much?"

"Aye," he turned back, looking up at her. "Me parents had me an' me braithurs an' sister all within six years, starting within a year o' their marriage. That last letter I got from home… 'Twas t' tell me Colin's been married a year an' he already has a son, while I…"

He sat up, shaking his head angrily, but who he was angry at, he wasn't certain.

"I've made love t' you e'ery night o' our marriage, Maria, as I promised, but…" He hesitated, then burst out, "…naithin's happened. I haven't used th' fishskin since our weddin' night." He gave a slight ironic laugh. "I imagine th' thing's unusable now. Still, *acushla*…" His eyes met hers, in a shockingly direct stare. "You haven't done anythin' t' prevent us from havin' a babe, have you?"

It took Maria several seconds before she answered. She was shocked Padraig would ask such a thing, as well as the suggestion she might know how. True, she hadn't actually thought of having a child, believing it would automatically happen…sometime…but that wasn't the same thing as preventing one, was it?

"Padraig, be assured I want a baby as much as you do." She gave him a gentle smile holding unintentional sympathy.

He saw it and looked away, as if he couldn't meet her gaze. "Can it be I'm…inadequate?"

The word hung in the air like an accusation.

"Of course not." Her answer was vehement, sharp and loud. She seized his shoulder, pulling Padraig around to face her. "There's nothing about you that's inadequate, Padraig McCoy, and you stop thinking that. Right now."

She gave him a little shake, relaxing slightly when he smiled sheepishly.

"If we don't have a child yet, it's because it isn't the time."

She put her arms around him and he gently touched her back.

"You think th' Good Lord's kept them from us because He thinks I'm not ready t' be a faithur?" Padraig sounded as if he'd never thought of that. "I want t' be, Maria. Shouldn't that make a difference?"

"It does," she soothed. "And it will." She lay down, clasping his face in her hands and kissing him. As usual, his moustache tickled her lip and she smoothed it with her fingers. "In the meantime…"

"In th' meantime?" he repeated.

"You'll just have to keep trying." She pulled him toward her.

That was the first time she ever used the intimacies of their marriage bed to distract and console him, but it wouldn't be the last.

In the morning, as soon as she heard Čik'ayela Wanáhča's moccasined footsteps on the stairs, Maria threw on one of the nightgowns Padraig had bought her but she'd never worn. Thrusting her arms into her wrapper, she followed the housekeeper down the stairs.

"Miz Maria, what you do here so early?" Čik'ayela Wanáhča stood with the spatterware cookpot in hand, preparing to brew the first coffee of the day.

"I've something to ask you," Maria said.

"What is it?" Čik'ayela Wanáhča set the pot on the worktable.

"Shh, don't speak so loudly." Maria put a finger to her lips. "I don't want Mr. Padraig to hear."

Čik'ayela Wanáhča didn't answer. She simply frowned and waited for Maria to explain.

The explanation was a while in coming. For several moments, Maria paced back and forth in the space between the stove and the worktable, wringing her hands while Čik'ayela Wanáhča waited patiently.

As last Maria turned and said, with the air of someone confessing a dreadful secret, "Mr. Padraig wants to have a child."

"Do you?" was all Čik'ayela Wanáhča asked.

"Of course." Maria looked slightly angry the housekeeper might think otherwise. "Even if I didn't," she added, "I love my husband and I'll do everything I can to give him a son."

"Yes," Čik'ayela Wanáhča agreed. "Men need sons."

"It's not that I haven't thought of it, too," Maria went on, seemingly speaking mostly to herself. "I simply didn't expect there to be a problem. I thought…"

She stopped, spun, and looked back at the housekeeper.

"I have to give him a child. A man like Padraig…he's…"

"He's proud," Čik'ayela Wanáhča finished for her. "To be childless will make him think himself less of a man."

"You understand, then?" Maria looked relieved.

"Miss Maria, why tell *me* this?"

"Because…I…" Maria shook her head as if she couldn't find the exact words. Her face blazed pink, then went white. "I thought you might know some way…Flying Bird once told me her…your people…know of herbs and…things. That could aid…fertility…" The words trailed away into silence.

"Ahh." Čik'ayela Wanáhča nodded as if everything was abruptly very clear. She looked around the kitchen. "There are some things here I could use."

"Really?" Maria looked around also, disappointed when she saw nothing immediately advertising itself as a cure for childlessness.

"Yes." The housekeeper walked to the pantry, pulling open the door. She disappeared inside and returned a few moments later, setting some things on the table.

Maria looked at the items. "Carrots? And…what's that?" She pointed to several shreds of something translucent and amber like hardened tree sap.

"Ginger," Čik'ayela Wanáhča answered. "Cookie says it's good in cakes. We got it in our government supplies, but I don't make cakes so well." She smiled slightly, then shrugged.

"That's no problem," Maria answered. "Your pies make up for it."

"I can put it in a pie." The housekeeper brightened. "The carrots go in soups and stews, or I can boil them with honey. I use them already."

"They must not be working." Maria was well aware she had eaten carrots on various occasions. "What else is there?"

"Other things, but not here. In the garden, there are raspberries. Near the river, I've seen agaric, and on the prairie, there are cornflowers, sunflowers, and milk thistle."

"If they're on the prairie," Maria persisted, "how will you…"

"When I visit my people," Čik'ayela Wanáhča answered. "I'll gather cornflowers, thistle, and sunflowers on the return trip." Remembering Padraig always rode with her, insisting on escorting her, she added, "I'll tell Mr. Padraig I need them for Cookie's medicine box."

"Oh, Čik'ayela Wanáhča, how can I ever thank you?" Maria clasped the woman's hand.

"Don't worry, Miz Maria, I'll help you give Mr. Padraig his son." Čik'ayela Wanáhča gave her a conspiratorial smile. "I'll make special food for both of you. Today…I think today for breakfast Mr. Padraig should have one of those omelets he likes so, with carrots and mushrooms."

Padraig declared his breakfast that morning was the best he'd had in some time.

Chapter 42

Early Spring, 1863

Time for another trail drive rolled around. Though he'd reluctantly gone on the previous one, this time Padraig was abruptly assailed with a presage of danger. For some reason even he couldn't explain, he became certain that, if he left Maria, something terrible would happen.

Because of that, he suggested Buck ride in his place, with Big Jack serving as trail boss as usual. Not wanting to alarm Maria by what he considered a premonition, he skirted telling her the real reason he chose to stay behind, giving various implausible reasons, such as too much needing his presence at the ranch, what with the town growing so in the past two years. The war was making McCoy's Crossing into a prosperous town—nay, now 'twas big enough to be called a city, and he and the council had many things to discuss concerning its expansion.

"Don't lie to me, Padraig." Even as she said that, Maria felt a twinge because she was the one lying in this marriage. Perhaps that gave her enough insight into knowing Padraig well enough to say that. "What's the real reason?"

Confronted like that, Padraig didn't intend further prevarication.

"I've a feelin'," he admitted, "of impendin' doom. I know that sounds dramatic, but 'tis th' way I feel, *acushla,* an' it started th' moment I thought of goin' on that drive."

"Is there any reason you should think such a thing?" Maria demanded. When he shook his head, she asked, "Do you have that Second Sight you told me some Irishmen do? Can you see the future?"

Secretly, she didn't believe in such, but if her husband did…

Again, he shook his head. "I don't have th' Sight, not as far as I know."

"You probably drank too much coffee this morning," Čik'ayela Wanáhča called from the kitchen.

She wasn't eavesdropping. They were standing in the parlor doorway and she couldn't help overhearing.

"I've noticed when anyone around here drinks much of that, they seem to get anxious."

She wondered if she'd put a little too much chickweed in his breakfast cup that morning. She decided she'd better lessen the dosage of fertility-aiding herbs a bit where Mr. Padraig was concerned. As far as she could tell, the amount of herbs she gave Maria was all right.

In the end, it took Maria two days of arguing, listening, sympathizing, and urging before Padraig changed his mind.

"Aye, I'll go, then, if you're certain?" Her assurance that she was made him add, "Then we'll leave in th' mornin'. I've some business in town I need t' take care of first. I'm sorry I've been such a worrier, lass."

With that, he saddled the pinto, kissed her, and rode into McCoy's Crossing.

Padraig went directly to John Blackstone's office. He greeted the lawyer, nodded to Benjamin True, who looked surprisingly comfortable in a frockcoat and cravat and seated at a nearby desk, then stated with no preamble, "John, I've come t' make out me will."

"Will?" That made Blackstone sit up from his recline behind his own desk. "You aren't ill, are you, Padraig?"

"Nay, but I'm goin' on anaithur cattle drive, an' 'tis occured t' me I've made one drive an' shouldn't make anaithur with naithin' in place should somethin' happen to me as it did Mr. Jessup."

"Good thinking," Blackstone replied, wondering why he hadn't realized this himself and suggested it to the younger man as soon as he heard of Padraig's marriage. He pulled a few sheets of foolscap from a desk drawer and opened his inkwell, selecting a pen. "What do you want it to say?"

"Guess we'd start off with th' usual lawyer talk," Padraig answered. "Th' bein' o' sound mind an' all that..." He waited while Blackstone wrote those phrases. "I make you executor o' me estate, John, because you're better equipped t' handle th' sort o' things I want done." He glanced at True. "With Benjamin as back-up, if needed."

The lawyer nodded, not really surprised. A good many of the businessmen as well as ranchers had named him their executor. When those men began dying, he was going to have his hands full administering their estates. He'd truly need Benjamin then.

"I leave e'erythin' t' Maria, o' course," Padraig continued. He mentioned a few bequests and then said, "I want th' ranch t' be sold."

"Are you sure of that?"

"Maria won't be able t' run it, e'en with Buck's help, an' I don't want some scoundrel comin' in an' buyin' it an' bilkin' her o' its true value. I know you'll be honest with her about sellin' th' property. Then she'll be set as far as money's concerned."

"What about where she'll live?" Blackstone asked.

"I've a letter here." Padraig took a letter from his breast pocket. "Would you mail it for me?"

Blackstone nodded and accepted it.

"'Tis t' me faithur, askin' him t' take Maria in an' care for her, an if she wishes t' remarry, help her find a good an' honest husband."

"Damn, Padraig." Benjamin looked astounded. "I don't know many men who'd go that far in providing for their wives."

"Maybe they don't love them as much as I do Maria."

Padraig sat silently as Blackstone meticulously wrote out his requests, making certain the entire document was legible. After he was finished, the lawyer copied the will onto another set of foolscap. He handed both papers to Padraig.

"Read over each to make certain I've copied it correctly."

While Padraig was reading, Blackstone went to the door of his office, opened it, and looked out. The boardwalks were filled with people, townsfolk, ranchers, and farmers walking about. The mayor went past, while on the other side of the street was Delsey speaking to someone in front of the general store.

"Bainbridge. Just the man I want to see." He motioned the mayor over, then called, "Delsey, hey!

Come over here. Got a favor to ask."

As the general store's owner waited for a horse and wagon to pass before crossing the street, Bainbridge turned and came back to where Blackstone stood.

"What do you need, Josiah?"

Blackstone waited until Delsey arrived before answering. "Need you two as witnesses to the signing of a will."

"Certainly," Delsey said. "Whose?"

Blackstone didn't answer, simply ushered them into his office.

"Padraig?" Bainbridge looked surprised, then nodded. "Excellent idea, my boy. Surprised you haven't already done this."

Padraig looked up, smiling a greeting. "I'm surprised I hadn't thought o' it before, Mayor."

"Everything in order?" Blackstone asked.

Padraig nodded and laid the two wills on the desk.

"Then sign at the X." Blackstone dipped the pen into the ink and held it out to him. Taking it, Padraig signed both sheets, then gave the pen to Bainbridge. The mayor and Delsey duly wrote their names in the spaces Blackstone had provided, and Delsey returned the pen to the lawyer.

"Thank you, gentlemen." Blackstone replaced the pen in its holder, took a blotter, and pressed it against the signatures. "Ben?"

The Lakota took something from his desk, brought it over, and picked up the sheets. He slid each one into the side of the little silver object that looked almost like the garlic press Padraig remembered his father's cook using. When he released it, there was an embossed mark on the paper. He did the same to the second.

"There. Both notarized."

Blackstone placed the original will in the safe behind his desk, then folded the other and gave it to Padraig. "Now, what say we adjourn to Trails End and have a drink to celebrate the responsibility Padraig here has given me?"

"Guess I'll stay here," Ben returned to his desk. "Trails End still has a 'No Indians Allowed' policy, even if I'm now an accepted lawyer."

"Why don't you hire yourself to fight that?" Padraig asked.

Ben shook his head. "I can't afford me, Padraig."

"Do you still want to go, Josiah?" Bainbridge asked. He looked as if he might decline also.

"Sorry I can't go with you gents, either," Padraig said. "Got t' get back t' th' ranch an' get ready if I'm leavin' in th' mornin'.

"Trail drive?" Bainbridge asked.

Padraig nodded.

"Making that will now is a truly smart move."

Though he didn't particularly wish to hear that, Padraig agreed. He thanked all four men and left the office.

****

12 March, 1863
Quinton Francis Xavier McCoy, Esquire
McCoy Hall
Tipperary, Ireland
The United Kingdom of Great Britain

Honoured Father,
It is time for me to make another cattle drive to Sedalia. If you'll hark back to one of my previous letters

in which I recounted to you the death of my employer, Mr. Jessup, which resulted in my buying his ranch, you can appreciate what I'm about to ask of you.

With the added responsibility of a wife, I now realize with each drive in what a dangerous situation I find myself. Therefore, I have made a will in the event something untoward should happen. The provisions are simple: With the exception of a few bequests, I leave everything to Maria, appointing my lawyer in McCoy's Crossing to administer my estate. I wish the ranch to be sold so she'll have enough money to provide for her. Father, I would ask you to offer Maria a home at McCoy Hall should she find herself my widow. She has no family, and I beg that you take her in and give her the same love and care you would Bridey, Felicity, or Colin's wife should either find herself so bereaved.

If she should find someone to console her, I would also hope you'd make certain he's a good and honest man and will truly care for her.

I write this trusting you won't let my past sins be passed to my wife and, if necessary, will honour this request I make of you in the name of blood ties and family.

Your son,
Padraig Aloysius Francis McCoy
Owner, The Shamrock Ranch
McCoy's Crossing, Nebraska Territory,
United States of America

Chapter 43

By the time Padraig got back to the ranch, the men had finished rounding up the cattle. The herd milled close to the gates through which they'd be driven to the trail leading southward. Cookie was putting the last supplies into the chuck wagon. All he needed to do was harness the horses.

The thirteen men going on the drive had picked out their horses, and the wrangler was ready to drive them into a remuda.

Buck was pacing in front of the ranch house, waiting for Padraig to return from whatever had taken him into town. Maria had told him the boss had an errand, but even she was unaware of its nature. He didn't walk onto the porch because he didn't want the sound of his boot heels on the boards bothering her.

Will and Sam and the others hovered near the bunkhouse, anxious as everyone else for Padraig's return.

"It ain't like he and Miss Maria are newlyweds," Will grumbled. "Dang it, I know he loves her. Hell, if I had a sweet little woman like that, I might find it hard to leave her, too, but damn it, Buck, he went on the drive before without this much trouble. Why now?"

Will's question went unanswered as the sound of hoofbeats made them look toward the road leading into the ranch yard.

Padraig rode the pinto to the hitching post, dismounted, and said, "I'll bed down me horse after supper."

He looked at Buck, who stopped his pacing but didn't speak.

"Guess you're goin' t' have t' put up with me ridin' along this time, too." He went into the house, calling out, "Maria...*a chroi*? I'm back."

Buck turned to look at the others. Will took off his hat and slapped his thigh.

"Thank God, Boss McCoy's back! Now we won't have to be bullied by you on the trail like you do here at the ranch."

He dodged the mock swing Buck took at him and ran back to the bunkhouse.

Inside, Padraig went directly to his office, putting the will into the little safe he'd had the architect build into the wall. Inside was also a copy of the deed to the Shamrock, his marriage certificate, and several hundred dollars in greenbacks. Closing the safe, he turned to see Maria standing in the doorway and hurried to take her in his arms.

"You got back just in time for supper," she said.

"An' 'tis very hungry I am." He swung her into his arms, walking out of the office. "What are we havin'?"

"I found a recipe called 'Irish Stew' though I imagine it's not like anything an Irishman ever ate," she replied.

"Ah...tha's me second favorite meal." He reached the first step going upstairs.

"What's your favorite?" she asked.

"We're ten steps away from your findin' out," he told her as he carried her up the stairs.

****

In the morning before the sun was barely peeping over the prairie's flat horizon, Buck, on his horse and leading the pinto, waited at the front door. In the pre-dawn quiet, the others were already mounted and guiding the herd down the road onto the prairie, the chuck wagon rolling along behind. Except for the eerie call of a mourning dove, a soft snort and an occasional complaint from one of the cattle were the only sounds breaking the silence.

The front door opened and Padraig came out. He was dressed for hard riding, in trail coat and chaps. Over his shoulder he'd slung his saddlebags, with his bedroll under his arm.

Maria followed.

He kissed her and said, "I'll see you when I get back, *acushla.*" Nodding to Buck, he swung into the saddle. "Let's get these steers on their way."

Chapter 44

The morning after Padraig and his men left on the drive, Čik'ayela Wanáhča was in the kitchen, preparing breakfast. Though most of the men were gone now, she still had to cook for the four remaining hands and Maria. Philosophically, she felt it was no more difficult preparing a meal for six than it was for twenty...or fifty when Mr. Padraig decided to have another of his parties.

There had been a good many parties after that housewarming. Mr. Padraig was definitely a man who liked gathering his friends around him. Cookie was a help then, she didn't deny.

She smiled as she thought of the chuck wagon cook. A good man, helpful and kind to her when he could've been very resentful of the way she'd taken his place after he was assured she was merely there to keep the house tidy and cook for the boss and his wife. A fairly good-looking man, too, and if she hadn't told herself she'd never take another husband...and certainly not a white man...Cookie might've found himself a likely candidate.

As it was, Čik'ayela Wanáhča found the cook as close to a friend as a white cowboy could be to a Lakota woman.

She might've taken on more work for herself by becoming cook for the entire ranch, but Čik'ayela Wanáhča found herself enjoying it. It was much different work from that she'd done at the encampment. Sewing and mending torn shirts and replacing buttons wasn't as difficult as softening an antelope hide by pounding it with a stone, then chewing it, but she never actually had to create a garment since the white men bought theirs ready-made at the place in town called the general store. Nevertheless, at the camp, she'd never had to dust or sweep and mop a tent floor, and there had always been others to help in cooking and preparing food.

Čik'ayela Wanáhča laughed quietly.

At least, she didn't have to help butcher a cow or dress it as she and the other women did the antelope, buffalo, or other game the men brought back from the areas they were allowed to hunt. Mr. Padraig took care of that when they needed more beef, though she did have to catch and kill a chicken if she decided to vary the meat from beef and pork on occasion.

As for the rest of it, when Mr. Padraig rode into town each month to get provisions, he generally took both her and Miz Maria with him. Čik'ayela Wanáhča quickly overcame her amazement at the act of simply walking into that general store, telling the man behind the counter what she wished, and having him bring it out and place it before her. She was also astonished by the way the man treated her, the same as did the others they might see outside the store. He was almost friendly. He never failed to ask her what she was planning to cook Mr. Padraig and Miz Maria that night, then saying he wished he was being invited for supper. So far, except for the parties, Padraig had never given anyone a dinner invitation, however.

Čik'ayela Wanáhča was beginning to think perhaps white men weren't as bad as she'd believed all these years. Except for the loss of her Flying Bird and her son, and the fact that she and her part of the Lakota were more or less confined to that small area near the Platte, she might actually believe it. Certainly the way she and Speaks Truth were now treated was evidence of that. She often saw Speaks Truth when she returned to the encampment, though he now dressed in white men's clothing. He returned often, also, bringing with him money, part of the salary the lawyer paid him, which he turned over to his father to be placed in a buckskin pouch Eagle-of-Iron kept under his sleeping mat.

She was relatively happy in her new home, no matter how it came about. Maria and Mr. Padraig were the main reason. She looked upon them both with an affection startling her in its intensity. Though she had a fondness for Maria, Padraig was her favorite. She saw him as both the independent rancher going about his business with self-assurance, as well as a slightly overgrown child needing pampering now and then, but in a way that wasn't obvious. His red hair fascinated her. She'd seen other men with light-colored hair but never one whose hair was such a brilliant copper.

As for Miz Maria…much as Čik'ayela Wanáhča was coming to care for Padraig's wife, she would be the first to admit *the girl is lazy.* Not that she'd ever say that to Padraig. She'd immediately seen through Maria's ploy of being too weak and delicate to do housework but never mentioned it. Why should she? Her own Flying Bird had been the same way. Even at the age of five, there were chores the child managed to convince someone else to do. Even her brother could be tricked into carrying water or helping to gather herbs.

Čik'ayela Wanáhča had to smile as she saw the way Maria had Padraig wrapped around her little finger, but it wasn't her place to speak of how he spoiled his wife. After all, it was that very trait bringing her here to the two people she was rapidly coming to care for as much as she had her own family.

During the day, while Čik'ayela Wanáhča worked in the kitchen, Maria sat with her, though she did no work. She explained that was what *being a companion* meant, having the housekeeper keep her company by talking to her while she worked.

The Lakota woman accepted that. She enjoyed it when the young woman spoke to her about her daughter, relating things happening at that white man's school, of things Flying Bird had said or done. She had no idea Maria was merely changing the story a bit, telling her mother of experiences she herself had in those years as she grew from a frightened five-year-old into the young eighteen-year-old determined to become something she wasn't.

She also was unaware how many times Maria wanted to say to her, *Mama...it's Flying Bird...I've come home to you*, but didn't dare because she'd sworn no one, not even her own mother, would ever know her real identity.

Maria lied and made her past life into the stories she told Čik'ayela Wanáhča, speaking of her younger self as of someone else. It made Čik'ayela Wanáhča happy, she rationalized, so what harm was there in that part of the lie?

****

Punctual as always, the remaining men trooped in, ate their meal, drank the coffee, told her how good it was...then left to do their chores. Even with the boss gone, there was plenty to keep them busy, and they all knew what to do without being watched over.

It was then Čik'ayela Wanáhča realized Maria had missed breakfast.

At first, she thought perhaps she was merely enjoying being in bed without her husband's demanding body beside her, and exercising her prerogative to sleep a little longer.

Čik'ayela Wanáhča had no disillusions concerning Padraig's lustiness in those evening hours before they slept. Hadn't she seen him kiss Miss Maria in plain sight enough? Hug her also? He wasn't quiet in his loving, and the sounds she often heard coming from the master bedroom at the other end of the hall definitely weren't the noise of quarrel but of tender marital joining.

That was why, as she finished washing the dishes and stacking them on the end of the worktable, ready to be used for the noon meal, she realized it was much later than it should be and Maria still hadn't appeared.

Something was wrong.

Hurrying down the hall and up the stairs, she knocked anxiously on the bedroom door.

"Miz Maria...are you all right?"

At first, there wasn't an answer. Then, very faintly, she heard, "Čik'ayela Wanáhča...help me..." followed by the sound of gagging.

She pushed open the door and rushed in.

Maria lay against the pillows, pale and limp. She had one arm across her forehead as if shielding her eyes from the light. The bosom of her nightgown was spattered and stained.

"Miz Maria, what's the matter?" The fear in Čik'ayela Wanáhča's voice was real. Maria's pallor frightened her.

"Oh, Čik'ayela Wanáhča..." The answer was faint as she struggled to sit up. She swallowed loudly. "I-I don't know. I felt fine when Padraig left. I was trying to decide if I should sleep a bit more when I heard you moving around in the kitchen, and the sound of bacon frying. It always smells so good, but this morning, when I took a deep breath..."

She broke off and began to gag again as if the very thought was enough to make her ill. Hand to her mouth, she leaned over the edge of the bed, reaching under it. Čik'ayela Wanáhča stooped and pulled the chamber pot from under the bed. It was nearly filled. Nevertheless, she brought it up as Maria began to vomit.

The upheaval was over quickly.

"What's the matter with me?" Maria fell back onto the pillow, tears of fear in her eyes. "I feel awful...my stomach's so..."

"Shh, you'll be all right."

Čik'ayela Wanáhča set the chamber pot back under the bed, reminding herself to empty it later. She hurried to the little washstand on the other side of the room where the ironstone pitcher and basin sat. Pouring water, she dipped the end of her apron in it, wrung it, and ran back to the bed.

"When did this start?" She pressed the damp apron against Maria's forehead, blotting her face and cheeks.

"I..." Maria frowned, thinking. "A few days ago...but I wasn't really sick that time, just...a little queasy. I love the smell of bacon and eggs when it floats up the stairs, but today...did you cook eggs this morning?"

"I always cook eggs for breakfast," Čik'ayela Wanáhča reminded her. She began to dry Maria's face, noting her color was slowly returning.

"The smell's never bothered me before…except as I said… Oh!" She glanced at the door. Čik'ayela Wanáhča had left it open, and the scents from the kitchen had followed her…eggs, bacon, biscuits… "Open the window, quick…get the smell out of here!"

Maria placed fingers against her nose and mouth as Čik'ayela Wanáhča hurried to the window and flung it open so quickly the upper sash crashed against the frame. She came back to the bed.

"I'll get you another nightgown to wear. This one is stained."

Opening one of the chest of drawers, she extracted another of the frilly gowns and deftly removed the one Maria wore, replacing it. As she smoothed the lacy collar, she continued, "You must stay in bed today. I'll make something to soothe your stomach…"

"I can't eat anything," Maria protested. "I'm sure I'll get sick again."

Čik'ayela Wanáhča shook her head. "You must eat. I make something…what is that word? Bland."

She reached behind Maria and fluffed the pillows.

Maria settled herself. She hiccoughed slightly, put a hand to her mouth, then her stomach, held her breath, and relaxed when nothing else happened.

"You'll be fine." Čik'ayela Wanáhča patted her shoulder as she tucked the quilt around her.

"Are you sure?" Maria asked anxiously. "You don't think I have that dreadful influenza Padraig told me about? He said people died from that, and the symptoms…"

"Is there anything you'd like me to cook for you?" Čik'ayela Wanáhča thought a moment, then changed the subject.

"Nothing." Maria looked away and moaned slightly. "At this moment, there's nothing in this world I want...no, wait...are the raspberries ripe yet? I'd like some raspberries..." She closed her eyes. "Yes, a nice, tart raspberry or two... I went to the garden a couple of days ago, but they weren't quite ready to be picked."

Čik'ayela Wanáhča nodded as if that confirmed something. "I think I may be able to find a few."

"Would you soak them in honey and...sprinkle some crushed red peppers over everything?" Maria sighed, actually licking her lower lip in anticipation as Čik'ayela Wanáhča looked startled by that particular combination. "That will taste so good."

"Don't worry, Miz Maria. You don't have this influenza."

"You sound very certain," Maria said.

"I am."

"Do you know what's wrong with me?"

"Yes, Miz Maria. I believe I do." Čik'ayela Wanáhča fell silent.

"What is it?" Maria cried out. "What terrible disease do I have?" She began to gag, looked frightened, then swallowed loudly and relaxed again.

"You have no disease," Čik'ayela Wanáhča answered. "My herbs have worked. That's all."

"Your herbs? What..." Maria stopped, her expression changing from fright to confusion to abrupt understanding. "You mean...oh!"

Čik'ayela Wanáhča placed a gentle hand on her belly. "You carry the little one Mr. Padraig wants, Miz Maria."

Maria's own hand covered hers, pressing against the

soft batiste of her gown. Her other hand went to her mouth. A single tear trickled down her cheek.

"Stay in bed today," Čik'ayela Wanáhča ordered. Her eyes twinkled. "Now, you have an excuse not to do housework."

"What do you mean?" Maria's own eyes flickered guiltily, then opened wide.

"I mean, you may have fooled Mr. Padraig and the others, but not Čik'ayela Wanáhča," the housekeeper said. "You're not as delicate as you pretend, Miz Maria...and now's the time to show exactly how strong you are."

Maria began to sob.

"Don't be afraid."

"I'm not afraid." Maria's damp eyes met hers. She wiped away the tears. "I'm simply so happy. I wish I'd known before Padraig left." She thought about that. "I guess my timing was bad. If I'd been sick yesterday..."

"Mr. Padraig definitely wouldn't have gone on that trail drive," Čik'ayela Wanáhča finished for her.

They both laughed.

"I go and make you some oatmeal," the housekeeper decided. "With a little honey...and raspberries, if there are any, and red pepper. There are still a few of those peppermint sticks Mr. Padraig brought from the last trip to the general store. I'll bring you one to suck on. That'll help you keep food down."

She hurried away.

Behind her came a loud, heartfelt sigh. Čik'ayela Wanáhča smiled.

It'll be good to have a little one in the house. She wondered which parent the baby would look like.

Chapter 45

Sam had been sent into town to get supplies. As if everyone was still in residence, Čik'ayela Wanáhča ordered staples and everything else to stock the pantry's shelves. It had been nearly six weeks since Padraig and the others rode out of the Shamrock, and she expected them back any time, starved for something other than Cookie's meals, which they'd always appreciated before she arrived.

With each meal she cooked for the men, she was still astonished Cookie never took exception to the compliments they gave her...and for that she was sincerely grateful.

She was startled to hear hoofbeats pounding, two horses running at breakneck speed. Carrying the mixing bowl in which she was stirring batter for biscuits, she hurried through the parlor to the front door. Maria, sitting on the settee, clumsily attempting to sew a little shirt to relieve her boredom during Padraig's absence, looked up.

"What is it?"

"Horses. Don't you hear?"

"Yes, but I thought it was Sam." Maria looked startled. "You don't think so?"

She got to her feet, dropping the shirt to the cushions as Maria opened the door.

The buckboard with Sam holding the reins careened

directly toward the porch steps. Čik'ayela Wanáhča took a step back inside as he pulled on the reins so roughly the horses were nearly jerked onto their haunches. He leaped from the wagon seat before either animal could recover, running to the ranch house as the housekeeper came onto the porch.

"Miz Maria...there's a telegram for you!" He held up a piece of paper, waving it.

"Telegram?" Maria whispered.

She pushed past Čik'ayela Wanáhča, reaching for the paper as Sam came up the steps.

"Stationmaster gave it to me. He was getting ready to send a rider out when I showed up to fetch the mail." Sam was panting as if he, and not the horses, had run all the way from town. "I brung it as fast as I could."

"I hope you didn't injure the horses." Maria surprised herself that she could think of the animals at that moment. *A telegram. That isn't good. A telegram's always bad news.*

She took the paper from him. It was folded. She didn't open it.

"Have you read it?"

"No, ma'am," Sam's eyes flicked away briefly as he admitted, "I can't read."

She shook her head in apology, staring at the folded sheet. She looked at Čik'ayela Wanáhča. The housekeeper shook her head, also.

"I can't read white man's writing, either. You must read it, Miz Maria." She looked at Sam. "Did the stationmaster say who it is from?"

"The boss." He nodded.

Taking a deep breath, Maria unfolded the paper.

START *My dear wife* STOP *little problem*

preventing my coming home STOP *will be a bit later than expected* STOP *do not worry* STOP *your loving husband Padraig* END

"Don't *worry*?" Maria looked up. "That means something's terribly wrong. What could it be?" She glanced at Sam. "There was nothing else?"

"No, ma'am." He shook his head. "That's all. Wasn't even any mail this time."

Maria didn't answer, staring at the words pasted on the yellow form as if they could tell her more than she already knew.

"Maybe it means he's having a hard time getting the price he wants," Sam offered. "I remember once he haggled three days with a buyer before they reached an agreement."

"I imagine that's it." Maria's tone indicated she believed no such thing. "Drive the wagon around to the kitchen." She looked at Čik'ayela Wanáhča, who clutched the mixing bowl, her own expression betraying concern. "Help Sam unload things. I'm going back inside. I think I need to sit down."

"Are you all right?" Čik'ayela Wanáhča shifted the bowl and placed a hand on her arm.

"I'm fine." Maria patted the hand. "I simply need to rest a bit, that's all. Hurrying out here is something I shouldn't have done."

She went inside, back to the settee where she picked up the tiny garment, studying the amateurish stitches and uneven hemming. Seamstressery had never been her strongpoint, and she'd often been punished for that while in school, a fact making her more resistant to becoming better.

She pressed the little shirt to her lips to stop their

314

trembling.

Oh, Padraig, what has happened?

Four more weeks passed before the day Maria came to the door to see Cookie's wagon roll into the yard with fourteen horsemen following it. Frantically, she scanned the faces—dusty, sunburned, bewhiskered—until she found the one she sought…as trail weary and dirty as the rest, his red hair powdered a dingy brown by prairie dust.

"Padraig…" She breathed, so softly Čik'ayela Wanáhča glanced at her sharply.

She was down the steps and starting toward him, only to stop when he didn't dismount but sat stiffly in the saddle. There was something odd about one of his arms.

It wasn't in the sleeve of his duster but strapped across his chest in a dingy sling wrapped around his neck.

Before Maria could ask, Buck was off his own horse, coming over and catching Padraig about the waist, easing him off the horse.

As if he's an old man. The thought shocked her.

Buck's movements were careful and gentle as if he were handling something very fragile. Padraig dropped the horse's reins and practically fell from the saddle, grasping the horn with his right hand.

It was then she realized he was riding a different horse and not the pinto. This one was the skewbald sorrel.

Buck set Padraig on his feet, steadied him, and stepped back. She heard Padraig mutter gratitude and look toward her.

"Hello, *acushla*." Even his voice sounded different, hollow and reedy.

"What happened?" She didn't return the greeting.

315

"Why is your arm wrapped like that? Where's the pinto?"

He took a step toward her. It was so shaky she thought he was going to fall. Buck must have also because he edged closer to Padraig, hands going out slightly, then dropping to his sides. The look he threw Maria was unreadable.

Apologetic?

"Pinto was getting old," Padraig rasped. "Needed a new horse."

"There was a stampede," Buck burst out. "The pinto went down. The boss was thrown clear but his horse didn't get up."

"Stampede? Padraig?" Maria felt a bolt of fear go through her. He'd told her how his former boss died. She remembered the tears in his eyes as he spoke. She took another step.

"I'm all right, sweet." With his good hand, Padraig removed his hat.

The brim had shaded his face. Now a massive empurpling around his left eye and down his cheek was visible. That side of his face was swollen above the heavy beard grown on the drive.

Maria stared. There was a sudden loud ringing in her ears. The sun became too bright. *What's happening?* Her vision narrowed, black swirling around its edges. Her knees buckled as her eyes rolled upward.

Padraig made a futile effort to catch her, grimacing in pain. He could only stand helplessly as his wife collapsed at his feet. Luckily Buck caught her before she hit the ground, scooping her into his arms.

"Bring her inside," Čik'ayela Wanáhča ordered, pulling open the screen door.

Hefting Maria's body, the foreman hurried up the steps. Inside, he laid her gently on the settee while Padraig clumsily followed, shouting over his shoulder, "Go on an' get yourselves settled, boys."

He was certain Maria would be embarrassed that his men had seen her react so. In the next moment, he forgot his men and anything except his wife.

"What happened? Damn it, I knew I should've sent her a letter. She's so damned delicate…and this shock…" He looked around, seeing Buck and taking out his fear on the foreman. "Damn it, Buck, why couldn't you keep your big mouth shut?"

"She had to know, Boss," Buck defended himself. "Would you ever tell her what really happened?"

Stung that he knew him so well, Padraig snapped, "It wasn't your place. Get out o' here! Get t' th' bunkhouse before I do somethin' I shouldn't."

"You got a broken arm, Boss. How much can you do?" Nevertheless, Buck left as fast as he could.

"Get me some water." Padraig ordered, coming around the settee and pulling Čik'ayela Wanáhča away from Maria, though that caused another grunt of pain as the movement of his body transferred itself to his injured arm. He dropped into the place she vacated.

There was something white lying on the floor, knocked there when Buck laid Maria on the settee. He picked it up, fingering the soft white fabric. A handkerchief? It had embroidery. Surely those awkward stitches had to be Maria's. She was sewing him a handkerchief? His heart did an uncharacteristic twinge at this sign of her love.

Čik'ayela Wanáhča reappeared with a small basin of water. He dipped the piece of cloth into it, brought it out dripping, and began to pat Maria's face.

She moved slightly, then came awake, blinking water out of her eyes. Pushing his hands away, she wiped her face.

"Stop…" She sat up, saw what he held, and burst into tears. "Oh, Padraig, you've ruined it!"

"Nay, lass." He dropped the sodden thing to the floor. "'Twill dry and be as good as a handkerchief can be."

"Handkerchief?" she shrieked. "It's not a handkerchief, you foolish man."

Behind him, he heard Čik'ayela Wanáhča make a sound suspiciously like a snicker.

"Nay? What is it then, an' why are you so upset?"

"I'm upset because I've just learned my husband was in a stampede in which his horse got killed and he broke his arm and…" Her hands went to his chest, fluttering downward. "Was anything else hurt?"

"Nay, and the doc in Sedalia says th' arm will be good as new in a couple more weeks."

To that, she slapped his unharmed one, and burst into tears again.

"I thought that might make you happy," he said. "It appears I've made it worse."

"It's not that…it's…" She picked up the wet bit of cloth, squeezed it and looked at the water dripping between her fingers onto the lap of her dress. "Čik'ayela Wanáhča, give us a moment alone, please. I need to speak to my husband privately."

The housekeeper didn't answer, simply nodded and disappeared through the doorway. Maria waited until she heard her steps in the kitchen.

She looked again at the wet piece of cloth she was

clutching so tightly.

"What is that thing anyway," Padraig asked, "if 'tisn't a handkerchief. Why are you so upset about it?"

"Because…" She dropped it to her lap, smoothing the damp cloth.

Now he could see it had a tiny collar and sleeves.

She sighed and looked up at him. "I hadn't wanted to tell you this way. I thought you'd come back in one piece."

"I still am," he assured her. "I'm all here."

"…and when we were alone, I'd say it."

"Say what, Maria? What does *it* have to do with *that*?" Frowning, he nodded at the little garment. "You know, that looks like those li'l shirts me maithur made before Colin…"

He looked up at her, mouth falling open.

"It is." She nodded. "It's a sacque. For our baby."

"Our…" He didn't get out another word, enveloping her in a one-handed but tight, rib-crushing hug, then pushed her away. "God, mustn't do that…don't' want t' shake loose th' l'il fella. You're all right?"

He seized her shoulder with his good hand, fingers anxiously tight.

"Th' shock o' seein' me, it didn't…"

"I'm fine." She assured him. "Padraig, you're holding me too tight."

"Oh. Sorry." He released her, sat on the sofa, and awkwardly pulled her onto his lap, leaning back. "Maria, I'm so happy, but…oh, damn!" He brushed lips against her cheek. "I'd planned a rousing homecomin' for t'night, and now…" His laugh was sheepish. "Guess that idea's thrown out th' window."

"There's no reason we can't have whatever

319

homecoming you wish," Maria told him, touching his cheek. "Once you get rid of *that*." She smiled at the bushy beard. "But, really, dearest, how much can you possibly do, with one arm in a sling?"

"You'd be surprised," Padraig answered. "But I'll be afraid t' touch you now, for fear…"

"I'm not china, and I won't break." Maria realized she was dispelling her fragile image as she spoke. "We'll see how it goes. But for now…"

She slid off his lap, taking his good hand in hers.

"I think you need to rest a bit."

She led him to the stairs.

"Čik'ayela Wanáhča," Padraig called. "I'm goin' upstairs for a bit of a lie-down." He laughed. "Sorry you're goin' t' have two invalids for a bit."

"*I'm* not an invalid," Maria corrected. "I'm merely in the family way."

Upstairs, she helped him out of his trail coat and pulled off his boots, then unbuckled the chaps and dropped everything to the floor. Getting off the shirt was more of a chore because she had to untie the sling, then ease his arm out of the sleeve. It hurt, though he attempted not to show it, but each little grunt and groan made Maria hesitate and actually made the process more painful.

When at last the shirt joined the other garments, she stood looking at Padraig's chest in dismay. A row of bruises flowed into each other, large, rounded shapes she told herself could only be hoof marks. His left shoulder was blackened, his forearm splinted with two slender wooden lathes wrapped and held in place with knotted strips of bandage.

Maria closed her eyes, envisioning what had

happened…Padraig falling from the pinto, landing on his left side, his face striking the hard earth as the maddened cows galloped and leaped over him, miraculously missing striking anything vital.

I won't faint this time. He's here. He's alive, and those marks will fade.

She opened her eyes. He was watching her anxiously.

"I'm sorry, love, truly. I thought it best t' tell you in person. I didn't think Buck would beat me t' it or that you might faint, an' I certainly didn't expect…" He nodded toward her waist, "…that."

He put an arm around her, holding her close. The heat of his bare body seeped through the cotton of her dress. Maria was startled to feel such a surge of desire she went weak all over again. She asked herself why she was surprised. No feelings had changed between them, certainly two and a half months of separation merely made their love stronger. The only difference was now she was carrying his child and he was recovering from what might've been his death.

"How long have you known?" he asked, softly.

"The day after you left." She made it an apology. "I wish I'd realized sooner."

"If you had, I wouldn't have gone." His next words were delivered as if in sudden realization. "An' I wouldn't be in this fix." He waved his splinted arm and winced. "Damn it, this is your fault, woman!"

Then he laughed and hugged her again.

"What are we going t' do about that homecomin' now?"

"We'll figure out something," she told him. "Aren't Irishmen supposed to be resourceful?"

"Aye, but…"

"We'll start by seeing how proficient you are in using one hand to help me out of this dress."

****

Padraig snuggled his wife against his side.

"That was a novel experience," he muttered. "Though I'm not certain I like me wife bein' th' one on top like that. Still, 'twas good betwixt us as always, so what does it matter who was where?"

He slid his hand down her ribs, pulling her closer so he could rest a hand on her belly. Maria shivered slightly.

"'Tis a wonder you're carryin' within you, darlin', a miracle. Are you afraid?

"Of course," Maria answered. "Both of us, my dear husband, are about to take on the responsibility of another person."

"Aye, one whose life we're goin' t' mold an' shape. 'Tis a terrible responsibility we've got, Maria. I hope I'm up t' th' task. I don't doubt *you* are."

"You're a good man, Padraig. If our son's anything like you, he'll be a good man, too."

"Pray God he doesn't take after me as I was when young. That was truly someone I'd ne'er want you t' meet, *acushla*. Anyway, who says 'tis goin' t' be a son? What if we have a beautiful li'l daughter?"

"Would that disappoint you? If it's a girl?"

"It'll please me whate'er 'tis." Padraig released her. Raising himself on one elbow, he pressed a kiss on Maria's belly, brushing his lips against her skin in a soft, sensual caress. "Bless you, me babe. You've got a da who can't wait t' meet you in person."

Downstairs in the kitchen, Čik'ayela Wanáhča shook her head as she heard Padraig's laughter. *That*

322

man! Gets himself trampled by cows and he still manages to laugh.

Chapter 46

In the middle of the war, talk of constructing a railroad across the entire country began. Consequently, a groundbreaking ceremony was held in Omaha, but it was two years later—with the ending of the war, before the first rail would be laid.

When that happened, men from both the North and the South, as well as now-emancipated slaves and many Chinese, found work laying tracks, facing freezing cold, broiling summers, illness, and attacks by hostile Lakota protesting the invaders who often laid iron rails and thick-timbered crossties over their sacred land.

It would be four more danger-frought years and the forfeiting of many lives before the project was completed, and the United States was finally connected from one ocean to another.

In 1869, travel by railroad across Nebraska finally became a fact.

****

Padraig still allowed Maria to ride into town with him when he went to get supplies. It was going to be one of the last chances she'd get to accompany him until after the baby was born, he decided. Her rounded belly was beginning to show and it wouldn't be proper for her to be out in polite society as it became more noticeable.

Besides, he didn't want her being bounced and jounced around on the buckboard's hard wooden seat on the long drive there and back.

With that in mind, he made the announcement to his men that pretty soon there was going to be another McCoy bossing them around, then told Buck to take the buckboard to the saddler. He had a heavily padded cushion covered in smooth leather attached to the wagon's seat so Maria would be protected when she was in the wagon, not that she was going to be in it very much, if he had anything to say.

He also curtailed her riding around the ranch with him, especially on that sidesaddle. Padraig patrolled the house, searching for anything that might cause Maria to trip or stumble. Throw rugs were relegated to the pantry, neatly folded on a shelf, to be brought out after the birth. The front step railings were checked to make certain they were sturdy and well-attached, though the house wasn't yet old enough to show deterioration. A second railing was added to the kitchen steps, also.

Padraig made certain there was nothing to cause harm to either his wife or his expected child. He also stayed close to home now, riding out to check on the men, then hurrying back to be near if he was needed. That continued for several weeks before Maria declared him unnecessary as well as underfoot.

"Go back to doing what you were doing before I told you about the baby," she ordered. "Nothing's changed, and I won't have you neglecting the ranch because of me."

Feeling properly chastised and perhaps a little hurt that she didn't seem to consider her condition as monumentally important as he did, Padraig obeyed. He still cut his workday shorter than usual, however, and was back at the ranch before the sun went down, no matter what his wife said.

Maria wasn't exactly enjoying parts of her pregnancy.

There was a lull in her condition after the dreadful bouts of nausea and morning upheavals dissipated, but then those odd and voracious cravings, noticed earlier, swept in full force.

It began with the sudden yen for raspberries marinated in honey and crushed pepper and ended with an overwhelming desire for boiled cabbage slathered with prepared mustard. Čik'ayela Wanáhča had so stripped the raspberry canes of fruit there were hardly any left for jam that year.

The first cravings were gone by the time Padraig returned from the drive, but with his appearance, the second wave replaced it, and though he himself liked cabbage with a good slice of corned beef, watching his wife pour mustard over it as if it were a rich golden gravy made his own stomach cringe.

"Lord, wife," he gasped as Maria thrust a forkful of the concoction into her mouth, chewed, swallowed, and sighed as if she's eaten a bit of ambrosia. "I sincerely hope that's going t' do somethin' good for our child, because I don't think I'll e'er like cabbage again."

Maria simply shook her head and speared another cabbage leaf.

"Cabbage guarantees good health," Čik'ayela Wanáhča informed him.

"Thank goodness for that," was all Padraig said.

So it went…for six more months, while Čik'ayela Wanáhča soothed and pampered Maria and was alternately amused and sympathetic of Padraig by turns.

Chapter 47

Padraig's son was born on a snow-filled December morning.

There was nothing particularly dramatic about his emergence into the world as far as births went. It was fairly normal and relatively easy...on the mother, that is.

The father suffered terribly.

Maria spent a restless night, seeming unable to find a comfortable spot in the bed. Padraig, sensitive as always to his wife's movements, woke every time she shifted. He pulled her into his arms, attempting to establish a gentle intimacy by cuddling her, though close contact was near impossible now. Nevertheless, his touch seemed to calm Maria, who eventually fell asleep again.

In the morning, however, as he helped her into one of the shapeless dresses he'd had Miss Sammons make to accommodate her widening girth, he noticed how she kept putting her hands to her back.

"Are you feelin' all right, love?"

"As well as can be expected, I suppose," she snapped. "Since I'm carrying around an extra ton or two."

At the sudden hurt flashing across his face, she forced a smile and patted his cheek.

"Don't worry, dearest. I'm joking. It's merely difficult to move about now and I find myself wishing your son would get tired of where he is and decide to change domiciles." She sighed heavily. "Truly, Padraig, I think now I must weigh as much as you, and if that's so, I don't understand how you ever manage to move so quickly."

"Oh, Maria." Padraig enveloped her in an awkward hug. "I'm selfish," he said. "I wish th' babe was here, also, so I could get t' know him…an' so I could again hug you without standin' three feet away."

That made her laugh and she pushed him away, lumbering to the bedroom door. He hurried after her, being careful to grasp her arm as she went down the stairs and into the kitchen.

With her pregnancy advancing, Maria had taken it into her head to eat in the kitchen with the hired hands again. It was as if by surrounding herself with over a dozen strong, brawny men, including her husband, she felt safe and protected. The men were a little cowed by her presence at first, as if they'd forgotten how, when she first arrived at the ranch, she and Padraig always took meals with them. Soon, however, the old camaraderie between boss's wife and his employees was reestablished. Everyone was once more at Maria's beck and call, this time because she definitely was delicate, fragile, and unable to do for herself.

This morning, Maria continued shifting uneasily in her chair. She also picked at her food, pushing aside the delicately browned biscuit Čik'ayela Wanáhča selected for her and carefully covered with a coating of creamy butter. She consumed bare morsels of egg and ham. Thinking she looked a little pale and the way she was eating might be an indication of incipient nausea, Čik'ayela Wanáhča went to the pantry for a peppermint stick, a staple during the course of Maria's pregnancy. Silently, she laid it by her plate.

"Thank you." Maria leaned back with a sigh, then placed a hand between her back and the chair. "Oh, my back hurts so."

Čik'ayela Wanáhča stiffened. "Miz Maria, how long has it hurt?"

"It started last…" Maria winced, crying out. "Oh! What…"

"Love, what is it?" Immediately Padraig was on his feet while the other men looked at each other in concern.

Maria stared at the sodden hem of her dress and then at the liquid puddling under her chair.

She staggered to her feet, only to cry out again as her hand once more went to her back. "Padraig?"

"Her water's broken," Čik'ayela Wanáhča declared impassively.

"Oh, Lord, Boss." Buck looked from Maria to Padraig, his own face going white. "The baby's coming?"

Padraig didn't answer. He simply pushed back his chair, ran around the table, and scooped his wife into his arms. Staggering slightly as he hefted her weight, he started down the hall.

"Sam," Buck said. "Saddle a horse and fetch Dr. Sheppard." He started after Padraig, ready to do whatever he was asked.

By the time he got upstairs, they were in the bedroom. Padraig set Maria on her feet. She clung to him as if she couldn't keep her balance.

"I'm sending Sam for the doc," Buck said.

"Doc? Uh…" Padraig gave the foreman a stunned look.

"Thank you, Buck." Maria looked over her husband's shoulder at the foreman. To Padraig, she said, "I think you should let Čik'ayela Wanáhča take over now. Change your shirt…"

Padraig glanced down. Below his chest all the way to the waist of his denims were damp where Maria's body had been hugged against his. He touched the wet fabric, staring at his fingers as if he didn't understand how they'd gotten that way.

"…and denims, then go downstairs. Buck, will you sit with him?"

"Yes, ma'am." Buck dragged Padraig across the room to the wardrobe. "Here, Boss, get something."

Obediently Padraig opened the chest and got out a fresh shirt. He looked back at Maria. "I can't leave. She needs me."

Holding onto the bedpost, Maria bit her lip, attempting not to show how much it hurt. That didn't last long.

"I'll…be…all right…" she gasped. "But I need you out of here, Padraig. Truly I do."

Čik'ayela Wanáhča hurried in, carrying a folded leather sheet. "Mr. Padraig. You go. Wait downstairs. Miz Maria and I can handle this until the doctor comes."

Buck pushed a protesting Padraig toward the stairs.

Čik'ayela Wanáhča turned back to Maria, saying softly, "Come, let's get you ready."

Padraig might've gone downstairs, but he didn't sit calmly. The moment his shirt and denims were buttoned and the soiled ones taken to the kitchen laundry tub, he was on his feet, pacing back and forth.

"Why doesn't Sam get back with th' doc?" he demanded. "How long's he been gone anyway?"

"Couple of hours," Buck supplied, unhelpfully. "Boss, you know how long it takes to get to town and back."

"God, Buck, she could have th' baby before he gets here."

"Would that be so bad?" Buck didn't seem to realize he wasn't helping a bit. "I mean..." he went on as Padraig stopped to glare at him, "...women have been having babies longer than there's been docs around to help them. Haven't they?'

"*Women* may have," Padraig replied icily, "but not me wife. I don't want anythin' t' go wrong. She's here with a ranch full o' men who don't know..."

"Čik'ayela Wanáhča's here," Buck added. "She told me she had two babies. She knows what's what."

"Aye, but..."

"She'll be all right, Boss." The foreman put a hand on Padraig's shoulder and pushed him onto the settee. "You'll see."

Padraig settled...for a moment. A sound from upstairs made him leap to his feet again. "What was that?"

A second sound came. This one high-pitched, just short of a scream.

"She's in pain."

"Well, yeah." Buck's tone implied that should be obvious. Again, he pushed Padraig onto the sofa. "She's having a baby. I reckon that's never pain-free."

All that got was a glance from his boss that would've skewered him to the parlor wall if it had held knives.

By the time the doctor did arrive, Padraig was wearing a hole in the hearth before the fireplace and

Buck was wringing his own hands and wanting to take refuge in the bunkhouse.

"Oh, God, what did I do?" Padraig alternately mumbled a prayer and berated himself. "Why did I want a child? What if she dies?" He looked at Buck, stricken. "I've killed her with me own selfishness."

It was then they heard horses' hooves and the rattle of a buckboard over the snow. In a moment, the front door flew open and Sam and Dr. Sheppard appeared, followed by an icy draft of air. They stamped snow from their boots as Sam shut the door.

Chapter 48

"Sam here says your wife's gone into labor." Sheppard set his bag on the floor and unwrapped the muffler from around his neck. He slid out of his wool coat, dropping it and his gloves over the back of the settee.

Sam didn't move, standing by the door as if waiting for further orders.

"This way." Padraig caught the doctor's arm and pulled him into the hallway, dragging him up the stairs.

Sheppard managed to snag his bag as he was swept away.

"How long ago did her pains start?" He wanted to know.

"We were at breakfast." Padraig had no idea how long ago it'd been.

In all that time he'd never once glanced at the clock on the mantel, not wanting to know for certain the length of time he'd listened to Maria's screams ranging from low moans to near-shrieks.

They were at the bedroom door now. Padraig pushed it open. "Maria, th' doctor's here…"

Sheppard rushed in, setting his instrument bag on the lamp table. Padraig had a brief glimpse of his nightgowned wife, lying propped against three pillows. Her hair was unbound and plastered to her forehead and cheeks in sweat-soaked tangles, face pale and twisted with pain. Her hands were above her head, gripping the center of the headboard. As he watched, she grimaced again and squeezed the carved section as tightly as she could, while gritting her teeth to suppress the scream trying to escape.

A movement from Čik'ayela Wanáhča made him glance at the housekeeper. She had her eyes closed and appeared to be chanting, her lips moving in a barely audible mutter. He became aware of an odd smell in the room, something herbal, light and not unpleasant. Then he saw the small saucer lying on the bedside table, smoke spiraling out of it from burning bits of what looked like dried weeds and chaff.

"What's this?" Sheppard waved a hand at the saucer.

Čik'ayela Wanáhča opened her eyes. "Herbs. I burn them to help the baby come easier."

"Doubt if they're going to help." Sheppard the medical man didn't scoff, but he plainly looked dubious. He pulled off his frock coat and slung it into a chair. "Can't hurt, I suppose. Is there somewhere I can wash my hands?"

Čik'ayela Wanáhča pointed to the ironstone pitcher and basin. Sheppard hurried over, poured water, and immersed his hands after rubbing them with the bar of soap lying in a little dish.

"Maria…" Padraig called to his wife.

She didn't react, except to close her eyes and release the headboard long enough to wipe at them. She inhaled quickly, drawing up her legs.

"Patrick, go back downstairs," Sheppard ordered. He dried his hands on a towel and dropped it to the wash table's top.

"But…"

Maria screamed.

Čik'ayela Wanáhča bent over her, pushing up Maria's nightgown to her knees. "Doctor, I think it is time."

Sheppard's elbow on Padraig's shoulder propelled him out of the room. The doctor slammed the door with the other elbow.

Trying not to listen to the sounds from inside, Padraig started down the stairs.

In the parlor, he found Buck had sent Sam to the bunkhouse.

Padraig tossed down the goblet of brandy the foreman poured him and held it out to be refilled. He tried to think of something, *anything* except what was happening upstairs. It was useless, the only thing coming into his mind other than the pain Maria was going through were half-remembered images of when Colin was born.

Padraig had been three, nearly four, then, and he hadn't really understood what was going on, except that Mama had gotten very fat, and then one afternoon, cried out and hurried to bed. There had been plenty of noise after that. Quinton told Nanny to take Padraig and Donal to the nursery and keep them busy and they'd gone with her obediently.

When Padraig asked if Mama was sick, Nanny told him she was getting ready for the angels to send down their new baby brother. Three hours later when Colin made his appearance, Padraig wondered why the angels sent something so ugly, red, and puny. He wondered if, when his new brother got older, the crying, squirming thing would be as beautiful as the angels who brought him.

Colin had been more than beautiful. Within a few hours, he truly looked like a little carrot-topped cherub. Padraig was so thankful he'd never spoken aloud to anyone, especially his mother and father, that his first thought upon seeing his brother had been how ugly he was.

Noon time came and went. Cookie tiptoed into the kitchen and made dinner for the men. He offered some to the boss but Padraig refused, asking instead for another glass of brandy. Buck, out of loyalty, had declined also, though he was now regretting it because his stomach was complaining loudly. While the men ate, Cookie stuck his head back into the parlor, asking for information, got it, then herded everyone back to the bunkhouse.

Many hours later, the longest in Padraig's life, upstairs got very quiet.

"She's dead!" Now into his fourth glass of brandy, he shot to his feet, wavered and nearly fell. "Me Maria's died!"

"Nah, Boss." Buck put out a steadying hand.

They heard footsteps on the stairs, slow, steady ones, not frantic and hurried as they'd be if someone was dead, at least Padraig hoped so.

Čik'ayela Wanáhča came through the doorway, holding a small blanket-wrapped bundle. From the flowers embroidered around the edges, Padraig recognized it as one of the little flour sack blankets Maria had painstakingly sewn.

"Is she all right?" He lurched toward the housekeeper, looking up the stairs.

"Miz Maria's fine," she replied. "So's the baby."

"I've got t' go t' her."

He staggered to the stairs. For some reason, there appeared to be two sets and he stepped up, only to miss and nearly fall. Grasping the rail, he planted his foot firmly on the third step.

"Maria?" He raised his voice, calling.

"Mr. Padraig."

He looked back at the housekeeper.

She raised the bundle. "Don't you want to see him?"

"Him?"

"Your son," she said, with a slightly impatient air.

"Oh. Right." He fell back down the stairs to flip open the blanket, staring blearily at the wizened bit of red-faced humanity. "Seen him."

He tossed the blanket over the baby's face and turned back to the stairs.

"Maria?"

Padraig ran up the steps, tripping on every other one.

Buck came into the hall. "Can I see the little fella?" His tone was so diffident and shy Čik'ayela Wanáhča couldn't keep from smiling.

She opened the blanket, folding back the edges Padraig had so roughly closed. Buck peered at the baby.

"Well. Kind of little to have caused such a fuss, ain't he?" He smiled as the baby yawned and wiggled slightly. "Hate to say it, but he don't look like the boss." Buck lowered his voice, though Padraig was in no condition to hear anything. "Here's hoping he grows up to be as big and tall as his pa anyway."

From upstairs, there was a loud crash.

Padraig had reached the top of the stairs and stumbled to the bedroom door, pushing it open. It struck the wall, rebounded and swung back, nearly striking him as he staggered inside.

Sheppard was bent over the bed.

"Maria?"

The doctor glanced over his shoulder. "Come in, Papa. Your wife will be presentable in a moment."

He was wiping Maria's face with a damp cloth. She looked pale but much better than the last time Padraig had seen her, if a trifle washed-out and tired. He hesitated. Maria opened her eyes and held out her hand.

He took it. Sheppard stepped out of the way and Padraig fell to his knees beside the bed, kissing Maria's hand.

"Have you seen him?" she asked.

"Seen who?" He looked around. "The doctor? O' course I have."

"The baby. Čik'ayela Wanáhča took him downstairs. To show you."

"Oh…" He had a vague memory of seeing something in the housekeeper's arms. "Aye…I think."

"Padraig? What's the matter?" She touched his cheek, then slid her hand to his shoulder and inhaled. "Are you…you're drunk!"

"Nay, *acushla*," he denied.

"Yes, you are. Oh, Padraig!"

"Just toastin' me child's birth a li'l early, that's all," he lied.

"We have a son. Just as you wanted. Why aren't you happy?"

"I *am* happy, love…happy you're all right…an'…" He tried to get his muddled thoughts together. *Baby…son…I have a son…* The thought came through. "I've a son. Good Lord! I barely looked at the lad."

He lurched to his feet.

"I've got t' get back down there an' make up for that.

Can't have th' babe think his da's ignorin' him. God, Maria, we've a…"

The brandy seized him. Padraig's knees buckled and he fell to the floor before Doc Sheppard could catch him.

With Buck's help, the doctor got Padraig settled in Maria's never-used bedroom.

Čik'ayela Wanáhča brought the baby back to his mother.

Maria accepted the little bundle, looking down at the baby and pressing a gentle kiss to his forehead.

"He looks like you," the housekeeper said. "Is Mr. Padraig disappointed?"

"I don't think he's realized it yet," Maria told her. "Becoming a father hasn't truly sunk in." Her arms tightened around the baby. "I thought he'd have red hair. I suppose I should've realized there was a chance he'd take after my side of the family."

Why, oh, why? Please God, don't let Padraig become suspicious. Let him think his son looks Spanish and not Lakota.

She would continue that prayer for many days to come.

Chapter 49

Two weeks later, Padraig's son was christened in the little church on the outskirts of McCoy's Crossing. While the proud parents beamed and the godparents, Josiah Blackstone and his wife, looked on, Cuilline Padraig Quinton McCoy was welcomed into God's flock. He wasn't particularly appreciative of the honor, squalling at the top of his lungs as the preacher dribbled water out of the marble baptismal fount onto his little head. The fount had been a gift from Padraig, ordered from a statuary company Back East, arriving in time for his son to be the first baby christened from it.

After that, with his dark hair plastered to his little skull, he proceeded to wet his diaper as well as his christening gown, sending Maria scurrying into the little choir room to the left of the altar to change both. Since she had anticipated a diaper change but not a complete wardrobe mishap, young Cuilline spent the rest of his christening day wearing nothing but the diaper.

"Here's hopin' this isn't a portent of things t' come," his proud father said at the party held after the christening. He raised a punch cup in a toast to his son, then passed out specially ordered cigars all around.

There was some confusion by a few guests about the baby's name.

"Colleen?" Mayor Bainbridge asked. "Isn't that a girl's name?"

"Ah, nay," Padraig corrected. "'Tis Cuilline." He spelled it. "'Tis me maithur's maiden name. Don't think any one's used it as yet, so th' lad'll be th' first."

"Is that what you're going to call him?" Blackstone asked. "Not Padraig Junior?"

"Good Lord, one o' me around is enough. I wouldn't want a duplicate. I'm thinkin' we'll shorten it a bit," Padraig answered. "Quill, maybe."

"Quill," Blackstone nodded. "Sounds almost Indian, if you'll forgive my saying so."

He looked up as Maria emerged from the choir room with the now-dry baby, who was sucking one of his fists.

"Hate t' say it, Padraig, but he doesn't look like you." He spoke quickly before Maria got within earshot. "He looks almost like a Lakota, no offense."

"Ah, now, that's where you're wrong." Padraig didn't take any insult. "He's Black Irish, just like me Uncle Seamus an' me cousin Connell...dark hair...dark eyes...aye, he's as Irish as they come, just th' dark kind."

"Black Irish?" Delsey had now joined the group. "Well, I never..."

"I imagine there's a lot you don't know about us Irish," Padraig rejoined. "Some say th' dark ones are descended from Spanish sailors who survived the sinkin' o' their Armada back in 1588, so he's got Spanish in him from both sides." He kissed Maria as she reached him, bouncing the baby. "He's me li'l *buachaill dubh*, me li'l black boy."

A little later, when they were alone a moment before more well-wishers surged around them, Maria whispered, "You're not angry? Because he isn't red-haired?'"

She'd heard his remark.

"Didn't I just say?" Padraig gave her a fond look. "It'd be nice to have him th' image o' meself, but he takes after anaithur branch o' th' family, so why should I be disappointed?"

He looked up to smile at someone approaching and didn't see Maria's look of relief.

****

15 December, 1863
Quinton Aloysius Francis Xavier McCoy, Esquire
McCoy Hall
Tipperary, Ireland
The United Kingdom of Great Britain

Most Honoured Father,
It is my proud duty to inform you that this branch of the McCoy family has been increased by one. Maria has given birth to a son.

I have taken the liberty of naming him Cuilline Padraig Quinton McCoy, after my mother and you, sir. I hope you approve.

Now you have two grandchildren, unless Donal has supplied another, but since I have not had any correspondence stating that happy event, I am supposing it hasn't yet occurred.

As to who the child resembles, I wish I might say he's my image, but you'll probably be relieved to learn that is not the case. In truth, he resembles Uncle Seamus, having dark hair and eyes, the latter which I believe will be hazel. Since Maria is Spanish and could also be mistaken for Black Irish, this shouldn't be a surprise.

Be happy for me, sir, and I hope someday I may be welcomed back into your home so you and your grandson may meet.

Your son,
Padraig Aloysius Francis McCoy
Owner, The Shamrock Ranch
McCoy's Crossing, Nebraska
United States of America

Chapter 50

"Come to your da!" Padraig laughed, holding out his hands as three-year-old Quill stumbled toward him on short fat legs. He caught the child, swinging him into the air and making Quill squeal with delight and burst into giggles. "Now then…"

He set the little boy down and dropped onto the front step so they were more or less eye to eye.

"What's this mean? *Dia duit, Da*?"

"It means 'God bless you, Pa,'" Quill replied promptly.

"An' God bless you, too, *mo mac*," Padraig replied, beaming at the child. "Do you know what that means? *Mo mac*?"

Quill shook his head, finger going into his mouth. He was cutting a jaw tooth and chewed on his forefinger so often Padraig feared he might bite it off.

"Don't do that, lad." Padraig pulled Quill's hand from his mouth. "It means 'me son.'"

"That's me." Quill punched his chest with the same fat forefinger.

"That's right." Padraig hugged the child. "*Sláinte chugat*, me boy."

"Good health to you, too, Pa," Quill replied dutifully.

"He's learned the language quick enough." Padraig looked back at Maria, watching from her rocker.

"I suppose." She studied the shirt on which she was struggling to sew a button. Maria's needlework hadn't gotten a bit better with time, not that she cared if it did or didn't. "Wherever is he going to use Gaillich in Nebraska, Padraig?"

"He won't," Padraig admitted, getting to his feet. "But he will when he takes a trip with his ma an' da back t' see his Grandpa Quinton and Grandma Màiri."

"A trip to Ireland?" Maria looked startled, then excited. "When will that be?"

"Don't start packin' yet. Not until Quill's a li'l older and hardy enough to brave an ocean voyage. Later, in a few years."

"Oh." She relaxed, looking disappointed.

"Here now, I didn't know you were so hopin' t' meet your in-laws."

"Of course I want to meet them," she protested. "Get to know them, have them see I didn't marry you for your money."

"Now, Maria." He stood, holding Quill in his arms. "No one…"

"Oh, I'm certain they've thought of it. What with there being such a distance between my age and yours."

"Old codger gettin' himself conied by a pretty young thin', eh? I hadn't thought o' that." He did now. "Sometimes, I forget I'm a dozen years older than you."

"You're not an old codger," she declared, glancing at Čik'ayela Wanáhča.

She didn't really want the housekeeper to hear that because it was one of Maria's secret fears, along with someone discovering her true heritage. She was afraid someone would think she was one of those women who trapped a man simply for his money and then proceeded to help him spend it all. She didn't realize anyone seeing how truly she loved Padraig and the way she was such a good hostess for his home and a loving mother to his son would never believe that.

"Glad you think so," he retorted." Because sometimes on a cold, wintry morn, I certainly feel as if I am. Forty's gettin' close, *a chroi*…an' then there's fifty, an'…"

"Oh, hush," she ordered, picking up the shirt again. "If you must talk about something, let it be Quill's language lesson." She glanced at Čik'ayela Wanáhča again, her heartbeat speeding up a bit as she suggested, "If he's going to learn foreign languages, perhaps he should learn Lakota, too."

"Not a bad idea." Padraig nodded. He set Quill on the porch railing so they were the same height, looking into the boy's hazel eyes. "So, let's see…what's th' word for *faithur*, Čik'ayela Wanáhča?"

"*Até*," the housekeeper replied.

"*Até*," Padraig repeated. To Quill, he asked, "Can you say that?"

"Unh-huh." Quill nodded, chewing on his finger.

"Unh-huh?" Padraig said and scowled dramatically. "What kind o' answer is that?"

"I mean, yes, sir," Quill amended.

Again, Padraig pulled the finger from his mouth. "Let's hear it."

Obediently, Quill repeated the word.

"Good lad. How about *maithur*? How does that go?" Padraig asked Čik'ayela Wanáhča.

"*Iná*," she supplied.

Padraig repeated the word and so did Quill.

Maria had been watching them silently. Now she

spoke something she'd often thought about, wondering if she dared. "What about *grandmother*?"

"That's *Uŋčí*," the housekeeper told her.

"*Uŋčí*," Quill repeated, without being asked. "*Até.*" He pointed to Padraig. "*Iná.*" He gestured to Maria. There was a silence as he looked around, then stabbed a chubby finger in Čik'ayela Wanáhča direction. "*Uŋčí.*"

"Eh, lad, I fear that's not quite correct," Padraig said.

He gave the housekeeper such a look, then turned one of the same sternness on Maria before looking back at Quill as if studying the child, that she felt her heart sink. She actually went pale.

Čik'ayela Wanáhča looked at her in alarm. "Miz Maria?"

"You know, that might not be such a bad idea." Padraig didn't seem to notice how his wife leaned back in her chair, biting her lip.

"What might?" Maria forced herself to ask, wondering why he didn't hear the weakness in her voice.

"Having th' lad here call Čik'ayela Wanáhča grandmaithur… After all, he sees her e'ery day an' 'twill be a long time before he meets his real one." He looked at the housekeeper, eyes gleaming. "Would you like t' be me son's surrogate grandmaithur?"

"I don't know what *surrogate* is," she replied.

"It means, a substitute, someone taking the place of the real thing," he explained.

"I don't think Čik'ayela Wanáhča would want to…" Maria was abruptly fearful of the repercussions of such a relationship.

"I'd be pleased, Miz Maria," Čik'ayela Wanáhča interrupted. "Mr. Padraig, I've mourned my son and daughter many years. When I came here, it was almost like having them with me again. Though you're a grown man and I last saw my son as a child, I hope he may have become a good person as you are." She looked at Maria. "I hope my Flying Bird is like you, Miz Maria." She smiled. "I'll always miss them, but you've helped close the hollow they made in my heart. I'd be proud to be this sur-ro-gate *Uŋčí* for your son."

"Did you hear that, Quill?" Padraig swung the child off the railing. "Now you have two grandmas, one here an' one in th' Auld Country." He looked thoughtful. "You know, I think I like *Uŋčí*, better, too. 'Tis easier t' say. May I call you *Uŋčí* also?"

Čik'ayela Wanáhča nodded.

"Then here, Grandma…take your surrogate grandson an' put him t' bed for his nap. I notice he's startin' t' droop."

With that, he passed Quill to the housekeeper, who clasped the child in her arms and went inside. Already half-asleep, Quill rested his head on her shoulder.

Maria stood, clutching the shirt.

"You aren't angry, are you?" Padraig asked belatedly.

"I was simply a little surprised, that's all." She smiled, startled by the elation she felt. *My son will call my mother by her rightful name, and she'll know the joy of a grandchild, but neither will be aware of the truth.* "I don't know why I didn't think of it. Čik'ayela Wanáhča has definitely been motherly to both of us."

"Nay, now." Padraig shook a finger at her. "Not Čik'ayela Wanáhča…Uŋčí," he corrected. "You have to say it, too."

"Uŋčí," Maria repeated obediently.

Padraig wound his arm around her waist and walked her inside. He bent so his mouth was close to her ear. "Say…while th' lad's taking his nap, why don't his da an' ma have a bit o' a rest, also?"

"How much rest will that be?" She heaved an exaggerated sigh, then smiled as he guided her to the stairs.

Chapter 51

With the end of the war, the people of McCoy's Crossing believed Padraig was truly able to foresee the future, for his predictions concerning the town began to happen.

As he'd said, many people began heading west, from both North and South, all attempting to escape the horrors still in their minds, as well as the struggles brought about by the aftermath of the war. Nebraska attained statehood and the capitol was moved from Omaha to Lancaster, its name changed to Lincoln in honor of the assassinated president.

There were thirty people living in Lancaster at that time, with barely that many more on surrounding ranches and farmsteads. In comparison, McCoy's Crossing had a lively population of seventy-five people in town, and perhaps a hundred more on the farms and ranches in the area.

Solitary men, families, and businesses headed west, many stopping at McCoy's Crossing. The seamstress's shop expanded into a ladies' dress and milliner's shop, and the barber shop and bath house was renovated to appeal to a more genteel class of customer and renamed a gentlemen's sartorial parlor. Delsey's general store was now Delsey's Mercantile and Emporium, enlarging not only its inventory but also its location, so the original building spanned half of one side of the boardwalk.

With the finishing of the railroad and the advent of trains passing regularly through town, the Crossroads Hotel became the place it previously aspired to be, where travelers staying overnight would have a choice between it and the boarding house that eventually became a permanent residence for unmarried men and several spinsters. The post office was converted to a railway station where telegraph wires had been strung. There was even a dentist, his shingle advertising Painless Dentistry.

****

Young Quill's childhood was uneventful and happy. Though he didn't bypass the usual juvenile diseases, the ones he contracted were the mildest cases imaginable.

Padraig was more in love with Maria than ever, and the ranch was prosperous.

Though there was no hint of another child to be the brother Quill kept asking for, Padraig didn't worry.

"P'rhaps this is God's way o' tellin' me this one's goin' t' be enough for me t' handle," he told Maria and his lack of other offspring didn't appear to bother him at all. He had his wife, his son, and the Shamrock. Padraig told himself he didn't need anything more.

Chapter 52

Mid-summer, 1869

Things remained steady until Quill was around six.

On one day when Maria and Padraig went to town for supplies, Quill wasn't present. He'd been naughty and his punishment was being denied the trip to McCoy's Crossing. This was a particularly severe penalty because everyone they saw while in town made a fuss over the child and Quill reveled in it.

The day before, Uŋčí had baked cookies. She was always keeping the family as well as the cowpokes supplied with pastries and sweets. This time it was molasses cookies, her specialty.

She gave Quill one, then placed the others in the crock cookie jar. When he kept eying them and she saw a little hand reach for the jar, she placed it in the pantry on one of the top shelves.

"No more before dinner."

Quill sulked all through dinner.

Later, there was a crash and she hurried to the pantry to find Quill on the floor, surrounded by the broken jar and shattered cookies.

While Uŋčí was busy discussing the supper menu with his mother, the child had dragged a chair into the pantry, climbed upon it and from there to the shelf, reaching up for the jar. He lost his balance, the jar slipped from his grasp, and both fell to the floor.

Once assured he wasn't harmed, Maria waited until Padraig arrived, telling him what his son had done. Perhaps remembering her own mistreatment at the eastern school, she'd never been able to punish Quill. Using the excuse that the father should handle discipline, she always foisted that chore onto Padraig, who was also unable to bring himself to perform corporal punishment. Instead, he decided to take away the privilege Quill loved.

Quill whined, Maria wheedled, but Padraig was firm. Quill was disobedient. He wasn't going with them.

When Padraig and Maria left the ranch the next morning, a teary-eyed Quill remained on the front porch, watching them ride away.

"You must learn to do what your father says," Uŋčí told him.

Quill looked at her as if he were totally betrayed, because his beloved Uŋčí, who always let him have his way and sometimes even circumvented his papa if it wasn't too serious, was siding with Padraig.

"I guess," he grudgingly agreed.

"You know." With that, she took his hand and led him back into the house. "You can sit in the kitchen and help me make biscuits."

Quill brightened. Making biscuits was almost as much fun as making mud pies.

In town, Padraig took the list to the mercantile. Then he and Maria proceeded to the depot where he gathered the mail.

The war had ended four years before. The last spike of the Transcontinental Railroad had been driven a few months earlier, and now the railway going from Omaha through Nebraska was open for business. As Padraig had predicted, there were a good many people heading west to escape the aftermath of Reconstruction, and some stopped in McCoy's Crossing…and stayed.

They had just come out of the station and were standing on the platform when the train arrived.

"There are quite a few passengers today," Maria said.

"Unh-huh." Padraig's answer was preoccupied as he looked up from the envelopes he was studying. Most were flyers, nothing of importance.

Black smoke billowed from the train's smokestack, mixing with steam pouring from the engine, changing it to a murky gray. The conductor's figure was barely discernable as he stepped from the train.

A man's figure emerged from the smoke. He was holding the hand of a little boy around eight years old. A woman held the child's other hand. They were all well-dressed, with the youngster wearing a blue velvet suit cut similar to the man's, down to the ruffles on his shirt.

A sudden breeze cleared away the smoke and the man raised his head just as Padraig looked in his direction.

Their eyes met.

"Lord God!" The letters fell from Padraig's hands, scattering on the platform. He stared. "Colin?"

"Padraig? What is it?" Maria's hand went to his arm.

He didn't answer, simply pulled away and ran down the steps toward the couple, who stopped as soon as they saw him. She was astonished to see her husband seize the stranger in his arms and begin pounding his back and the stranger returning the gesture. They backed away from each other, laughing.

Lifting her skirts, Maria carefully picked her way down the steps and hurried to them.

As she neared, she heard Padraig say, "What in th' name o' God are you doin' here?"

"Comin' t' visit me braithur," the man replied in an accent matching her husband's. "Didn't you get me letter?"

"I've gotten naithin' from home in o'er a year," Padraig replied. "Wells Fargo must've lost it somewhere 'twixt here an' th' last station. You should've sent a telegram."

"Nay matter." Colin shrugged. "We're here."

Padraig stepped back. "Let me look at you. Lord, you're fully man-grown now!"

"O' course I am," Colin retorted. "'Tis been near twenty years. Did you think I'd stay a child fore'er?" He looked past Padraig to Maria, who had reached them. "Is this me sister-in-law?"

"Aye." Padraig turned back to put his arm around her waist. "Maria, this is me baby braithur, Colin. Still full o' surprises."

Colin removed his top hat, bowing formally. Without it, his red hair gleamed in the sun and his resemblance to Padraig was remarkable, though he was nearly four years younger.

"Maria, so pleased t' finally meet you. You can't imagine how I've waited for this moment." He looked back at Padraig. "Da was past flabbergasted when he received that letter about your marriage." He laughed. "Stomped around for days, he did, frettin'."

"I didn't think th' news would upset him so. He worried?" Padraig looked surprised.

"Oh, not about you. 'Twas your wife. He said he

hoped th' poor girl knew what she was in for." Colin's eyes twinkled. "An' then t' hear you had a babe."

He shook his head.

Digging into a waistcoat pocket, he brought out a small box similar to a jeweler's case. He held it out to Padraig.

"What's this?"

"A christening gift."

Padraig took it.

"Late, I know," Colin went on. "But Da was afraid it might get lost in that United States postal system or whate'er 'tis called, so he decided t' hold it against th' day you came back t' visit. If me letter was lost, I guess 'tis a good thin' he did. When we left, he asked me t' deliver it in person."

"So this is from Da an' not you?" That was Padraig's subtle way of reminding Colin he'd sent *his* son a christening gift.

"Colin…" The woman with him plucked at his sleeve before he could answer.

Colin glanced at her. "Excuse me ill manners. This is me wife, Fiona."

She nodded, shyly.

"…and this is…" He looked around. "Where'd the lad go? Liam? Son?"

There was movement behind Fiona. The boy had taken refuge behind his mother, looking shyly at them from the protection of her skirts. Colin hauled him out, scooping him up.

"This is me son, Liam."

"Hello, Liam." Padraig gave a hearty laugh.

Liam cringed and hid his face against his father's neck. He was as red-haired as Colin, with a slight smattering of freckles across his nose and cheeks over skin as fair as any Englishman's, and green McCoy eyes.

Like me son should look, Padraig thought, and immediately felt a twinge of guilt because he'd never had that thought before until now.

"Here now." Colin didn't appear angry but was nevertheless a little embarrassed by the child's reaction. "There's naught t' be afeared. This is your Uncle Padraig an' Aunt Maria, whom we've come all this far t' see. Don't know what's th' matter with th' lad. He's usually bold as brass," he told Padraig. "He's been lookin' forward t' gettin' here."

Liam straightened, turning slightly so he could peer at Padraig again. Deciding the stranger wasn't a threat, he raised his head. "You look like me da."

"That's because your da and I are braithurs," Padraig explained. He noticed something pinned to the lapel of the child's jacket. "I see you're wearing that eagle feather I sent you."

One plump hand went to the silver stickpin, fingers brushing across it. "You made this for me?"

"*I* didn't make it," Padraig replied. "I had one of the Lakota people fashion it. For me brand-new nephew."

"I pinned it to the side of his crib," Fiona explained. She spoke quietly, almost timidly as if a little cowed by Padraig's presence. "When Liam was old enough to ask about it, he insisted on wearing it. Everywhere."

"Eagles wepwesent honor, twuf, wisdom, an' couwage," Liam told him. "Da wead that from a letter me Uncle Padwaig sent me." He looked surprised as the realization struck. A pudgy finger pointed. "That's you!"

"Aye, 'tis," Padraig agreed. "I'm glad you like it, nephew." He looked at Colin again. "So you've come for

357

a visit. Wish I'd known, I'd have been here with th' McCoy's Crossin' Civic Band t' welcome you. Good thing th' train was on time. Two minutes later an' we'd have been on our way home."

"Then 'tis a good thing it arrived when it did," Colin agreed. "You say you're on your way now? Can't wait t' see th' ranch. What's it called again? Shamrock? An' your lad?" He looked around. "Where is he?"

"At home. Bein' punished for doin' somethin' he was told not ta." Padraig didn't go into detail, but Colin's nod told him he remembered well the many punishments his older brother had suffered at their father's hands for his own disobedience. "How much luggage do you have?"

Padraig and Colin, holding Liam's hand, wandered back to where the conductor was directing a porter in placing suitcases and other items on a cart.

Maria looked at Fiona. An awkward moment passed between them, two strangers confronting each other.

"I guess we've been abandoned."

"It's all right, I suppose. After all, they haven't seen each other in nearly twenty years. Colin was only eighteen when Padraig was…left home." Fiona smiled an apology for mentioning how Padraig was sent away.

When Maria smiled back, the moment disappeared, and they watched silently as Padraig and Colin loaded the large trunk into the wagon bed with Liam standing by. Afterward, the three came back to where they stood.

"You're certain there's still room for those supplies you say you have t' get?" Colin asked.

"Positive. I'm more worried about where we're going t' put e'eryone," Padraig replied. "I suppose I can hire a horse an' ride, an' you can drive. That seat'll hold three, I think. As for you…" He glanced at Liam, standing by his father's side. "Would you like t' ride with me, do you think? Before me on me saddle?"

"I guess." Liam didn't sound too certain, but after being so cowed upon first meeting his uncle, he was now putting on a brave face for his father's sake.

"Good enough, then." Padraig threw an arm across Colin's shoulders. "Think you can handle a buckboard, li'l braithur?'

"I imagine. I've got me own team back in Tipperary, y'know, an' I won e'ery curricle race I was in while I was at university."

"You mean you managed to graduate?" Padraig leaned back as if awed. "My, my…an' stealin' me thunder as a driver, too? But then, you *are* a McCoy, an' if there's anythin' we're good at, 'tis being horsemen…an' lovers." This last was added in a low tone so Fiona wouldn't hear. "Hope you haven't let our reputation down in that department."

"Quiet, now." Colin glanced back at Fiona, who was busily chatting with Maria.

Liam had run ahead and taken her hand and was walking between his mother and his aunt.

"I'll have you know I'm a settled married man."

"Hell, so am I, but I wasn't always, y'know." Padraig threw an arm across Colin's shoulders.

"Aye, I do." Colin smiled, then added, under his breath, "Unfortunately."

Padraig laughed. "Come on, then, let's see how you handle th' reins."

It wasn't Colin who ended up driving the team, however, for once at the livery stable, after Padraig had introduced his brother to Olsen, Fiona spoke up.

"You may not know it, Padraig, but I know how to handle horses also, and I think you and my husband should both ride." She appeared surprised that she'd said so much information in one sentence. "That way you can get reacquainted while I drive the team."

"Are you serious, lass?" Padraig looked shocked. He glanced at Colin. "She can drive a team?"

"Did you think I'd marry a lass who didn't know her way around horses?" Colin demanded. "I taught her meself."

The ride back to the ranch wasn't a silent one. After a few complaints about the configuration of the western saddle, Colin seemed to settle in. He and Padraig rode ahead, their voices trailing back to the two women, along with an occasional laugh from Liam, perched in front of Padraig, clasping the saddle horn tightly.

"Your Fiona doesn't speak much, does she?" Padraig glanced behind him at the wagon, noting how expertly Colin's wife was handling the reins.

"She's a quiet one," Colin admitted. "Wasn't that way at first, not when I was courtin' her, but after we settled at McCoy Hall...I guess Da intimidates her a li'l. You know how loud an' blustery he is."

"Hasn't changed in that respect, eh?"

"She expresses herself much better when we're alone." Colin winked and smiled. "I'm hopin' being away from him an' in this country where e'eryone speaks his mind so freely, e'en th' females, she'll manage to be a li'l more outspoken."

"What's outspoken?" Liam abruptly piped up.

"Ne'er you mind." Colin leaned over and tousled his son's bright curls. "You've plenty o' that already." He looked at Padraig. "Guess we'd better watch what we say. A certain li'l pitcher with big ears has a habit o' repeatin' thin's t' his ma."

Chapter 53

At the ranch, Uŋčí greeted them at the front door.

"Mr. Padraig, you bring guests?" She studied Colin. "This one looks like you. He is of your tribe? From that Ireland?"

"You might say that," Padraig replied. "This is me braithur, Colin. Colin, this li'l lady is me housekeeper. Her name's Čik'ayela Wanáhča, but we call her Uŋčí. She's Lakota an' she runs me household."

"Ma'am." Colin again doffed his top hat, revealing the bright red hair and further confirming his relationship to Padraig. "Please forgive me if I stumble o'er your name. 'Tis a bit much for me t' wrap me tongue around at first sight."

"You must call me Uŋčí also, Mr. Colin," she replied. "Since you are part of Mr. Padraig's family."

Padraig introduced Fiona, who gave the housekeeper a timid smile, and then Liam. After the child's reaction to meeting him, he expected the little boy to be fearful of the housekeeper, but Liam looked up at her with a surprisingly bold stare.

"Uncle Padwaig says you're a Injun. You ain't no Injun," he declared.

"Yes." She looked down at him, returning his unsmiling gaze. "I am."

"Nay." He shook his head, making the curls bounce. "Where's your fedders an' war paint?"

"Forgive th' lad," Colin said. "He only knows what he's heard."

Uŋčí ignored him, her attention on Liam. "I don't wear those when I'm cooking dinner," she told the child. "Or when I'm baking cookies."

"You have cookies?" The green gaze brightened even more.

She nodded. "It is a new recipe. It would please me if you'd eat one and tell me if they're any good."

Liam thought about that. "I fink I will." He stopped, looking back at Colin. "Da?"

"Go on in," Padraig urged. "I imagine Quill's in the kitchen?"

Uŋčí nodded.

"You can meet your cousin Quill while you eat your cookie."

Grasping Uŋčí's hand, Liam allowed himself to be led into the house.

"I think she's made a conquest," Colin observed. "The way t' Liam's affection is definitely though his li'l belly."

Padraig looked back at Maria and Fiona. "Why don't you two go on in while Colin an' I get Buck an' one o' th' hands t' unload the wagon an' put your trunk in a guest room?"

Inside, Liam ignored the interior of the house completely, stopping stock still as he saw the child sitting at the table.

Quill stared back at him. "Hey, who are you?" He slid out of the chair, looking at the housekeeper. "Uŋčí, who's he?"

Before she could answer, Liam said, "I'm Liam McCoy an' I've come t' visit me cousin Quill." He looked around. "Where is he?"

"I'm Quill."

"Nay, you can't be." Liam shook his head.

"I guess I can," Quill retorted, shoving the rest of the biscuit he was eating into his mouth and smearing butter on his chin. "My pa owns this ranch, so I can be whoever I want."

"You're me cousin?" Liam was thoroughly astonished. "Cuilline Padwaig Quinton McCoy?" His lisp made a mishmash of Quill's name.

"That's me," Quill replied. He wiped his hand on his shirtfront and held it out as Padraig had taught him. "Da says my name's bigger'n I am."

Liam studied the hand but made no move to grasp it. "If you're a McCoy, why are you so dark? Why is your hair black?"

"Da says I'm Black Irish, like Great-Uncle Seamus."

"Huh." Liam thought about that. He'd met Great-Uncle Seamus once, but the man was now in his mid-sixties and his once-black hair was white. He'd also met Uncle Connell, who was Seamus' son and he did have black hair, as dark as this little boy's. "You sure you ain't a Injun…like Miss Uŋčí here?"

He nodded at the housekeeper, who was watching them with amusement. A step in the doorway told her Maria and Fiona were also studying the two children.

"I'm positive," Quill replied, nodding his head emphatically. "We call her just Uŋčí. That's Lakota for 'grandmother.' " He leaned forward slightly, saying in a loud whisper, "She's my surry-gate grandmother."

"What's a suwwy-gate?" Liam asked.

"It's a subby-tute. For my grandma in Ireland."

"Oh. I see." Liam glanced at Uŋčí. "Then I guess I can call her that, too, since Grandma's still in Ireland an' I'm here." He grasped the hand Quill still held out. "Please t' meet you, Quill McCoy. I'm your cousin Uilliam Coilin Fionn McCoy. They call me Liam."

Quill gave him a sharp and steady look. "You got any brothers?"

"Nay. I want one, but Da says God ran out o' bwaithurs for his bwanch o' th' McCoy family an' nane o' his orders for one have been filled."

"I don't have any brothers, either. I guess God ran out for our side, too."

"We're cousins," Liam said philosophically. "Guess we can pwetend we're bwaithurs."

"Good idea." Quill nodded. "Want a biscuit?" He gestured toward the platter on the table and sat down again.

"I'd wather have a cookie," Liam decided. "Uŋčí said I could."

"I can't have cookies," Quill told him. "I've been wayward and that's part of my punishment."

"Then I won't have cookies, ithur," Liam decided. "Us bwaithurs got t' stick t'gether, don't we?" He picked up a biscuit and bit into it. "This is good." He smiled. "Kind of like a scone."

"What's a scone?" Quill wanted to know, starting on his second biscuit.

"It's a sort of biscuit but with jelly on top. Me Gwandmaithur Cleary gives them to me when we have tea. She's a lady," he added, as if in afterthought.

"So's Uŋčí." Thinking Liam was insulting her, Quill defended the Lakota.

"Nay, I mean that's part of her name," Liam

explained. "Lady Alisdaire. 'Tis because me gwandfaithur's nobility."

"Is she like a queen?" Quill's hazel eyes rounded in wonder. For a moment, he forgot to chew his biscuit.

"Pwetty close," Liam admitted. "Me maithur's The Honouwable Fiona."

"Do I have to call her that?"

"I guess 'Aunt Fiona' will do. No one at McCoy Hall calls her 'The Honouwable.' "

Quill thought about that, chewing hurriedly. "Does that make you a prince or something?"

Liam shook his head. "I'm just me, 'cause me da's a commoner."

"If he's my pa's brother, he can't be too common," Quill decided.

Uŋčí returned to her chores, lost in thought as to how she should change tonight's meal, since Miz Maria was obviously so involved with their guests she hadn't bothered to discuss it with her. The two children ate in silence a moment before Quill spoke again.

"Will you answer me something?" He finished his biscuit and reached for another.

"Sure."

"Why are you wearing such a sissy-prissy suit?"

"'Tis what e'eryone wears where I come fwom," Liam declared, touching the soft nap of his jacket protectively.

"But you ain't there now, are you?" Quill snickered. "Guess you'd better find some *real* clothes, Cousin. I'll loan you a pair of my denims."

Chapter 54

Colin and Fiona were placed in one of the two bedrooms between Maria's sewing room and the small room at the end of the hall that was Uŋčí's. There was a whispered protest from Fiona at being housed next to a servant, but Colin shushed her before Padraig could hear. Liam was given the bedroom next to Quill's.

"You mean, we can't bunk together?" Quill protested. "But, Da…"

"It may be Liam doesn't want to share a room," Padraig suggested. "He might want some privacy."

"No, I don't," Liam assured him quickly. "I don't need pwibacy."

The look on his face made Padraig wonder if he actually knew what the word meant.

"I don't know…" He looked at his brother. "What do you think, Colin?"

After a great deal of whining and promising, Quill and his cousin convinced their parents they wanted to share Quill's bedroom.

"Very well." Colin finally gave in to Liam's pleas. He glanced at Quill. "When your da and I say 'tis time for th' lamps t' go out an' you two t' sleep, I don't want t' hear any gigglin' or horsin' aroun'."

As Padraig reinforced his brother's orders, there were assurances from both boys that whatever their fathers said would be immediately obeyed. Colin muttered he saw a conspiratorial glance exchanged between the cousins.

The trunk in his parents' bedroom was opened and Liam and Quill spent the next half hour trotting to and from there and Quill's room, carrying Liam's clothing to the wardrobe. Liam dumped them inside and Quill chose substitutes for his cousin from his own clothing.

That night in the dining room, Uŋčí served garden peas and carrots, baked potatoes, biscuits, and freshly carved pork chops from one of the sides of pork in the smokehouse. Padraig sat at the head of the table, lord of the manor in his very bearing, while Maria faced him at its foot. Colin and Fiona sat on one side of the table, with the boys, each bolstered by cushions from the sofa, seated on the other. Quill was proudly displaying the gift Quinton had sent him, a watch fob.

"He's a bit young as well as rough yet to be carryin' a watch," Padraig had decided, but when Quill stated he wanted to wear his Grandpa's gift, he placed it on a rawhide string. The child was now wearing it around his neck.

When he looked at Colin and asked, "What did *you* bring me, Uncle Colin?" Padraig immediately admonished him for being greedy.

"Nay, 'tis all right," Colin answered. "I've brought ourselves, Quill—myself, your Aunt Fiona, and Liam— to come visit you."

Quill thought about that a moment. "I guess that's good enough, 'cause you brought me Liam to play with."

He would never know how those words made his uncle feel.

Before anyone could fill a plate, however, the kitchen door opened and the tramping of boots floated up the hall.

"Who's that?" Colin looked toward the door. "You expectin' guests, braithur?"

"Just th' hired hands," Padraig explained.

"They eat here?" Fiona, paused in taking a biscuit from the platter Uŋčí set before her.

Colin shot her a warning glance, shaking his head. She bit her lip and averted her gaze, though her expression said plainly she was adding this to her list of minor lifestyle differences to ignore. Luckily, neither Padraig nor Maria saw.

"In th' kitchen," Padraig explained. "The table's near as big as this one, an' they've always eaten there. I think some o' th' ranches have a mess hall, but Mr. Jessup set it up this way an' I saw no need t' change. Maria an' I used t' eat with them before th' house was enlarged."

"I thought if we were going to have a dining room, we should utilize it," Maria said. Her tone was slightly defensive.

"Does Uŋčí cook for them, too?" Colin asked.

"Only when they're here. I've a chuck wagon cook for th' drives," Padraig explained. He reached for the platter of chops, selected one, and dropped it onto his plate, passing it to Colin.

"Drive?"

"A cattle drive. I think I mentioned that in one o' me letters t' Da. In th' spring when the calves from th' previous year are old enough, we drive them south t' th' stockyards t' be sold. Having th' railroad come through eases that a bit now. We don't have t' go so far an' don't walk as much fat off th' beeves."

"An' this chuck wagon cook..." Colin looked

fascinated.

"He drives th' wagon carryin' our supplies, an' he cooks our meals. Does th' doctorin' too, if any needs it. When I was hurt…"

"I don't think Colin needs a history of a cattle drive right now," Maria interrupted, not wanting to hear a recounting of that terrible day when a cattle stampede injured Padraig and killed his horse. "Especially not while we're eating."

"Sorry, o' course not," Padraig acquiesced.

"Think your men'd mind havin' a couple o' intruders at th' table t'night?" Colin got to his feet, picking up the delicate china plate before him. "I've met Buck and Pete. Now I'd like t' meet th' rest o' your employees, braithur."

"Colin! You aren't suggesting…" Fiona didn't finish.

Plate in hand, her husband was out the door, Padraig following.

For several seconds, no one else moved, then Liam slid from the chair in which he'd been sitting, gathering his cushion. Quill did the same. The boys looked at each other, then at their mothers.

Fiona sighed, her expression despairing. "Go ahead."

As they carefully balanced cushions and plates and scurried out the door, she shook her head. "No use saying no. When Colin gets an idea into his head, he'll have his way no matter what."

"It's the same with Padraig," Maria agreed. "We appear to have married two men equally willful." She smiled ruefully as she gathered her own empty plate and napkin. "Shall we?"

"I'm thankful so far he's not thought of anything so harebrained it's dangerous," Fiona muttered.

She and Maria followed their husbands and sons down the hall.

"I swear, Uŋčí, you're a better cook than me faithur's own Mrs. Hennessey who's been preparing meals for us as long as I can remember."

"Thank you, Mr. Colin," Uŋčí replied, glancing solemnly around the table and letting her gaze rest on the chuck wagon cook. "You are kind to say that."

"Hey," Cookie protested. "I always tell you how good you cook. And the others, too." He glanced around. "Well...most of them, anyway."

"I tease you, Cookie," Uŋčí replied. She reached for Colin's plate. "You are finished, Mr. Colin?"

"Couldn't eat another bite," he patted his vest, which he'd unbuttoned so he could have a third helping of buttered peas and carrots and a fourth biscuit. "Now I've got t' sleep this off so I can prepare meself for breakfast."

"I'm afraid you'll have to eat Cookie's food tomorrow," she told him.

"You're not givin' notice, are you?" He pretended distress, glancing at Padraig, who grinned at his younger brother's antics. "Braithur, stop her!"

Accustomed to Padraig's mock dramatics, Uŋčí knew he wasn't serious. "I don't know what *notice* is, but tomorrow's the day I visit my people. Cookie takes over cooking that day."

"There's an Indian encampment near here?" Colin looked interested.

"About five miles, near the banks o' th' Platte," Padraig answered. "I always escort Uŋčí there and back."

"I tell Mr. Padraig it's unnecessary, but he insists," Uŋčí explained.

"I insist because 'tis in me nature as a gentleman t' ride with an unprotected female when she goes visitin'," Padraig said.

"Would you mind havin' two escorts t'morrow?" Colin asked.

"You want t' ride with us?" Padraig looked surprised, frowning at Fiona's abruptly worried expression. He'd noticed how his sister-in-law said very little but reacted with various expressions, mostly negative ones, to whatever was said.

"If Uŋčí wouldn't mind," Colin answered, looking back at the housekeeper.

"No, Mr. Colin, I don't mind."

"Hey, Uncle Padwaig," Liam swallowed the portion of potato he'd just stuffed into his mouth. "Can I go, too?"

"Don't see why not," Padraig answered.

"Can I wide wiv you on th' horse again?"

"You could ride with me," Colin said.

"Nay, Da. I'd wather wide with Uncle Padwaig. He lets me hold th' weins."

"Well, then…" Colin gave a grimace of mock disappointment.

"If Liam's going, can I, too," Quill protested. "Da?"

Before Padraig could answer, Maria spoke up. "I don't think Quill needs to go."

"But *I* can? Wight?" Liam persisted.

He glanced from his mother to his father, neither of whom had spoken. Colin looked enthusiastic. Fiona appeared dismayed.

"So I can see a weal Injun, with fedders an'

e'erythin'?"

"If Liam goes…" Padraig glanced at Maria, then at Quill, whose face was primping into a pout. "'Tis only fair that Quill go with us, too." He ruffled the child's dark straight hair. Looking down the table, his gaze met Maria's as he said, "Of course you can, son."

"You can wide wiv me da," Liam told him. "An' I'll wide wiv yours."

Padraig turned to Colin. "After we get back, I'll give you a tour o' th' ranch."

Maria didn't speak. On her side of the table, neither did Fiona.

Later, after the men returned to the bunkhouse, Cookie insisted on staying behind and helping Uŋčí finish the chores.

"More people to feed means more dishes and pots and pans to wash," he said. "You'll be here all night otherwise."

Uŋčí couldn't argue with that.

Maria and Fiona retired to the parlor where Maria was wrestling with yet another shirt, this one having a torn sleeve cuff where Padraig had caught it on barbed wire earlier in the week. Padraig and Colin were on the porch, sharing glasses of brandy, getting reacquainted and reliving old times. Occasionally raised voices filtered through the screen. Other times the sound dropped to whispers, then bursts of laughter.

"Uŋčí says I shouldn't have to worry about mending," Maria said. "I feel guilty that I never learned how."

That was a lie. Along with their letters and ciphers, one of the first things the girl children had been taught at the school she attended was how to cook and sew.

Embroidery as well as other genteel pastimes were also stressed when her foster parents sent her to the school for young ladies.

Fiona took a second shirt out of the mending basket. It was one of Quill's, three buttons missing. "I see Quill's as rough on clothing as Liam is."

She selected a needle, found a thimble and spool, and began to thread it before looking up.

"Your hired men…they're…"

"A bit crude and coarse, I know," Maria supplied. She'd notice how Fiona watched the men furtively as she ate, occasionally wincing at their ungrammatical speech. It had amused her while making her also feel sympathetic.

"I was going to say *rough*," Fiona corrected apologetically. "Nevertheless, I sense an odd kindness under their manner. They were truly nice to me."

She didn't add how appalled she'd been that she, a nobleman's daughter, was sitting at table with the hired help, men comparable to laborers. Fiona realized quick enough that would mark her as a snob and lower her in her brother-in-law's estimation. Colin's sharp words, though spoken in an undertone, had underscored that.

She didn't want such a thing to happen. From the little she'd seen of him, she liked her brother-in-law, who'd already erased the opinion she'd formed over the years from hearing about his younger self's escapades. She didn't want to insult him by bringing up their cultural differences.

"They're good men," Maria told her. "They have to be rough, and hardy, too, to live in a place like this. It demands it."

"Padraig isn't so changed," Fiona pointed out.

"That's because he wasn't born here, I think. I imagine he's quite different from the way he was when he arrived, however."

"I'm glad we won't be staying all that long," Fiona went on. "Not that I'm in such a hurry to leave your and Padraig's company," she added hastily, so Maria wouldn't get the wrong idea. "But I'd hate to think Colin might be changed by his surroundings. He's a gentleman, not a-a…cowboy."

"I consider Padraig a gentleman," Maria pointed out.

A short, embarrassed silence fell.

Fiona decided she'd best change the subject before she found herself in her sister-in-law's bad graces. She also told herself to watch what she said. She was now in a country where employer and employee were on a more even status than in Ireland and she'd better not forget it.

"You aren't worried about them going to that Indian camp?"

"There's nothing dangerous between here and the encampment."

"B-but those Indians…" Fiona protested. "What if they decide to attack and…they scalp people, don't they?" Her eyes went wide, as if she envisioned two bright and bloody copper falls of hair hanging from a scalp pole before a Lakota tent.

"The Lakota around here have been peaceful." Maria was so far into her own deception she felt no insult at Fiona's words. *They are no longer my people. My people are somewhere in Alta California.* "Besides, Uŋčí's with them. They would never have let Uŋčí come to work for Padraig if they were hostile."

"You *did* tell Padraig you didn't think Quill should

go," Fiona pointed out.

"That's only because he's so small." Maria answered. "I wasn't worried about his safety."

"I hope you're right," Fiona still looked doubtful.

"When they come back, unharmed, you'll see I am."

"I'm sorry," Fiona apologized. "I suppose you think I'm foolish, worrying so…it's just that…Colin does things on the spur of the moment, then thinks about the consequences later." She laughed quietly. "When we were courting, it was exciting…because I never knew what he was going to do, but later…like coming here…"

She gestured around, then busied herself searching through the button jar. Selecting one as similar to those on the shirt as she could find, she began sewing it into place.

"He got a bee in his bonnet about seeing his older brother. Truly, he and Father Quinton argued about it most loudly. Finally, Father Quinton said, '*Go then…see that rapscallion son o' mine and get your fill o' him,*' and Colin said, '*Thanks, Da, I will,*' and came upstairs to our bedchamber and said, '*Fiona, I'm going to America.*'" She looked up, giving a slightly quavering smile showing the shock she'd felt. "I didn't realize he meant all three of us."

"…and you didn't want to come here." Maria gave her a sympathetic smile, thinking if all McCoy men were as strong-willed as Padraig, the family must stay in a state of perpetual turmoil.

Fiona nodded and didn't speak.

"You could've refused to come with him."

"No." Fiona met her eyes. "I couldn't."

From outside, as if underscoring her words, came Colin's laughter.

****

Colin looked out across the front yard and past it to the road leading across the prairie.

"I hope no one was insulted by how timid Fiona acted," he said. "'Twas obvious she was shocked by eating with people she considers servants. I can see there's a familiar feeling 'twixt you an' your men, but Fiona doesn't understand that yet. She's got t' learn th' class system in Ireland doesn't exist as rigidly here in America."

He sighed and leaned against the porch railing.

"Is it as you imagined?" Padraig asked.

"Nay, naithin' like I saw in me mind," Colin denied. The look he turned on his brother held sheer wonder. "How could I e'er think o' anythin' this vast an' beautiful? 'Tis breath-takin'." He gestured at the sky. "Look at that sunset! I thought seeing th' sun set back in Tipperary was a beautiful sight, but this...'tis fantastic, Padraig."

"Fiona seemed a bit dismayed about you ridin' with me tomorrow." After what Colin had just said, Padraig hesitantly broached something he sensed might be a delicate subject.

"Ah...she's a female, always worryin' o'er her men," Colin brushed aside his wife's fears. "You should've heard her when I took Liam down t' the river t' teach th' lad t' swim."

"Th' same one where you and I learnt t' swim?"

"Aye. You'd have thought I was going t' tie him t' a plank an send him sailin' out t' sea." He laughed. "That or some giant trout was going t' swallow him whole as that whale did Jonah."

"Maithurs worry about their babes," Padraig spoke

with a more sympathetic tone, thinking of the many times he'd seen Maria stifle her own protests where Quill was concerned. "An' wives about the husbands they love."

"So why didn't Maria argue against you takin' Quill?" Liam pointed out.

"Because she knows if I want, I'll take him anyway," Padraig answered. "If I want t' go somewhere, I'll do that, too."

"Exactly." Colin struck the bannister with a fist as if he'd scored a point in some argument. "That's why Liam an' I are goin'. Besides," he added, "'tis difficult t' say *nay* t' th' lad."

"Same here," Padraig confessed.

"You've impressed me son. I could be jealous o' how he wants t' ride with you instead o' me...but I won't. I know 'tis just th' novelty."

Padraig laughed. "Think that fine Irish arse o' yours can tolerate sittin' that western saddle for ten miles there an' back?"

"I think me arse is accommodatin' its fine Irish self t' th' western saddle easily enough, thank you." Colin raised his brandy glass.

"Sounds like somethin' Da would say."

"Where do you think I heard it?"

"Can you see Da ridin' western-style?"

"Not really."

"I miss him. E'en after all this time." Padraig swallowed a little loudly. "How's Mama?"

"Doin' all right. Still tryin' t' keep Da from gettin' apoplectic. She an' Lady Alisdaire do a good bit o' charity work in th' villages."

"And Bridey?"

"Pretty as ev'er, though gettin' a bit on the plump side."

"How about Donal? Is he still hidin' behind that British exterior?"

"Like John Bull hisself, but you wouldn't recognize him. You knew about his excursions, didn't you?"

"Took all me will power not t' tell Da," Padraig confessed. "Is he…"

Colin shook his head. "He's as much in love with Felicity as I am with Fiona. As I think you are with Maria."

That confession was followed by silence.

"Oh, God, 'tis good t' see you again, Colin." Abruptly, Padraig was filled with such joy he thought he might actually burst into tears, thinking how much he'd miss this kind of banter with his siblings. Quelling that desire, he seized his brother and hugged him tightly, then raised his own glass in salute. "Why don't we go in now? Our wives will be thinkin' we've abandoned them."

"Padraig," Maria said as they came through the door. "I think tomorrow, after you and Colin return from taking Unčí to her visit, you should include Fiona in your tour of the ranch. I'm certain she'd like to see it, too. I'll ride along, also."

She glanced at Fiona as she said that.

"Uh…yes, I would." Fiona's confirmation seemed a bit reluctant. She immediately followed that with a more hopeful, "Oh, but I didn't bring my riding habit."

"And we've only one side saddle," Padraig added. It was plain he didn't want to include women but wanted more time alone with Colin.

"I guess that means I can't…" Fiona turned an apologetic gaze on Maria.

"No matter." Maria cut her off in mid-sentence, determined Fiona was going to be exposed to more of Nebraska than she'd seen so far. She hoped to overcome her sister-in-law's unspoken resistance. "You can use mine."

She didn't add Padraig disliked her riding sidesaddle.

"My riding habit as well. I think we're of a size. I have a western saddle I sometimes use. I'll wear my dungarees."

"You...you ride astride?" Fiona looked shocked. "Wearing breeches?"

"I do that sometimes," Maria admitted. Her eyes twinkled and she leaned toward Fiona, confiding in a loud whisper, "Padraig likes that."

Colin exchanged a smirk with his brother.

"Well, then..." Padraig covered his dismay at having his sister-in-law accompanying them. "Guess we'd best turn in. Sunrise comes early."

"Earlier than it does in Tipperary?" Colin tapped his glass against Padraig's and finished the last swallow of brandy.

"Much earlier," Padraig assured him.

****

The next morning after breakfast, however, Colin immediately disappeared upstairs to change, coming down shortly after to join everyone in the parlor. His appearance was met by exclamations from Buck, who had come in to speak with Padraig.

"Gawdalmighty, Colin, what's that you're wearing?" Buck shouted.

Even Padraig stared. His brother was dressed in black riding boots, fawn-colored riding trousers, and a scarlet coat with a black silk ascot, all topped by a black top hat.

"Just me huntin' pink, is all," Colin replied. He looked around at the slightly stunned expressions. "Won't it do?"

"I'm afraid not," Padraig replied. "You're liable t' have every bull calf in th' herd chargin' us when they see that red coat."

"Hm." Colin considered that. "What do you suggest?"

"That I loan you some o' me own clothes for this trip." Padraig put an arm across his brother's shoulders and steered him back up the stairs. "I think we're most th' same size now. Lord, I remember when you were such a li'l mite. "We'll finish our talk later," he called to Buck over his shoulder. "Right now, I've got to get me braithur into the proper clothes."

When Colin came downstairs again, he was wearing Padraig's second-best sombrero as well as one of his brother's cambric shirts, with a red bandana tied around his neck, all contrasting dramatically with his riding pants and shining leather knee boots.

Chapter 56

By now, Eagle-of-Iron was accustomed to seeing the red-haired white man ride into the camp with Čik'ayela Wanáhča. Padraig always greeted the chief in Lakota, using one of the few phrases he'd learned during Quill's lessons. After assisting the housekeeper in dismounting, though she could've done so by herself, he'd ride away, promising to return to escort her back to the ranch just before sundown.

The chief had once asked her why Padraig insisted on helping her from her horse. "Does he think you're a weakling who can't get off a horse's back by yourself?"

"He's being a gentleman," Uŋčí replied. "He helps Miz Maria all the time. That's what gentlemen do in Mr. Padraig's country."

"What's a gentleman?" Eagle-of-Iron frowned.

"A man who helps a woman from a horse's back." Uŋčí answered, shrugging. "They also open doors for women, and sometimes carry packages and other heavy things, and even do household chores for them."

She thought back to the many times Cookie had shouldered her aside with the statement, "That's too heavy for a little thing like you. Let a man do it."

Eagle-of-Iron looked shocked. "These gentlemen actually do woman's work?"

Uŋčí nodded.

"White men are strange." He shook his head.

Now Eagle-of-Iron asked, "Who is this?" and nodded at Colin as Padraig released reins to Uŋčí's brother-in-law, who tied the horse to the rope fence keeping their own animals penned.

"This is me braithur, Colin." Padraig gestured. "The li'l ones are me nephew an' me son, Liam and Quill."

"Pleased to meet you." Colin doffed his hat.

Liam tentatively raised a hand. "Hullo."

Quill merely stared. He might've spoken bravely about accompanying his father to the encampment, but now they were here, the presence of so many Lakota, with their long dark hair and buckskin clothing, was a little overwhelming to the child who was accustomed to fair-skinned men in flannel shirts and denims.

Eagle-of-Iron studied Colin, who hadn't dismounted but returned the Lakota's stare with a smile. "I can see you are of the same tribe. Do all of your blood have red hair, Padraig McCoy?"

"Not all, just those blessed." Padraig laughed and remounted. "See you around sunset."

"Yes, Mr. Padraig," Uŋčí replied.

He and Colin rode away.

Eagle-of-Iron turned from watching Padraig and Colin ride away and asked, "Padraig McCoy called the Lakota boy his nephew. His brother has a woman from our people?"

That appeared to worry him.

"What Lakota boy?" Uŋčí asked.

"You saw." He gestured in the direction Colin and Padraig had ridden. "The child before his brother on the saddle.

"The dark child is Mr. Padraig's son." Uŋčí's answer was patient. "The red-haired boy is Mr. Colin's."

"That one is of this Irish also?" Eagle-of-Iron was shocked. "He looks Lakota."

"Mr. Padraig says there are dark ones among his own people. Black Irish he calls them. Quill is Black Irish."

"Quill. It sounds Lakota," Eagle-of-Iron protested.

"I think Quill takes after his mother," Uŋčí continued. "Miz Maria is Spanish."

"Spanish," Eagle-of-Iron repeated. "They are Sioux?"

She shook her head. "Spanish live far away, at the other end of this country. Too far to ride in three days. They are white, too."

Eagle-of-Iron didn't answer. The idea of a red-haired man having a child who looked so much like his own people, and the fact of people somewhere who also were dark but considered white was too much to comprehend.

Chapter 57

It was near noon by the time they returned to the ranch. Fiona was already dressed to ride.

There had been a bit of a to-do as Liam and Quill decided they wanted to ride along with their parents and Padraig and Colin had adamantlysaid they would not.

At that point, Fiona and Maria stepped in, decreeing that it was time for naps, assuring the two youngsters that when they awoke, their parents would be back from their tour. "…and, if we're not," Maria said, before either could protest, "Big Jack or Buck will let you ride one of the horses inside the corral." She shot a look at Padraig who appeared about to comment. "I've already talked it over with them, and believe it or not, Big Jack actually volunteered."

"So, when I wake, I can wide a weal cowpony?" Liam's green eyes went wide.

"Yes, dear," Fiona's assurance sound a bit weary as if she were conceding some victory to an opponent.

They left the boys snuggling into Quill's bed, feigning loud snores. Fiona had changed into Maria's riding habit, which looked fetching on her, and Colin said so, while Padraig thought silently that Maria, in denims and one of his work shirts and wearing a sombrero with a twined string under her chin, made him want to cancel the entire trip and take her back upstairs. He managed not to say that, however, as she mounted her horse and rode it to his side.

"Be sure to show Fiona something scenic," Maria whispered, as Colin help his wife onto her horse and waited for her to adjust the sidesaddle before her swung back onto his own mount. "Let her see Nebraska isn't all flatland and grass."

With that in mind, Padraig led them through a section of prairie abloom with flowers, to Fiona's delight. She demanded to know the names of all she saw and Padraig called off as many as he could remember, with Maria supplying others.

"If 'twas time t' ride back inta McCoy's Crossin' for supplies, I'd show you th' salt flats," he said, pleased by her enthusiasm for the flowers and heeding his wife's words.

"Salt flats?"

"They're 'twixt here an' town. Salt deposits so thick it looks as if 'tis snowed." He explained. "If you're here at th' end o' th' month, you can see them then."

"I'm sure we may be," Colin said.

Fiona shot him a sharp glance that didn't go unnoticed by either Padraig or Maria, though neither remarked on it.

They came to a grove of trees with a little creek running through it.

"We're lucky the Shamrock has its own water supply," Padraig said as they entered the grove. In sharp contrast to the prairie, the air rising from the creek and the shade of the trees made the area dark and cool. "We've got this creek an' a couple o' springs."

"Aye." Colin spoke up. "I saw th' big windmill an' I was wonderin' where your mill was."

"That runs water t' th' sink in th' kitchen, as well as

a pump in th' yard. It supplies water for th' corrals, an' th' bunkhouse, too."

"I'd like t' see that bunkhouse," Colin said. "Is it like the servants' quarters back home?"

"Not quite." Padraig laughed. "I'll take you there later." He glanced at his sister-in-law. "I doubt Fiona'll want to see that…twelve or so men stashed in a room together."

Ahead of them, Fiona and Maria had stopped their horses at the creek's edge where it widened into a little pool.

"Colin," Fiona looked over her shoulder at her husband. "This reminds me of that pond where you taught me—I mean, Liam—to swim."

"Damn if it isn't like it." Colin looked around in mock surprise, ignoring his brother's raised brows. "Trees are a bit different, but it *is* similar." He laughed.

"What kind of trees are these?" Fiona asked, looking at one hanging over the water as if peering at its reflection.

"Mostly cottonwoods," Padraig replied. "All the trees around here were brought in by settlers. I think Mr. Jessup had these imported as saplings from Kansas City. He brought in th' apple trees, too. Where'er you see trees on th' plains, you can be sure there's water an' people nearby because that's where th' trees are planted."

"Too bad we didn't pack a picnic basket," Colin said. "This would be a good place t' lay out a supper."

"No time for picnics today," Padraig answered. "We still have t' ride back an' get Uŋčí, an' Cookie'll be making supper tonight."

"Ah well…don't tell him I said so, but e'en if he *is* a good cook, that li'l woman's much better." Colin laughed.

"Come on, ladies." Padraig turned the skewbald's head and trotted the horse out of the grove.

****

"What are they doing?" Fiona asked as they stopped their horses near a section of the herd separated from the others.

One of the hands was wrestling a calf to the ground while another helped him drag it to a fire. Buck, squatting near the fire, lifted a long stick-like item from the coals.

"They're branding th' calves," Padraig explained.

A bawl of pain interrupted what he was saying as the branding iron was pressed against the calf's flank.

Fiona flinched.

"Padraig, I don't think..." Maria began, wincing also as the wind changed and the scent of burning hair wafted toward them.

By now, Padraig was realizing perhaps this hadn't been the most prudent choice of something to show them.

"Bull calf," one of the cowboys holding the calf called.

Buck reached for something lying near the fire. It flashed silver in the sun as they flipped the calf onto its back, its legs kicking. One cowboy caught its hind legs. The blade snicked downward and up again. The calf shrieked this time, a sound of near-mortal pain. Buck tossed something red and dripping into a nearby barrel, then scooped a handful of mud from a puddle and slapped it onto the wound.

The calf was set on its feet and released. It tottered a moment, stumbled, then wobbled back to its mother, dripping mud and blood down its legs.

"Padraig? Did he just…"

Padraig was startled to see his brother's face pale slightly. Behind them, Fiona was paper-white and even Maria had lost a bit of color.

Now he was certain he'd made a mistake.

"Aye. Looks like the boys'll be having quite a feast tonight." He nodded at the barrel, speaking nonchalantly, trying to gloss over his mistake.

"Feast? You mean, they eat…" Colin stopped, swallowing loudly.

"Aye…consider it a delicacy, in fact. Call them mountain oysters."

"We won't be expected t'…" Again Colin couldn't finish. "I mean, you don't…"

"O' course not!" Padraig's denial was vehement. He glanced at Maria, who was shaking her head as if he were Quill who'd committed some very naughty act in polite company, like spitting on the rug. "Do you think I've turned Scot, droolin' over haggis? If that's on tonight's menu, we'll ride inta town an' eat at th' Sylvestre House."

Another calf was dragged to the fire. Its wail was as sharp as the first. The scent of blood and singed hair became even stronger.

"Please…" Fiona's weak request floated to him as she flapped a hand in front of her face before pressing it against her lips. "Can we go?"

"Of course." Padraig was quick to apologize. "Sorry, Fiona. I didn't think."

He wheeled the skewbald. Maria rode her own horse to his side.

"Honestly, Padraig. How could you?" She snapped

at him in an undertone making certain neither Fiona nor Colin heard.

Glancing back, she saw Colin leaning toward his wife, speaking softly. He had given her his bandana and she wiped her eyes with it.

"How could you be so thoughtless?

"Sorry, love, I didn't…"

"Well, make sure you *do*, no matter whatever you show them next. I think it's obvious Fiona isn't too happy about this trip and I'm doing my best to keep her pacified. Let something else like this happen, and she may be on the next train east!"

Sufficiently chastened, Padraig slowed the skewbald and rode back to Fiona.

"I apologize, Fiona. Sometime I forget not e'eryone in th' world's as inured t' ranch life as I've become. I've upset you an' I'm sorry."

She looked at him from behind the shield of Colin's bandanna. "I… It's just that…"

"Fiona has a soft heart," Colin put in. "She can't bear t' see anythin' hurt, e'en when 'tis necessary, an' I imagine *that*…" He nodded over his shoulder at the herd. "…is."

"That's true," Padraig answered. "We have t' brand th' cattle t' prove ownership in case any are stolen, an' th' ithur…well, th' cattle we sell don't need t' be bulls since we won't be usin' them for breedin'…"

"Please," Fiona groaned.

"I think you're making it worse." Maria joined them.

"Why don't you take Fiona back t' th' ranch house an' let her lie down for a bit?" Padraig suggested. He backed the skewbald away from Fiona's horse, as if afraid she might try to slap him.

With a nod, Maria said, "Excellent idea. Come on, Fiona."

She moved so Fiona could guide her horse forward, then rode beside her. Padraig saw she was speaking quickly and earnestly to her sister-in-law.

"Well, I did that up proud," he muttered.

"It certainly wasn't good," Colin agreed. He laughed and the sound was rueful. "Even gave me a twinge or two, it did, an' I've gone with Da an' watched th' shepherds do th' nuttin' o' the sheep a couple o' times."

"I'm sorry, Col."

"Don't be. Fiona's soft-hearted, as I said. Sometimes, too much." Colin brushed aside his wife's sensitivities. "While we're here, she'll simply have t' accept thin's, that's all. Now then, what say we get along with our tour? What's next?"

He looked around eagerly.

****

Padraig pulled the skewbald to a halt next to a length of barbed wire.

"This is the extent o' me property on this side," he said. He nodded to a bare, hard-trodden strip of land beyond the fence. "That bit's eminent domain, still owned by th' State o' Nebraska, right-o'-way for stages, travelers an' herders t' use."

"Whose land is that on th' ithur side?" Colin asked.

"Th' T-Bar. Used t' belong to me friend, Rance Terry," Padraig explained. "He died in that influenza epidemic I wrote Da about, so now 'tis his widow's. Ranch has been going downhill e'er since Terry died."

Colin didn't reply.

"They lost a lot o' calves this past winter, an' what

they do have aren't up t'grade. They're breedin' Texas longhorns, when what they need t' do is get a couple o' good Herefords like I have or maybe some o' those Scottish Angus like that Mr. Grant's usin' down in Kansas." Padraig paused and sighed. "Mrs. Terry's been tryin t' sell. She'd like t' go back to Kansas an' live with her family, but so far there's been no takers. I'm surprised, for 'twas a good ranch, an' it could be again, with th' right manager."

"What does a ranch like that go for?" Colin wondered aloud.

"I hear she's asking three dollars an acre. There's about eight thousand acres, I think. I know 'tis smaller than me ranch, anyhow."

"How many acres do *you* have?"

"Around ten thousand. I paid th' asking price for mine, a flat sum."

Colin looked around, then nodded. "I'll take it."

"What?"

"I said, *I'll take it*. I want t' buy th' T-Bar. Does th' Widow Terry have a solicitor?"

"They call them lawyers here," Padraig said, automatically. "Colin, I know you're enthralled by all th' newness an' p'rhaps th' idea o' th' adventure o' livin' in such a wild an' still untamed place, but think this through."

"I have thou—" Colin didn't get to finish.

"Nebraska may look good now, but you haven't been through a winter yet. You may change your mind when th' water freezes in th' wash basin because 'tis so cold outside…or when one o' those tornados comes through an' flattens e'erythin'. We've been lucky in that respect because the weather's been mild these past years, but it can still happen. Don't go makin' such a rash…"

"Do you think this is a spur o' th' moment thin', Padraig?" What Colin said next was astonishing. "Nay, this is what I came here for. T' buy a ranch, near yours if possible. I thought this out long before I got here."

"Does Da know about this?"

"It doesn't matter whether he does or nay. Da doesn't run me life…at least, not any more. I decided that before I left. Yes, he knows. I told him so. We talked…argued, rather. Then he told me t' do as I wished…an' this is what I wish. I came here with his blessing, not his permission. 'Tis what I want. T' own a ranch, p'rhaps t' be partners in its runnin' with me braithur."

Padraig didn't answer.

"'Tis been me dream for some time now, Padraig," Colin went on, voice quiet but urgent. "I've missed you so much, braithur, an' I can't think of a better way t' have you back in me life."

"In that case…" Padraig took a deep breath. "We'll ride inta McCoy's Crossin' tomorrow an' speak t' me lawyer about handlin' th' transaction. He was Terry's lawyer, too. In th' meantime…"

He glanced at the sun, seeing how low it was in the sky.

"I think 'tis time we went t' fetch Uŋčí."

Chapter 58

"I'm glad you decided to come back." Maria met them at the door. "Poor Fiona was about to go into a panic, thinking you'd been waylaid somewhere by a Sioux war party."

"'Twas so late we decided t' ride out an' get Uŋčí an' then come back t' th' ranch," Padraig explained.

He stepped aside so the housekeeper could walk around him and make her way to the kitchen.

"Smells like Cookie's already started supper, Uŋčí." He raised his head, sniffing. "Do I smell cabbage an' bacon?"

"Let's eat!" Colin pushed past them, aiming for the hallway and the kitchen.

Fiona, sitting on the settee, watched him go past, then leaped to her feet, following nearly at a run. "Colin? Don't I get a 'hello'? Where are your manners?"

"He's flushed," Maria commented, lowering her voice. "What's happened?"

"Naithin'."

"Padraig…"

"'Tisn't for me t' say, love. That's Colin's business," Padraig answered. "When he's ready."

"Ready for what?"

He didn't answer, merely took her arm and escorted her to the kitchen.

The men were at the table, Liam and Quill,

chattering about their horseback rides, were on their cushion-piled chairs. Uŋčí seated herself next to Big Jack while Cookie brought the big pot of cabbage and green bacon to the table already holding a platter of porkchops, biscuits, and a bowl of baked squash and onions. Colin was at the place he'd had that morning, Fiona sat herself beside him, giving him furious but silent stares.

They paused in passing around the bowls long enough for Padraig and Maria to take their places. Before Padraig could take the first bite, however, Colin was on his feet. Padraig looked at his brother. Maria was right. His fair face was flushed as if he'd just run a race, and he was breathing quickly, obviously excited.

"Gentlemen…" He raised the cup of cider Cookie set by his plate. "I wish t' propose a toast."

Everyone quieted, giving him their attention.

"Here's t' th' newest rancher in McCoy's Crossin'."

"Who's that, Colin?" Buck asked.

"Meself, o' course." Colin beamed. "I'm buyin' th' T-Bar."

"You what?" Fiona's fork fell to her plate, the clatter loud in the silence of the room. "How can you run a ranch from across the ocean?"

"I won't be running it from across an ocean," he replied.

"What does that mean?" Her voice shrilled, like a knife drilling the question into the air.

"It means we'll be living here and not in Ireland," he answered.

She stared at him. Fiona couldn't have looked more stunned if he'd slapped her. "Colin, how could you?"

Without another word, she put hands to her mouth, and with a choked sob, leaped to her feet. Pushing back her chair with a clatter, she ran from the room.

The men didn't speak, looking at each other in confusion. For once, Padraig was at a loss as to what to say as the stamp of Fiona's shoes on the stairs came back to them.

"Sorry." Colin looked around. "Guess I'd better speak with me wife. Privately."

He pushed back his chair and started to leave the room, then turned back as if suddenly remembering his manners. "Excuse me, please." His own footsteps followed in the echo of Fiona's.

"Is Mama mad at Da?" In the silence, Liam's question was as shrill as Fiona's had been.

Maria got to her feet. "I should…"

"Nay." Padraig caught her arm. "You shouldn't. This is 'twixt Colin an' Fiona." He pulled her back into her chair and sat in his own. "Let's eat, lads. Don't let th' comin' li'l domestic disturbance spoil your supper. Eat up."

With that, he began to spoon squash from the bowl in front of him.

The men resumed eating, though it was with less than their usual relish. When loud voices floated down the stairs, easily recognizable as Colin's and then Fiona's, raised in high tones almost to shrieks, dying to soft sobbing, that quelled their usual banter. They finished the meal in embarrassed silence except for near-whispered requests to "Pass the biscuits," or "Can I have another chop, Cookie?"

Afterward, in a body, one and all rose, nodded good night to Padraig and Maria, and trailed out the backdoor to the bunkhouse.

Padraig and Maria went into the parlor, leaving Uŋčí

and Cookie tending to the cleaning-up. They took Liam and Quill with them, getting a picture book from one of the bookcases, telling both boys to look at it.

A short time later, a red-faced Colin and tear-stained Fiona came down the stairs.

"Braithur…?" Colin glanced at Padraig, then stamped out onto the porch, letting the screen slam behind him.

Fiona didn't speak but simply sank onto the sofa.

"Ma?" Liam looked up. "What's th' matter with Da?"

Fiona didn't answer, shaking her head.

"Quill, I think 'tis time for you an' Liam t' get ready for bed," Padraig said.

"But, Pa, it's only seven o'clock," Quill protested, glancing at the clock on the mantel.

"Ne'er mind the time. I say you two should be abed," Padraig answered. "Now go. No arguments," he continued as Quill started to do exactly that.

Silently, Quill laid down the book. "Come on, Liam."

"But I want t' know why Da…"

"Liam," Fiona snapped at the child. "Do as your Uncle Padraig says."

"Aye, Ma." Obediently, but with obvious reluctance, Liam followed Quill up the stairs.

"I wish we'd never come here," Fiona looked at Padraig as she said it.

Tears trickled down her cheeks. She began to sob. Maria patted her hand.

Padraig didn't answer. Instead, he wheeled and slung open the screen, walking out onto the porch.

****

"You mean she, didn't know?" Padraig shouted at his brother. "Damn it, Colin, no wonder she's so upset. Spring somethin' like that on her…an' in front o' a group o' strangers, too? Have you no sense at all?"

"I'd spoken o' th' idea once or twice," Colin defended himself.

"But not in earnest, I'll wager," Padraig retorted. "I'll bet e'ery time you told her, you said you simply *wished* it would happen, or *what if,* or somethin' like that?"

"Well, aye, but…"

"An' you went t' Da with th idea, instead o' to your wife? Lord, what an imbecile I have for a braithur."

"You've no right t' say that o' me!" Colin flared. "I wasn't th one pluggin' that English lord's wife an' threatenin' Da's position so Da had t' pay you t' go away an' ne'er come back."

"Aye, now, that's a low blow." Padraig struggled to control his temper. "I'm not e'en going t' answer that."

"Doubt you can, anyway," Colin retorted. His tone changed, becoming *very* earnest. "Padraig, you've no idea how it's been…all these years…e'eryone lookin' at me and watchin' to see if I'd turn out like you…waitin' for me t' take that first fatal step… All my life, I've felt like a fly on a pin!"

"Colin…" Padraig was momentarily appalled by the anguish in his brother's words. "I had no idea…"

"An' would it have made any difference, if you had?"

Padraig didn't answer. Instead, he stuttered a moment but found nothing he could say, as he remembered facing that same question with Quinton and his answer then. At last, he huffed, "Anyway, we're not talkin' about me here, but you…an' what you've done."

"Aye, there's that," Colin admitted. "Truly, I don't want us t' fight, Padraig."

"Then tell me what are you goin' t' do?"

"What's there t' do?" Colin asked. "I'm buyin' th' ranch, as I said."

"An' Fiona?"

"She's me wife. She'll accept that an' not complain. Eventually."

"Seems she's already done th' complainin'. You're still goin' ahead with it?"

"I am. I'm th' head o' me family. This is one time I'm doin' what *I* want and I don't care what anyone says. Da didn't stop me from comin' here, an' naithur is me wife goin' t' keep me from stayin'. She doesn't run me life as Mar…"

Colin stopped.

"As…?" Padraig prompted. "As Maria does mine? Is that what you were about t' say? You think I'm skirt-whipped?"

"Well, you do give in t' her a bit," Colin answered. "E'en in two days I've seen it. She says something an' you jump t' do it."

"Me wife doesn't tell me what t' do!" Padraig exclaimed. "Aye, a good many times I do what she suggests, an' I let her have her way a good bit, but that's because I love her. But she doesn't boss me around an' where me life an me ranch are concerned, I make me own decisions."

"I'm sorry, Padraig."

"You'd best be sayin' that to Fiona, not me," Padraig snapped. "An' you'd better be givin' her more consideration in your decisions from now on. This country is a place where both men an' women have t' work together, Colin, an' if you don't realize an' accept that now, you may as well take th' next train east an' board a ship for Ireland."

He realized Colin was staring at him, green eyes wide.

"What th' hell is it?"

"God, you're th' image o' Da in one o' his frenzies. I ne'er realized how much alike you two are." He began to laugh, and in a moment, Padraig was laughing along with him. "'Twas like bein' at home. I'm sorry, Padraig. E'erythin' you said's true. I was only thinkin' o' meself, ne'er o' Fiona or Liam." He looked earnest, before adding, "Do you think she can forgive me?"

"One way t' find out," Padraig replied. "That's t' get in there an' start includin' her in your future plans."

He pushed Colin toward the door.

****

Maria caught Fiona's hands in her own.

"It won't be so bad," she soothed.

"No offense, Maria, but I don't want to live here," Fiona wailed. "I want to live in Tipperary."

"I'm afraid if Colin's made up his mind, you're going to stay here," Maria said practically. "It appears your husband's like his brother in stubbornness, and I don't think you can change his mind once it's set."

"He's never acted like this before."

Fiona stared at the fingers entwined with hers. A tear dropped onto Maria's hand.

"You had no idea?"

"He mentioned it a couple of times, but I thought it was in jest, something a person says when he'd bored or tired of routine, not for real. But…" She sighed and there was defeat in the sound. "Didn't I say when he gets an idea, there's no stopping him?"

"In that case, fair warning..." Maria said. "Colin may have quite a bit bottled up that'll come pouring out now that he's taken that first step."

"Oh, my God..." Fiona moaned.

"The Terrys' ranch house is bigger than our original one," Maria said, trying to find some spot of optimism. "You might want to renovate, though. Padraig practically tore down this one because he felt it was too small. There's a good architect in town. Padraig told him to build the house however I wanted it. That's why we have a ballroom and a dining room. I'm sure Colin will let you do the same..." She paused, then added, "...with the right encouragement. You can make it look exactly like the one in Tipperary, if you wish. And furnish it however you want. You can order furniture from Chicago or New York or even Europe."

She thought she saw a gleam of interest in Fiona's eyes at that.

"You won't be bored, Fiona, or alone. The women around here are friendly. They'll welcome you with open arms. Padraig's always having parties and dances, and you can too. We'll give them together. And...you'll have me, Fiona. We'll be friends."

"Thank you." Fiona wiped away a last tear and looked up. She hugged Maria. "Thank you for that. I'll need a friend," she muttered.

Just then Padraig and Colin came back into the parlor.

Chapter 59

The following morning, Colin and Padraig rode into McCoy's Crossing. With them they took the horse Padraig had hired from Olsen, as well as the tack. After returning them to the livery stable, they continued to the bank, where Padraig introduced his brother to Mr. Bainbridge and explained he wanted a draft drawn on his account.

"'Twill be better for th' money to come from me own account than waitin' for a cheque t' clear from yours in Tipperary. Quicker and safer. You can open your own later."

Colin agreed, admitting he imagined his brother knew more about US transactions than he. Once that was accomplished, they went to Blackstone's office. After the customary introductions were made and more preamble of conversation plus Padraig asking after Benjamin True, who was currently absent from the office, Colin told the lawyer what he wanted.

It was accomplished with remarkable speed. Blackstone had all the papers ready, simply waiting for a buyer to appear. All he had to do was place Colin's name in the proper blanks in the document.

"You certain she's all right with th' price?" Colin interrupted Blackstone's explanation. "I mean, I don't want t' cheat th' lady just because she's after a quick sale. P'rhaps I should offer more than three dollars an acre."

"I assure you, Mr. McCoy..." Where he used Padraig's given name, Blackstone was formal with Colin. "This price is reasonable and Mrs. Terry won't suffer because of it. She's the widow of a friend, so I won't let her be cheated. Now then...when would you like to take possession?"

"I don't want t' hurry th' lady. She can have three months to vacate," Colin was still attempting to be fair. "She can take whate'er she wishes from th' house or leave it if she wants. I'll also want th' hired hands an' foreman to stay if they wish."

"We need you t' draw up some papers o' partnership, also," Padraig spoke up, banking on Colin still adhering to the idea he'd expressed the night before. "Colin an' I are goin' inta business together."

With Blackstone's assurances he'd tend to everything and notify the widow of the sale forthwith, Colin and Padraig were on their way.

"Lord, I can't believe it!" Colin exclaimed. "Padraig, I'm a cattle baron now."

"Not yet." Padraig couldn't help but smile at his brother's excitement. "But you will be. Soon."

Colin acted as he had on Christmas morn, except this time the gift St. Nicholas had brought was more than a pony or that set of trains he wanted. This was something that would take a great deal of hard work.

"You've got t' earn that title," Padraig said. "I warn you, 'twon't be easy."

"I will," Colin promised. "With you showin' me what t' do."

"It'll be hard work, I want you to know that," Padraig cautioned.

"I'm ready, braithur," Colin answered. "After all, I'm a McCoy."

Back at the ranch, Fiona greeted them with a tearful, "So you've done it."

"It won't be so bad, lass," he soothed.

"You say that, now," she sniffled. "But just wait…Maria's been telling me of the life a rancher's wife leads, and…"

Colin looked at Maria, who raised her chin slightly, as if in defiance. "I hope you didn't make it sound too hellish?"

"I merely told her the truth, Colin." Maria reached for Padraig hand as she spoke. Her husband tactfully kept silent.

"Come, lass, let's talk this over." Fiona didn't answer as Colin took her hand and led her up the stairs.

Padraig and Maria were left alone in the parlor.

"Where are th' lads?" Padraig asked.

"Supposedly taking naps," Maria replied. "I thought it might be best if they were out of the way for…" She glanced upwards as if she could see into Colin and Fiona's bedroom. "…whatever was coming. They protested, of course." She laughed. "Quill actually said if he slept any more today, he was going to change his name to Rip Van Winkle, but they quieted after I promised they could play there instead of sleeping if they were quiet and didn't come out until they were told."

She looked anxious. "They know something's up, but Fiona and I have tried to keep it from them. If there's any problem between her and Colin, she doesn't want Liam to know about it. She's as protective of him as I am of Quill," she added softly.

"Has there been any problem 'twixt us you've

shielded from me son?" Padraig asked.

"No, but if we were t' argue...badly...I'd try t' keep him from knowin' about it."

"Don't worry about Colin an' Fiona." Padraig put his arms around her and drew her close. "I've had my say, and now 'tis their problem an' they have t' solve it, by talkin' it over, fightin' about it, or howe'er it goes. They have t' settle it themselves."

"And if they don't?"

"Then they don't." He shrugged. "Aithur way, solve it or not, Colin's a grown man now an' he has t' take care o' his problems himself. He doesn't need a big braithur or his faithur hoverin' o'er him. I think he's had enough o' that." He kissed her forehead. "I'd much rather talk o' us."

"What about us?" She frowned slightly.

"Maria, me dear, I got t' thinkin' while I was standin' in Blackstone's office listenin' t' Colin go o'er th' sale an' such with Josiah, an' I've somethin' t' ask you."

"What?" Now she looked a bit worried, and anxious.

"What Colin did t' Fiona was unforgivable, at least from her point o' view. I hope they can set this aside, but it made me wonder. What would you do if I told you I wanted t' sell th' ranch, pack up, an' return home?"

"Home? You mean, to Ireland?"

"That's right."

"I'd go with you, of course." Her reply was prompt. She didn't even seem to think about it, the concern on her face disappearing.

"Nay, lass. I don't want you t' say what you think I want t' hear. I want you t' answer me truthfully. What would you *really* do?"

"That *is* the truth, Padraig. The way we met and married may have been unusual, but I do love *you*...not this ranch or all the things you've bought me or any of our possessions."

Once I might have, she thought, *but now I love only you*, and it was the truth.

"Just you. The Shamrock is simply a *place*. You're the man I love. Without you, it's nothing. If you say we're moving to Ireland, then, I'll be like Ruth...*whither thou goest, I will go...*"

"Ah, lass, thank you. That's what I wanted t' hear."

"Are we going to Ireland?" Nevertheless, she sounded as if she wanted to be reassured.

"Someday, but no time soon, I don't imagine. Home's here, Maria, with you an' Quill. For me, it'll always be where you two are. I loved you th' moment I saw you, an' that love keeps gettin' stronger th' longer we're together. Now, then, *a chroi*, why don't we go upstairs an' celebrate that love?"

With that, cattle baron Padraig McCoy swung his wife into his arms and started up the stairs.

A word about the author...

Toni V. Sweeney has lived thirty years in the South, a score in the Middle West, and a decade on the Pacific Coast, and now she's trying for her second thirty on the Great Plains.

Since the publication of her first novel in 1989, Toni has written 94 novels, with 90 of them published. This includes several series.

Visit Toni at:
https://www.facebook.com/profile.php?id=
100048587829251

Thank you for purchasing
this publication of The Wild Rose Press, Inc.

For questions or more information
contact us at
info@thewildrosepress.com.

The Wild Rose Press, Inc.